*Follow the yellow brick road to your nearest bookstore
and discover the magic of a land called*

OZ

OZ, the COMPLETE COLLECTION, VOLUME 1
The WONDERFUL WIZARD of OZ
The MARVELOUS LAND of OZ
OZMA of OZ

OZ, the COMPLETE COLLECTION, VOLUME 2
DOROTHY and the WIZARD in OZ
The ROAD to OZ
The EMERALD CITY of OZ

OZ, the COMPLETE COLLECTION, VOLUME 3
The PATCHWORK GIRL of OZ
TIK-TOK of OZ
The SCARECROW of OZ

OZ, the COMPLETE COLLECTION, VOLUME 4
RINKITINK in OZ
The LOST PRINCESS of OZ
The TIN WOODMAN of OZ

OZ, the COMPLETE COLLECTION, VOLUME 5
The MAGIC of OZ
GLINDA of OZ
The ROYAL BOOK of OZ

Read them all!

Oz

The Complete

COLLECTION

VOLUME

3

L. Frank Baum

Includes:

The PATCHWORK GIRL of Oz

TIK-TOK of Oz

The SCARECROW of Oz

SIMON AND SCHUSTER

This edition published in Great Britain by Simon & Schuster UK Ltd, 2013
A CBS COMPANY

Published in the USA by Aladdin, an imprint of
Simon & Schuster Children's Publishing, 2013

The Patchwork Girl originally published in 1913
Tik-Tok of Oz originally published in 1914
The Scarecrow of Oz originally published in 1915

These titles were previously published individually.

1 3 5 7 9 10 8 6 4 2

Simon & Schuster UK Ltd
1st Floor
222 Gray's Inn Road
London
WC1X 8HB

www.simonandschuster.co.uk

Simon & Schuster Australia, Sydney
Simon & Schuster India, New Delhi

A CIP catalogue record for this book is available from the British Library

PB ISBN 978-1-4711-1718-3
E-Book ISBN 978-1-4711-1719-0

Printed and bound by CPI Group (UK) Ltd, Croydon, CR0 4YY

Contents

The
Patchwork
Girl
of
Oz

Affectionately dedicated to my young friend
Sumner Hamilton Britton of Chicago

Through the kindness of Dorothy Gale of Kansas, afterward Princess Dorothy of Oz, an humble writer in the United States of America was once appointed Royal Historian of Oz, with the privilege of writing the chronicle of that wonderful fairyland. But after making six books about the adventures of those interesting but queer people who live in the Land of Oz, the Historian learned with sorrow that by an edict of the Supreme Ruler, Ozma of Oz, her country would thereafter be rendered invisible to all who lived outside its borders and that all communication with Oz would, in the future, be cut off.

The children who had learned to look for the books about Oz and who loved the stories about the gay and happy people inhabiting that favored country, were as sorry as their Historian that there would be no more books of Oz stories. They wrote many letters asking if the Historian did not know of some adventures to write about that had happened before the Land of Oz was shut out from all the rest of the world. But he did not know of any. Finally one of the children inquired why we couldn't hear from Princess Dorothy by wireless telegraph, which would enable her to communicate to the Historian whatever happened in the far-off Land of Oz without his seeing her, or even knowing just where Oz is.

That seemed a good idea; so the Historian rigged up a high tower in his back yard, and took lessons in wireless telegraphy until he understood it, and then began to call "Princess Dorothy of Oz" by sending messages into the air.

Now, it wasn't likely that Dorothy would be looking for wireless messages or would heed the call; but one thing the Historian was sure of, and that was that the powerful Sorceress, Glinda, would know what he was doing and that he desired to communicate with Dorothy. For Glinda has a big book in which is recorded every event that takes place anywhere in the world, just the moment that it happens, and so of course the book would tell her about the wireless message.

And that was the way Dorothy heard that the Historian wanted to speak with her, and there was a Shaggy Man in the Land of Oz who knew how to telegraph a wireless reply. The result was that the Historian begged so hard to be told the latest news of Oz, so that he could write it down for the children to read, that Dorothy asked permission of Ozma, and Ozma graciously consented.

That is why, after two long years of waiting, another Oz story is now presented to the children of America. This would not have been possible had not some clever man invented the "wireless" and an equally clever child suggested the idea of reaching the mysterious Land of Oz by its means.

L. Frank Baum

"Ozcot" at Hollywood in California

Chapter 1

OJO and UNC NUNKIE

Where's the butter, Unc Nunkie?" asked Ojo.
Unc looked out of the window and
stroked his long beard. Then he turned to
the Munchkin boy and shook his head.

"Isn't," said he.

"Isn't any butter? That's too bad, Unc. Where's the jam
then?" inquired Ojo, standing on a stool so he could look
through all the shelves of the cupboard. But Unc Nunkie
shook his head again.

"Gone," he said.

"No jam, either? And no cake—no jelly—no apples—
nothing but bread?"

"All," said Unc, again stroking his beard as he gazed from the window.

The little boy brought the stool and sat beside his uncle, munching the dry bread slowly and seeming in deep thought.

"Nothing grows in our yard but the bread tree," he mused, "and there are only two more loaves on that tree; and they're not ripe yet. Tell me, Unc; why are we so poor?"

The old Munchkin turned and looked at Ojo. He had kindly eyes, but he hadn't smiled or laughed in so long that the boy had forgotten that Unc Nunkie could look any other way than solemn. And Unc never spoke any more words than he was obliged to, so his little nephew, who lived alone with him, had learned to understand a great deal from one word.

"Why are we so poor, Unc?" repeated the boy.

"Not," said the old Munchkin.

"I think we are," declared Ojo. "What have we got?"

"House," said Unc Nunkie.

"I know; but everyone in the Land of Oz has a place to live. What else, Unc?"

"Bread."

"I'm eating the last loaf that's ripe. There; I've put aside your share, Unc. It's on the table, so you can eat it when you get hungry. But when that is gone, what shall we eat, Unc?"

The old man shifted in his chair but merely shook his head.

"Of course," said Ojo, who was obliged to talk because his uncle would not, "no one starves in the Land of Oz, either.

There is plenty for everyone, you know; only, if it isn't just where you happen to be, you must go where it is."

The aged Munchkin wriggled again and stared at his small nephew as if disturbed by his argument.

"By to-morrow morning," the boy went on, "we must go where there is something to eat, or we shall grow very hungry and become very unhappy."

"Where?" asked Unc.

"Where shall we go? I don't know, I'm sure," replied Ojo. "But *you* must know, Unc. You must have traveled, in your time, because you're so old. I don't remember it, because ever since I could remember anything we've lived right here in this lonesome, round house, with a little garden back of it and the thick woods all around. All I've ever seen of the great Land of Oz, Unc dear, is the view of that mountain over at the south, where they say the Hammerheads live—who won't let any-body go by them—and that mountain at the north, where they say nobody lives."

"One," declared Unc, correcting him.

"Oh, yes; one family lives there, I've heard. That's the Crooked Magician, who is named Dr. Pipt, and his wife Margolotte. One year you told me about them; I think it took you a whole year, Unc, to say as much as I've just said about the Crooked Magician and his wife. They live high up on the mountain, and the good Munchkin Country, where the fruits and flowers grow, is just the other side. It's funny you and I should live here all alone, in the middle of the forest, isn't it?"

"Yes," said Unc.

"Then let's go away and visit the Munchkin Country and its jolly, good-natured people. I'd love to get a sight of something besides woods, Unc Nunkie."

"Too little," said Unc.

"Why, I'm not so little as I used to be," answered the boy earnestly. "I think I can walk as far and as fast through the woods as you can, Unc. And now that nothing grows in our back yard that is good to eat, we must go where there is food."

Unc Nunkie made no reply for a time. Then he shut down the window and turned his chair to face the room, for the sun was sinking behind the tree-tops and it was growing cool.

By and by Ojo lighted the fire and the logs blazed freely in the broad fireplace. The two sat in the firelight a long time— the old, white-bearded Munchkin and the little boy. Both were thinking. When it grew quite dark outside, Ojo said:

"Eat your bread, Unc, and then we will go to bed."

But Unc Nunkie did not eat the bread; neither did he go directly to bed. Long after his little nephew was sound asleep in the corner of the room the old man sat by the fire, thinking.

·····◄ Chapter 2 ►·····

The CROOKED MAGICIAN

Just at dawn next morning Unc Nunkie laid his hand tenderly on Ojo's head and awakened him.

"Come," he said.

Ojo dressed. He wore blue silk stockings, blue knee-pants with gold buckles, a blue ruffled waist and a jacket of bright blue braided with gold. His shoes were of blue leather and turned up at the toes, which were pointed. His hat had a peaked crown and a flat brim, and around the brim was a row of tiny golden bells that tinkled when he moved. This was the native costume of those who inhabited the Munchkin Country of the Land of Oz, so Unc Nunkie's dress was much like that of his nephew. Instead of shoes, the old man wore boots with turnover tops and his blue coat had wide cuffs of gold braid.

The boy noticed that his uncle had not eaten the bread, and supposed the old man had not been hungry. Ojo was hungry, though; so he divided the piece of bread upon the table and ate his half for breakfast, washing it down with fresh, cool water from the brook. Unc put the other piece of bread in his jacket pocket, after which he again said, as he walked out through the doorway: "Come."

Ojo was well pleased. He was dreadfully tired of living all alone in the woods and wanted to travel and see people. For a long time he had wished to explore the beautiful Land of Oz in which they lived. When they were outside, Unc simply latched the door and started up the path. No one would disturb their little house, even if anyone came so far into the thick forest while they were gone.

At the foot of the mountain that separated the Country of the Munchkins from the Country of the Gillikins, the path divided. One way led to the left and the other to the right— straight up the mountain. Unc Nunkie took this right-hand path and Ojo followed without asking why. He knew it would take them to the house of the Crooked Magician, whom he had never seen but who was their nearest neighbor.

All the morning they trudged up the mountain path and at noon Unc and Ojo sat on a fallen tree-trunk and ate the last of the bread which the old Munchkin had placed in his pocket. Then they started on again and two hours later came in sight of the house of Dr. Pipt.

It was a big house, round, as were all the Munchkin houses, and painted blue, which is the distinctive color of the Munchkin Country of Oz. There was a pretty garden around the house, where blue trees and blue flowers grew in abundance and in one place were beds of blue cabbages, blue carrots and blue lettuce, all of which were delicious to eat. In Dr. Pipt's garden grew bun-trees, cake-trees, cream-puff bushes, blue buttercups which yielded excellent blue butter and a row of chocolate-caramel plants. Paths of blue gravel divided the vegetable and flower beds and a wider path led up to the front door. The place was in a clearing on the mountain, but a little way off was the grim forest, which completely surrounded it.

Unc knocked at the door of the house and a chubby, pleasant-faced woman, dressed all in blue, opened it and greeted the visitors with a smile.

"Ah," said Ojo; "you must be Dame Margolotte, the good wife of Dr. Pipt."

"I am, my dear, and all strangers are welcome to my home."

"May we see the famous Magician, Madam?"

"He is very busy just now," she said, shaking her head doubtfully. "But come in and let me give you something to eat, for you must have traveled far in order to get our lonely place."

"We have," replied Ojo, as he and Unc entered the house.

"We have come from a far lonelier place than this."

"A lonelier place! And in the Munchkin Country?" she exclaimed. "Then it must be somewhere in the Blue Forest."

"It is, good Dame Margolotte."

"Dear me!" she said, looking at the man, "you must be Unc Nunkie, known as the Silent One." Then she looked at the boy. "And you must be Ojo the Unlucky," she added.

"Yes," said Unc.

"I never knew I was called the Unlucky," said Ojo, soberly; "but it is really a good name for me."

"Well," remarked the woman, as she bustled around the room and set the table and brought food from the cupboard, "you were unlucky to live all alone in that dismal forest, which is much worse than the forest around here; but perhaps your luck will change, now you are away from it. If, during your travels, you can manage to lose that 'Un' at the beginning of your name 'Unlucky,' you will then become Ojo the Lucky, which will be a great improvement."

"How can I lose that 'Un,' Dame Margolotte?"

"I do not know how, but you must keep the matter in mind and perhaps the chance will come to you," she replied.

Ojo had never eaten such a fine meal in all his life. There was a savory stew, smoking hot, a dish of blue peas, a bowl of sweet milk of a delicate blue tint and a blue pudding with blue plums in it. When the visitors had eaten heartily of this fare the woman said to them:

"Do you wish to see Dr. Pipt on business or for pleasure?"

Unc shook his head.

"We are traveling," replied Ojo, "and we stopped at your house just to rest and refresh ourselves. I do not think Unc Nunkie cares very much to see the famous Crooked Magician; but for my part I am curious to look at such a great man."

The woman seemed thoughtful.

"I remember that Unc Nunkie and my husband used to be friends, many years ago," she said, "so perhaps they will be glad to meet again. The Magician is very busy, as I said, but if you will promise not to disturb him you may come into his workshop and watch him prepare a wonderful charm."

"Thank you," replied the boy, much pleased. "I would like to do that."

She led the way to a great domed hall at the back of the house, which was the Magician's workshop. There was a row of windows extending nearly around the sides of the circular room, which rendered the place very light, and there was a back door in addition to the one leading to the front part of the house. Before the row of windows a broad seat was built and there were some chairs and benches in the room besides. At one end stood a great fireplace, in which a blue log was blazing with a blue flame, and over the fire hung four kettles in a row, all bubbling and steaming at a great rate. The Magician was stirring all four of these kettles at the same time, two with his hands and two with his feet, to the latter, wooden ladles being strapped, for this man was so very crooked that his legs were as handy as his arms.

Unc Nunkie came forward to greet his old friend, but not being able to shake either his hands or his feet, which were all occupied in stirring, he patted the Magician's bald head and asked: "What?"

"Ah, it's the Silent One," remarked Dr. Pipt, without looking up, "and he wants to know what I'm making. Well, when it is quite finished this compound will be the wonderful Powder of Life, which no one knows how to make but myself. Whenever it is sprinkled on anything, that thing will at once come to life, no matter what it is. It takes me several years to make this magic powder, but at this moment I am pleased to say it is nearly done. You see, I am making it for my good wife Margolotte, who wants to use some of it for a purpose of her own. Sit down and make yourself comfortable, Unc Nunkie, and after I've finished my task I will talk to you."

"You must know," said Margolotte, when they were all seated together on the broad window-seat, "that my husband foolishly gave away all the Powder of Life he first made to old Mombi the Witch, who used to live in the Country of the Gillikins, to the north of here. Mombi gave to Dr. Pipt a Powder of Perpetual Youth in exchange for his Powder of Life, but she cheated him wickedly, for the Powder of Youth was no good and could work no magic at all."

"Perhaps the Powder of Life couldn't either," said Ojo.

"Yes; it is perfection," she declared. "The first lot we tested on our Glass Cat, which not only began to live but has lived ever since. She's somewhere around the house now."

"A Glass Cat!" exclaimed Ojo, astonished.

"Yes; she makes a very pleasant companion, but admires herself a little more than is considered modest, and she positively refuses to catch mice," explained Margolotte. "My husband made the cat some pink brains, but they proved to be too high-bred and particular for a cat, so she thinks it is undignified in her to catch mice. Also she has a pretty blood-red heart, but it is made of stone—a ruby, I think—and so is rather hard and unfeeling. I think the next Glass Cat the Magician makes will have neither brains nor heart, for then it will not object to catching mice and may prove of some use to us."

"What did old Mombi the Witch do with the Powder of Life your husband gave her?" asked the boy.

"She brought Jack Pumpkinhead to life, for one thing," was the reply. "I suppose you've heard of Jack Pumpkinhead. He is now living near the Emerald City and is a great favorite with the Princess Ozma, who rules all the Land of Oz."

"No; I've never heard of him," remarked Ojo. "I'm afraid I don't know much about the Land of Oz. You see, I've lived all my life with Unc Nunkie, the Silent One, and there was no one to tell me anything."

"That is one reason you are Ojo the Unlucky," said the woman, in a sympathetic tone. "The more one knows, the luckier he is, for knowledge is the greatest gift in life."

"But tell me, please, what you intend to do with this new lot of the Powder of Life, which Dr. Pipt is making. He said his wife wanted it for some especial purpose."

"So I do," she answered. "I want it to bring my Patchwork Girl to life."

"Oh! A Patchwork Girl? What is that?" Ojo asked, for this seemed even more strange and unusual than a Glass Cat.

"I think I must show you my Patchwork Girl," said Margolotte, laughing at the boy's astonishment, "for she is rather difficult to explain. But first I will tell you that for many years I have longed for a servant to help me with the housework and to cook the meals and wash the dishes. No servant will come here because the place is so lonely and out-of-the-way, so my clever husband, the Crooked Magician, proposed that I make a girl out of some sort of material and he would make her live by sprinkling over her the Powder of Life. This seemed an excellent suggestion and at once Dr. Pipt set to work to make a new batch of his magic powder. He has been at it a long, long while, and so I have had plenty of time to make the girl. Yet that task was not so easy as you may suppose. At first I couldn't think what to make her of, but finally in searching through a chest I came across an old patchwork quilt, which my grandmother once made when she was young."

"What is a patchwork quilt?" asked Ojo.

"A bed-quilt made of patches of different kinds and colors of cloth, all neatly sewed together. The patches are of all shapes and sizes, so a patchwork quilt is a very pretty and gorgeous thing to look at. Sometimes it is called a 'crazy-quilt,' because the patches and colors are so mixed up. We never have used my grandmother's many-colored patchwork quilt, handsome as it is, for we Munchkins do not care for any color other than blue, so it has been packed away in the chest for about a hundred years. When I found it, I said to myself that it would do nicely for my servant girl, for when she was brought to life she would not be proud nor haughty, as the Glass Cat is, for such a dreadful mixture of colors would discourage her from trying to be as dignified as the blue Munchkins are."

"Is blue the only respectable color, then?" inquired Ojo.

"Yes, for a Munchkin. All our country is blue, you know. But in other parts of Oz the people favor different colors. At the Emerald City, where our Princess Ozma lives, green is the popular color. But all Munchkins prefer blue to anything else and when my housework girl is brought to life she will find herself to be of so many unpopular colors that she'll never dare be rebellious or impudent, as servants are sometimes liable to be when they are made the same way their mistresses are."

Unc Nunkie nodded approval.

"Good i-dea," he said; and that was a long speech for Unc Nunkie because it was two words.

"So I cut up the quilt," continued Margolotte, "and made

from it a very well-shaped girl, which I stuffed with cotton-wadding. I will show you what a good job I did," and she went to a tall cupboard and threw open the doors.

Then back she came, lugging in her arms the Patchwork Girl, which she set upon the bench and propped up so that the figure would not tumble over.

..——..◂ Chapter 3 ▸..——..

The PATCHWORK GIRL

O jo examined this curious contrivance with wonder. The Patchwork Girl was taller than he, when she stood upright, and her body was plump and rounded because it had been so neatly stuffed with cotton. Margolotte had first made the girl's form from the patchwork quilt and then she had dressed it with a patchwork skirt and an apron with pockets in it—using the same gay material throughout. Upon the feet she had sewn a pair of red leather shoes with pointed toes. All the fingers and thumbs of the girl's hands had been carefully formed and stuffed and stitched at the edges, with gold plates at the ends to serve as finger-nails.

"She will have to work, when she comes to life," said Margolotte.

The head of the Patchwork Girl was the most curious part of her. While she waited for her husband to finish making his Powder of Life the woman had found ample time to complete the head as her fancy dictated, and she realized that a good servant's head must be properly constructed. The hair was of brown yarn and hung down on her neck in several neat braids. Her eyes were two silver suspender-buttons cut from a pair of the Magician's old trousers, and they were sewed on with black threads, which formed the pupils of the eyes. Margolotte had puzzled over the ears for some time, for these were important if the servant was to hear distinctly, but finally she had made them out of thin plates of gold and attached them in place by means of stitches through tiny holes bored in the metal. Gold is the most common metal in the Land of Oz and is used for many purposes because it is soft and pliable.

The woman had cut a slit for the Patchwork Girl's mouth and sewn two rows of white pearls in it for teeth, using a strip of scarlet plush for a tongue. This mouth Ojo considered very artistic and lifelike, and Margolotte was pleased when the boy praised it. There were almost too many patches on the face of the girl for her to be considered strictly beautiful, for one cheek was yellow and the other red, her chin blue, her forehead purple and the center, where her nose had been formed and padded, a bright yellow.

"You ought to have had her face all pink," suggested the boy.

"I suppose so; but I had no pink cloth," replied the woman. "Still, I cannot see as it matters much, for I wish my Patchwork Girl to be useful rather than ornamental. If I get tired looking at her patched face I can whitewash it."

"Has she any brains?" asked Ojo.

"No; I forgot all about the brains!" exclaimed the woman. "I am glad you reminded me of them, for it is not too late to supply them, by any means. Until she is brought to life I can do anything I please with this girl. But I must be careful not to give her too much brains, and those she has must be such as are fitted to the station she is to occupy in life. In other words, her brains mustn't be very good."

"Wrong," said Unc Nunkie.

"No; I am sure I am right about that," returned the woman.

"He means," explained Ojo, "that unless your servant has good brains she won't know how to obey you properly, nor do the things you ask her to do."

"Well, that may be true," agreed Margolotte; "but, on the contrary, a servant with too much brains is sure to become independent and high-and-mighty and feel above her work. This is a very delicate task, as I said, and I must take care to give the girl just the right quantity of the right sort of brains. I want her to know just enough, but not too much."

With this she went to another cupboard which was filled

with shelves. All the shelves were lined with blue glass bottles, neatly labeled by the Magician to show what they contained. One whole shelf was marked: "Brain Furniture," and the bottles on this shelf were labeled as follows: "Obedience," "Cleverness," "Judgment," "Courage," "Ingenuity," "Amiability," "Learning," "Truth," "Poesy," "Self Reliance."

"Let me see," said Margolotte; "of those qualities she must have 'Obedience' first of all," and she took down the bottle bearing that label and poured from it upon a dish several grains of the contents. "'Amiability' is also good and 'Truth.'" She poured into the dish a quantity from each of these bottles. "I think that will do," she continued, "for the other qualities are not needed in a servant."

Unc Nunkie, who with Ojo stood beside her, touched the bottle marked "Cleverness."

"Little," said he.

"A little 'Cleverness'? Well, perhaps you are right, sir," said she, and was about to take down the bottle when the Crooked Magician suddenly called to her excitedly from the fireplace.

"Quick, Margolotte! Come and help me."

She ran to her husband's side at once and helped him lift the four kettles from the fire. Their contents had all boiled away, leaving in the bottom of each kettle a few grains of fine white powder. Very carefully the Magician removed this powder, placing it all together in a golden dish, where he mixed it with a golden spoon. When the mixture was complete there was scarcely a handful, all told.

"That," said Dr. Pipt, in a pleased and triumphant tone, "is the wonderful Powder of Life, which I alone in the world know how to make. It has taken me nearly six years to prepare these precious grains of dust, but the little heap on that dish is worth the price of a kingdom and many a King would give all he has to possess it. When it has become cooled I will place it in a small bottle; but meantime I must watch it carefully, lest a gust of wind blow it away or scatter it."

Unc Nunkie, Margolotte and the Magician all stood looking at the marvelous powder, but Ojo was more interested just then in the Patchwork Girl's brains. Thinking it both unfair and unkind to deprive her of any good qualities that were handy, the boy took down every bottle on the shelf and poured some of the contents in Margolotte's dish. No one saw him do this, for all were looking at the Powder of Life; but soon the woman remembered what she had been doing, and came back to the cupboard.

"Let's see," she remarked; "I was about to give my girl a little 'Cleverness,' which is the Doctor's substitute for 'Intelligence'—a quality he has not yet learned how to manufacture." Taking down the bottle of "Cleverness" she added some of the powder to the heap on the dish. Ojo became a bit uneasy at this, for he had already put quite a lot of the "Cleverness" powder in the dish; but he dared not interfere and so he comforted himself with the thought that one cannot have too much cleverness.

Margolotte now carried the dish of brains to the bench. Ripping the seam of the patch on the girl's forehead, she placed the powder within the head and then sewed up the seam as neatly and securely as before.

"My girl is all ready for your Powder of Life, my dear," she said to her husband. But the Magician replied:

"This powder must not be used before to-morrow morning; but I think it is now cool enough to be bottled."

He selected a small gold bottle with a pepper-box top, so that the powder might be sprinkled on any object through the small holes. Very carefully he placed the Powder of Life in the gold bottle and then locked it up in a drawer of his cabinet.

"At last," said he, rubbing his hands together gleefully, "I have ample leisure for a good talk with my old friend Unc Nunkie. So let us sit down cosily and enjoy ourselves. After stirring those four kettles for six years I am glad to have a little rest."

"You will have to do most of the talking," said Ojo, "for Unc is called the Silent One and uses few words."

"I know; but that renders your uncle a most agreeable companion and gossip," declared Dr. Pipt. "Most people talk too much, so it is a relief to find one who talks too little."

Ojo looked at the Magician with much awe and curiosity.

"Don't you find it very annoying to be so crooked?" he asked.

"No; I am quite proud of my person," was the reply. "I suppose I am the only Crooked Magician in all the world. Some others are accused of being crooked, but I am the only genuine."

He was really very crooked and Ojo wondered how he managed to do so many things with such a twisted body. When he sat down upon a crooked chair that had been made to fit him, one knee was under his chin and the other near the small of his back; but he was a cheerful man and his face bore a pleasant and agreeable expression.

"I am not allowed to perform magic, except for my own amusement," he told his visitors, as he lighted a pipe with a crooked stem and began to smoke. "Too many people were working magic in the Land of Oz, and so our lovely Princess Ozma put a stop to it. I think she was quite right. There were several wicked Witches who caused a lot of trouble; but now they are all out of business and only the great Sorceress, Glinda the Good, is permitted to practice her arts, which never harm anybody. The Wizard of Oz, who used to be a humbug and knew no magic at all, has been taking lessons from Glinda, and I'm told he is getting to be a pretty good Wizard; but he is merely the assistant of the great Sorceress. I've the right to make a servant girl for my wife, you know, or a Glass Cat to catch our mice—which she refuses to do—but I am forbidden to work magic for others, or to use it as a profession."

"Magic must be a very interesting study," said Ojo.

"It truly is," asserted the Magician. "In my time I've performed some magical feats that were worthy of the skill of Glinda the Good. For instance, there's the Powder of Life, and my Liquid of Petrifaction, which is contained in that bottle on the shelf yonder—over the window."

"What does the Liquid of Petrifaction do?" inquired the boy.

"Turns everything it touches to solid marble. It's an invention of my own, and I find it very useful. Once two of those dreadful Kalidahs, with bodies like bears and heads like tigers, came here from the forest to attack us; but I sprinkled some of that Liquid on them and instantly they turned to marble. I now use them as ornamental statuary in my garden. This table looks to you like wood, and once it really was wood; but I sprinkled a few drops of the Liquid of Petrifaction on it and now it is marble. It will never break nor wear out."

"Fine!" said Unc Nunkie, wagging his head and stroking his long grey beard.

"Dear me; what a chatterbox you're getting to be, Unc," remarked the Magician, who was pleased with the compliment. But just then there came a scratching at the back door and a shrill voice cried:

"Let me in! Hurry up, can't you? Let me in!"

Margolotte got up and went to the door.

"Ask like a good cat, then," she said.

"Mee-ee-ow-w-w! There; does that suit your royal highness?" asked the voice, in scornful accents.

"Yes; that's proper cat talk," declared the woman, and opened the door.

At once a cat entered, came to the center of the room and stopped short at the sight of strangers. Ojo and Unc Nunkie both stared at it with wide open eyes, for surely no such curious creature had ever existed before—even in the Land of Oz.

·····◄ Chapter 4 ►·····

The GLASS CAT

The cat was made of glass, so clear and transparent that you could see through it as easily as through a window. In the top of its head, however, was a mass of delicate pink balls which looked like jewels, and it had a heart made of a blood-red ruby. The eyes were two large emeralds, but aside from these colors all the rest of the animal was clear glass, and it had a spun-glass tail that was really beautiful.

"Well, Doc Pipt, do you mean to introduce us, or not?" demanded the cat, in a tone of annoyance. "Seems to me you are forgetting your manners."

"Excuse me," returned the Magician. "This is Unc Nunkie,

the descendant of the former Kings of the Munchkins, before this country became a part of the Land of Oz."

"He needs a haircut," observed the cat, washing its face.

"True," replied Unc, with a low chuckle of amusement.

"But he has lived alone in the heart of the forest for many years," the Magician explained; "and, although that is a barbarous country, there are no barbers there."

"Who is the dwarf?" asked the cat.

"That is not a dwarf, but a boy," answered the Magician. "You have never seen a boy before. He is now small because he is young. With more years he will grow big and become as tall as Unc Nunkie."

"Oh. Is that magic?" the glass animal inquired.

"Yes; but it is Nature's magic, which is more wonderful than any art known to man. For instance, my magic made you, and made you live; and it was a poor job because you are useless and a bother to me; but I can't make you grow. You will always be the same size—and the same saucy, inconsiderate Glass Cat, with pink brains and a hard ruby heart."

"No one can regret more than I the fact that you made me," asserted the cat, crouching upon the floor and slowly swaying its spun-glass tail from side to side. "Your world is a very uninteresting place. I've wandered through your gardens and in the forest until I'm tired of it all, and when I come into the house the conversation of your fat wife and of yourself bores me dreadfully."

"That is because I gave you different brains from those we ourselves possess—and much too good for a cat," returned Dr. Pipt.

"Can't you take 'em out, then, and replace 'em with pebbles, so that I won't feel above my station in life?" asked the cat, pleadingly.

"Perhaps so. I'll try it, after I've brought the Patchwork Girl to life," he said.

The cat walked up to the bench on which the Patchwork Girl reclined and looked at her attentively.

"Are you going to make that dreadful thing live?" she asked.

The Magician nodded.

"It is intended to be my wife's servant maid," he said. "When she is alive she will do all our work and mind the house. But you are not to order her around, Bungle, as you do us. You must treat the Patchwork Girl respectfully."

"I won't. I couldn't respect such a bundle of scraps under any circumstances."

"If you don't, there will be more scraps than you will like," cried Margolotte, angrily.

"Why didn't you make her pretty to look at?" asked the cat. "You made me pretty—very pretty, indeed—and I love to watch my pink brains roll around when they're working, and to see my precious red heart beat." She went to a long mirror, as she said this, and stood before it, looking at herself with an air of much pride. "But that poor patched thing will hate herself, when she's once alive," continued the cat. "If I were you I'd use her for a mop, and make another servant that is prettier."

"You have a perverted taste," snapped Margolotte, much annoyed at this frank criticism. "I think the Patchwork Girl is beautiful, considering what she's made of. Even the rainbow hasn't as many colors, and you must admit that the rainbow is a pretty thing."

The Glass Cat yawned and stretched herself upon the floor.

"Have your own way," she said. "I'm sorry for the Patch-work Girl, that's all."

Ojo and Unc Nunkie slept that night in the Magician's house, and the boy was glad to stay because he was anxious to see the Patchwork Girl brought to life. The Glass Cat was also a wonderful creature to little Ojo, who had never seen or known anything of magic before, although he had lived in the Fairyland of Oz ever since he was born. Back there in the woods nothing unusual ever happened. Unc Nunkie, who might have been King of the Munchkins, had not his people united with all the other countries of Oz in acknowledging Ozma as their sole Ruler, had retired into this forgotten forest nook with his baby nephew and they had lived all alone there. Only that the neglected garden had failed to grow food for them, they would always have lived in the solitary Blue Forest;

but now they had started out to mingle with other people, and the first place they came to proved so interesting that Ojo could scarcely sleep a wink all night.

Margolotte was an excellent cook and gave them a fine breakfast. While they were all engaged in eating, the good woman said:

"This is the last meal I shall have to cook for some time, for right after breakfast Dr. Pipt has promised to bring my new servant to life. I shall let her wash the breakfast dishes and sweep and dust the house. What a relief it will be!"

"It will, indeed, relieve you of much drudgery," said the Magician. "By the way, Margolotte, I thought I saw you getting some brains from the cupboard, while I was busy with my kettles. What qualities have you given your new servant?"

"Only those that an humble servant requires," she answered. "I do not wish her to feel above her station, as the Glass Cat does. That would make her discontented and unhappy, for of course she must always be a servant."

Ojo was somewhat disturbed as he listened to this, and the boy began to fear he had done wrong in adding all those different qualities of brains to the lot Margolotte had prepared for the servant. But it was too late now for regret, since all the brains were securely sewn up inside the Patchwork Girl's head. He might have confessed what he had done and thus allowed Margolotte and her husband to change the brains; but he was afraid of incurring their anger. He believed that Unc had seen him add to the brains, and Unc had not said a word against it; but then, Unc never did say anything unless it was absolutely necessary.

As soon as breakfast was over they all went into the Magician's big workshop, where the Glass Cat was lying before the mirror and the Patchwork Girl lay limp and lifeless upon the bench.

"Now, then," said Dr. Pipt, in a brisk tone, "we shall perform one of the greatest feats of magic possible to man, even in this marvelous Land of Oz. In no other country could it be done at all. I think we ought to have a little music while the Patchwork Girl comes to life. It is pleasant to reflect that the first sounds her golden ears will hear will be delicious music."

As he spoke he went to a phonograph, which was screwed fast to a small table, and wound up the spring of the instrument and adjusted the big gold horn.

"The music my servant will usually hear," remarked Margolotte, "will be my orders to do her work. But I see no harm in allowing her to listen to this unseen band while she wakens to her first realization of life. My orders will beat the band, afterward."

The phonograph was now playing a stirring march tune and the Magician unlocked his cabinet and took out the gold bottle containing the Powder of Life.

They all bent over the bench on which the Patchwork Girl reclined. Unc Nunkie and Margolotte stood behind, near the windows, Ojo at one side and the Magician in front, where he would have freedom to sprinkle the powder. The Glass Cat came near, too, curious to watch the important scene.

"All ready?" asked Dr. Pipt.

"All is ready," answered his wife.

So the Magician leaned over and shook from the bottle some grains of the wonderful powder, and they fell directly on the Patchwork Girl's head and arms.

...——·« Chapter 5 »·——...

A TERRIBLE ACCIDENT

It will take a few minutes for this powder to do its work," remarked the Magician, sprinkling the body up and down with much care.

But suddenly the Patchwork Girl threw up one arm, which knocked the bottle of powder from the crooked man's hand and sent it flying across the room. Unc Nunkie and Margolotte were so startled that they both leaped backward and bumped together, and Unc's head joggled the shelf above them and upset the bottle containing the Liquid of Petrifaction.

The Magician uttered such a wild cry that Ojo jumped away and the Patchwork Girl sprang after him and clasped her stuffed arms around him in terror. The Glass Cat snarled and hid under the table, and so it was that when the powerful Liquid of Petrifaction was spilled it fell only upon the wife of the Magician and the uncle of Ojo. With these two the charm worked promptly. They stood motionless and stiff as marble statues, in exactly the positions they were in when the Liquid struck them.

Ojo pushed the Patchwork Girl away and ran to Unc Nunkie, filled with a terrible fear for the only friend and protector he had ever known. When he grasped Unc's hand it was cold and hard. Even the long grey beard was solid marble. The Crooked Magician was dancing around the room in a frenzy of despair, calling upon his wife to forgive him, to speak to him, to come to life again!

The Patchwork Girl, quickly recovering from her fright, now came nearer and looked from one to another of the people with deep interest. Then she looked at herself and laughed. Noticing the mirror, she stood before it and examined her extraordinary features with amazement—her button eyes, pearl bead teeth and puffy nose. Then, addressing her reflection in the glass, she exclaimed:

> *"Whee, but there's a gaudy dame!*
> *Makes a paint-box blush with shame.*
> *Razzle-dazzle, fizzle-fazzle!*
> *Howdy-do, Miss What's-your-name?"*

She bowed, and the reflection bowed. Then she laughed again, long and merrily, and the Glass Cat crept out from under the table and said:

"I don't blame you for laughing at yourself. Aren't you horrid?"

"Horrid?" she replied. "Why, I'm thoroughly delightful. I'm an Original, if you please, and therefore incomparable. Of all the comic, absurd, rare and amusing creatures the world contains, I must be the supreme freak. Who but poor Margolotte could have managed to invent such an unreasonable being as I? But I'm glad—I'm awfully glad!—that I'm just what I am, and nothing else."

"Be quiet, will you?" cried the frantic Magician; "be quiet and let me think! If I don't think I shall go mad."

"Think ahead," said the Patchwork Girl, seating herself in a chair. "Think all you want to. I don't mind."

"Gee! but I'm tired playing that tune," called the phonograph, speaking through its horn in a brazen, scratchy voice. "If you don't mind, Pipt, old boy, I'll cut it out and take a rest."

The Magician looked gloomily at the music-machine.

"What dreadful luck!" he wailed, despondently. "The Powder of Life must have fallen on the phonograph."

He went up to it and found that the gold bottle that contained the precious powder had dropped upon the stand and scattered its life-giving grains over the machine. The phonograph was very much alive, and began dancing a jig with the legs of the table to which it was attached, and this dance so annoyed Dr. Pipt that he kicked the thing into a corner and pushed a bench against it, to hold it quiet.

"You were bad enough before," said the Magician, resentfully; "but a live phonograph is enough to drive every sane person in the Land of Oz stark crazy."

"No insults, please," answered the phonograph in a surly tone. "You did it, my boy; don't blame me."

"You've bungled everything, Dr. Pipt," added the Glass Cat, contemptuously.

"Except me," said the Patchwork Girl, jumping up to whirl merrily around the room.

"I think," said Ojo, almost ready to cry through grief over Unc Nunkie's sad fate, "it must all be my fault, in some way. I'm called Ojo the Unlucky, you know."

"That's nonsense, kiddie," retorted the Patchwork Girl cheerfully. "No one can be unlucky who has the intelligence to direct his own actions. The unlucky ones are those who beg for a chance to think, like poor Dr. Pipt here. What's the row about, anyway, Mr. Magic-maker?"

"The Liquid of Petrifaction has accidentally fallen upon my dear wife and Unc Nunkie and turned them into marble," he sadly replied.

"Well, why don't you sprinkle some of that powder on them and bring them to life again?" asked the Patchwork Girl.

The Magician gave a jump.

"Why, I hadn't thought of that!" he joyfully cried, and grabbed up the golden bottle, with which he ran to Margolotte.

Said the Patchwork Girl:

"Higgledy, piggledy, dee—
What fools magicians be!
His head's so thick
He can't think quick,
So he takes advice from me."

Standing upon the bench, for he was so crooked he could not reach the top of his wife's head in any other way, Dr. Pipt began shaking the bottle. But not a grain of powder came out. He pulled off the cover, glanced within, and then threw the bottle from him with a wail of despair.

"Gone—gone! Every bit gone," he cried. "Wasted on that miserable phonograph when it might have saved my dear wife!"

Then the Magician bowed his head on his crooked arms and began to cry.

Ojo was sorry for him. He went up to the sorrowful man and said softly:

"You can make more Powder of Life, Dr. Pipt."

"Yes; but it will take me six years—six long, weary years of stirring four kettles with both feet and both hands," was the agonized reply. "Six years! while poor Margolotte stands watching me as a marble image."

"Can't anything else be done?" asked the Patchwork Girl.

The Magician shook his head. Then he seemed to remember something and looked up.

"There is one other compound that would destroy the magic spell of the Liquid of Petrifaction and restore my wife and Unc Nunkie to life," said he. "It may be hard to find the things I need to make this magic compound, but if they were found I could do in an instant what will otherwise take six long, weary years of stirring kettles with both hands and both feet."

"All right; let's find the things, then," suggested the Patchwork Girl. "That seems a lot more sensible than those stirring times with the kettles."

"That's the idea, Scraps," said the Glass Cat, approvingly. "I'm glad to find you have decent brains. Mine are exceptionally good. You can see 'em work; they're pink."

"Scraps?" repeated the girl. "Did you call me 'Scraps'? Is that my name?"

"I—I believe my poor wife had intended to name you 'Angeline,'" said the Magician.

"But I like 'Scraps' best," she replied with a laugh. "It fits me better, for my patchwork is all scraps, and nothing else. Thank you for naming me, Miss Cat. Have you any name of your own?"

"I have a foolish name that Margolotte once gave me, but which is quite undignified for one of my importance," answered the cat. "She called me 'Bungle.'"

"Yes," sighed the Magician; "you were a sad bungle, taken all in all. I was wrong to make you as I did, for a more useless, conceited and brittle thing never before existed."

"I'm not so brittle as you think," retorted the cat. "I've been alive a good many years, for Dr. Pipt experimented on me with the first magic Powder of Life he ever made, and so far I've never broken or cracked or chipped any part of me."

"You seem to have a chip on your shoulder," laughed the Patchwork Girl, and the cat went to the mirror to see.

"Tell me," pleaded Ojo, speaking to the Crooked Magician, "what must we find to make the compound that will save Unc Nunkie?"

"First," was the reply, "I must have a six-leaved clover. That can only be found in the green country around the Emerald City, and six-leaved clovers are very scarce, even there."

"I'll find it for you," promised Ojo.

"The next thing," continued the Magician, "is the left wing of a yellow butterfly. That color can only be found in the yellow country of the Winkies, West of the Emerald City."

"I'll find it," declared Ojo. "Is that all?"

"Oh, no; I'll get my Book of Recipes and see what comes next."

Saying this, the Magician unlocked a drawer of his cabinet

and drew out a small book covered with blue leather. Looking through the pages he found the recipe he wanted and said: "I must have a gill of water from a dark well."

"What kind of a well is that, sir?" asked the boy.

"One where the light of day never penetrates. The water must be put in a gold bottle and brought to me without any light ever reaching it."

"I'll get the water from the dark well," said Ojo.

"Then I must have three hairs from the tip of a Woozy's tail, and a drop of oil from a live man's body."

Ojo looked grave at this.

"What is a Woozy, please?" he inquired.

"Some sort of an animal. I've never seen one, so I can't describe it," replied the Magician.

"If I can find a Woozy, I'll get the hairs from its tail," said Ojo. "But is there ever any oil in a man's body?"

The Magician looked in the book again, to make sure.

"That's what the recipe calls for," he replied, "and of course we must get everything that is called for, or the charm won't work. The book doesn't say 'blood'; it says 'oil,' and there must be oil somewhere in a live man's body or the book wouldn't ask for it."

"All right," returned Ojo, trying not to feel discouraged; "I'll try to find it."

The Magician looked at the little Munchkin boy in a doubtful way and said:

"All this will mean a long journey for you; perhaps several long journeys; for you must search through several of the different countries of Oz in order to get the things I need."

"I know it, sir; but I must do my best to save Unc Nunkie."

"And also my poor wife Margolotte. If you save one you will save the other, for both stand there together and the same compound will restore them both to life. Do the best you can, Ojo, and while you are gone I shall begin the six years' job of making a new batch of the Powder of Life. Then, if you should unluckily fail to secure any one of the things needed, I will have lost no time. But if you succeed you must return here as quickly as you can, and that will save me much tiresome stirring of four kettles with both feet and both hands."

"I will start on my journey at once, sir," said the boy.

"And I will go with you," declared the Patchwork Girl.

"No, no!" exclaimed the Magician. "You have no right to leave this house. You are only a servant and have not been discharged."

Scraps, who had been dancing up and down the room, stopped and looked at him.

"What is a servant?" she asked.

"One who serves. A—a sort of slave," he explained.

"Very well," said the Patchwork Girl, "I'm going to serve you and your wife by helping Ojo find the things you need. You need a lot, you know, such as are not easily found."

"It is true," sighed Dr. Pipt. "I am well aware that Ojo has undertaken a serious task."

Scraps laughed, and resuming her dance she said:

> *"Here's a job for a boy of brains:*
> *A drop of oil from a live man's veins;*
> *A six-leaved clover; three nice hairs*
> *From a Woozy's tail, the book declares*
> *Are needed for the magic spell,*
> *And water from a pitch-dark well.*
> *The yellow wing of a butterfly*
> *To find must Ojo also try,*
> *And if he gets them without harm,*
> *Doc Pipt will make the magic charm;*
> *But if he doesn't get 'em, Unc*
> *Will always stand a marble chunk."*

The Magician looked at her thoughtfully.

"Poor Margolotte must have given you some of the quality of poesy, by mistake," he said. "And, if that is true, I didn't make a very good article when I prepared it, or else you got an overdose or an underdose. However, I believe I shall let you go with Ojo, for my poor wife will not need your services until she is restored to life. Also I think you may be able to help the boy, for your head seems to contain some thoughts I did not expect to find in it. But be very careful of yourself, for you're a souvenir of my dear Margolotte. Try not to get ripped, or your stuffing may fall out. One of your eyes seems loose, and you may have to sew it on tighter. If you talk too much you'll wear out your scarlet plush tongue, which ought to have been hemmed on the edges. And remember you belong to me and must return here as soon as your mission is accomplished."

"I'm going with Scraps and Ojo," announced the Glass Cat.

"You can't," said the Magician.

"Why not?"

"You'd get broken in no time, and you couldn't be a bit of use to the boy and the Patchwork Girl."

"I beg to differ with you," returned the cat, in a haughty tone. "Three heads are better than two, and my pink brains are beautiful. You can see 'em work."

"Well, go along," said the Magician, irritably. "You're only an annoyance, anyhow, and I'm glad to get rid of you."

"Thank you for nothing, then," answered the cat, stiffly.

Dr. Pipt took a small basket from a cupboard and packed several things in it. Then he handed it to Ojo.

"Here is some food and a bundle of charms," he said. "It is all I can give you, but I am sure you will find friends on your journey who will assist you in your search. Take care of the Patchwork Girl and bring her safely back, for she ought to prove useful to my wife. As for the Glass Cat—properly named Bungle—if she bothers you I now give you my permission to break her in two, for she is not respectful and does not obey me. I made a mistake in giving her the pink brains, you see."

Then Ojo went to Unc Nunkie and kissed the old man's marble face very tenderly.

"I'm going to try to save you, Unc," he said, just as if the marble image could hear him; and then he shook the crooked hand of the Crooked Magician, who was already busy hanging the four kettles in the fireplace, and picking up his basket left the house.

The Patchwork Girl followed him, and after them came the Glass Cat.

⸺⸱⸪ ◯hapter 6 ⸱⸪⸺⸱

The JOURNEY

Ojo had never traveled before and so he only knew that the path down the mountainside led into the open Munchkin Country, where large numbers of people dwelt. Scraps was quite new and not supposed to know anything of the Land of Oz, while the Glass Cat admitted she had never wandered very far away from the Magician's house. There was only one path before them, at the beginning, so they could not miss their way, and for a time they walked through the thick forest in silent thought, each one impressed with the importance of the adventure they had undertaken.

Suddenly the Patchwork Girl laughed. It was funny to see her laugh, because her cheeks wrinkled up, her nose tipped, her silver button eyes twinkled and her mouth curled at the corners in a comical way.

"Has something pleased you?" asked Ojo, who was feeling solemn and joyless through thinking upon his uncle's sad fate.

"Yes," she answered. "Your world pleases me, for it's a queer world, and life in it is queerer still. Here am I, made from an old bedquilt and intended to be a slave to Margolotte, rendered free as air by an accident that none of you could foresee. I am enjoying life and seeing the world, while the woman who made me is standing helpless as a block of wood. If that isn't funny enough to laugh at, I don't know what is."

"You're not seeing much of the world yet, my poor, innocent Scraps," remarked the Cat. "The world doesn't consist wholly of the trees that are on all sides of us."

"But they're part of it; and aren't they pretty trees?" returned Scraps, bobbing her head until her brown yarn curls fluttered in the breeze. "Growing between them I can see lovely ferns and wild-flowers, and soft green mosses. If the rest of your world is half as beautiful I shall be glad I'm alive."

"I don't know what the rest of the world is like, I'm sure," said the cat; "but I mean to find out."

"I have never been out of the forest," Ojo added; "but to me the trees are gloomy and sad and the wild-flowers seem lonesome. It must be nicer where there are no trees and there is room for lots of people to live together."

"I wonder if any of the people we shall meet will be as splendid as I am," said the Patchwork Girl. "All I have seen, so far, have pale, colorless skins and clothes as blue as the country they live in, while I am of many gorgeous colors—face and body and clothes. That is why I am bright and contented, Ojo, while you are blue and sad."

"I think I made a mistake in giving you so many sorts of brains," observed the boy. "Perhaps, as the Magician said, you have an overdose, and they may not agree with you."

"What had you to do with my brains?" asked Scraps.

"A lot," replied Ojo. "Old Margolotte meant to give you only a few—just enough to keep you going—but when she wasn't looking I added a good many more, of the best kinds I could find in the Magician's cupboard."

"Thanks," said the girl, dancing along the path ahead of Ojo and then dancing back to his side. "If a few brains are good, many brains must be better."

"But they ought to be evenly balanced," said the boy, "and I had no time to be careful. From the way you're acting, I guess the dose was badly mixed."

"Scraps hasn't enough brains to hurt her, so don't worry," remarked the cat, which was trotting along in a very dainty and graceful manner. "The only brains worth considering are mine, which are pink. You can see 'em work."

After walking a long time they came to a little brook that trickled across the path, and here Ojo sat down to rest and eat something from his basket. He found that the Magician had given him part of a loaf of bread and a slice of cheese. He broke off some of the bread and was surprised to find the loaf just as large as it was before. It was the same way with the cheese: however much he broke off from the slice, it remained exactly the same size.

"Ah," said he, nodding wisely; "that's magic. Dr. Pipt has enchanted the bread and the cheese, so it will last me all through my journey, however much I eat."

"Why do you put those things into your mouth?" asked Scraps, gazing at him in astonishment. "Do you need more stuffing? Then why don't you use cotton, such as I am stuffed with?"

"I don't need that kind," said Ojo.

"But a mouth is to talk with, isn't it?"

"It is also to eat with," replied the boy. "If I didn't put food into my mouth, and eat it, I would get hungry and starve.

"Ah, I didn't know that," she said. "Give me some."

Ojo handed her a bit of the bread and she put it in her mouth.

"What next?" she asked, scarcely able to speak.

"Chew it and swallow it," said the boy.

Scraps tried that. Her pearl teeth were unable to chew the bread and beyond her mouth there was no opening. Being unable to swallow she threw away the bread and laughed.

"I must get hungry and starve, for I can't eat," she said.

"Neither can I," announced the cat; "but I'm not fool enough to try. Can't you understand that you and I are superior people and not made like these poor humans?"

"Why should I understand that, or anything else?" asked the girl. "Don't bother my head by asking conundrums, I beg of you. Just let me discover myself in my own way."

With this she began amusing herself by leaping across the brook and back again.

"Be careful, or you'll fall in the water," warned Ojo.

"Never mind."

"You'd better. If you get wet you'll be soggy and can't walk. Your colors might run, too," he said.

"Don't my colors run whenever I run?" she asked.

"Not in the way I mean. If they get wet, the reds and greens and yellows and purples of your patches might run into each other and become just a blur—no color at all, you know."

"Then," said the Patchwork Girl, "I'll be careful, for if I spoiled my splendid colors I would cease to be beautiful."

"Pah!" sneered the Glass Cat, "such colors are not beautiful; they're ugly, and in bad taste. Please notice that my body has no color at all. I'm transparent, except for my exquisite red heart and my lovely pink brains—you can see 'em work."

"Shoo—shoo—shoo!" cried Scraps, dancing around and laughing. "And your horrid green eyes, Miss Bungle! You can't see your eyes, but we can, and I notice you're very proud of what little color you have. Shoo, Miss Bungle, shoo—shoo—shoo! If you were all colors and many colors, as I am, you'd be too stuck up for anything." She leaped over the cat and back again, and the startled Bungle crept close to a tree to escape her. This made Scraps laugh more heartily than ever, and she said:

> *"Whoop-te-doodle-doo!*
> *The cat has lost her shoe.*
> *Her tootsie's bare, but she don't care,*
> *So what's the odds to you?"*

"Dear me, Ojo," said the cat; "don't you think the creature is a little bit crazy?"

"It may be," he answered, with a puzzled look.

"If she continues her insults I'll scratch off her suspender-button eyes," declared the cat.

"Don't quarrel, please," pleaded the boy, rising to resume the journey. "Let us be good comrades and as happy and cheerful as possible, for we are likely to meet with plenty of trouble on our way."

It was nearly sundown when they came to the edge of the forest and saw spread out before them a delightful landscape. There were broad blue fields stretching for miles over the valley, which was dotted everywhere with pretty, blue domed houses, none of which, however, was very near to the place where they stood. Just at the point where the path left the forest stood a tiny house covered with leaves from the trees, and before this stood a Munchkin man with an axe in his hand. He seemed very much surprised when Ojo and Scraps and the Glass Cat came out of the woods, but as the Patchwork Girl approached nearer he sat down upon a bench and laughed so hard that he could not speak for a long time.

This man was a woodchopper and lived all alone in the little house. He had bushy blue whiskers and merry blue eyes and his blue clothes were quite old and worn.

"Mercy me!" exclaimed the woodchopper, when at last he could stop laughing. "Who would think such a funny harlequin lived in the Land of Oz? Where did you come from, Crazy-quilt?"

"Do you mean me?" asked the Patchwork Girl.

"Of course," he replied.

"You misjudge my ancestry. I'm not a crazy-quilt; I'm patchwork," she said.

"There's no difference," he replied, beginning to laugh again. "When my old grandmother sews such things together she calls it a crazy-quilt; but I never thought such a jumble could come to life."

"It was the magic powder that did it," explained Ojo.

"Oh, then you have come from the Crooked Magician on the mountain. I might have known it, for—Well, I declare! here's a glass cat. But the Magician will get in trouble for this;

it's against the Law for anyone to work magic except Glinda the Good and the royal Wizard of Oz. If you people—or things—or glass spectacles—or crazy-quilts—or whatever you are, go near the Emerald City, you'll be arrested."

"We're going there, anyhow," declared Scraps, sitting upon the bench and swinging her stuffed legs.

> *"If any of us takes a rest,*
> *We'll be arrested sure,*
> *And get no restitution*
> *'Cause the rest we must endure."*

"I see," said the woodchopper, nodding; "you're as crazy as the crazy-quilt you're made of."

"She really *is* crazy," remarked the Glass Cat. "But that isn't to be wondered at when you remember how many different things she's made of. For my part, I'm made of pure glass—except my jewel heart and my pretty pink brains. Did you notice my brains, stranger? You can see 'em work."

"So I can," replied the woodchopper; "but I can't see that they accomplish much. A glass cat is a useless sort of thing, but a Patchwork Girl is really useful. She makes me laugh, and laughter is the best thing in life. There was once a woodchopper, a friend of mine, who was made all of tin, and I used to laugh every time I saw him."

"A tin woodchopper?" said Ojo. "That is strange."

"My friend wasn't always tin," said the man, "but he was careless with his axe, and used to chop himself very badly. Whenever he lost an arm or a leg he had it replaced with tin; so after a while he was all tin."

"And could he chop wood then?" asked the boy.

"He could if he didn't rust his tin joints. But one day he met Dorothy in the forest and went with her to the Emerald City, where he made his fortune. He is now one of the favorites of Princess Ozma, and she has made him the Emperor of the Winkies—the Country where all is yellow."

"Who is Dorothy?" inquired the Patchwork Girl.

"A little maid who used to live in Kansas, but is now a Princess of Oz. She's Ozma's best friend, they say, and lives with her in the royal palace."

"Is Dorothy made of tin?" inquired Ojo.

"Is she patchwork, like me?" inquired Scraps.

"No," said the man; "Dorothy is flesh, just as I am. I know of only one tin person, and that is Nick Chopper, the Tin Woodman; and there will never be but one Patchwork Girl, for any magician that sees you will refuse to make another one like you."

"I suppose we shall see the Tin Woodman, for we are going to the Country of the Winkies," said the boy.

"What for?" asked the woodchopper.

"To get the left wing of a yellow butterfly."

"It is a long journey," declared the man, "and you will go

through lonely parts of Oz and cross rivers and traverse dark forests before you get there."

"Suits me all right," said Scraps. "I'll get a chance to see the country."

"You're crazy, girl. Better crawl into a rag-bag and hide there; or give yourself to some little girl to play with. Those who travel are likely to meet trouble; that's why I stay at home."

The woodchopper then invited them all to stay the night at his little hut, but they were anxious to get on and so left him and continued along the path, which was broader, now, and more distinct.

They expected to reach some other house before it grew dark, but the twilight was brief and Ojo soon began to fear they had made a mistake in leaving the woodchopper.

"I can scarcely see the path," he said at last. "Can you see it, Scraps?"

"No," replied the Patchwork Girl, who was holding fast to the boy's arm so he could guide her.

"I can see," declared the Glass Cat. "My eyes are better than yours, and my pink brains—"

"Never mind your pink brains, please," said Ojo hastily; "just run ahead and show us the way. Wait a minute and I'll tie a string to you; for then you can lead us."

He got a string from his pocket and tied it around the cat's neck, and after that the creature guided them along the path. They had proceeded in this way for about an hour when a twinkling blue light appeared ahead of them.

"Good! there's a house at last," cried Ojo. "When we reach it the good people will surely welcome us and give us a night's lodging." But however far they walked the light seemed to get no nearer, so by and by the cat stopped short, saying:

"I think the light is traveling, too, and we shall never be able to catch up with it. But here is a house by the roadside, so why go farther?"

"Where is the house, Bungle?"

"Just here beside us, Scraps."

Ojo was now able to see a small house near the pathway. It was dark and silent, but the boy was tired and wanted to rest, so he went up to the door and knocked.

"Who is there?" cried a voice from within.

"I am Ojo the Unlucky, and with me are Miss Scraps Patchwork and the Glass Cat," he replied.

"What do you want?" asked the Voice.

"A place to sleep," said Ojo.

"Come in, then; but don't make any noise, and you must go directly to bed," returned the Voice.

Ojo unlatched the door and entered. It was very dark inside and he could see nothing at all. But the cat exclaimed: "Why, there's no one here!"

"There must be," said the boy. "Some one spoke to me."

"I can see everything in the room," replied the cat, "and

no one is present but ourselves. But here are three beds, all made up, so we may as well go to sleep."

"What is sleep?" inquired the Patchwork Girl.

"It's what you do when you go to bed," said Ojo.

"But why do you go to bed?" persisted the Patchwork Girl.

"Here, here! You are making altogether too much noise," cried the Voice they had heard before. "Keep quiet, strangers, and go to bed."

The cat, which could see in the dark, looked sharply around for the owner of the Voice, but could discover no one, although the Voice had seemed close beside them. She arched her back a little and seemed afraid. Then she whispered to Ojo: "Come!" and led him to a bed.

With his hands the boy felt the bed and found it was big and soft, with feather pillows and plenty of blankets. So he took off his shoes and hat and crept into the bed. Then the cat led Scraps to another bed and the Patchwork Girl was puzzled to know what to do with it.

"Lie down and keep quiet," whispered the cat, warningly.

"Can't I sing?" asked Scraps.

"No."

"Can't I whistle?" asked Scraps.

"No."

"Can't I dance till morning, if I want to?" asked Scraps.

"You must keep quiet," said the cat, in a soft voice.

"I don't want to," replied the Patchwork Girl, speaking as loudly as usual. "What right have you to order me around? If I want to talk, or yell, or whistle—"

Before she could say anything more an unseen hand seized her firmly and threw her out of the door, which closed behind her with a sharp slam. She found herself bumping and rolling in the road and when she got up and tried to open the door of the house again she found it locked.

"What has happened to Scraps?" asked Ojo.

"Never mind. Let's go to sleep, or something will happen to us," answered the Glass Cat.

So Ojo snuggled down in his bed and fell asleep, and he was so tired that he never wakened until broad daylight.

..—..◄ Chapter 7 ►..—..

The TROUBLESOME PHONOGRAPH

When the boy opened his eyes next morning he looked carefully around the room. These small Munchkin houses seldom had more than one room in them. That in which Ojo now found himself had three beds, set all in a row on one side of it. The Glass Cat lay asleep on one bed, Ojo was in the second, and the third was neatly made up and smoothed for the day. On the other side of the room was a round table on which breakfast was already placed, smoking hot. Only one chair was drawn up to the table, where a place was set for one person. No one seemed to be in the room except the boy and Bungle.

Ojo got up and put on his shoes. Finding a toilet stand at

the head of his bed he washed his face and hands and brushed his hair. Then he went to the table and said:

"I wonder if this is my breakfast?"

"Eat it!" commanded a Voice at his side, so near that Ojo jumped. But no person could he see.

He was hungry, and the breakfast looked good; so he sat down and ate all he wanted. Then, rising, he took his hat and wakened the Glass Cat.

"Come on, Bungle," said he; "we must go."

He cast another glance about the room and, speaking to the air, he said: "Whoever lives here has been kind to me, and I'm much obliged."

There was no answer, so he took his basket and went out the door, the cat following him. In the middle of the path sat the Patchwork Girl, playing with pebbles she had picked up.

"Oh, there you are!" she exclaimed cheerfully. "I thought you were never coming out. It has been daylight a long time."

"What did you do all night?" asked the boy.

"Sat here and watched the stars and the moon," she replied. "They're interesting. I never saw them before, you know."

"Of course not," said Ojo.

"You were crazy to act so badly and get thrown outdoors," remarked Bungle, as they renewed their journey.

"That's all right," said Scraps. "If I hadn't been thrown out I wouldn't have seen the stars, nor the big grey wolf."

"What wolf?" inquired Ojo.

"The one that came to the door of the house three times during the night."

"I don't see why that should be," said the boy, thoughtfully; "there was plenty to eat in that house, for I had a fine breakfast, and I slept in a nice bed."

"Don't you feel tired?" asked the Patchwork Girl, noticing that the boy yawned.

"Why, yes; I'm as tired as I was last night; and yet I slept very well."

"And aren't you hungry?"

"It's strange," replied Ojo. "I had a good breakfast, and yet I think I'll now eat some of my crackers and cheese."

Scraps danced up and down the path. Then she sang:

> *"Kizzle-kazzle-kore;*
> *The wolf is at the door,*
> *There's nothing to eat but a bone without meat,*
> *And a bill from the grocery store."*

"What does that mean?" asked Ojo.

"Don't ask me," replied Scraps. "I say what comes into my head, but of course I know nothing of a grocery store or bones without meat or—very much else."

"No," said the cat; "she's stark, staring, raving crazy, and her brains can't be pink, for they don't work properly."

"Bother the brains!" cried Scraps. "Who cares for 'em, anyhow? Have you noticed how beautiful my patches are in this sunlight?"

Just then they heard a sound as of footsteps pattering along the path behind them and all three turned to see what was coming. To their astonishment they beheld a small round table running as fast as its four spindle legs could carry it, and to the top was screwed fast a phonograph with a big gold horn.

"Hold on!" shouted the phonograph. "Wait for me!"

"Goodness me; it's that music thing which the Crooked Magician scattered the Powder of Life over," said Ojo.

"So it is," returned Bungle, in a grumpy tone of voice; and then, as the phonograph overtook them, the Glass Cat added sternly: "What are you doing here, anyhow?"

"I've run away," said the music thing. "After you left, old Dr. Pipt and I had a dreadful quarrel and he threatened to smash me to pieces if I didn't keep quiet. Of course I wouldn't do that, because a talking-machine is supposed to talk and make a noise—and sometimes music. So I slipped out of the house while the Magician was stirring his four kettles and I've been running after you all night. Now that I've found such pleasant company, I can talk and play tunes all I want to."

Ojo was greatly annoyed by this unwelcome addition to their party. At first he did not know what to say to the new-comer, but a little thought decided him not to make friends.

"We are traveling on important business," he declared,

"and you'll excuse me if I say we can't be bothered."

"How very impolite!" exclaimed the phonograph.

"I'm sorry; but it's true," said the boy. "You'll have to go somewhere else."

"This is very unkind treatment, I must say," whined the phonograph, in an injured tone. "Everyone seems to hate me, and yet I was intended to amuse people."

"It isn't you we hate, especially," observed the Glass Cat; "it's your dreadful music. When I lived in the same room with you I was much annoyed by your squeaky horn. It growls and grumbles and clicks and scratches so it spoils the music, and your machinery rumbles so that the racket drowns every tune you attempt."

"That isn't my fault; it's the fault of my records. I must admit that I haven't a clear record," answered the machine.

"Just the same, you'll have to go away," said Ojo.

"Wait a minute," cried Scraps. "This music thing interests me. I remember to have heard music when I first came to life, and I would like to hear it again. What is your name, my poor abused phonograph?"

"Victor Columbia Edison," it answered.

"Well, I shall call you 'Vic' for short," said the Patchwork Girl. "Go ahead and play something."

"It'll drive you crazy," warned the cat.

"I'm crazy now, according to your statement. Loosen up and reel out the music, Vic."

"The only record I have with me," explained the phonograph, "is one the Magician attached just before we had our quarrel. It's a highly classical composition."

"A what?" inquired Scraps.

"It is classical music, and is considered the best and most puzzling ever manufactured. You're supposed to like it, whether you do or not, and if you don't, the proper thing is to look as if you did. Understand?"

"Not in the least," said Scraps.

"Then, listen!"

At once the machine began to play and in a few minutes Ojo put his hands to his ears to shut out the sounds and the cat snarled and Scraps began to laugh.

"Cut it out, Vic," she said. "That's enough."

But the phonograph continued playing the dreary tune, so Ojo seized the crank, jerked it free and threw it into the road. However, the moment the crank struck the ground it bounded back to the machine again and began winding it up. And still the music played.

"Let's run!" cried Scraps, and they all started and ran down the path as fast as they could go. But the phonograph was right behind them and could run and play at the same time. It called out, reproachfully:

"What's the matter? Don't you love classical music?"

"No, Vic," said Scraps, halting. "We will passical the classical and preserve what joy we have left. I haven't any nerves, thank goodness, but your music makes my cotton shrink."

"Then turn over my record. There's a rag-time tune on the other side," said the machine.

"What's rag-time?"

"The opposite of classical."

"All right," said Scraps, and turned over the record.

The phonograph now began to play a jerky jumble of sounds which proved so bewildering that after a moment Scraps stuffed her patchwork apron into the gold horn and cried: "Stop—stop! That's the other extreme. It's extremely bad!"

Muffled as it was, the phonograph played on.

"If you don't shut off that music I'll smash your record," threatened Ojo.

The music stopped, at that, and the machine turned its horn from one to another and said with great indignation: "What's the matter now? Is it possible you can't appreciate rag-time?"

"Scraps ought to, being rags herself," said the cat; "but I simply can't stand it; it makes my whiskers curl."

"It is, indeed, dreadful!" exclaimed Ojo, with a shudder.

"It's enough to drive a crazy lady mad," murmured the Patchwork Girl. "I'll tell you what, Vic," she added as she smoothed out her apron and put it on again, "for some reason or other you've missed your guess. You're not a concert; you're a nuisance."

"Music hath charms to soothe the savage breast," asserted the phonograph sadly.

"Then we're not savages. I advise you to go home and beg the Magician's pardon."

"Never! He'd smash me."

"That's what we shall do, if you stay here," Ojo declared.

"Run along, Vic, and bother some one else," advised Scraps. "Find some one who is real wicked, and stay with him till he repents. In that way you can do some good in the world."

The music thing turned silently away and trotted down a side path, toward a distant Munchkin village.

"Is that the way we go?" asked Bungle anxiously.

"No," said Ojo; "I think we shall keep straight ahead, for this path is the widest and best. When we come to some house we will inquire the way to the Emerald City."

Chapter 8

Chapter 8

The FOOLISH OWL and the WISE DONKEY

O n they went, and half an hour's steady walking brought them to a house somewhat better than the two they had already passed. It stood close to the roadside and over the door was a sign that read: "Miss Foolish Owl and Mr. Wise Donkey: Public Advisers."

When Ojo read this sign aloud Scraps said laughingly: "Well, here is a place to get all the advice we want, maybe more than we need. Let's go in."

The boy knocked at the door.

"Come in!" called a deep bass voice.

So they opened the door and entered the house, where a

little light-brown donkey, dressed in a blue apron and a blue cap, was engaged in dusting the furniture with a blue cloth. On a shelf over the window sat a great blue owl with a blue sun-bonnet on her head, blinking her big round eyes at the visitors.

"Good morning," said the donkey, in his deep voice, which seemed bigger than he was. "Did you come to us for advice?"

"Why, we came, anyhow," replied Scraps, "and now we are here we may as well have some advice. It's free, isn't it?"

"Certainly," said the donkey. "Advice doesn't cost anything—unless you follow it. Permit me to say, by the way, that you are the queerest lot of travelers that ever came to my shop. Judging you merely by appearances, I think you'd better talk to the Foolish Owl yonder."

They turned to look at the bird, which fluttered its wings and stared back at them with its big eyes.

"Hoot-ti-toot-ti-toot!" cried the owl.

> "Fiddle-cum-foo,
> Howdy-do?
> Riddle-cum, tiddle-cum,
> Too-ra-la-loo!"

"That beats your poetry, Scraps," said Ojo.

"It's just nonsense!" declared the Glass Cat.

"But it's good advice for the foolish," said the donkey, admiringly. "Listen to my partner, and you can't go wrong."

Said the owl in a grumbling voice:

"Patchwork Girl has come to life;
No one's sweetheart, no one's wife;
Lacking sense and loving fun,
She'll be snubbed by everyone."

"Quite a compliment! Quite a compliment, I declare," exclaimed the donkey, turning to look at Scraps. "You are certainly a wonder, my dear, and I fancy you'd make a splendid pincushion. If you belonged to me, I'd wear smoked glasses when I looked at you."

"Why?" asked the Patchwork Girl.

"Because you are so gay and gaudy."

"It is my beauty that dazzles you," she asserted. "You Munchkin people all strut around in your stupid blue color, while I—"

"You are wrong in calling me a Munchkin," interrupted the donkey, "for I was born in the Land of Mo and came to visit the Land of Oz on the day it was shut off from all the rest of the world. So here I am obliged to stay, and I confess it is a very pleasant country to live in."

"Hoot-ti-toot!" cried the owl;

"Ojo's searching for a charm,
'Cause Unc Nunkie's come to harm.

> *Charms are scarce; they're hard to get;*
> *Ojo's got a job, you bet!"*

"Is the owl so very foolish?" asked the boy.

"Extremely so," replied the donkey. "Notice what vulgar expressions she uses. But I admire the owl for the reason that she *is* positively foolish. Owls are supposed to be so very wise, generally, that a foolish one is unusual, and you perhaps know that anything or anyone unusual is sure to be interesting to the wise."

The owl flapped its wings again, muttering these words:

> *"It's hard to be a glassy cat—*
> *No cat can be more hard than that;*
> *She's so transparent, every act*
> *Is clear to us, and that's a fact."*

"Have you noticed my pink brains?" inquired Bungle, proudly. "You can see 'em work."

"Not in the daytime," said the donkey. "She can't see very well by day, poor thing. But her advice is excellent. I advise you all to follow it."

"The owl hasn't given us any advice, as yet," the boy declared.

"No? Then what do you call all those sweet poems?"

"Just foolishness," replied Ojo. "Scraps does the same thing."

"Foolishness! Of course! To be sure! The Foolish Owl must be foolish or she wouldn't be the Foolish Owl. You are very complimentary to my partner, indeed," asserted the donkey, rubbing his front hoofs together as if highly pleased.

"The sign says that *you* are wise," remarked Scraps to the donkey. "I wish you would prove it."

"With great pleasure," returned the beast. "Put me to the test, my dear Patches, and I'll prove my wisdom in the wink of an eye."

"What is the best way to get to the Emerald City?" asked Ojo.

"Walk," said the donkey.

"I know; but what road shall I take?" was the boy's next question.

"The road of yellow bricks, of course. It leads directly to the Emerald City."

"And how shall we find the road of yellow bricks?"

"By keeping along the path you have been following. You'll come to the yellow bricks pretty soon, and you'll know them when you see them because they're the only yellow things in the blue country."

"Thank you," said the boy. "At last you have told me something."

"Is that the extent of your wisdom?" asked Scraps.

"No," replied the donkey; "I know many other things, but they wouldn't interest you. So I'll give you a last word of advice: move on, for the sooner you do that the sooner you'll get to the Emerald City of Oz."

"Hoot-ti-toot-ti-toot-ti-too!" screeched the owl;

> *"Off you go! fast or slow,*
> *Where you're going you don't know.*
> *Patches, Bungle, Munchkin lad,*
> *Facing fortunes good and bad,*
> *Meeting dangers grave and sad,*
> *Sometimes worried, sometimes glad—*
> *Where you're going you don't know,*
> *Nor do I, but off you go!"*

"Sounds like a hint, to me," said the Patchwork Girl.

"Then let's take it and go," replied Ojo.

They said good-bye to the Wise Donkey and the Foolish Owl and at once resumed their journey.

····• Chapter 9 •····

THEY MEET the WOOZY

There seem to be very few houses around here, after all," remarked Ojo, after they had walked for a time in silence.

"Never mind," said Scraps; "we are not looking for houses, but rather the road of yellow bricks. Won't it be funny to run across something yellow in this dismal blue country?"

"There are worse colors than yellow in this country," asserted the Glass Cat, in a spiteful tone.

"Oh; do you mean the pink pebbles you call your brains, and your red heart and green eyes?" asked the Patchwork Girl.

"No; I mean you, if you must know it," growled the cat.

"You're jealous!" laughed Scraps. "You'd give your whiskers for a lovely variegated complexion like mine."

"I wouldn't!" retorted the cat. "I've the clearest complexion in the world, and I don't employ a beauty-doctor, either."

"I see you don't," said Scraps.

"Please don't quarrel," begged Ojo. "This is an important journey, and quarreling makes me discouraged. To be brave, one must be cheerful, so I hope you will be as good-tempered as possible."

They had traveled some distance when suddenly they faced a high fence which barred any further progress straight ahead. It ran directly across the road and enclosed a small forest of tall trees, set close together. When the group of adventurers peered through the bars of the fence they thought this forest looked more gloomy and forbidding than any they had ever seen before.

They soon discovered that the path they had been following now made a bend and passed around the enclosure, but what made Ojo stop and look thoughtful was a sign painted on the fence which read:

BEWARE OF THE WOOZY!

"That means," he said, "that there's a Woozy inside that fence, and the Woozy must be a dangerous animal or they wouldn't tell people to beware of it."

"Let's keep out, then," replied Scraps. "That path is outside the fence, and Mr. Woozy may have all his little forest to himself, for all we care."

"But one of our errands is to find a Woozy," Ojo explained. "The Magician wants me to get three hairs from the end of a Woozy's tail."

"Let's go on and find some other Woozy," suggested the cat. "This one is ugly and dangerous, or they wouldn't cage him up. Maybe we shall find another that is tame and gentle."

"Perhaps there isn't any other, at all," answered Ojo. "The sign doesn't say: 'Beware *a* Woozy'; it says: 'Beware *the* Woozy,' which may mean there's only one in all the Land of Oz."

"Then," said Scraps, "suppose we go in and find him? Very likely if we ask him politely to let us pull three hairs out of the tip of his tail he won't hurt us."

"It would hurt *him*, I'm sure, and that would make him cross," said the cat.

"You needn't worry, Bungle," remarked the Patchwork Girl; "for if there is danger you can climb a tree. Ojo and I are not afraid; are we, Ojo?"

"I am, a little," the boy admitted; "but this danger must be faced, if we intend to save poor Unc Nunkie. How shall we get over the fence?"

"Climb," answered Scraps, and at once she began climbing up the rows of bars. Ojo followed and found it more easy than he had expected. When they got to the top of the fence they began to get down on the other side and soon were in the forest. The Glass Cat, being small, crept between the lower bars and joined them.

Here there was no path of any sort, so they entered the woods, the boy leading the way, and wandered through the trees until they were nearly in the center of the forest. They now came upon a clear space in which stood a rocky cave.

So far they had met no living creature, but when Ojo saw the cave he knew it must be the den of the Woozy.

It is hard to face any savage beast without a sinking of the heart, but still more terrifying is it to face an unknown beast, which you have never seen even a picture of. So there is little wonder that the pulses of the Munchkin boy beat fast as he and his companions stood facing the cave. The opening was perfectly square, and about big enough to admit a goat.

"I guess the Woozy is asleep," said Scraps. "Shall I throw in a stone, to waken him?"

"No; please don't," answered Ojo, his voice trembling a little. "I'm in no hurry."

But he had not long to wait, for the Woozy heard the sound of voices and came trotting out of his cave. As this is the only Woozy that has ever lived, either in the Land of Oz or out of it, I must describe it to you.

The creature was all squares and flat surfaces and edges. Its head was an exact square, like one of the building-blocks a child plays with; therefore it had no ears, but heard sounds through two openings in the upper corners. Its nose, being in the center of a square surface, was flat, while the mouth was formed by the opening of the lower edge of the block. The body of the Woozy was much larger than its head, but was likewise block-shaped—being twice as long as it was wide and high. The tail was square and stubby and perfectly straight, and the four legs were made in the same way, each being four-sided. The animal was covered with a thick, smooth skin and had no hair at all except at the extreme end of its tail, where there grew exactly three stiff, stubby hairs. The beast was dark blue in color and his face was not fierce nor ferocious in expression, but rather good-humored and droll.

Seeing the strangers, the Woozy folded his hind legs as if they had been hinged and sat down to look his visitors over.

"Well, well," he exclaimed; "what a queer lot you are! At first I thought some of those miserable Munchkin farmers had come to annoy me, but I am relieved to find you in their stead. It is plain to me that you are a remarkable group—as remarkable in your way as I am in mine—and so you are welcome to my domain. Nice place, isn't it? But lonesome—dreadfully lonesome."

"Why did they shut you up here?" asked Scraps, who was regarding the queer, square creature with much curiosity.

"Because I eat up all the honey-bees which the Munchkin farmers who live around here keep to make them honey."

"Are you fond of eating honey-bees?" inquired the boy.

"Very. They are really delicious. But the farmers did not like to lose their bees and so they tried to destroy me. Of course they couldn't do that."

"Why not?"

"My skin is so thick and tough that nothing can get through it to hurt me. So, finding they could not destroy me, they drove me into this forest and built a fence around me. Unkind, wasn't it?"

"But what do you eat now?" asked Ojo.

"Nothing at all. I've tried the leaves from the trees and the mosses and creeping vines, but they don't seem to suit my taste. So, there being no honey-bees here, I've eaten nothing for years."

"You must be awfully hungry," said the boy. "I've got some bread and cheese in my basket. Would you like that kind of food?"

"Give me a nibble and I will try it; then I can tell you better whether it is grateful to my appetite," returned the Woozy.

So the boy opened his basket and broke a piece off the loaf of bread. He tossed it toward the Woozy, who cleverly caught it in his mouth and ate it in a twinkling.

"That's rather good," declared the animal. "Any more?"

"Try some cheese," said Ojo, and threw down a piece.

The Woozy ate that, too, and smacked its long, thin lips.

"That's mighty good!" it exclaimed. "Any more?"

"Plenty," replied Ojo. So he sat down on a Stump and fed the Woozy bread and cheese for a long time; for, no matter how much the boy broke off, the loaf and the slice remained just as big.

"That'll do," said the Woozy, at last; "I'm quite full. I hope the strange food won't give me indigestion."

"I hope not," said Ojo. "It's what I eat."

"Well, I must say I'm much obliged, and I'm glad you came," announced the beast. "Is there anything I can do in return for your kindness?"

"Yes," said Ojo earnestly, "you have it in your power to do me a great favor, if you will."

"What is it?" asked the Woozy. "Name the favor and I will grant it."

"I—I want three hairs from the tip of your tail," said Ojo, with some hesitation.

"Three hairs! Why, that's all I have—on my tail or anywhere else," exclaimed the beast.

"I know; but I want them very much."

"They are my sole ornaments, my prettiest feature," said the Woozy, uneasily. "If I give up those three hairs I—I'm just a blockhead."

"Yet I must have them," insisted the boy, firmly, and he then told the Woozy all about the accident to Unc Nunkie and Margolotte, and how the three hairs were to be a part of the magic charm that would restore them to life. The beast listened with attention and when Ojo had finished the recital it said, with a sigh:

"I always keep my word, for I pride myself on being square. So you may have the three hairs, and welcome. I think, under such circumstances, it would be selfish in me to refuse you."

"Thank you! Thank you very much," cried the boy, joyfully. "May I pull out the hairs now?"

"Any time you like," answered the Woozy.

So Ojo went up to the queer creature and taking hold of one of the hairs began to pull. He pulled harder. He pulled with all his might; but the hair remained fast.

"What's the trouble?" asked the Woozy, which Ojo had dragged here and there all around the clearing in his endeavor to pull out the hair.

"It won't come," said the boy, panting.

"I was afraid of that," declared the beast. "You'll have to pull harder."

"I'll help you," exclaimed Scraps, coming to the boy's side. "You pull the hair, and I'll pull you, and together we ought to get it out easily."

"Wait a jiffy," called the Woozy, and then it went to a tree and hugged it with its front paws, so that its body couldn't be dragged around by the pull. "All ready, now. Go ahead!"

Ojo grasped the hair with both hands and pulled with all his strength, while Scraps seized the boy around his waist and added her strength to his. But the hair wouldn't budge. Instead, it slipped out of Ojo's hands and he and Scraps both rolled upon the ground in a heap and never stopped until they bumped against the rocky cave.

"Give it up," advised the Glass Cat, as the boy arose and assisted the Patchwork Girl to her feet. "A dozen strong men couldn't pull out those hairs. I believe they're clinched on the under side of the Woozy's thick skin."

"Then what shall I do?" asked the boy, despairingly. "If on our return I fail to take these three hairs to the Crooked Magician, the other things I have come to seek will be of no use at all, and we cannot restore Unc Nunkie and Margolotte to life."

"They're goners, I guess," said the Patchwork Girl.

"Never mind," added the cat. "I can't see that old Unc and Margolotte are worth all this trouble, anyhow."

But Ojo did not feel that way. He was so disheartened that he sat down upon a stump and began to cry.

The Woozy looked at the boy thoughtfully.

"Why don't you take me with you?" asked the beast. "Then, when at last you get to the Magician's house, he can surely find some way to pull out those three hairs."

Ojo was overjoyed at this suggestion.

"That's it!" he cried, wiping away the tears and springing to his feet with a smile. "If I take the three hairs to the Magician, it won't matter if they are still in your body."

"It can't matter in the least," agreed the Woozy.

"Come on, then," said the boy, picking up his basket; "let us start at once. I have several other things to find, you know."

But the Glass Cat gave a little laugh and inquired in her scornful way:

"How do you intend to get the beast out of this forest?"

That puzzled them all for a time.

"Let us go to the fence, and then we may find a way," suggested Scraps. So they walked through the forest to the fence, reaching it at a point exactly opposite that where they had entered the enclosure.

"How did you get in?" asked the Woozy.

"We climbed over," answered Ojo.

"I can't do that," said the beast. "I'm a very swift runner, for I can overtake a honey-bee as it flies; and I can jump very high, which is the reason they made such a tall fence to keep me in. But I can't climb at all, and I'm too big to squeeze between the bars of the fence."

Ojo tried to think what to do.

"Can you dig?" he asked.

"No," answered the Woozy, "for I have no claws. My feet are quite flat on the bottom of them. Nor can I gnaw away the boards, as I have no teeth."

"You're not such a terrible creature, after all," remarked Scraps.

"You haven't heard me growl, or you wouldn't say that," declared the Woozy. "When I growl, the sound echoes like thunder all through the valleys and woodlands, and children tremble with fear, and women cover their heads with their aprons, and big men run and hide. I suppose there is nothing in the world so terrible to listen to as the growl of a Woozy."

"Please don't growl, then," begged Ojo, earnestly.

"There is no danger of my growling, for I am not angry. Only when angry do I utter my fearful, ear-splitting, soul-shuddering growl. Also, when I am angry, my eyes flash fire, whether I growl or not."

"Real fire?" asked Ojo.

"Of course, real fire. Do you suppose they'd flash imitation fire?" inquired the Woozy, in an injured tone.

"In that case, I've solved the riddle," cried Scraps, dancing with glee. "Those fence-boards are made of wood, and if the Woozy stands close to the fence and lets his eyes flash fire, they might set fire to the fence and burn it up. Then he could walk away with us easily, being free."

"Ah, I have never thought of that plan, or I would have been free long ago," said the Woozy. "But I cannot flash fire from my eyes unless I am very angry."

"Can't you get angry 'bout something, please?" asked Ojo.

"I'll try. You just say 'Krizzle-Kroo' to me."

"Will that make you angry?" inquired the boy.

"Terribly angry."

"What does it mean?" asked Scraps.

"I don't know; that's what makes me so angry," replied the Woozy.

He then stood close to the fence, with his head near one of the boards, and Scraps called out "Krizzle-Kroo!" Then Ojo said "Krizzle-Kroo!" and the Glass Cat said "Krizzle-Kroo!" The Woozy began to tremble with anger and small sparks darted from his eyes. Seeing this, they all cried "Krizzle-Kroo!" together, and that made the beast's eyes flash fire so fiercely that the fence-board caught the sparks and began to smoke. Then it burst into flame, and the Woozy stepped back and said triumphantly:

"Aha! That did the business, all right. It was a happy thought for you to yell all together, for that made me as angry as I have ever been. Fine sparks, weren't they?"

"Reg'lar fireworks," replied Scraps, admiringly.

In a few moments the board had burned to a distance of several feet, leaving an opening big enough for them all to pass through. Ojo broke some branches from a tree and with them whipped the fire until it was extinguished.

"We don't want to burn the whole fence down," said he, "for the flames would attract the attention of the Munchkin farmers, who would then come and capture the Woozy again. I guess they'll be rather surprised when they find he's escaped."

"So they will," declared the Woozy, chuckling gleefully. "When they find I'm gone the farmers will be badly scared, for they'll expect me to eat up their honey-bees, as I did before."

"That reminds me," said the boy, "that you must promise not to eat honey-bees while you are in our company."

"None at all?"

"Not a bee. You would get us all into trouble, and we can't afford to have any more trouble than is necessary. I'll feed you all the bread and cheese you want, and that must satisfy you."

"All right; I'll promise," said the Woozy, cheerfully. "And when I promise anything you can depend on it, 'cause I'm square."

"I don't see what difference that makes," observed the Patchwork Girl, as they found the path and continued their journey. "The shape doesn't make a thing honest, does it?"

"Of course it does," returned the Woozy, very decidedly. "No one could trust that Crooked Magician, for instance, just because he *is* crooked; but a square Woozy couldn't do anything crooked if he wanted to."

"I am neither square nor crooked," said Scraps, looking down at her plump body.

"No; you're round, so you're liable to do anything," asserted the Woozy. "Do not blame me, Miss Gorgeous, if I regard you with suspicion. Many a satin ribbon has a cotton back."

Scraps didn't understand this, but she had an uneasy misgiving that she had a cotton back herself. It would settle down, at times, and make her squat and dumpy, and then she had to roll herself in the road until her body stretched out again.

Chapter 10

SHAGGY MAN
to the RESCUE

They had not gone very far before Bungle, who had run on ahead, came bounding back to say that the road of yellow bricks was just before them. At once they hurried forward to see what this famous road looked like.

It was a broad road, but not straight, for it wandered over hill and dale and picked out the easiest places to go. All its length and breadth was paved with smooth bricks of a bright yellow color, so it was smooth and level except in a few places where the bricks had crumbled or been removed, leaving holes that might cause the unwary to stumble.

"I wonder," said Ojo, looking up and down the road, "which way to go."

"Where are you bound for?" asked the Woozy.

"The Emerald City," he replied.

"Then go west," said the Woozy. "I know this road pretty well, for I've chased many a honey-bee over it."

"Have you ever been to the Emerald City?" asked Scraps.

"No. I am very shy by nature, as you may have noticed, so I haven't mingled much in society."

"Are you afraid of men?" inquired the Patchwork Girl.

"Me? With my heart-rending growl—my horrible, shudderful growl? I should say not. I am not afraid of anything," declared the Woozy.

"I wish I could say the same," sighed Ojo. "I don't think we need be afraid when we get to the Emerald City, for Unc Nunkie has told me that Ozma, our girl Ruler, is very lovely and kind, and tries to help everyone who is in trouble. But they say there are many dangers lurking on the road to the great Fairy City, and so we must be very careful."

"I hope nothing will break me," said the Glass Cat, in a nervous voice. "I'm a little brittle, you know, and can't stand many hard knocks."

"If anything should fade the colors of my lovely patches it would break my heart," said the Patchwork Girl.

"I'm not sure you have a heart," Ojo reminded her.

"Then it would break my cotton," persisted Scraps. "Do you think they are all fast colors, Ojo?" she asked anxiously.

"They seem fast enough when you run," he replied; and then, looking ahead of them, he exclaimed: "Oh, what lovely trees!"

They were certainly pretty to look upon and the travelers hurried forward to observe them more closely.

"Why, they are not trees at all," said Scraps; "they are just monstrous plants."

That is what they really were: masses of great broad leaves which rose from the ground far into the air, until they towered twice as high as the top of the Patchwork Girl's head, who was a little taller than Ojo. The plants formed rows on both sides of the road and from each plant rose a dozen or more of the big broad leaves, which swayed continually from side to side, although no wind was blowing. But the most curious thing about the swaying leaves was their color. They seemed to have a general groundwork of blue, but here and there other colors glinted at times through the blue—gorgeous yellows, turning to pink, purple, orange and scarlet, mingled with more sober browns and greys—each appearing as a blotch or stripe anywhere on a leaf and then disappearing, to be replaced by some other color of a different shape.

The changeful coloring of the great leaves was very beautiful, but it was bewildering, as well, and the novelty of the scene drew our travelers close to the line of plants, where they stood watching them with rapt interest.

Suddenly a leaf bent lower than usual and touched the Patchwork Girl. Swiftly it enveloped her in its embrace, covering her completely in its thick folds, and then it swayed back upon its stem.

"Why, she's gone!" gasped Ojo, in amazement, and listening carefully he thought he could hear the muffled screams of Scraps coming from the center of the folded leaf. But, before he could think what he ought to do to save her, another leaf bent down and captured the Glass Cat, rolling around the little creature until she was completely hidden, and then straightening up again upon its stem.

"Look out," cried the Woozy. "Run! Run fast, or you are lost."

Ojo turned and saw the Woozy running swiftly up the road. But the last leaf of the row of plants seized the beast even as he ran and instantly he disappeared from sight.

The boy had no chance to escape. Half a dozen of the great leaves were bending toward him from different directions and as he stood hesitating one of them clutched him in its embrace. In a flash he was in the dark. Then he felt himself gently lifted until he was swaying in the air, with the folds of the leaf hugging him on all sides.

At first he struggled hard to escape, crying out in anger: "Let me go! Let me go!" But neither struggles nor protests had any effect whatever. The leaf held him firmly and he was a prisoner.

Then Ojo quieted himself and tried to think. Despair fell upon him when he remembered that all his little party had been captured, even as he was, and there was none to save them.

"I might have expected it," he sobbed, miserably. "I'm Ojo the Unlucky, and something dreadful was sure to happen to me."

He pushed against the leaf that held him and found it to be soft, but thick and firm. It was like a great bandage all around him and he found it difficult to move his body or limbs in order to change their position.

The minutes passed and became hours. Ojo wondered how long one could live in such a condition and if the leaf would gradually sap his strength and even his life, in order to feed itself. The little Munchkin boy had never heard of any person dying in the Land of Oz, but he knew one could suffer a great deal of pain. His greatest fear at this time was that he would always remain imprisoned in the beautiful leaf and never see the light of day again.

No sound came to him through the leaf; all around was intense silence. Ojo wondered if Scraps had stopped screaming, or if the folds of the leaf prevented his hearing her. By and by he thought he heard a whistle, as of some one whistling a tune. Yes; it really must be some one whistling, he decided, for he could follow the strains of a pretty Munchkin melody that Unc Nunkie used to sing to him. The sounds were low and sweet and, although they reached Ojo's ears very faintly, they were clear and harmonious.

Could the leaf whistle, Ojo wondered? Nearer and nearer came the sounds and then they seemed to be just the other side of the leaf that was hugging him.

Suddenly the whole leaf toppled and fell, carrying the boy with it, and while he sprawled at full length the folds slowly relaxed and set him free. He scrambled quickly to his feet and found that a strange man was standing before him—a man so curious in appearance that the boy stared with round eyes.

He was a big man, with shaggy whiskers, shaggy eyebrows, shaggy hair—but kindly blue eyes that were gentle as those of a cow. On his head was a green velvet hat with a jeweled band, which was all shaggy around the brim. Rich but shaggy laces were at his throat; a coat with shaggy edges was decorated with diamond buttons; the velvet breeches had jeweled buckles at the knees and shags all around the bottoms. On his breast hung a medallion bearing a picture of Princess Dorothy of Oz, and in his hand, as he stood looking at Ojo, was a sharp knife shaped like a dagger.

"Oh!" exclaimed Ojo, greatly astonished at the sight of this stranger; and then he added: "Who has saved me, sir?"

"Can't you see?" replied the other, with a smile; "I'm the Shaggy Man."

"Yes; I can see that," said the boy, nodding. "Was it you who rescued me from the leaf?"

"None other, you may be sure. But take care, or I shall have to rescue you again."

Ojo gave a jump, for he saw several broad leaves leaning toward him; but the Shaggy Man began to whistle again, and at the sound the leaves all straightened up on their stems and kept still.

The man now took Ojo's arm and led him up the road, past the last of the great plants, and not till he was safely beyond their reach did he cease his whistling.

"You see, the music charms 'em," said he. "Singing or whistling—it doesn't matter which—makes 'em behave, and nothing else will. I always whistle as I go by 'em and so they always let me alone. To-day as I went by, whistling, I saw a leaf curled and knew there must be something inside it. I cut down the leaf with my knife and—out you popped. Lucky I passed by, wasn't it?"

"You were very kind," said Ojo, "and I thank you. Will you please rescue my companions, also?"

"What companions?" asked the Shaggy Man.

"The leaves grabbed them all," said the boy. "There's a Patchwork Girl and—"

"A what?"

"A girl made of patchwork, you know. She's alive and her name is Scraps. And there's a Glass Cat—"

"Glass?" asked the Shaggy Man.

"All glass."

"And alive?"

"Yes," said Ojo; "she has pink brains. And there's a Woozy—"

"What's a Woozy?" inquired the Shaggy Man.

"Why, I—I—can't describe it," answered the boy, greatly perplexed. "But it's a queer animal with three hairs on the tip of its tail that won't come out and—"

"What won't come out?" asked the Shaggy Man; "the tail?"

"The hairs won't come out. But you'll see the Woozy, if you'll please rescue it, and then you'll know just what it is."

"Of course," said the Shaggy Man, nodding his shaggy head. And then he walked back among the plants, still whistling, and found the three leaves which were curled around Ojo's traveling companions. The first leaf he cut down released Scraps, and on seeing her the Shaggy Man threw back his shaggy head, opened wide his mouth and laughed so shaggily and yet so merrily that Scraps liked him at once. Then he took off his hat and made her a low bow, saying:

"My dear, you're a wonder. I must introduce you to my friend the Scarecrow."

When he cut down the second leaf he rescued the Glass Cat, and Bungle was so frightened that she scampered away like a streak and soon had joined Ojo, when she sat beside him panting and trembling. The last plant of all the row had captured the Woozy, and a big bunch in the center of the curled leaf showed plainly where he was. With his sharp knife the Shaggy Man sliced off the stem of the leaf and as it fell and unfolded out trotted the Woozy and escaped beyond the reach of any more of the dangerous plants.

Chapter 11

A GOOD FRIEND

Soon the entire party was gathered on the road of yellow bricks, quite beyond the reach of the beautiful but treacherous plants. The Shaggy Man, staring first at one and then at the other, seemed greatly pleased and interested.

"I've seen queer things since I came to the Land of Oz," said he, "but never anything queerer than this band of adventurers. Let us sit down a while, and have a talk and get acquainted."

"Haven't you always lived in the Land of Oz?" asked the Munchkin boy.

"No; I used to live in the big, outside world. But I came here once with Dorothy, and Ozma let me stay."

"How do you like Oz?" asked Scraps. "Isn't the country and the climate grand?"

"It's the finest country in all the world, even if it is a fairyland, and I'm happy every minute I live in it," said the Shaggy Man. "But tell me something about yourselves."

So Ojo related the story of his visit to the house of the Crooked Magician, and how he met there the Glass Cat, and how the Patchwork Girl was brought to life and of the terrible accident to Unc Nunkie and Margolotte. Then he told how he had set out to find the five different things which the Magician needed to make a charm that would restore the marble figures to life, one requirement being three hairs from a Woozy's tail.

"We found the Woozy," explained the boy, "and he agreed to give us the three hairs; but we couldn't pull them out. So we had to bring the Woozy along with us."

"I see," returned the Shaggy Man, who had listened with interest to the story. "But perhaps I, who am big and strong, can pull those three hairs from the Woozy's tail."

"Try it, if you like," said the Woozy.

So the Shaggy Man tried it, but pull as hard as he could he failed to get the hairs out of the Woozy's tail. So he sat down again and wiped his shaggy face with a shaggy silk handkerchief and said:

"It doesn't matter. If you can keep the Woozy until you get the rest of the things you need, you can take the beast and his three hairs to the Crooked Magician and let him find a way to extract 'em. What are the other things you are to find?"

"One," said Ojo, "is a six-leaved clover."

"You ought to find that in the fields around the Emerald City," said the Shaggy Man. "There is a Law against picking six-leaved clovers, but I think I can get Ozma to let you have one."

"Thank you," replied Ojo. "The next thing is the left wing of a yellow butterfly."

"For that you must go to the Winkie Country," the Shaggy Man declared. "I've never noticed any butterflies there, but that is the yellow country of Oz and it's ruled by a good friend of mine, the Tin Woodman."

"Oh, I've heard of him!" exclaimed Ojo. "He must be a wonderful man."

"So he is, and his heart is wonderfully kind. I'm sure the Tin Woodman will do all in his power to help you to save your Unc Nunkie and poor Margolotte."

"The next thing I must find," said the Munchkin boy, "is a gill of water from a dark well."

"Indeed! Well, that is more difficult," said the Shaggy Man, scratching his left ear in a puzzled way. "I've never heard of a dark well; have you?"

"No," said Ojo.

"Do you know where one may be found?" inquired the Shaggy Man.

"I can't imagine," said Ojo.

"Then we must ask the Scarecrow."

"The Scarecrow! But surely, sir, a scarecrow can't know anything."

"Most scarecrows don't, I admit," answered the Shaggy Man. "But this Scarecrow of whom I speak is very intelligent. He claims to possess the best brains in all Oz."

"Better than mine?" asked Scraps.

"Better than mine?" echoed the Glass Cat. "Mine are pink, and you can see 'em work."

"Well, you can't see the Scarecrow's brains work, but they do a lot of clever thinking," asserted the Shaggy Man. "If anyone knows where a dark well is, it's my friend the Scarecrow."

"Where does he live?" inquired Ojo.

"He has a splendid castle in the Winkie Country, near to the palace of his friend the Tin Woodman, and he is often to be found in the Emerald City, where he visits Dorothy at the royal palace."

"Then we will ask him about the dark well," said Ojo.

"But what else does this Crooked Magician want?" asked the Shaggy Man.

"A drop of oil from a live man's body."

"Oh; but there isn't such a thing."

"That is what I thought," replied Ojo; "but the Crooked Magician said it wouldn't be called for by the recipe if it couldn't be found, and therefore I must search until I find it."

"I wish you good luck," said the Shaggy Man, shaking his head doubtfully; "but I imagine you'll have a hard job getting a drop of oil from a live man's body. There's blood in a body, but no oil."

"There's cotton in mine," said Scraps, dancing a little jig.

"I don't doubt it," returned the Shaggy Man admiringly. "You're a regular comforter and as sweet as patchwork can be. All you lack is dignity."

"I hate dignity," cried Scraps, kicking a pebble high in the air and then trying to catch it as it fell. "Half the fools and all the wise folks are dignified, and I'm neither the one nor the other."

"She's just crazy," explained the Glass Cat.

The Shaggy Man laughed.

"She's delightful, in her way," he said. "I'm sure Dorothy will be pleased with her, and the Scarecrow will dote on her. Did you say you were traveling toward the Emerald City?"

"Yes," replied Ojo. "I thought that the best place to go, at first, because the six-leaved clover may be found there."

"I'll go with you," said the Shaggy Man, "and show you the way."

"Thank you," exclaimed Ojo. "I hope it won't put you out any."

"No," said the other, "I wasn't going anywhere in particular. I've been a rover all my life, and although Ozma has given me a suite of beautiful rooms in her palace I still get the wandering fever once in a while and start out to roam the country over. I've been away from the Emerald City several weeks, this time, and now that I've met you and your friends I'm sure it will interest me to accompany you to the great city of Oz and introduce you to my friends."

"That will be very nice," said the boy, gratefully.

"I hope your friends are not dignified," observed Scraps.

"Some are, and some are not," he answered; "but I never criticise my friends. If they are really true friends, they may be anything they like, for all of me."

"There's some sense in that," said Scraps, nodding her queer head in approval. "Come on, and let's get to the Emerald City as soon as possible." With this she ran up the path, skipping and dancing, and then turned to await them.

"It is quite a distance from here to the Emerald City," remarked the Shaggy Man, "so we shall not get there to-day, nor to-morrow. Therefore let us take the jaunt in an easy manner. I'm an old traveler and have found that I never gain anything by being in a hurry. 'Take it easy' is my motto. If you can't take it easy, take it as easy as you can."

After walking some distance over the road of yellow bricks Ojo said he was hungry and would stop to eat some bread and cheese. He offered a portion of the food to the Shaggy Man, who thanked him but refused it.

"When I start out on my travels," said he, "I carry along enough square meals to last me several weeks. Think I'll indulge in one now, as long as we're stopping anyway."

Saying this, he took a bottle from his pocket and shook from it a tablet about the size of one of Ojo's finger-nails.

"That," announced the Shaggy Man, "is a square meal, in condensed form. Invention of the great Professor Wogglebug, of the Royal College of Athletics. It contains soup, fish, roast meat, salad, apple-dumplings, ice cream and chocolate-drops, all boiled down to this small size, so it can be conveniently carried and swallowed when you are hungry and need a square meal."

"I'm square," said the Woozy. "Give me one, please."

So the Shaggy Man gave the Woozy a tablet from his bottle and the beast ate it in a twinkling.

"You have now had a six course dinner," declared the Shaggy Man.

"Pshaw!" said the Woozy, ungratefully, "I want to taste something. There's no fun in that sort of eating."

"One should only eat to sustain life," replied the Shaggy Man, "and that tablet is equal to a peck of other food."

"I don't care for it. I want something I can chew and taste," grumbled the Woozy.

"You are quite wrong, my poor beast," said the Shaggy Man in a tone of pity. "Think how tired your jaws would get chewing a square meal like this, if it were not condensed to the size of a small tablet—which you can swallow in a jiffy."

"Chewing isn't tiresome; it's fun," maintained the Woozy.

"I always chew the honey-bees when I catch them. Give me some bread and cheese, Ojo."

"No, no! You've already eaten a big dinner!" protested the Shaggy Man.

"May be," answered the Woozy; "but I guess I'll fool myself by munching some bread and cheese. I may not be hungry, having eaten all those things you gave me, but I consider this eating business a matter of taste, and I like to realize what's going into me."

Ojo gave the beast what he wanted, but the Shaggy Man shook his shaggy head reproachfully and said there was no animal so obstinate or hard to convince as a Woozy.

At this moment a patter of footsteps was heard, and looking up they saw the live phonograph standing before them. It seemed to have passed through many adventures since Ojo and his comrades last saw the machine, for the varnish of its wooden case was all marred and dented and scratched in a way that gave it an aged and disreputable appearance.

"Dear me!" exclaimed Ojo, staring hard. "What has happened to you?"

"Nothing much," replied the phonograph in a sad and depressed voice. "I've had enough things thrown at me, since I left you, to stock a department store and furnish half a dozen bargain-counters."

"Are you so broken up that you can't play?" asked Scraps.

"No; I still am able to grind out delicious music. Just now

I've a record on tap that is really superb," said the phonograph, growing more cheerful.

"That is too bad," remarked Ojo. "We've no objection to you as a machine, you know; but as a music-maker we hate you."

"Then why was I ever invented?" demanded the machine, in a tone of indignant protest.

They looked at one another inquiringly, but no one could answer such a puzzling question. Finally the Shaggy Man said:

"I'd like to hear the phonograph play."

Ojo sighed. "We've been very happy since we met you, sir," he said.

"I know. But a little misery, at times, makes one appreciate happiness more. Tell me, Phony, what is this record like, which you say you have on tap?"

"It's a popular song, sir. In all civilized lands the common people have gone wild over it."

"Makes civilized folks wild folks, eh? Then it's dangerous."

"Wild with joy, I mean," explained the phonograph. "Listen. This song will prove a rare treat to you, I know. It made the author rich—for an author. It is called 'My Lulu.'"

Then the phonograph began to play. A strain of odd, jerky sounds was followed by these words, sung by a man through his nose with great vigor of expression:

> *"Ah wants mah Lulu, mah coal-black Lulu;*
> *Ah wants mah loo-loo, loo-loo, loo-loo, Lu!*

Ah loves mah Lulu, mah coal-black Lulu,
There ain't nobody else loves loo-loo, Lu!"

"Here—shut that off!" cried the Shaggy Man, springing to his feet. "What do you mean by such impertinence?"

"It's the latest popular song," declared the phonograph, speaking in a sulky tone of voice.

"A popular song?"

"Yes. One that the feeble-minded can remember the words of and those ignorant of music can whistle or sing. That makes a popular song popular, and the time is coming when it will take the place of all other songs."

"That time won't come to us, just yet," said the Shaggy Man, sternly: "I'm something of a singer myself, and I don't intend to be throttled by any Lulus like your coal-black one. I shall take you all apart, Mr. Phony, and scatter your pieces far and wide over the country, as a matter of kindness to the people you might meet if allowed to run around loose. Having performed this painful duty I shall—"

But before he could say more the phonograph turned and dashed up the road as fast as its four table-legs could carry it, and soon it had entirely disappeared from their view.

The Shaggy Man sat down again and seemed well pleased. "Some one else will save me the trouble of scattering that phonograph," said he; "for it is not possible that such a music-maker can last long in the Land of Oz. When you are rested, friends, let us go on our way."

During the afternoon the travelers found themselves in a lonely and uninhabited part of the country. Even the fields were no longer cultivated and the country began to resemble a wilderness. The road of yellow bricks seemed to have been neglected and became uneven and more difficult to walk upon. Scrubby underbrush grew on either side of the way, while huge rocks were scattered around in abundance.

But this did not deter Ojo and his friends from trudging on, and they beguiled the journey with jokes and cheerful conversation. Toward evening they reached a crystal spring which gushed from a tall rock by the roadside and near this spring stood a deserted cabin. Said the Shaggy Man, halting here:

"We may as well pass the night here, where there is shelter for our heads and good water to drink. Road beyond here is pretty bad; worst we shall have to travel; so let's wait until morning before we tackle it."

They agreed to this and Ojo found some brushwood in the cabin and made a fire on the hearth. The fire delighted Scraps, who danced before it until Ojo warned her she might set fire to herself and burn up. After that the Patchwork Girl kept at a respectful distance from the darting flames, but the Woozy lay down before the fire like a big dog and seemed to enjoy its warmth.

For supper the Shaggy Man ate one of his tablets, but Ojo

stuck to his bread and cheese as the most satisfying food. He also gave a portion to the Woozy.

When darkness came on and they sat in a circle on the cabin floor, facing the firelight—there being no furniture of any sort in the place—Ojo said to the Shaggy Man:

"Won't you tell us a story?"

"I'm not good at stories," was the reply; "but I sing like a bird."

"Raven, or crow?" asked the Glass Cat.

"Like a song bird. I'll prove it. I'll sing a song I composed myself. Don't tell anyone I'm a poet; they might want me to write a book. Don't tell 'em I can sing, or they'd want me to make records for that awful phonograph. Haven't time to be a public benefactor, so I'll just sing you this little song for your own amusement."

They were glad enough to be entertained, and listened with interest while the Shaggy Man chanted the following verses to a tune that was not unpleasant:

> *"I'll sing a song of Ozland, where wondrous creatures dwell*
> *And fruits and flowers and shady bowers abound in every dell,*
> *Where magic is a science and where no one shows surprise*
> *If some amazing thing takes place before his very eyes.*
>
> *Our Ruler's a bewitching girl whom fairies love to please;*
> *She's always kept her magic sceptre to enforce decrees*

To make her people happy, for her heart is kind and true
And to aid the needy and distressed is what she longs to do.

And then there's Princess Dorothy, as sweet as any rose,
A lass from Kansas, where they don't grow fairies, I suppose;
And there's the brainy Scarecrow, with a body stuffed with
*   straw,*
Who utters words of wisdom rare that fill us all with awe.

I'll not forget Nick Chopper, the Woodman made of Tin,
Whose tender heart thinks killing time is quite a dreadful sin,
Nor old Professor Wogglebug, who's highly magnified
And looks so big to everyone that he is filled with pride.

Jack Pumpkinhead's a dear old chum who might be called
*   a chump,*
But won renown by riding round upon a magic Gump;
The Sawhorse is a splendid steed and though he's made of
*   wood*
He does as many thrilling stunts as any meat horse could.

And now I'll introduce a beast that ev'ryone adores—
The Cowardly Lion shakes with fear 'most ev'ry time he
*   roars,*
And yet he does the bravest things that any lion might,
Because he knows that cowardice is not considered right.

> *There's Tik-Tok—he's a clockwork man and quite a funny*
>   *sight—*
> *He talks and walks mechanically, when he's wound up*
>   *tight;*
> *And we've a Hungry Tiger who would babies love to eat*
> *But never does because we feed him other kinds of meat.*
>
> *It's hard to name all of the freaks this noble Land's acquired;*
> *'Twould make my song so very long that you would soon be*
>   *tired;*
> *But give attention while I mention one wise Yellow Hen*
> *And Nine fine Tiny Piglets living in a golden pen.*
>
> *Just search the whole world over—sail the seas from coast*
>   *to coast—*
> *No other nation in creation queerer folk can boast;*
> *And now our rare museum will include a Cat of Glass,*
> *A Woozy, and—last but not least—a crazy Patchwork*
>   *Lass."*

Ojo was so pleased with this song that he applauded the singer by clapping his hands, and Scraps followed suit by clapping her padded fingers together, although they made no noise. The cat pounded on the floor with her glass paws—gently, so as not to break them—and the Woozy, which had been asleep, woke up to ask what the row was about.

"I seldom sing in public, for fear they might want me to start an opera company," remarked the Shaggy Man, who was pleased to know his effort was appreciated. "Voice, just now, is a little out of training; rusty, perhaps."

"Tell me," said the Patchwork Girl earnestly, "do all those queer people you mention really live in the Land of Oz?"

"Every one of 'em. I even forgot one thing: Dorothy's Pink Kitten."

"For goodness sake!" exclaimed Bungle, sitting up and looking interested. "A Pink Kitten? How absurd! Is it glass?"

"No; just ordinary kitten."

"Then it can't amount to much. I have pink brains, and you can see 'em work."

"Dorothy's kitten is all pink—brains and all—except blue eyes. Name's Eureka. Great favorite at the royal palace," said the Shaggy Man, yawning.

The Glass Cat seemed annoyed.

"Do you think a pink kitten—common meat—is as pretty as I am?" she asked.

"Can't say. Tastes differ, you know," replied the Shaggy Man, yawning again. "But here's a pointer that may be of service to you: make friends with Eureka and you'll be solid at the palace."

"I'm solid now; solid glass."

"You don't understand," rejoined the Shaggy Man, sleepily. "Anyhow, make friends with the Pink Kitten and you'll be all right. If the Pink Kitten despises you, look out for break-ers."

"Would anyone at the royal palace break a Glass Cat?"

"Might. You never can tell. Advise you to purr soft and look humble—if you can. And now I'm going to bed."

Bungle considered the Shaggy Man's advice so carefully that her pink brains were busy long after the others of the party were fast asleep.

······◄ Chapter 12 ►······

The GIANT PORCUPINE

Next morning they started out bright and early
to follow the road of yellow bricks toward the
Emerald City. The little Munchkin boy was
beginning to feel tired from the long walk, and
he had a great many things to think of and consider besides the
events of the journey. At the wonderful Emerald City, which
he would presently reach, were so many strange and curious
people that he was half afraid of meeting them and wondered
if they would prove friendly and kind. Above all else, he could
not drive from his mind the important errand on which he
had come, and he was determined to devote every energy to

finding the things that were necessary to prepare the magic recipe. He believed that until dear Unc Nunkie was restored to life he could feel no joy in anything, and often he wished that Unc could be with him, to see all the astonishing things Ojo was seeing. But alas Unc Nunkie was now a marble statue in the house of the Crooked Magician and Ojo must not falter in his efforts to save him.

The country through which they were passing was still rocky and deserted, with here and there a bush or a tree to break the dreary landscape. Ojo noticed one tree, especially, because it had such long, silky leaves and was so beautiful in shape. As he approached it he studied the tree earnestly, wondering if any fruit grew on it or if it bore pretty flowers.

Suddenly he became aware that he had been looking at that tree a long time—at least for five minutes—and it had remained in the same position, although the boy had continued to walk steadily on. So he stopped short, and when he stopped, the tree and all the landscape, as well as his companions, moved on before him and left him far behind.

Ojo uttered such a cry of astonishment that it aroused the Shaggy Man, who also halted. The others then stopped, too, and walked back to the boy.

"What's wrong?" asked the Shaggy Man.

"Why, we're not moving forward a bit, no matter how fast we walk," declared Ojo. "Now that we have stopped, we are moving backward! Can't you see? Just notice that rock."

Scraps looked down at her feet and said: "The yellow bricks are not moving."

"But the whole road is," answered Ojo.

"True; quite true," agreed the Shaggy Man. "I know all about the tricks of this road, but I have been thinking of something else and didn't realize where we were."

"It will carry us back to where we started from," predicted Ojo, beginning to be nervous.

"No," replied the Shaggy Man; "it won't do that, for I know a trick to beat this tricky road. I've traveled this way before, you know. Turn around, all of you, and walk backward."

"What good will that do?" asked the cat.

"You'll find out, if you obey me," said the Shaggy Man.

So they all turned their backs to the direction in which they wished to go and began walking backward. In an instant Ojo noticed they were gaining ground and as they proceeded in this curious way they soon passed the tree which had first attracted his attention to their difficulty.

"How long must we keep this up, Shags?" asked Scraps, who was constantly tripping and tumbling down, only to get up again with a laugh at her mishap.

"Just a little way farther," replied the Shaggy Man.

A few minutes later he called to them to turn about quickly and step forward, and as they obeyed the order they found themselves treading solid ground.

"That task is well over," observed the Shaggy Man. "It's

a little tiresome to walk backward, but that is the only way to pass this part of the road, which has a trick of sliding back and carrying with it anyone who is walking upon it."

With new courage and energy they now trudged forward and after a time came to a place where the road cut through a low hill, leaving high banks on either side of it. They were traveling along this cut, talking together, when the Shaggy Man seized Scraps with one arm and Ojo with another and shouted: "Stop!"

"What's wrong now?" asked the Patchwork Girl.

"See there!" answered the Shaggy Man, pointing with his finger.

Directly in the center of the road lay a motionless object that bristled all over with sharp quills, which resembled arrows. The body was as big as a ten-bushel-basket, but the projecting quills made it appear to be four times bigger.

"Well, what of it?" asked Scraps.

"That is Chiss, who causes a lot of trouble along this road," was the reply.

"Chiss! What is Chiss?

"I think it is merely an overgrown porcupine, but here in Oz they consider Chiss an evil spirit. He's different from a reg'lar porcupine, because he can throw his quills in any direction, which an American porcupine cannot do. That's what makes old Chiss so dangerous. If we get too near, he'll fire those quills at us and hurt us badly."

"Then we will be foolish to get too near," said Scraps.

"I'm not afraid," declared the Woozy. "The Chiss is cowardly, I'm sure, and if it ever heard my awful, terrible, frightful growl, it would be scared stiff."

"Oh; can you growl?" asked the Shaggy Man.

"That is the only ferocious thing about me," asserted the Woozy with evident pride. "My growl makes an earthquake blush and the thunder ashamed of itself. If I growled at that creature you call Chiss, it would immediately think the world had cracked in two and bumped against the sun and moon, and that would cause the monster to run as far and as fast as its legs could carry it."

"In that case," said the Shaggy Man, "you are now able to do us all a great favor. Please growl."

"But you forget," returned the Woozy; "my tremendous growl would also frighten you, and if you happen to have heart disease you might expire."

"True; but we must take that risk," decided the Shaggy Man, bravely. "Being warned of what is to occur we must try to bear the terrific noise of your growl; but Chiss won't expect it, and it will scare him away."

The Woozy hesitated.

"I'm fond of you all, and I hate to shock you," it said.

"Never mind," said Ojo.

"You may be made deaf."

"If so, we will forgive you."

"Very well, then," said the Woozy in a determined voice, and advanced a few steps toward the giant porcupine. Pausing to look back, it asked: "All ready?"

"All ready!" they answered.

"Then cover up your ears and brace yourselves firmly. Now, then—look out!"

The Woozy turned toward Chiss, opened wide its mouth and said:

"Quee-ee-ee-eek."

"Go ahead and growl," said Scraps.

"Why, I—I *did* growl!" retorted the Woozy, who seemed much astonished.

"What, that little squeak?" she cried.

"It is the most awful growl that ever was heard, on land or sea, in caverns or in the sky," protested the Woozy. "I wonder you stood the shock so well. Didn't you feel the ground tremble? I suppose Chiss is now quite dead with fright."

The Shaggy Man laughed merrily.

"Poor Wooz!" said he; "your growl wouldn't scare a fly."

The Woozy seemed to be humiliated and surprised. It hung its head a moment, as if in shame or sorrow, but then it said with renewed confidence: "Anyhow, my eyes can flash fire; and good fire, too; good enough to set fire to a fence!"

"That is true," declared Scraps; "I saw it done myself. But your ferocious growl isn't as loud as the tick of a beetle—or one of Ojo's snores when he's fast asleep."

"Perhaps," said the Woozy, humbly, "I have been mistaken about my growl. It has always sounded very fearful to me, but that may have been because it was so close to my ears."

"Never mind," Ojo said soothingly; "it is a great talent to be able to flash fire from your eyes. No one else can do that."

As they stood hesitating what to do Chiss stirred and suddenly a shower of quills came flying toward them, almost filling the air, they were so many. Scraps realized in an instant that they had gone too near to Chiss for safety, so she sprang in front of Ojo and shielded him from the darts, which stuck their points into her own body until she resembled one of those targets they shoot arrows at in archery games. The Shaggy Man dropped flat on his face to avoid the shower, but one quill struck him in the leg and went far in. As for the Glass Cat, the quills rattled off her body without making even a scratch, and the skin of the Woozy was so thick and tough that he was not hurt at all.

When the attack was over they all ran to the Shaggy Man, who was moaning and groaning, and Scraps promptly pulled the quill out of his leg. Then up he jumped and ran over to Chiss, putting his foot on the monster's neck and holding it a prisoner. The body of the great porcupine was now as smooth as leather, except for the holes where the quills had been, for it had shot every single quill in that one wicked shower.

"Let me go!" it shouted angrily. "How dare you put your foot on Chiss?"

"I'm going to do worse than that, old boy," replied the Shaggy Man. "You have annoyed travelers on this road long enough, and now I shall put an end to you."

"You can't!" returned Chiss. "Nothing can kill me, as you know perfectly well."

"Perhaps that is true," said the Shaggy Man in a tone of disappointment. "Seems to me I've been told before that you can't be killed. But if I let you go, what will you do?"

"Pick up my quills again," said Chiss in a sulky voice.

"And then shoot them at more travelers? No; that won't do. You must promise me to stop throwing quills at people."

"I won't promise anything of the sort," declared Chiss.

"Why not?"

"Because it is my nature to throw quills, and every animal must do what Nature intends it to do. It isn't fair for you to blame me. If it were wrong for me to throw quills, then I wouldn't be made with quills to throw. The proper thing for you to do is to keep out of my way."

"Why, there's some sense in that argument," admitted the Shaggy Man, thoughtfully; "but people who are strangers, and don't know you are here, won't be able to keep out of your way."

"Tell you what," said Scraps, who was trying to pull the quills out of her own body, "let's gather up all the quills and take them away with us; then old Chiss won't have any left to throw at people."

"Ah, that's a clever idea. You and Ojo must gather up the quills while I hold Chiss a prisoner; for, if I let him go, he will get some of his quills and be able to throw them again."

So Scraps and Ojo picked up all the quills and tied them in a bundle so they might easily be carried. After this the Shaggy Man released Chiss and let him go, knowing that he was harmless to injure anyone.

"It's the meanest trick I ever heard of," muttered the porcupine gloomily. "How would you like it, Shaggy Man, if I took all your shags away from you?"

"If I threw my shags and hurt people, you would be welcome to capture them," was the reply.

Then they walked on and left Chiss standing in the road sullen and disconsolate. The Shaggy Man limped as he walked, for his wound still hurt him, and Scraps was much annoyed because the quills had left a number of small holes in her patches.

When they came to a flat stone by the roadside the Shaggy Man sat down to rest, and then Ojo opened his basket and took out the bundle of charms the Crooked Magician had given him.

"I am Ojo the Unlucky," he said, "or we would never have met that dreadful porcupine. But I will see if I can find anything among these charms which will cure your leg."

Soon he discovered that one of the charms was labelled: "For flesh wounds," and this the boy separated from the others.

It was only a bit of dried root, taken from some unknown shrub, but the boy rubbed it upon the wound made by the quill and in a few moments the place was healed entirely and the Shaggy Man's leg was as good as ever.

"Rub it on the holes in my patches," suggested Scraps, and Ojo tried it, but without any effect.

"The charm you need is a needle and thread," said the Shaggy Man. "But do not worry, my dear; those holes do not look badly, at all."

"They'll let in the air, and I don't want people to think I'm airy, or that I've been stuck up," said the Patchwork Girl.

"You were certainly stuck up until we pulled out those quills," observed Ojo, with a laugh.

So now they went on again and coming presently to a pond of muddy water they tied a heavy stone to the bundle of quills and sunk it to the bottom of the pond, to avoid carrying it farther.

·····◄ Chapter 13 ►·····

SCRAPS and the SCARECROW

From here on the country improved and the desert places began to give way to fertile spots; still no houses were yet to be seen near the road. There were some hills, with valleys between them, and on reaching the top of one of these hills the travelers found before them a high wall, running to the right and the left as far as their eyes could reach. Immediately in front of them, where the wall crossed the roadway, stood a gate having stout iron bars that extended from top to bottom. They found, on coming nearer, that this gate was locked with a great padlock, rusty through lack of use.

"Well," said Scraps, "I guess we'll stop here."

"It's a good guess," replied Ojo. "Our way is barred by this great wall and gate. It looks as if no one had passed through in many years."

"Looks are deceiving," declared the Shaggy Man, laughing at their disappointed faces, "and this barrier is the most deceiving thing in all Oz."

"It prevents our going any farther, anyhow," said Scraps. "There is no one to mind the gate and let people through, and we've no key to the padlock."

"True," replied Ojo, going a little nearer to peep through the bars of the gate. "What shall we do, Shaggy Man? If we had wings we might fly over the wall, but we cannot climb it and unless we get to the Emerald City I won't be able to find the things to restore Unc Nunkie to life."

"All very true," answered the Shaggy Man, quietly; "but I know this gate, having passed through it many times."

"How?" they all eagerly inquired.

"I'll show you how," said he. He stood Ojo in the middle of the road and placed Scraps just behind him, with her padded hands on his shoulders. After the Patchwork Girl came the Woozy, who held a part of her skirt in his mouth. Then, last of all, was the Glass Cat, holding fast to the Woozy's tail with her glass jaws.

"Now," said the Shaggy Man, "you must all shut your eyes tight, and keep them shut until I tell you to open them."

"I can't," objected Scraps. "My eyes are buttons, and they won't shut."

So the Shaggy Man tied his red handkerchief over the Patchwork Girl's eyes and examined all the others to make sure they had their eyes fast shut and could see nothing.

"What's the game, anyhow—blind-man's-buff?" asked Scraps.

"Keep quiet!" commanded the Shaggy Man, sternly. "All ready? Then follow me."

He took Ojo's hand and led him forward over the road of yellow bricks, toward the gate. Holding fast to one another they all followed in a row, expecting every minute to bump against the iron bars. The Shaggy Man also had his eyes closed, but marched straight ahead, nevertheless, and after he had taken one hundred steps, by actual count, he stopped and said:

"Now you may open your eyes."

They did so, and to their astonishment found the wall and the gateway far behind them, while in front the former Blue Country of the Munchkins had given way to green fields, with pretty farm-houses scattered among them.

"That wall," explained the Shaggy Man, "is what is called an optical illusion. It is quite real while you have your eyes open, but if you are not looking at it the barrier doesn't exist at all. It's the same way with many other evils in life; they seem to exist, and yet it's all seeming and not true. You will notice that the wall—or what we thought was a wall—separates the Munchkin Country from the green country that surrounds the Emerald City, which lies exactly in the center of Oz. There are two roads of yellow bricks through the Munchkin Country, but the one we followed is the best of the two. Dorothy once traveled the other way, and met with more dangers than we did. But all our troubles are over for the present, as another day's journey will bring us to the great Emerald City."

They were delighted to know this, and proceeded with new courage. In a couple of hours they stopped at a farm-house, where the people were very hospitable and invited them to dinner. The farm folk regarded Scraps with much curiosity but no great astonishment, for they were accustomed to seeing extraordinary people in the Land of Oz.

The woman of this house got her needle and thread and sewed up the holes made by the porcupine quills in the Patchwork Girl's body, after which Scraps was assured she looked as beautiful as ever.

"You ought to have a hat to wear," remarked the woman, "for that would keep the sun from fading the colors of your face. I have some patches and scraps put away, and if you will wait two or three days I'll make you a lovely hat that will match the rest of you."

"Never mind the hat," said Scraps, shaking her yarn braids; "it's a kind offer, but we can't stop. I can't see that my colors have faded a particle, as yet; can you?"

"Not much," replied the woman. "You are still very gorgeous, in spite of your long journey."

The children of the house wanted to keep the Glass Cat to play with, so Bungle was offered a good home if she would remain; but the cat was too much interested in Ojo's adventures and refused to stop.

"Children are rough playmates," she remarked to the Shaggy Man, "and although this home is more pleasant than that of the Crooked Magician I fear I would soon be smashed to pieces by the boys and girls."

After they had rested themselves they renewed their journey, finding the road now smooth and pleasant to walk upon and the country growing more beautiful the nearer they drew to the Emerald City.

By and by Ojo began to walk on the green grass, looking carefully around him.

"What are you trying to find?" asked Scraps.

"A six-leaved clover," said he.

"Don't do that!" exclaimed the Shaggy Man, earnestly. "It's against the Law to pick a six-leaved clover. You must wait until you get Ozma's consent."

"She wouldn't know it," declared the boy.

"Ozma knows many things," said the Shaggy Man. "In her room is a Magic Picture that shows any scene in the Land of Oz where strangers or travelers happen to be. She may be watching the picture of us even now, and noticing everything that we do."

"Does she always watch the Magic Picture?" asked Ojo.

"Not always, for she has many other things to do; but, as I said, she may be watching us this very minute."

"I don't care," said Ojo, in an obstinate tone of voice; "Ozma's only a girl."

The Shaggy Man looked at him in surprise.

"You ought to care for Ozma," said he, "if you expect to save your uncle. For, if you displease our powerful Ruler, your journey will surely prove a failure; whereas, if you make a friend of Ozma, she will gladly assist you. As for her being a girl, that is another reason why you should obey her Laws, if you are courteous and polite. Everyone in Oz loves Ozma and hates her enemies, for she is as just as she is powerful."

Ojo sulked a while, but finally returned to the road and kept away from the green clover. The boy was moody and bad tempered for an hour or two afterward, because he could really see no harm in picking a six-leaved clover, if he found one, and in spite of what the Shaggy Man had said he considered Ozma's Law to be unjust.

They presently came to a beautiful grove of tall and stately trees, through which the road wound in sharp curves—first one way and then another. As they were walking through this grove they heard some one in the distance singing, and the sounds grew nearer and nearer until they could distinguish the words, although the bend in the road still hid the singer. The song was something like this:

> "Here's to the hale old bale of straw
> That's cut from the waving grain,
> The sweetest sight man ever saw
> In forest, dell or plain.
> It fills me with a crunkling joy
> A straw-stack to behold,
> For then I pad this lucky boy
> With strands of yellow gold."

"Ah!" exclaimed the Shaggy Man; "here comes my friend the Scarecrow."

"What, a live Scarecrow?" asked Ojo.

"Yes; the one I told you of. He's a splendid fellow, and very intelligent. You'll like him, I'm sure."

Just then the famous Scarecrow of Oz came around the bend in the road, riding astride a Wooden Sawhorse which was so small that its rider's legs nearly touched the ground.

The Scarecrow wore the blue dress of the Munchkins, in which country he was made, and on his head was set a peaked hat with a flat brim trimmed with tinkling bells. A rope was tied around his waist to hold him in shape, for he was stuffed with straw in every part of him except the top of his head, where at one time the Wizard of Oz had placed sawdust, mixed with needles and pins, to sharpen his wits. The head itself was merely a bag of cloth, fastened to the body at the neck, and on the front of this bag was painted the face—ears, eyes, nose and mouth.

The Scarecrow's face was very interesting, for it bore a comical and yet winning expression, although one eye was a bit larger than the other and the ears were not mates. The Munchkin farmer who had made the Scarecrow had neglected to sew him together with close stitches and therefore some of the straw with which he was stuffed was inclined to stick out between the seams. His hands consisted of padded white gloves, with the fingers long and rather limp, and on his feet he wore Munchkin boots of blue leather with broad turns at the tops of them.

The Sawhorse was almost as curious as its rider. It had been rudely made, in the beginning, to saw logs upon, so that its body was a short length of a log, and its legs were stout branches fitted into four holes made in the body. The tail was formed by a small branch that had been left on the log, while the head was a gnarled bump on one end of the body. Two knots of wood formed the eyes, and the mouth was a gash chopped in the log. When the Sawhorse first came to life it had no ears at all, and so could not hear; but the boy who then owned him had whittled two ears out of bark and stuck them in the head, after which the Sawhorse heard very distinctly.

This queer wooden horse was a great favorite with Princess Ozma, who had caused the bottoms of its legs to be shod with plates of gold, so the wood would not wear away. Its saddle was made of cloth-of-gold richly encrusted with precious gems. It had never worn a bridle.

As the Scarecrow came in sight of the party of travelers, he reined in his wooden steed and dismounted, greeting the Shaggy Man with a smiling nod. Then he turned to stare at the Patchwork Girl in wonder, while she in turn stared at him.

"Shags," he whispered, drawing the Shaggy Man aside, "pat me into shape, there's a good fellow!"

While his friend punched and patted the Scarecrow's body, to smooth out the humps, Scraps turned to Ojo and whispered: "Roll me out, please; I've sagged down dreadfully from walking so much and men like to see a stately figure."

She then fell upon the ground and the boy rolled her back and forth like a rolling-pin, until the cotton had filled all the spaces in her patchwork covering and the body had lengthened to its fullest extent. Scraps and the Scarecrow both finished their hasty toilets at the same time, and again they faced each other.

"Allow me, Miss Patchwork," said the Shaggy Man, "to present my friend, the Right Royal Scarecrow of Oz. Scarecrow, this is Miss Scraps Patches; Scraps, this is the Scarecrow. Scarecrow—Scraps; Scraps—Scarecrow."

They both bowed with much dignity.

"Forgive me for staring so rudely," said the Scarecrow, "but you are the most beautiful sight my eyes have ever beheld."

"That is a high compliment from one who is himself so beautiful," murmured Scraps, casting down her suspender-button eyes by lowering her head. "But, tell me, good sir, are you not a trifle lumpy?"

"Yes, of course; that's my straw, you know. It bunches up, sometimes, in spite of all my efforts to keep it even. Doesn't your straw ever bunch?"

"Oh, I'm stuffed with cotton," said Scraps. "It never bunches, but it's inclined to pack down and make me sag."

"But cotton is a high-grade stuffing. I may say it is even more stylish, not to say aristocratic, than straw," said the Scarecrow politely. "Still, it is but proper that one so entrancingly lovely should have the best stuffing there is going. I—er—I'm *so* glad I've met you, Miss Scraps! Introduce us again, Shaggy."

"Once is enough," replied the Shaggy Man, laughing at his friend's enthusiasm.

"Then tell me where you found her, and—Dear me, what a queer cat! What are *you* made of—gelatine?"

"Pure glass," answered the cat, proud to have attracted the Scarecrow's attention. "I am much more beautiful than the Patchwork Girl. I'm transparent, and Scraps isn't; I've pink brains—you can see 'em work; and I've a ruby heart, finely polished, while Scraps hasn't any heart at all."

"No more have I," said the Scarecrow, shaking hands with Scraps, as if to congratulate her on the fact. "I've a friend, the Tin Woodman, who has a heart, but I find I get along pretty well without one. And so—Well, well! here's a little Munchkin boy, too. Shake hands, my little man. How are you?"

Ojo placed his hand in the flabby stuffed glove that served the Scarecrow for a hand, and the Scarecrow pressed it so cordially that the straw in his glove crackled.

Meantime, the Woozy had approached the Sawhorse and begun to sniff at it. The Sawhorse resented this familiarity and with a sudden kick pounded the Woozy squarely on its head with one gold-shod foot.

"Take that, you monster!" it cried angrily.

The Woozy never even winked.

"To be sure," he said; "I'll take anything I have to. But don't make me angry, you wooden beast, or my eyes will flash fire and burn you up."

The Sawhorse rolled its knot eyes wickedly and kicked again, but the Woozy trotted away and said to the Scarecrow:

"What a sweet disposition that creature has! I advise you to chop it up for kindling-wood and use me to ride upon. My back is flat and you can't fall off."

"I think the trouble is that you haven't been properly introduced," said the Scarecrow, regarding the Woozy with much wonder, for he had never seen such a queer animal before. "The Sawhorse is the favorite steed of Princess Ozma, the Ruler of the Land of Oz, and he lives in a stable decorated with pearls and emeralds, at the rear of the royal palace. He is swift as the wind, untiring, and is kind to his friends. All the people of Oz respect the Sawhorse highly, and when I visit Ozma she sometimes allows me to ride him—as I am doing to-day. Now you know what an important personage the Sawhorse is, and if some one—perhaps yourself—will tell me your name, your rank and station, and your history, it will give me pleasure to relate them to the Sawhorse. This will lead to mutual respect and friendship."

The Woozy was somewhat abashed by this speech and did not know how to reply. But Ojo said:

"This square beast is called the Woozy, and he isn't of much importance except that he has three hairs growing on the tip of his tail."

The Scarecrow looked and saw that this was true.

"But," said he, in a puzzled way, "what makes those three hairs important? The Shaggy Man has thousands of hairs, but no one has ever accused him of being important."

So Ojo related the sad story of Unc Nunkie's transformation into a marble statue, and told how he had set out to find the things the Crooked Magician wanted, in order to make a charm that would restore his uncle to life. One of the requirements was three hairs from a Woozy's tail, but not being able to pull out the hairs they had been obliged to take the Woozy with them.

The Scarecrow looked grave as he listened and he shook his head several times, as if in disapproval.

"We must see Ozma about this matter," he said. "That Crooked Magician is breaking the Law by practicing magic without a license, and I'm not sure Ozma will allow him to restore your uncle to life."

"Already I have warned the boy of that," declared the Shaggy Man.

At this Ojo began to cry. "I want my Unc Nunkie!" he exclaimed. "I know how he can be restored to life, and I'm going to do it—Ozma or no Ozma! What right has this girl Ruler to keep my Unc Nunkie a statue forever?"

"Don't worry about that just now," advised the Scarecrow. "Go on to the Emerald City, and when you reach it have the Shaggy Man take you to see Dorothy. Tell her your story and I'm sure she will help you. Dorothy is Ozma's best friend, and if you can win her to your side your uncle is pretty safe to live again." Then he turned to the Woozy and said: "I'm afraid you are not important enough to be introduced to the Sawhorse, after all."

"I'm a better beast than he is," retorted the Woozy, indignantly. "My eyes can flash fire, and his can't."

"Is this true?" inquired the Scarecrow, turning to the Munchkin boy.

"Yes," said Ojo, and told how the Woozy had set fire to the fence.

"Have you any other accomplishments?" asked the Scarecrow.

"I have a most terrible growl—that is, *sometimes*," said the Woozy, as Scraps laughed merrily and the Shaggy Man smiled. But the Patchwork Girl's laugh made the Scarecrow forget all about the Woozy. He said to her:

"What an admirable young lady you are, and what jolly good company! We must be better acquainted, for never before have I met a girl with such exquisite coloring or such natural, artless manners."

"No wonder they call you the Wise Scarecrow," replied Scraps.

"When you arrive at the Emerald City I will see you again," continued the Scarecrow. "Just now I am going to call upon an old friend—an ordinary young lady named Jinjur—who has promised to repaint my left ear for me. You may have noticed that the paint on my left ear has peeled off and faded, which affects my hearing on that side. Jinjur always fixes me up when I get weather-worn."

"When do you expect to return to the Emerald City?" asked the Shaggy Man.

"I'll be there this evening, for I'm anxious to have a long talk with Miss Scraps. How is it, Sawhorse; are you equal to a swift run?"

"Anything that suits you suits me," returned the wooden horse.

So the Scarecrow mounted to the jeweled saddle and waved his hat, when the Sawhorse darted away so swiftly that they were out of sight in an instant.

OJO BREAKS the LAW

"What a queer man," remarked the Munchkin boy, when the party had resumed its journey.

"And so nice and polite," added Scraps, bobbing her head. "I think he is the handsomest man I've seen since I came to life."

"Handsome is as handsome does," quoted the Shaggy Man; "but we must admit that no living scarecrow is handsomer. The chief merit of my friend is that he is a great thinker, and in Oz it is considered good policy to follow his advice."

"I didn't notice any brains in his head," observed the Glass Cat.

"You can't see 'em work, but they're there, all right," declared the Shaggy Man. "I hadn't much confidence in his brains myself, when first I came to Oz, for a humbug Wizard gave them to him; but I was soon convinced that the Scarecrow is really wise; and, unless his brains make him so, such wisdom is unaccountable."

"Is the Wizard of Oz a humbug?" asked Ojo.

"Not now. He was once, but he has reformed and now assists Glinda the Good, who is the Royal Sorceress of Oz and the only one licensed to practice magic or sorcery. Glinda has taught our old Wizard a good many clever things, so he is no longer a humbug."

They walked a little while in silence and then Ojo said:

"If Ozma forbids the Crooked Magician to restore Unc Nunkie to life, what shall I do?"

The Shaggy Man shook his head.

"In that case you can't do anything," he said. "But don't be discouraged yet. We will go to Princess Dorothy and tell her your troubles, and then we will let her talk to Ozma. Dorothy has the kindest little heart in the world, and she has been through so many troubles herself that she is sure to sympathize with you."

"Is Dorothy the little girl who came here from Kansas?" asked the boy.

"Yes. In Kansas she was Dorothy Gale. I used to know her there, and she brought me to the Land of Oz. But now Ozma has made her a Princess, and Dorothy's Aunt Em and Uncle Henry are here, too." Here the Shaggy Man uttered a long sigh, and then he continued: "It's a queer country, this Land of Oz; but I like it, nevertheless."

"What is queer about it?" asked Scraps.

"You, for instance," said he.

"Did you see no girls as beautiful as I am in your own country?" she inquired.

"None with the same gorgeous, variegated beauty," he confessed. "In America a girl stuffed with cotton wouldn't be alive, nor would anyone think of making a girl out of a patchwork quilt."

"What a queer country America must be!" she exclaimed in great surprise. "The Scarecrow, whom you say is wise, told me I am the most beautiful creature he has ever seen."

"I know; and perhaps you are—from a scarecrow point of view," replied the Shaggy Man; but why he smiled as he said it Scraps could not imagine.

As they drew nearer to the Emerald City the travelers were filled with admiration for the splendid scenery they beheld. Handsome houses stood on both sides of the road and each had a green lawn before it as well as a pretty flower garden.

"In another hour," said the Shaggy Man, "we shall come in sight of the walls of the Royal City."

He was walking ahead, with Scraps, and behind them came the Woozy and the Glass Cat. Ojo had lagged behind, for in spite of the warnings he had received the boy's eyes were fastened on the clover that bordered the road of yellow bricks and he was eager to discover if such a thing as a six-leaved clover really existed.

Suddenly he stopped short and bent over to examine the ground more closely. Yes; here at last was a clover with six spreading leaves. He counted them carefully, to make sure. In an instant his heart leaped with joy, for this was one of the important things he had come for—one of the things that would restore dear Unc Nunkie to life.

He glanced ahead and saw that none of his companions was looking back. Neither were any other people about, for it was midway between two houses. The temptation was too strong to be resisted.

"I might search for weeks and weeks, and never find another six-leaved clover," he told himself, and quickly pluck-ing the stem from the plant he placed the prized clover in his basket, covering it with the other things he carried there. Then, trying to look as if nothing had happened, he hurried forward and overtook his comrades.

The Emerald City, which is the most splendid as well as the most beautiful city in any fairyland, is surrounded by a high, thick wall of green marble, polished smooth and set with glistening emeralds. There are four gates, one facing the Munchkin Country, one facing the Country of the Winkies, one facing the Country of the Quadlings and one facing the Country of the Gillikins. The Emerald City lies directly in the center of these four important countries of Oz. The gates had bars of pure gold, and on either side of each gateway were built high towers, from which floated gay banners. Other towers were set at distances along the walls, which were broad enough for four people to walk abreast upon.

This enclosure, all green and gold and glittering with precious gems, was indeed a wonderful sight to greet our travelers, who first observed it from the top of a little hill; but beyond the wall was the vast city it surrounded, and hundreds of jeweled spires, domes and minarets, flaunting flags and banners, reared their crests far above the towers of the gateways. In the center of the city our friends could see the tops of many magnificent trees, some nearly as tall as the spires of the buildings, and the Shaggy Man told them that these trees were in the royal gardens of Princess Ozma.

They stood a long time on the hilltop, feasting their eyes on the splendor of the Emerald City.

"Whee!" exclaimed Scraps, clasping her padded hands in ecstacy, "that'll do for me to live in, all right. No more of the Munchkin Country for these patches—and no more of the Crooked Magician!"

"Why, you belong to Dr. Pipt," replied Ojo, looking at her in amazement. "You were made for a servant, Scraps, so you are personal property and not your own mistress."

"Bother Dr. Pipt! If he wants me, let him come here and get me. I'll not go back to his den of my own accord; that's certain. Only one place in the Land of Oz is fit to live in, and that's the Emerald City. It's lovely! It's almost as beautiful as I am, Ojo."

"In this country," remarked the Shaggy Man, "people live wherever our Ruler tells them to. It wouldn't do to have everyone live in the Emerald City, you know, for some must plow the land and raise grains and fruits and vegetables, while others chop wood in the forests, or fish in the rivers, or herd the sheep and the cattle."

"Poor things!" said Scraps.

"I'm not sure they are not happier than the city people," replied the Shaggy Man. "There's a freedom and independence in country life that not even the Emerald City can give one. I know that lots of the city people would like to get back to the land. The Scarecrow lives in the country, and so do the Tin Woodman and Jack Pumpkinhead; yet all three would be welcome to live in Ozma's palace if they cared to. Too much splendor becomes tiresome, you know. But, if we're to reach the Emerald City before sundown, we must hurry, for it is yet a long way off."

The entrancing sight of the city had put new energy into

them all and they hurried forward with lighter steps than before. There was much to interest them along the roadway, for the houses were now set more closely together and they met a good many people who were coming or going from one place or another. All these seemed happy-faced, pleasant people, who nodded graciously to the strangers as they passed, and exchanged words of greeting.

At last they reached the great gateway, just as the sun was setting and adding its red glow to the glitter of the emeralds on the green walls and spires. Somewhere inside the city a band could be heard playing sweet music; a soft, subdued hum, as of many voices, reached their ears; from the neighboring yards came the low mooing of cows waiting to be milked.

They were almost at the gate when the golden bars slid back and a tall soldier stepped out and faced them. Ojo thought he had never seen so tall a man before. The Soldier wore a handsome green and gold uniform, with a tall hat in which was a waving plume, and he had a belt thickly encrusted with jewels. But the most peculiar thing about him was his long green beard, which fell far below his waist and perhaps made him seem taller than he really was.

"Halt!" said the Soldier with the Green Whiskers, not in a stern voice but rather in a friendly tone.

They halted before he spoke and stood looking at him.

"Good evening, Colonel," said the Shaggy Man. "What's the news since I left? Anything important?"

"Billina has hatched out thirteen new chickens," replied the Soldier with the Green Whiskers, "and they're the cutest little fluffy yellow balls you ever saw. The Yellow Hen is mighty proud of those children, I can tell you."

"She has a right to be," agreed the Shaggy Man. "Let me see; that's about seven thousand chicks she has hatched out; isn't it, General?"

"That, at least," was the reply. "You will have to visit Billina and congratulate her."

"It will give me pleasure to do that," said the Shaggy Man. "But you will observe that I have brought some strangers home with me. I am going to take them to see Dorothy."

"One moment, please," said the Soldier, barring their way as they started to enter the gate. "I am on duty, and I have orders to execute. Is anyone in your party named Ojo the Unlucky?"

"Why, that's me!" cried Ojo, astonished at hearing his name on the lips of a stranger.

The Soldier with the Green Whiskers nodded. "I thought so," said he, "and I am sorry to announce that it is my painful duty to arrest you."

"Arrest me!" exclaimed the boy. "What for?"

"I haven't looked to see," answered the Soldier. Then he

drew a paper from his breast pocket and glanced at it. "Oh, yes; you are to be arrested for willfully breaking one of the Laws of Oz."

"Breaking a Law!" said Scraps. "Nonsense, Soldier; you're joking."

"Not this time," returned the Soldier, with a sigh. "My dear child—what are you, a rummage sale or a guess-me-quick?—in me you behold the Body-Guard of our gracious Ruler, Princess Ozma, as well as the Royal Army of Oz and the Police Force of the Emerald City."

"And only one man!" exclaimed the Patchwork Girl.

"Only one, and plenty enough. In my official positions I've had nothing to do for a good many years—so long that I began to fear I was absolutely useless—until to-day. An hour ago I was called to the presence of her Highness, Ozma of Oz, and told to arrest a boy named Ojo the Unlucky, who was journeying from the Munchkin Country to the Emerald City and would arrive in a short time. This command so astonished me that I nearly fainted, for it is the first time anyone has merited arrest since I can remember. You are rightly named Ojo the Unlucky, my poor boy, since you have broken a Law of Oz.

"But you are wrong," said Scraps. "Ozma is wrong—you are all wrong—for Ojo has broken no Law."

"Then he will soon be free again," replied the Soldier with the Green Whiskers. "Anyone accused of crime is given a fair trial by our Ruler and has every chance to prove his innocence. But just now Ozma's orders must be obeyed."

With this he took from his pocket a pair of handcuffs made of gold and set with rubies and diamonds, and these he snapped over Ojo's wrists.

···—·‹ Chapter 15 ›·—···

OZMA'S PRISONER

The boy was so bewildered by this calamity that he made no resistance at all. He knew very well he was guilty, but it surprised him that Ozma also knew it. He wondered how she had found out so soon that he had picked the six-leaved clover. He handed his basket to Scraps and said:

"Keep that, until I get out of prison. If I never get out, take it to the Crooked Magician, to whom it belongs."

The Shaggy Man had been gazing earnestly in the boy's face, uncertain whether to defend him or not; but something he read in Ojo's expression made him draw back and refuse to interfere to save him. The Shaggy Man was greatly surprised and grieved, but he knew that Ozma never made mistakes and so Ojo must really have broken the Law of Oz.

The Soldier with the Green Whiskers now led them all through the gate and into a little room built in the wall. Here sat a jolly little man, richly dressed in green and having around his neck a heavy gold chain to which a number of great golden keys were attached. This was the Guardian of the Gates and at the moment they entered his room he was playing a tune upon a mouth-organ.

"Listen!" he said, holding up his hand for silence. "I've just composed a tune called 'The Speckled Alligator.' It's in patch-time, which is much superior to rag-time, and I've composed it in honor of the Patchwork Girl, who has just arrived."

"How did you know I had arrived?" asked Scraps, much interested.

"It's my business to know who's coming, for I'm the Guardian of the Gates. Keep quiet while I play you 'The Speckled Alligator.'"

It wasn't a very bad tune, nor a very good one, but all listened respectfully while he shut his eyes and swayed his head from side to side and blew the notes from the little instrument. When it was all over the Soldier with the Green Whiskers said:

"Guardian, I have here a prisoner."

"Good gracious! A prisoner?" cried the little man, jumping up from his chair. "Which one? Not the Shaggy Man?"

"No; this boy."

"Ah; I hope his fault is as small as himself," said the Guardian of the Gates. "But what can he have done, and what made him do it?"

"Can't say," replied the Soldier. "All I know is that he has broken the Law."

"But no one ever does that!"

"Then he must be innocent, and soon will be released. I hope you are right, Guardian. Just now I am ordered to take him to prison. Get me a prisoner's robe from your Official Wardrobe."

The Guardian unlocked a closet and took from it a white robe, which the Soldier threw over Ojo. It covered him from head to foot, but had two holes just in front of his eyes, so he could see where to go. In this attire the boy presented a very quaint appearance.

As the Guardian unlocked a gate leading from his room into the streets of the Emerald City, the Shaggy Man said to Scraps:

"I think I shall take you directly to Dorothy, as the Scarecrow advised, and the Glass Cat and the Woozy may come with us. Ojo must go to prison with the Soldier with the Green Whiskers, but he will be well treated and you need not worry about him."

"What will they do with him?" asked Scraps.

"That I cannot tell. Since I came to the Land of Oz no one

has ever been arrested or imprisoned—until Ojo broke the Law."

"Seems to me that girl Ruler of yours is making a big fuss over nothing," remarked Scraps, tossing her yarn hair out of her eyes with a jerk of her patched head. "I don't know what Ojo has done, but it couldn't be anything very bad, for you and I were with him all the time."

The Shaggy Man made no reply to this speech and presently the Patchwork Girl forgot all about Ojo in her admiration of the wonderful city she had entered.

They soon separated from the Munchkin boy, who was led by the Soldier with the Green Whiskers down a side street toward the prison. Ojo felt very miserable and greatly ashamed of himself, but he was beginning to grow angry because he was treated in such a disgraceful manner. Instead of entering the splendid Emerald City as a respectable traveler who was entitled to a welcome and to hospitality, he was being brought in as a criminal, handcuffed and in a robe that told all he met of his deep disgrace.

Ojo was by nature gentle and affectionate and if he had disobeyed the Law of Oz it was to restore his dear Unc Nunkie to life. His fault was more thoughtless than wicked, but that did not alter the fact that he had committed a fault. At first he had felt sorrow and remorse, but the more he thought about the unjust treatment he had received—unjust merely because he considered it so—the more he resented his arrest, blaming

Ozma for making foolish Laws and then punishing folks who broke them. Only a six-leaved clover! A tiny green plant growing neglected and trampled under foot. What harm could there be in picking it? Ojo began to think Ozma must be a very bad and oppressive Ruler for such a lovely fairyland as Oz. The Shaggy Man said the people loved her; but how could they?

The little Munchkin boy was so busy thinking these things—which many guilty prisoners have thought before him—that he scarcely noticed all the splendor of the city streets through which they passed. Whenever they met any of the happy, smiling people, the boy turned his head away in shame, although none knew who was beneath the robe.

By and by they reached a house built just beside the great city wall, but in a quiet, retired place. It was a pretty house, neatly painted and with many windows. Before it was a garden filled with blooming flowers. The Soldier with the Green Whiskers led Ojo up the gravel path to the front door, on which he knocked.

A woman opened the door and, seeing Ojo in his white robe, exclaimed:

"Goodness me! A prisoner at last. But what a small one, Soldier."

"The size doesn't matter, Tollydiggle, my dear. The fact remains that he is a prisoner," said the Soldier. "And, this being the prison, and you the jailer, it is my duty to place the prisoner in your charge."

"True. Come in, then, and I'll give you a receipt for him."

They entered the house and passed through a hall to a large circular room, where the woman pulled the robe off from Ojo and looked at him with kindly interest. The boy, on his part, was gazing around him in amazement, for never had he dreamed of such a magnificent apartment as this in which he stood. The roof of the dome was of colored glass, worked into beautiful designs. The walls were paneled with plates of gold decorated with gems of great size and many colors, and upon the tiled floor were soft rugs delightful to walk upon. The furniture was framed in gold and upholstered in satin brocade and it consisted of easy chairs, divans and stools in great variety. Also there were several tables with mirror tops and cabinets filled with rare and curious things. In one place a case filled with books stood against the wall, and elsewhere Ojo saw a cupboard containing all sorts of games.

"May I stay here a little while before I go to prison?" asked the boy, pleadingly.

"Why, this is your prison," replied Tollydiggle, "and in me behold your jailor. Take off those handcuffs, Soldier, for it is impossible for anyone to escape from this house."

"I know that very well," replied the Soldier and at once unlocked the handcuffs and released the prisoner.

The woman touched a button on the wall and lighted a big chandelier that hung suspended from the ceiling, for it was growing dark outside. Then she seated herself at a desk and asked:

"What name?"

"Ojo the Unlucky," answered the Soldier with the Green Whiskers.

"Unlucky? Ah, that accounts for it," said she. "What crime?"

"Breaking a Law of Oz."

"All right. There's your receipt, Soldier; and now I'm responsible for the prisoner. I'm glad of it, for this is the first time I've ever had anything to do, in my official capacity," remarked the jailer, in a pleased tone.

"It's the same with me, Tollydiggle," laughed the Soldier. "But my task is finished and I must go and report to Ozma that I've done my duty like a faithful Police Force, a loyal Army and an honest Body-Guard—as I hope I am."

Saying this, he nodded farewell to Tollydiggle and Ojo and went away.

"Now, then," said the woman briskly, "I must get you some supper, for you are doubtless hungry. What would you prefer: planked whitefish, omelet with jelly or mutton-chops with gravy?"

Ojo thought about it. Then he said: "I'll take the chops, if you please."

"Very well; amuse yourself while I'm gone; I won't be long," and then she went out by a door and left the prisoner alone.

Ojo was much astonished, for not only was this unlike any

prison he had ever heard of, but he was being treated more as a guest than a criminal. There were many windows and they had no locks. There were three doors to the room and none were bolted. He cautiously opened one of the doors and found it led into a hallway. But he had no intention of trying to escape. If his jailor was willing to trust him in this way he would not betray her trust, and moreover a hot supper was being prepared for him and his prison was very pleasant and comfortable. So he took a book from the case and sat down in a big chair to look at the pictures.

This amused him until the woman came in with a large tray and spread a cloth on one of the tables. Then she arranged his supper, which proved the most varied and delicious meal Ojo had ever eaten in his life.

Tollydiggle sat near him while he ate, sewing on some fancy work she held in her lap. When he had finished she cleared the table and then read to him a story from one of the books.

"Is this really a prison?" he asked, when she had finished reading.

"Indeed it is," she replied. "It is the only prison in the Land of Oz."

"And am I a prisoner?"

"Bless the child! Of course."

"Then why is the prison so fine, and why are you so kind to me?" he earnestly asked.

Tollydiggle seemed surprised by the question, but she presently answered:

"We consider a prisoner unfortunate. He is unfortunate in two ways—because he has done something wrong and because he is deprived of his liberty. Therefore we should treat him kindly, because of his misfortune, for otherwise he would become hard and bitter and would not be sorry he had done wrong. Ozma thinks that one who has committed a fault did so because he was not strong and brave; therefore she puts him in prison to make him strong and brave. When that is accomplished he is no longer a prisoner, but a good and loyal citizen and everyone is glad that he is now strong enough to resist doing wrong. You see, it is kindness that makes one strong and brave; and so we are kind to our prisoners."

Ojo thought this over very carefully. "I had an idea," said he, "that prisoners were always treated harshly, to punish them."

"That would be dreadful!" cried Tollydiggle. "Isn't one punished enough in knowing he has done wrong? Don't you wish, Ojo, with all your heart, that you had not been disobedient and broken a Law of Oz?"

"I—I hate to be different from other people," he admitted.

"Yes; one likes to be respected as highly as his neighbors are," said the woman. "When you are tried and found guilty, you will be obliged to make amends, in some way. I don't know just what Ozma will do to you, because this is the first time one of us has broken a Law; but you may be sure she will be just and merciful. Here in the Emerald City people are too happy and contented ever to do wrong; but perhaps you came from some faraway corner of our land, and having no love for Ozma carelessly broke one of her Laws."

"Yes," said Ojo, "I've lived all my life in the heart of a lonely forest, where I saw no one but dear Unc Nunkie."

"I thought so," said Tollydiggle. "But now we have talked enough, so let us play a game until bedtime."

Chapter 16

PRINCESS DOROTHY

Dorothy Gale was sitting in one of her rooms in the royal palace, while curled up at her feet was a little black dog with a shaggy coat and very bright eyes. She wore a plain white frock, without any jewels or other ornaments except an emerald-green hair-ribbon, for Dorothy was a simple little girl and had not been in the least spoiled by the magnificence surrounding her. Once the child had lived on the Kansas prairies, but she seemed marked for adventure, for she had made several trips to the Land of Oz before she came to live there for good. Her very best friend was the beautiful Ozma of Oz, who loved Dorothy so well that she kept her in her own palace, so as to be near her. The girl's Uncle Henry and Aunt Em—the only relatives she had in the world—had also been brought here by Ozma and given a pleasant home. Dorothy knew almost everybody in Oz, and it was she who had discovered the Scarecrow, the Tin Woodman and the Cowardly Lion, as well as Tik-Tok the Clockwork Man. Her life was very pleasant now, and although she had been made a Princess of Oz by her friend Ozma she did not care much to be a Princess and remained as sweet as when she had been plain Dorothy Gale of Kansas.

Dorothy was reading in a book this evening when Jellia Jamb, the favorite servant-maid of the palace, came to say that the Shaggy Man wanted to see her.

"All right," said Dorothy; "tell him to come right up."

"But he has some queer creatures with him—some of the queerest I've ever laid eyes on," reported Jellia.

"Never mind; let 'em all come up," replied Dorothy.

But when the door opened to admit not only the Shaggy Man, but Scraps, the Woozy and the Glass Cat, Dorothy jumped up and looked at her strange visitors in amazement. The Patchwork Girl was the most curious of all and Dorothy was uncertain at first whether Scraps was really alive or only a dream or a nightmare. Toto, her dog, slowly uncurled himself and going to the Patchwork Girl sniffed at her inquiringly; but soon he lay down again, as if to say he had no interest in such an irregular creation.

"You're a new one to me," Dorothy said reflectively,

addressing the Patchwork Girl. "I can't imagine where you've come from."

"Who, me?" asked Scraps, looking around the pretty room instead of at the girl. "Oh, I came from a bed-quilt, I guess. That's what they say, anyhow. Some call it a crazy-quilt and some a patchwork quilt. But my name is Scraps—and now you know all about me."

"Not quite all," returned Dorothy with a smile. "I wish you'd tell me how you came to be alive."

"That's an easy job," said Scraps, sitting upon a big upholstered chair and making the springs bounce her up and down. "Margolotte wanted a slave, so she made me out of an old bed-quilt she didn't use. Cotton stuffing, suspender-button eyes, red velvet tongue, pearl beads for teeth. The Crooked Magician made a Powder of Life, sprinkled me with it and— here I am. Perhaps you've noticed my different colors. A very refined and educated gentleman named the Scarecrow, whom I met, told me I am the most beautiful creature in all Oz, and I believe it."

"Oh! Have you met our Scarecrow, then?" asked Dorothy, a little puzzled to understand the brief history related.

"Yes; isn't he jolly?"

"The Scarecrow has many good qualities," replied Dorothy. "But I'm sorry to hear all this 'bout the Crooked Magician. Ozma'll be mad as hops when she hears he's been doing magic again. She told him not to."

"He only practices magic for the benefit of his own family," explained Bungle, who was keeping at a respectful distance from the little black dog.

"Dear me," said Dorothy; "I hadn't noticed you before. Are you glass, or what?"

"I'm glass, and transparent, too, which is more than can be said of some folks," answered the cat. "Also I have some lovely pink brains; you can see 'em work."

"Oh; is that so? Come over here and let me see."

The Glass Cat hesitated, eyeing the dog.

"Send that beast away and I will," she said.

"Beast! Why, that's my dog Toto, an' he's the kindest dog in all the world. Toto knows a good many things, too; 'most as much as I do, I guess."

"Why doesn't he say anything?" asked Bungle.

"He can't talk, not being a fairy dog," explained Dorothy. "He's just a common United States dog; but that's a good deal; and I understand him, and he understands me, just as well as if he could talk."

Toto, at this, got up and rubbed his head softly against Dorothy's hand, which she held out to him, and he looked up into her face as if he had understood every word she had said.

"This cat, Toto," she said to him, "is made of glass, so you mustn't bother it, or chase it, any more than you do my Pink Kitten. It's prob'ly brittle and might break if it bumped against anything."

"Woof!" said Toto, and that meant he understood.

The Glass Cat was so proud of her pink brains that she ventured to come close to Dorothy, in order that the girl might "see 'em work." This was really interesting, but when Dorothy patted the cat she found the glass cold and hard and unresponsive, so she decided at once that Bungle would never do for a pet.

"What do you know about the Crooked Magician who lives on the mountain?" asked Dorothy.

"He made me," replied the cat; "so I know all about him. The Patchwork Girl is new—three or four days old—but I've lived with Dr. Pipt for years; and, though I don't much care for him, I will say that he has always refused to work magic for any of the people who come to his house. He thinks there's no harm in doing magic things for his own family, and he made me out of glass because the meat cats drink too much milk. He also made Scraps come to life so she could do the housework for his wife Margolotte."

"Then why did you both leave him?" asked Dorothy.

"I think you'd better let me explain that," interrupted the Shaggy Man, and then he told Dorothy all of Ojo's story and how Unc Nunkie and Margolotte had accidentally been turned to marble by the Liquid of Petrifaction. Then he related how the boy had started out in search of the things needed to make the magic charm, which would restore the unfortunates to life, and how he had found the Woozy and taken him along because he could not pull the three hairs out of its tail. Dorothy listened to all this with much interest, and thought that so far Ojo had acted very well. But when the Shaggy Man told her of the Munchkin boy's arrest by the Soldier with the Green Whiskers, because he was accused of wilfully breaking a Law of Oz, the little girl was greatly shocked.

"What do you s'pose he's done?" she asked.

"I fear he has picked a six-leaved clover," answered the Shaggy Man, sadly. "I did not see him do it, and I warned him that to do so was against the Law; but perhaps that is what he did, nevertheless."

"I'm sorry 'bout that," said Dorothy gravely, "for now there will be no one to help his poor uncle and Margolotte 'cept this Patchwork Girl, the Woozy and the Glass Cat."

"Don't mention it," said Scraps. "That's no affair of mine. Margolotte and Unc Nunkie are perfect strangers to me, for the moment I came to life they came to marble."

"I see," remarked Dorothy with a sigh of regret; "the woman forgot to give you a heart."

"I'm glad she did," retorted the Patchwork Girl. "A heart must be a great annoyance to one. It makes a person feel sad or sorry or devoted or sympathetic—all of which sensations interfere with one's happiness."

"I have a heart," murmured the Glass Cat. "It's made of a ruby; but I don't imagine I shall let it bother me about helping Unc Nunkie and Margolotte."

"That's a pretty hard heart of yours," said Dorothy. "And the Woozy, of course—"

"Why, as for me," observed the Woozy, who was reclining on the floor with his legs doubled under him, so that he looked much like a square box, "I have never seen those unfortunate people you are speaking of, and yet I am sorry for them, having at times been unfortunate myself. When I was shut up in that forest I longed for some one to help me, and by and by Ojo came and did help me. So I'm willing to help his uncle. I'm only a stupid beast, Dorothy, but I can't help that, and if you'll tell me what to do to help Ojo and his uncle, I'll gladly do it."

Dorothy walked over and patted the Woozy on his square head.

"You're not pretty," she said, "but I like you. What are you able to do; anything 'special?"

"I can make my eyes flash fire—real fire—when I'm angry. When anyone says 'Krizzle-Kroo' to me I get angry, and then my eyes flash fire."

"I don't see as fireworks could help Ojo's uncle," remarked Dorothy. "Can you do anything else?"

"I—I thought I had a very terrifying growl," said the Woozy, with hesitation; "but perhaps I was mistaken."

"Yes," said the Shaggy Man, "you were certainly wrong about that." Then he turned to Dorothy and added: "What will become of the Munchkin boy?"

"I don't know," she said, shaking her head thoughtfully. "Ozma will see him 'bout it, of course, and then she'll punish him. But how, I don't know, 'cause no one ever has been punished in Oz since I knew anything about the place. Too bad, Shaggy Man, isn't it?"

While they were talking Scraps had been roaming around the room and looking at all the pretty things it contained. She had carried Ojo's basket in her hand, until now, when she decided to see what was inside it. She found the bread and cheese, which she had no use for, and the bundle of charms, which were curious but quite a mystery to her. Then, turning these over, she came upon the six-leaved clover which the boy had plucked.

Scraps was quick-witted, and although she had no heart she recognized the fact that Ojo was her first friend. She knew at once that because the boy had taken the clover he had been imprisoned, and she understood that Ojo had given her the basket so they would not find the clover in his possession and have proof of his crime. So, turning her head to see that no one noticed her, she took the clover from the basket and dropped it into a golden vase that stood on Dorothy's table. Then she came forward and said to Dorothy:

"I wouldn't care to help Ojo's uncle, but I will help Ojo. He did not break the Law—no one can prove he did—and that green-whiskered Soldier had no right to arrest him."

"Ozma ordered the boy's arrest," said Dorothy, "and of

course she knew what she was doing. But if you can prove Ojo is innocent they will set him free at once."

"They'll have to prove him guilty, won't they?" asked Scraps.

"I s'pose so."

"Well, they can't do that," declared the Patchwork Girl.

As it was nearly time for Dorothy to dine with Ozma, which she did every evening, she rang for a servant and ordered the Woozy taken to a nice room and given plenty of such food as he liked best.

"That's honey-bees," said the Woozy.

"You can't eat honey-bees, but you'll be given something just as nice," Dorothy told him. Then she had the Glass Cat taken to another room for the night and the Patchwork Girl she kept in one of her own rooms, for she was much interested in the strange creature and wanted to talk with her again and try to understand her better.

····◄ Chapter 17 ►···——·

OZMA and HER FRIENDS

The Shaggy Man had a room of his own in the royal palace, so there he went to change his shaggy suit of clothes for another just as shaggy but not so dusty from travel. He selected a costume of pea-green and pink satin and velvet, with embroidered shags on all the edges and iridescent pearls for ornaments. Then he bathed in an alabaster pool and brushed his shaggy hair and whiskers the wrong way to make them still more shaggy. This accomplished, and arrayed in his splendid shaggy garments, he went to Ozma's banquet hall and found the Scarecrow, the Wizard and Dorothy already assembled there. The Scarecrow had made a quick trip and returned to the Emerald City with his left ear freshly painted.

A moment later, while they all stood in waiting, a servant threw open a door, the orchestra struck up a tune and Ozma of Oz entered.

Much has been told and written concerning the beauty of person and character of this sweet girl Ruler of the Land of Oz— the richest, the happiest and most delightful fairyland of which we have any knowledge. Yet with all her queenly qualities Ozma was a real girl and enjoyed the things in life that other real girls enjoy. When she sat on her splendid emerald throne in the great Throne Room of her palace and made Laws and settled disputes and tried to keep all her subjects happy and contented, she was as dignified and demure as any Queen might be; but when she had thrown aside her jeweled robe of state and her sceptre, and had retired to her private apartments, the girl—joyous, light-hearted and free—replaced the sedate Ruler.

In the banquet hall to-night were gathered only old and trusted friends, so here Ozma was herself—a mere girl. She greeted Dorothy with a kiss, the Shaggy Man with a smile, the little old Wizard with a friendly handshake and then she pressed the Scarecrow's stuffed arm and cried merrily:

"What a lovely left ear! Why, it's a hundred times better than the old one."

"I'm glad you like it," replied the Scarecrow, well pleased. "Jinjur did a neat job, didn't she? And my hearing is now perfect. Isn't it wonderful what a little paint will do, if it's properly applied?"

"It really *is* wonderful," she agreed, as they all took their seats; "but the Sawhorse must have made his legs twinkle to have carried you so far in one day. I didn't expect you back before to-morrow, at the earliest."

"Well," said the Scarecrow, "I met a charming girl on the road and wanted to see more of her, so I hurried back."

Ozma laughed.

"I know," she returned; "it's the Patchwork Girl. She is certainly bewildering, if not strictly beautiful."

"Have you seen her, then?" the straw man eagerly asked.

"Only in my Magic Picture, which shows me all scenes of interest in the Land of Oz."

"I fear the picture didn't do her justice," said the Scarecrow.

"It seemed to me that nothing could be more gorgeous," declared Ozma. "Whoever made that patchwork quilt, from which Scraps was formed, must have selected the gayest and brightest bits of cloth that ever were woven."

"I am glad you like her," said the Scarecrow in a satisfied tone. Although the straw man did not eat, not being made so he could, he often dined with Ozma and her companions, merely for the pleasure of talking with them. He sat at the table and had a napkin and plate, but the servants knew better than to offer him food. After a little while he asked: "Where is the Patchwork Girl now?"

"In my room," replied Dorothy. "I've taken a fancy to her; she's so queer and—and—uncommon."

"She's half crazy, I think," added the Shaggy Man.

"But she is so beautiful!" exclaimed the Scarecrow, as if that fact disarmed all criticism. They all laughed at his enthusiasm, but the Scarecrow was quite serious. Seeing that he was interested in Scraps they forbore to say anything against her. The little band of friends Ozma had gathered around her was so quaintly assorted that much care must be exercised to avoid hurting their feelings or making any one of them unhappy. It was this considerate kindness that held them close friends and enabled them to enjoy one another's society.

Another thing they avoided was conversing on unpleasant subjects, and for that reason Ojo and his troubles were not mentioned during the dinner. The Shaggy Man, however, related his adventures with the monstrous plants which had seized and enfolded the travelers, and told how he had robbed Chiss, the giant porcupine, of the quills which it was accustomed to throw at people. Both Dorothy and Ozma were pleased with this exploit and thought it served Chiss right.

Then they talked of the Woozy, which was the most remarkable animal any of them had ever before seen—except, perhaps, the live Sawhorse. Ozma had never known that her dominions contained such a thing as a Woozy, there being but one in existence and this being confined in his forest for many years. Dorothy said she believed the Woozy was a good beast, honest and faithful; but she added that she did not care much for the Glass Cat.

"Still," said the Shaggy Man, "the Glass Cat is very pretty and if she were not so conceited over her pink brains no one would object to her as a companion."

The Wizard had been eating silently until now, when he looked up and remarked:

"That Powder of Life which is made by the Crooked Magician is really a wonderful thing. But Dr. Pipt does not know its true value and he uses it in the most foolish ways."

"I must see about that," said Ozma, gravely. Then she smiled again and continued in a lighter tone: "It was Dr. Pipt's famous Powder of Life that enabled me to become the Ruler of Oz."

"I've never heard that story," said the Shaggy Man, looking at Ozma questioningly.

"Well, when I was a baby girl I was stolen by an old Witch named Mombi and transformed into a boy," began the girl Ruler. "I did not know who I was and when I grew big enough to work, the Witch made me wait upon her and carry wood for the fire and hoe in the garden. One day she came back from a journey bringing some of the Powder of Life, which Dr. Pipt had given her. I had made a pumpkinheaded man and set it up in her path to frighten her, for I was fond of fun and hated the Witch. But she knew what the figure was and to test her Powder of Life she sprinkled some of it on the man I had made. It came to life and is now our dear friend Jack Pumpkinhead. That night I ran away with Jack to escape punishment, and I took old Mombi's Powder of Life with me. During our journey we came upon a Wooden Sawhorse standing by the road and I used the magic powder to bring it to life. The Sawhorse has been with me ever since. When I got to the Emerald City the good Sorceress, Glinda, knew who I was and restored me to my proper person, when I became the rightful Ruler of this land. So you see had not old Mombi brought home the Powder of Life I might never have run away from her and become Ozma of Oz, nor would we have had Jack Pumpkinhead and the Sawhorse to comfort and amuse us."

That story interested the Shaggy Man very much, as well as the others, who had often heard it before. The dinner being now concluded, they all went to Ozma's drawing-room, where they passed a pleasant evening before it came time to retire.

·····◄ Chapter 18 ►·····

OJO Is FORGIVEN

The next morning the Soldier with the Green Whiskers went to the prison and took Ojo away to the royal palace, where he was summoned to appear before the girl Ruler for judgment. Again the Soldier put upon the boy the jeweled handcuffs and white prisoner's robe with the peaked top and holes for the eyes. Ojo was so ashamed, both of his disgrace and the fault he had committed, that he was glad to be covered up in this way, so that people could not see him or know who he was. He followed the Soldier with the Green Whiskers very willingly, anxious that his fate might be decided as soon as possible.

The inhabitants of the Emerald City were polite people

and never jeered at the unfortunate; but it was so long since they had seen a prisoner that they cast many curious looks toward the boy and many of them hurried away to the royal palace to be present during the trial.

When Ojo was escorted into the great Throne Room of the palace he found hundreds of people assembled there. In the magnificent emerald throne, which sparkled with countless jewels, sat Ozma of Oz in her Robe of State, which was embroidered with emeralds and pearls. On her right, but a little lower, was Dorothy, and on her left the Scarecrow. Still lower, but nearly in front of Ozma, sat the wonderful Wizard of Oz and on a small table beside him was the golden vase from Dorothy's room, into which Scraps had dropped the stolen clover.

At Ozma's feet crouched two enormous beasts, each the largest and most powerful of its kind. Although these beasts were quite free, no one present was alarmed by them; for the Cowardly Lion and the Hungry Tiger were well known and respected in the Emerald City and they always guarded the Ruler when she held high court in the Throne Room. There was still another beast present, but this one Dorothy held in her arms, for it was her constant companion, the little dog Toto. Toto knew the Cowardly Lion and the Hungry Tiger and often played and romped with them, for they were good friends.

Seated on ivory chairs before Ozma, with a clear space between them and the throne, were many of the nobility of the

Emerald City, lords and ladies in beautiful costumes, and officials of the kingdom in the royal uniforms of Oz. Behind these courtiers were others of less importance, filling the great hall to the very doors.

At the same moment that the Soldier with the Green Whiskers arrived with Ojo, the Shaggy Man entered from a side door, escorting the Patchwork Girl, the Woozy and the Glass Cat. All these came to the vacant space before the throne and stood facing the Ruler.

"Hullo, Ojo," said Scraps; "how are you?"

"All right," he replied; but the scene awed the boy and his voice trembled a little with fear. Nothing could awe the Patchwork Girl, and although the Woozy was somewhat uneasy in these splendid surroundings the Glass Cat was delighted with the sumptuousness of the court and the impressiveness of the occasion—pretty big words but quite expressive.

At a sign from Ozma the Soldier removed Ojo's white robe and the boy stood face to face with the girl who was to decide his punishment. He saw at a glance how lovely and sweet she was, and his heart gave a bound of joy, for he hoped she would be merciful.

Ozma sat looking at the prisoner a long time. Then she said gently:

"One of the Laws of Oz forbids anyone to pick a six-leaved clover. You are accused of having broken this Law, even after you had been warned not to do so."

Ojo hung his head and while he hesitated how to reply the Patchwork Girl stepped forward and spoke for him.

"All this fuss is about nothing at all," she said, facing Ozma unabashed. "You can't prove he picked the six-leaved clover, so you've no right to accuse him of it. Search him, if you like, but you won't find the clover; look in his basket and you'll find it's not there. He hasn't got it, so I demand that you set this poor Munchkin boy free."

The people of Oz listened to this defiance in amazement and wondered at the queer Patchwork Girl who dared talk so boldly to their Ruler. But Ozma sat silent and motionless and it was the little Wizard who answered Scraps.

"So the clover hasn't been picked, eh?" he said. "I think it has. I think the boy hid it in his basket, and then gave the basket to you. I also think you dropped the clover into this vase, which stood in Princess Dorothy's room, hoping to get rid of it so it would not prove the boy guilty. You're a stranger here, Miss Patches, and so you don't know that nothing can be hidden from our powerful Ruler's Magic Picture—nor from the watchful eyes of the humble Wizard of Oz. Look, all of you!" With these words he waved his hands toward the vase on the table, which Scraps now noticed for the first time.

From the mouth of the vase a plant sprouted, slowly growing before their eyes until it became a beautiful bush, and on the topmost branch appeared the six-leaved clover which Ojo had unfortunately picked.

The Patchwork Girl looked at the clover and said: "Oh, so you've found it. Very well; prove he picked it, if you can."

Ozma turned to Ojo.

"Did you pick the six-leaved clover?" she asked.

"Yes," he replied. "I knew it was against the Law, but I wanted to save Unc Nunkie and I was afraid if I asked your consent to pick it you would refuse me."

"What caused you to think that?" asked the Ruler.

"Why, it seemed to me a foolish Law, unjust and unreasonable. Even now I can see no harm in picking a six-leaved clover. And I—I had not seen the Emerald City, then, nor you, and I thought a girl who would make such a silly Law would not be likely to help anyone in trouble."

Ozma regarded him musingly, her chin resting upon her hand; but she was not angry. On the contrary she smiled a little at her thoughts and then grew sober again.

"I suppose a good many Laws seem foolish to those people who do not understand them," she said; "but no Law is ever made without some purpose, and that purpose is usually to protect all the people and guard their welfare. As you are a stranger, I will explain this Law which to you seems so foolish. Years ago there were many Witches and Magicians in the Land of Oz, and one of the things they often used in making their magic charms and transformations was a six-leaved clover. These Witches and Magicians caused so much trouble among my people, often using their powers for evil rather than good, that I decided to forbid anyone to practice magic or sorcery except Glinda the Good and her assistant, the Wizard of Oz, both of whom I can trust to use their arts only to benefit my people and to make them happier. Since I issued that Law the Land of Oz has been far more peaceful and quiet; but I learned that some of the Witches and Magicians were still practicing magic on the sly and using the six-leaved clovers to make their potions and charms. Therefore I made another Law forbidding anyone from plucking a six-leaved clover or from gathering other plants and herbs which the Witches boil in their kettles to work magic with. That has almost put an end to wicked sorcery in our land, so you see the Law was not a foolish one, but wise and just; and, in any event, it is wrong to disobey a Law."

Ojo knew she was right and felt greatly mortified to realize he had acted and spoken so ridiculously. But he raised his head and looked Ozma in the face, saying:

"I am sorry I have acted wrongly and broken your Law. I did it to save Unc Nunkie, and thought I would not be found out. But I am guilty of this act and whatever punishment you think I deserve I will suffer willingly."

Ozma smiled more brightly, then, and nodded graciously.

"You are forgiven," she said. "For, although you have committed a serious fault, you are now penitent and I think you have been punished enough. Soldier, release Ojo the Lucky and—"

"I beg your pardon; I'm Ojo the *Un*lucky," said the boy.

"At this moment you are lucky," said she. "Release him, Soldier, and let him go free."

The people were glad to hear Ozma's decree and murmured their approval. As the royal audience was now over, they began to leave the Throne Room and soon there were none remaining except Ojo and his friends and Ozma and her favorites.

The girl Ruler now asked Ojo to sit down and tell her all his story, which he did, beginning at the time he had left his home in the forest and ending with his arrival at the Emerald City and his arrest. Ozma listened attentively and was thoughtful for some moments after the boy had finished speaking. Then she said:

"The Crooked Magician was wrong to make the Glass Cat and the Patchwork Girl, for it was against the Law. And if he had not unlawfully kept the bottle of Liquid of Petrifaction standing on his shelf, the accident to his wife Margolotte and to Unc Nunkie could not have occurred. I can understand, however, that Ojo, who loves his uncle, will be unhappy unless he can save him. Also I feel it is wrong to leave those two victims standing as marble statues, when they ought to be alive. So I propose we allow Dr. Pipt to make the magic charm which will save them, and that we assist Ojo to find the things he is seeking. What do you think, Wizard?"

"That is perhaps the best thing to do," replied the Wizard.

"But after the Crooked Magician has restored those poor people to life you must take away his magic powers."

"I will," promised Ozma.

"Now tell me, please, what magic things must you find?" continued the Wizard, addressing Ojo.

"The three hairs from the Woozy's tail I have," said the boy. "That is, I have the Woozy, and the hairs are in his tail. The six-leaved clover I—I—"

"You may take it and keep it," said Ozma. "That will not be breaking the Law, for it is already picked, and the crime of picking it is forgiven."

"Thank you!" cried Ojo gratefully. Then he continued: "The next thing I must find is a gill of water from a dark well."

The Wizard shook his head. "That," said he, "will be a hard task, but if you travel far enough you may discover it."

"I am willing to travel for years, if it will save Unc Nunkie," declared Ojo, earnestly.

"Then you'd better begin your journey at once," advised the Wizard.

Dorothy had been listening with interest to this conversation. Now she turned to Ozma and asked: "May I go with Ojo, to help him?"

"Would you like to?" returned Ozma.

"Yes. I know Oz pretty well, but Ojo doesn't know it at all. I'm sorry for his uncle and poor Margolotte and I'd like to help save them. May I go?"

"If you wish to," replied Ozma.

"If Dorothy goes, then I must go to take care of her," said the Scarecrow, decidedly. "A dark well can only be discovered in some out-of-the-way place, and there may be dangers there."

"You have my permission to accompany Dorothy," said Ozma. "And while you are gone I will take care of the Patchwork Girl."

"I'll take care of myself," announced Scraps, "for I'm going with the Scarecrow and Dorothy. I promised Ojo to help him find the things he wants and I'll stick to my promise."

"Very well," replied Ozma. "But I see no need for Ojo to take the Glass Cat and the Woozy."

"I prefer to remain here," said the cat. "I've nearly been nicked half a dozen times, already, and if they're going into dangers it's best for me to keep away from them."

"Let Jellia Jamb keep her till Ojo returns," suggested Dorothy. "We won't need to take the Woozy, either, but he ought to be saved because of the three hairs in his tail."

"Better take me along," said the Woozy. "My eyes can flash fire, you know, and I can growl—a little."

"I'm sure you'll be safer here," Ozma decided, and the Woozy made no further objection to the plan.

After consulting together they decided that Ojo and his party should leave the very next day to search for the gill of water from a dark well, so they now separated to make preparations for the journey.

Ozma gave the Munchkin boy a room in the palace for that night and the afternoon he passed with Dorothy—getting acquainted, as she said—and receiving advice from the Shaggy Man as to where they must go. The Shaggy Man had wandered in many parts of Oz, and so had Dorothy, for that matter, yet neither of them knew where a dark well was to be found.

"If such a thing is anywhere in the settled parts of Oz," said Dorothy, "we'd prob'ly have heard of it long ago. If it's in the wild parts of the country, no one there would need a dark well. P'raps there isn't such a thing."

"Oh, there must be!" returned Ojo, positively; "or else the recipe of Dr. Pipt wouldn't call for it."

"That's true," agreed Dorothy; "and, if it's anywhere in the Land of Oz, we're bound to find it."

"Well, we're bound to *search* for it, anyhow," said the Scarecrow. "As for finding it, we must trust to luck."

"Don't do that," begged Ojo, earnestly. "I'm called Ojo the Unlucky, you know."

TROUBLE with the
TOTTENHOTS

A day's journey from the Emerald City brought the little band of adventurers to the home of Jack Pumpkinhead, which was a house formed from the shell of an immense pumpkin. Jack had made it himself and was very proud of it. There was a door, and several windows, and through the top was stuck a stovepipe that led from a small stove inside. The door was reached by a flight of three steps and there was a good floor on which was arranged some furniture that was quite comfortable.

It is certain that Jack Pumpkinhead might have had a much finer house to live in had he wanted it, for Ozma loved the stupid fellow, who had been her earliest companion; but

Jack preferred his pumpkin house, as it matched himself very well, and in this he was not so stupid, after all.

The body of this remarkable person was made of wood, branches of trees of various sizes having been used for the purpose. This wooden framework was covered by a red shirt—with white spots in it—blue trousers, a yellow vest, a jacket of green-and-gold, and stout leather shoes. The neck was a sharpened stick on which the pumpkin head was set, and the eyes, ears, nose and mouth were carved on the skin of the pumpkin, very like a child's jack-o'-lantern.

The house of this interesting creation stood in the center of a vast pumpkin-field, where the vines grew in profusion and bore pumpkins of extraordinary size as well as those which were smaller. Some of the pumpkins now ripening on the vines were almost as large as Jack's house, and he told Dorothy he intended to add another pumpkin to his mansion.

The travelers were cordially welcomed to this quaint domicile and invited to pass the night there, which they had planned to do. The Patchwork Girl was greatly interested in Jack and examined him admiringly.

"You are quite handsome," she said; "but not as really beautiful as the Scarecrow."

Jack turned, at this, to examine the Scarecrow critically, and his old friend slyly winked one painted eye at him.

"There is no accounting for tastes," remarked the Pumpkin-head, with a sigh. "An old crow once told me I was very fascinating, but of course the bird might have been mistaken. Yet I have noticed that the crows usually avoid the Scarecrow, who is a very honest fellow, in his way, but stuffed. I am not stuffed, you will observe; my body is good solid hickory."

"I adore stuffing," said the Patchwork Girl.

"Well, as for that, my head is stuffed with pumpkin-seeds," declared Jack. "I use them for brains, and when they are fresh I am intellectual. Just now, I regret to say, my seeds are rattling a bit, so I must soon get another head."

"Oh; do you change your head?" asked Ojo.

"To be sure. Pumpkins are not permanent, more's the pity, and in time they spoil. That is why I grow such a great field of pumpkins—that I may select a new head whenever necessary."

"Who carves the faces on them?" inquired the boy.

"I do that myself. I lift off my old head, place it on a table before me, and use the face for a pattern to go by. Sometimes the faces I carve are better than others—more expressive and cheerful, you know—but I think they average very well."

Before she had started on the journey Dorothy had packed a knapsack with the things she might need, and this knapsack the Scarecrow carried strapped to his back. The little girl wore a plain gingham dress and a checked sunbonnet, as she knew they were best fitted for travel. Ojo also had brought along his basket, to which Ozma had added a bottle of "Square Meal Tablets" and some fruit. But Jack Pumpkinhead grew a lot of things in his garden besides pumpkins, so he cooked for them a fine vegetable soup and gave Dorothy, Ojo and Toto, the only ones who found it necessary to eat, a pumpkin pie and some green cheese. For beds they must use the sweet dried grasses which Jack had strewn along one side of the room, but that satisfied Dorothy and Ojo very well. Toto, of course, slept beside his little mistress.

The Scarecrow, Scraps and the Pumpkinhead were tireless and had no need to sleep, so they sat up and talked together all night; but they stayed outside the house, under the bright stars, and talked in low tones so as not to disturb the sleepers. During the conversation the Scarecrow explained their quest for a dark well, and asked Jack's advice where to find it.

The Pumpkinhead considered the matter gravely.

"That is going to be a difficult task," said he, "and if I were you I'd take any ordinary well and enclose it, so as to make it dark."

"I fear that wouldn't do," replied the Scarecrow. "The well must be naturally dark, and the water must never have seen the light of day, for otherwise the magic charm might not work at all."

"How much of the water do you need?" asked Jack.

"A gill."

"How much is a gill?"

"Why—a gill is a gill, of course," answered the Scarecrow, who did not wish to display his ignorance.

"I know!" cried Scraps. "Jack and Jill went up the hill to fetch—"

"No, no; that's wrong," interrupted the Scarecrow. "There are two kinds of gills, I think; one is a girl, and the other is—"

"A gillyflower," said Jack.

"No; a measure."

"How big a measure?"

"Well, I'll ask Dorothy."

So next morning they asked Dorothy, and she said:

"I don't just know how much a gill is, but I've brought along a gold flask that holds a pint. That's more than a gill, I'm sure, and the Crooked Magician may measure it to suit himself. But the thing that's bothering us most, Jack, is to find the well."

Jack gazed around the landscape, for he was standing in the doorway of his house.

"This is a flat country, so you won't find any dark wells here," said he. "You must go into the mountains, where rocks and caverns are."

"And where is that?" asked Ojo.

"In the Quadling Country, which lies south of here," replied the Scarecrow. "I've known all along that we must go to the mountains."

"So have I," said Dorothy.

"But—goodness me!—the Quadling Country is full of dangers," declared Jack. "I've never been there myself, but—"

"I have," said the Scarecrow. "I've faced the dreadful Hammerheads, which have no arms and butt you like a goat; and I've faced the Fighting Trees, which bend down their branches to pound and whip you, and had many other adventures there."

"It's a wild country," remarked Dorothy, soberly, "and if we go there we're sure to have troubles of our own. But I guess we'll have to go, if we want that gill of water from the dark well."

So they said good-bye to the Pumpkinhead and resumed their travels, heading now directly toward the South Country, where mountains and rocks and caverns and forests of great trees abounded. This part of the Land of Oz, while it belonged to Ozma and owed her allegiance, was so wild and secluded that many queer peoples hid in its jungles and lived in their own way, without even a knowledge that they had a Ruler in the Emerald City. If they were left alone, these creatures never troubled the inhabitants of the rest of Oz, but those who invaded their domains encountered many dangers from them.

It was a two days journey from Jack Pumpkinhead's house to the edge of the Quadling Country, for neither Dorothy nor Ojo could walk very fast and they often stopped by the wayside to rest. The first night they slept on the broad fields, among the buttercups and daisies, and the Scarecrow covered the children with a gauze blanket taken from his knapsack, so they would not be chilled by the night air. Toward evening of the second day they reached a sandy plain where walking was difficult; but some distance before them they saw a group of palm trees, with many curious black dots under them; so they trudged bravely on to reach that place by dark and spend the night under the shelter of the trees.

The black dots grew larger as they advanced and although the light was dim Dorothy thought they looked like big kettles turned upside down. Just beyond this place a jumble of huge, jagged rocks lay scattered, rising to the mountains behind them.

Our travelers preferred to attempt to climb these rocks by daylight, and they realized that for a time this would be their last night on the plains.

Twilight had fallen by the time they came to the trees, beneath which were the black, circular objects they had marked from a distance. Dozens of them were scattered around and Dorothy bent near to one, which was about as tall as she was, to examine it more closely. As she did so the top flew open and out popped a dusky creature, rising its length into the air and then plumping down upon the ground just beside the little girl. Another and another popped out of the circular, pot-like dwelling, while from all the other black objects came popping more creatures—very like jumping-jacks when their boxes are unhooked—until fully a hundred stood gathered around our little group of travelers.

By this time Dorothy had discovered they were people, tiny and curiously formed, but still people. Their skins were dusky and their hair stood straight up, like wires, and was brilliant scarlet in color. Their bodies were bare except for skins fastened around their waists and they wore bracelets on their ankles and wrists, and necklaces, and great pendant earrings.

Toto crouched beside his mistress and wailed as if he did not like these strange creatures a bit. Scraps began to mutter something about "hoppity, poppity, jumpity, dump!" but no one paid any attention to her. Ojo kept close to the Scarecrow and the Scarecrow kept close to Dorothy; but the little girl turned to the queer creatures and asked:

"Who are you?"

They answered this question all together, in a sort of chanting chorus, the words being as follows:

> *"We're the jolly Tottenhots;*
> *We do not like the day,*
> *But in the night 'tis our delight*
> *To gambol, skip and play.*

> *"We hate the sun and from it run,*
> *The moon is cool and clear,*
> *So on this spot each Tottenhot*
> *Waits for it to appear.*

> *"We're ev'ry one chock full of fun,*
> *And full of mischief, too;*

But if you're gay and with us play
We'll do no harm to you.

"Glad to meet you, Tottenhots," said the Scarecrow solemnly. "But you mustn't expect us to play with you all night, for we've traveled all day and some of us are tired."

"And we never gamble," added the Patchwork Girl. "It's against the Law."

These remarks were greeted with shouts of laughter by the impish creatures and one seized the Scarecrow's arm and was astonished to find the straw man whirl around so easily. So the Tottenhot raised the Scarecrow high in the air and tossed him over the heads of the crowd. Some one caught him and tossed him back, and so with shouts of glee they continued throwing the Scarecrow here and there, as if he had been a basket-ball.

Presently another imp seized Scraps and began to throw her about, in the same way. They found her a little heavier than the Scarecrow but still light enough to be tossed like a sofa-cushion, and they were enjoying the sport immensely when Dorothy, angry and indignant at the treatment her friends were receiving, rushed among the Tottenhots and began slapping and pushing them until she had rescued the Scarecrow and the Patchwork Girl and held them close on either side of her. Perhaps she would not have accomplished this victory so easily had not Toto helped her, barking and snapping at the bare legs of the imps until they were glad to flee from his attack. As for Ojo, some of the creatures had attempted to toss him, also, but finding his body too heavy they threw him to the ground and a row of the imps sat on him and held him from assisting Dorothy in her battle.

The little brown folks were much surprised at being attacked by the girl and the dog, and one or two who had been slapped hardest began to cry. Then suddenly they gave a shout, all together, and disappeared in a flash into their various houses, the tops of which closed with a series of pops that sounded like a bunch of firecrackers being exploded.

The adventurers now found themselves alone, and Dorothy asked anxiously:

"Is anybody hurt?"

"Not me," answered the Scarecrow. "They have given my straw a good shaking up and taken all the lumps out of it. I am now in splendid condition and am really obliged to the Tottenhots for their kind treatment."

"I feel much the same way," said Scraps. "My cotton stuffing had sagged a good deal with the day's walking and they've loosened it up until I feel as plump as a sausage. But the play was a little rough and I'd had quite enough of it when you interfered."

"Six of them sat on me," said Ojo, "but as they are so little they didn't hurt me much."

Just then the roof of the house in front of them opened and

a Tottenhot stuck his head out, very cautiously, and looked at the strangers.

"Can't you take a joke?" he asked, reproachfully; "haven't you any fun in you at all?"

"If I had such a quality," replied the Scarecrow, "your people would have knocked it out of me. But I don't bear grudges. I forgive you."

"So do I," added Scraps. "That is, if you behave yourselves after this."

"It was just a little rough-house, that's all," said the Tottenhot. "But the question is not if we will behave, but if you will behave? We can't be shut up here all night, because this is our time to play; nor do we care to come out and be chewed up by a savage beast or slapped by an angry girl. That slapping hurts like sixty; some of my folks are crying about it. So here's the proposition: you let us alone and we'll let you alone."

"You began it," declared Dorothy.

"Well, you ended it, so we won't argue the matter. May we come out again? Or are you still cruel and slappy?"

"Tell you what we'll do," said Dorothy. "We're all tired and want to sleep until morning. If you'll let us get into your house, and stay there until daylight, you can play outside all you want to."

"That's a bargain!" cried the Tottenhot eagerly, and he gave a queer whistle that brought his people popping out of their houses on all sides. When the house before them was vacant, Dorothy and Ojo leaned over the hole and looked in, but could see nothing because it was so dark. But if the Tottenhots slept there all day the children thought they could sleep there at night, so Ojo lowered himself down and found it was not very deep.

"There's a soft cushion all over," said he. "Come on in."

Dorothy handed Toto to the boy and then climbed in herself. After her came Scraps and the Scarecrow, who did not wish to sleep but preferred to keep out of the way of the mischievous Tottenhots.

There seemed no furniture in the round den, but soft cushions were strewn about the floor and these they found made very comfortable beds. They did not close the hole in the roof but left it open to admit air. It also admitted the shouts and ceaseless laughter of the impish Tottenhots as they played outside, but Dorothy and Ojo, being weary from their journey, were soon fast asleep.

Toto kept an eye open, however, and uttered low, threatening growls whenever the racket made by the creatures outside became too boisterous; and the Scarecrow and the Patchwork Girl sat leaning against the wall and talked in whispers all night long. No one disturbed the travelers until daylight, when in popped the Tottenhot who owned the place and invited them to vacate his premises.

Chapter 20

The CAPTIVE YOOP

As they were preparing to leave, Dorothy asked:
"Can you tell us where there is a dark well?"

"Never heard of such a thing," said the Tottenhot. "We live our lives in the dark, mostly, and sleep in the daytime; but we've never seen a dark well, or anything like one."

"Does anyone live on those mountains beyond here?" asked the Scarecrow.

"Lots of people. But you'd better not visit them. We never go there," was the reply.

"What are the people like?" Dorothy inquired.

"Can't say. We've been told to keep away from the mountain

paths, and so we obey. This sandy desert is good enough for us, and we're not disturbed here," declared the Tottenhot.

So they left the man snuggling down to sleep in his dusky dwelling, and went out into the sunshine, taking the path that led toward the rocky places. They soon found it hard climbing, for the rocks were uneven and full of sharp points and edges, and now there was no path at all. Clambering here and there among the boulders they kept steadily on, gradually rising higher and higher until finally they came to a great rift in a part of the mountain, where the rock seemed to have split in two and left high walls on either side.

"S'pose we go this way," suggested Dorothy; "it's much easier walking than to climb over the hills."

"How about that sign?" asked Ojo.

"What sign?" she inquired.

The Munchkin boy pointed to some words painted on the wall of rock beside them, which Dorothy had not noticed. The words read:

LOOK OUT FOR YOOP.

The girl eyed this sign a moment and turned to the Scarecrow, asking:

"Who is Yoop; or what is Yoop?"

The straw man shook his head. Then looked at Toto and the dog said "Woof!"

"Only way to find out is to go on," said Scraps.

This being quite true, they went on. As they proceeded, the walls of rock on either side grew higher and higher. Presently they came upon another sign which read:

BEWARE THE CAPTIVE YOOP.

"Why, as for that," remarked Dorothy, "if Yoop is a captive there's no need to beware of him. Whatever Yoop happens to be, I'd much rather have him a captive than running around loose."

"So had I," agreed the Scarecrow, with a nod of his painted head.

"Still," said Scraps, reflectively:

"Yoop-te-hoop-te-loop-te-goop!
Who put noodles in the soup?
We may beware but we don't care,
And dare go where we scare the Yoop."

"Dear me! Aren't you feeling a little queer, just now?" Dorothy asked the Patchwork Girl.

"Not queer, but crazy," said Ojo. "When she says those things I'm sure her brains get mixed somehow and work the wrong way.

"I don't see why we are told to beware the Yoop unless he

is dangerous," observed the Scarecrow in a puzzled tone.

"Never mind; we'll find out all about him when we get to where he is," replied the little girl.

The narrow canyon turned and twisted this way and that, and the rift was so small that they were able to touch both walls at the same time by stretching out their arms. Toto had run on ahead, frisking playfully, when suddenly he uttered a sharp bark of fear and came running back to them with his tail between his legs, as dogs do when they are frightened.

"Ah," said the Scarecrow, who was leading the way, "we must be near Yoop."

Just then, as he rounded a sharp turn, the straw man stopped so suddenly that all the others bumped against him.

"What is it?" asked Dorothy, standing on tip-toes to look over his shoulder. But then she saw what it was and cried "Oh!" in a tone of astonishment.

In one of the rock walls—that at their left—was hollowed a great cavern, in front of which was a row of thick iron bars, the tops and bottoms being firmly fixed in the solid rock. Over this cavern was a big sign, which Dorothy read with much curiosity, speaking the words aloud that all might know what they said:

MISTER YOOP—HIS CAVE

The Largest Untamed Giant in Captivity.

Height, 21 Feet.—(And yet he has but 2 feet.)

Weight, 1640 Pounds.—(But he waits all the time.)

Age, 400 Years 'and Up' (as they say in the
Department Store advertisements).
Temper, Fierce and Ferocious.—(Except when asleep.)
Appetite, Ravenous.—(Prefers Meat People and
Orange Marmalade.)
STRANGERS APPROACHING THIS CAVE
DO SO AT THEIR OWN PERIL!
P.S.—Don't feed the Giant yourself.

"Very well," said Ojo, with a sigh; "let's go back."

"It's a long way back," declared Dorothy.

"So it is," remarked the Scarecrow, "and it means a tedious climb over those sharp rocks if we can't use this passage. I think it will be best to run by the Giant's cave as fast as we can go. Mister Yoop seems to be asleep just now."

But the Giant wasn't asleep. He suddenly appeared at the front of his cavern, seized the iron bars in his great hairy hands and shook them until they rattled in their sockets. Yoop was so tall that our friends had to tip their heads way back to look into his face, and they noticed he was dressed all in pink velvet, with silver buttons and braid. The Giant's boots were of pink leather and had tassels on them and his hat was decorated with an enormous pink ostrich feather, carefully curled.

"Yo-ho!" he said in a deep bass voice; "I smell dinner."

"I think you are mistaken," replied the Scarecrow. "There is no orange marmalade around here."

"Ah, but I eat other things," asserted Mister Yoop. "That is, I eat them when I can get them. But this is a lonely place, and no good meat has passed by my cave for many years; so I'm hungry."

"Haven't you eaten anything in many years?" asked Dorothy.

"Nothing except six ants and a monkey. I thought the monkey would taste like meat people, but the flavor was different. I hope you will taste better, for you seem plump and tender."

"Oh, I'm not going to be eaten," said Dorothy.

"Why not?"

"I shall keep out of your way," she answered.

"How heartless!" wailed the Giant, shaking the bars again. "Consider how many years it is since I've eaten a single plump little girl! They tell me meat is going up, but if I can manage to catch you I'm sure it will soon be going down. And I'll catch you if I can."

With this the Giant pushed his big arms, which looked like tree-trunks (except that tree-trunks don't wear pink velvet) between the iron bars, and the arms were so long that they touched the opposite wall of the rock passage. Then he extended them as far as he could reach toward our travelers and found he could almost touch the Scarecrow—but not quite.

"Come a little nearer, please," begged the Giant.

"I'm a Scarecrow."

"A Scarecrow? Ugh! I don't care a straw for a scarecrow. Who is that bright-colored delicacy behind you?"

"Me?" asked Scraps. "I'm a Patchwork Girl, and I'm stuffed with cotton."

"Dear me," sighed the Giant in a disappointed tone; "that reduces my dinner from four to two—and the dog. I'll save the dog for dessert."

Toto growled, keeping a good distance away.

"Back up," said the Scarecrow to those behind him. "Let us go back a little way and talk this over."

So they turned and went around the bend in the passage, where they were out of sight of the cave and Mister Yoop could not hear them.

"My idea," began the Scarecrow, when they had halted, "is to make a dash past the cave, going on a run."

"He'd grab us," said Dorothy.

"Well, he can't grab but one at a time, and I'll go first. As soon as he grabs me the rest of you can slip past him, out of his reach, and he will soon let me go because I am not fit to eat."

They decided to try this plan and Dorothy took Toto in her arms, so as to protect him. She followed just after the Scarecrow. Then came Ojo, with Scraps the last of the four. Their hearts beat a little faster than usual as they again approached the Giant's cave, this time moving swiftly forward.

It turned out about the way the Scarecrow had planned. Mister Yoop was quite astonished to see them come flying toward him, and thrusting his arms between the bars he seized the Scarecrow in a firm grip. In the next instant he realized, from the way the straw crunched between his fingers, that he had captured the non-eatable man, but during that instant of delay Dorothy and Ojo had slipped by the Giant and were out of reach. Uttering a howl of rage the monster threw the Scarecrow after them with one hand and grabbed Scraps with the other.

The poor Scarecrow went whirling through the air and so cleverly was he aimed that he struck Ojo's back and sent the boy tumbling head over heels, and he tripped Dorothy and sent her, also, sprawling upon the ground. Toto flew out of the little girl's arms and landed some distance ahead, and all were so dazed that it was a moment before they could scramble to their feet again. When they did so they turned to look toward the Giant's cave, and at that moment the ferocious Mister Yoop threw the Patchwork Girl at them.

Down went all three again, in a heap, with Scraps on top. The Giant roared so terribly that for a time they were afraid he had broken loose; but he hadn't. So they sat in the road and looked at one another in a rather bewildered way, and then began to feel glad.

"We did it!" exclaimed the Scarecrow, with satisfaction. "And now we are free to go on our way."

"Mister Yoop is very impolite," declared Scraps. "He jarred me terribly. It's lucky my stitches are so fine and strong, for otherwise such harsh treatment might rip me up the back."

"Allow me to apologize for the Giant," said the Scarecrow, raising the Patchwork Girl to her feet and dusting her skirt with his stuffed hands. "Mister Yoop is a perfect stranger to me, but I fear, from the rude manner in which he has acted, that he is no gentleman."

Dorothy and Ojo laughed at this statement and Toto barked as if he understood the joke, after which they all felt better and resumed the journey in high spirits.

"Of course," said the little girl, when they had walked a way along the passage, "it was lucky for us the Giant was caged; for, if he had happened to be loose, he—he—"

"Perhaps, in that case, he wouldn't be hungry any more," said Ojo gravely.

Chapter 21

HIP HOPPER the CHAMPION

They must have had good courage to climb all those rocks, for after getting out of the canyon they encountered more rock hills to be surmounted. Toto could jump from one rock to another quite easily, but the others had to creep and climb with care, so that after a whole day of such work Dorothy and Ojo found themselves very tired.

As they gazed upward at the great mass of tumbled rocks that covered the steep incline, Dorothy gave a little groan and said:

"That's going to be a ter'ble hard climb, Scarecrow. I wish we could find the dark well without so much trouble."

"Suppose," said Ojo, "you wait here and let me do the climbing, for it's on my account we're searching for the dark well. Then, if I don't find anything, I'll come back and join you."

"No," replied the little girl, shaking her head positively, "we'll all go together, for that way we can help each other. If you went alone, something might happen to you, Ojo."

So they began the climb and found it indeed difficult, for a way. But presently, in creeping over the big crags, they found a path at their feet which wound in and out among the masses of rock and was quite smooth and easy to walk upon. As the path gradually ascended the mountain, although in a round-about way, they decided to follow it.

"This must be the road to the Country of the Hoppers," said the Scarecrow.

"Who are the Hoppers?" asked Dorothy.

"Some people Jack Pumpkinhead told me about," he replied.

"I didn't hear him," replied the girl.

"No; you were asleep," explained the Scarecrow. "But he told Scraps and me that the Hoppers and the Horners live on this mountain."

"He said *in* the mountain," declared Scraps; "but of course he meant on it."

"Didn't he say what the Hoppers and Horners were like?" inquired Dorothy.

"No; he only said they were two separate nations, and that the Horners were the most important."

"Well, if we go to their country we'll find out all about 'em," said the girl. "But I've never heard Ozma mention those people, so they can't be *very* important."

"Is this mountain in the Land of Oz?" asked Scraps.

"Course it is," answered Dorothy. "It's in the South Country of the Quadlings. When one comes to the edge of Oz, in any direction, there is nothing more to be seen at all. Once you could see sandy desert all around Oz; but now it's diff'rent, and no other people can see us, any more than we can see them."

"If the mountain is under Ozma's rule, why doesn't she know about the Hoppers and the Horners?" Ojo asked.

"Why, it's a fairyland," explained Dorothy, "and lots of queer people live in places so tucked away that those in the Emerald City never even hear of 'em. In the middle of the country it's diff'rent, but when you get around the edges you're sure to run into strange little corners that surprise you. I know, for I've traveled in Oz a good deal, and so has the Scarecrow."

"Yes," admitted the straw man, "I've been considerable of a traveler, in my time, and I like to explore strange places. I find I learn much more by traveling than by staying at home."

During this conversation they had been walking up the steep pathway and now found themselves well up on the mountain. They could see nothing around them, for the rocks beside their path were higher than their heads. Nor could they see far in front of them, because the path was so crooked. But suddenly they stopped, because the path ended and there was no place to go. Ahead was a big rock lying against the side of the mountain, and this blocked the way completely.

"There wouldn't be a path, though, if it didn't go somewhere," said the Scarecrow, wrinkling his forehead in deep thought.

"This is somewhere, isn't it?" asked the Patchwork Girl, laughing at the bewildered looks of the others.

> "The path is locked, the way is blocked,
> Yet here we've innocently flocked;
> And now we're here it's rather queer
> There's no front door that can be knocked."

"Please don't, Scraps," said Ojo. "You make me nervous."

"Well," said Dorothy, "I'm glad of a little rest, for that's a drea'ful steep path."

As she spoke she leaned against the edge of the big rock that stood in their way. To her surprise it slowly swung backward and showed behind it a dark hole that looked like the mouth of a tunnel.

"Why, here's where the path goes to!" she exclaimed.

"So it is," answered the Scarecrow. "But the question is, do we want to go where the path does?"

"It's underground; right inside the mountain," said Ojo, peering into the dark hole. "Perhaps there's a well there; and, if there is, it's sure to be a dark one."

"Why, that's true enough!" cried Dorothy with eagerness. "Let's go in, Scarecrow; 'cause, if others have gone, we're pretty safe to go, too."

Toto looked in and barked, but he did not venture to enter until the Scarecrow had bravely gone first. Scraps followed closely after the straw man and then Ojo and Dorothy timidly stepped inside the tunnel. As soon as all of them had passed the big rock, it slowly turned and filled up the opening again; but now they were no longer in the dark, for a soft, rosy light enabled them to see around them quite distinctly.

It was only a passage, wide enough for two of them to walk abreast—with Toto in between them—and it had a high, arched roof. They could not see where the light which flooded the place so pleasantly came from, for there were no lamps anywhere visible. The passage ran straight for a little way and then made a bend to the right and another sharp turn to the left, after which it went straight again. But there were no side passages, so they could not lose their way.

After proceeding some distance, Toto, who had gone on ahead, began to bark loudly. They ran around a bend to see what was the matter and found a man sitting on the floor of the passage and leaning his back against the wall. He had probably been asleep before Toto's barks aroused him, for he was now rubbing his eyes and staring at the little dog with all his might.

There was something about this man that Toto objected to, and when he slowly rose to his foot they saw what it was. He had but one leg, set just below the middle of his round, fat body; but it was a stout leg and had a broad, flat foot at the bottom of it, on which the man seemed to stand very well. He had never had but this one leg, which looked something like a pedestal, and when Toto ran up and made a grab at the man's ankle he hopped first one way and then another in a very active manner, looking so frightened that Scraps laughed aloud.

Toto was usually a well behaved dog, but this time he was angry and snapped at the man's leg again and again. This filled the poor fellow with fear, and in hopping out of Toto's reach he suddenly lost his balance and tumbled heel over head upon the floor. When he sat up he kicked Toto on the nose and made the dog howl angrily, but Dorothy now ran forward and caught Toto's collar, holding him back.

"Do you surrender?" she asked the man.

"Who? Me?" asked the Hopper.

"Yes; you," said the little girl.

"Am I captured?" he inquired.

"Of course. My dog has captured you," she said.

"Well," replied the man, "if I'm captured I must surrender, for it's the proper thing to do. I like to do everything proper, for it saves one a lot of trouble."

"It does, indeed," said Dorothy. "Please tell us who you are."

"I'm Hip Hopper—Hip Hopper, the Champion."

"Champion what?" she asked in surprise.

"Champion wrestler. I'm a very strong man, and that ferocious animal which you are so kindly holding is the first living thing that has ever conquered me."

"And you are a Hopper?" she continued.

"Yes. My people live in a great city not far from here. Would you like to visit it?"

"I'm not sure," she said with hesitation. "Have you any dark wells in your city?"

"I think not. We have wells, you know, but they're all well lighted, and a well lighted well cannot well be a dark well. But there may be such a thing as a very dark well in the Horner Country, which is a black spot on the face of the earth."

"Where is the Horner Country?" Ojo inquired.

"The other side of the mountain. There's a fence between the Hopper Country and the Horner Country, and a gate in the fence; but you can't pass through just now, because we are at war with the Horners."

"That's too bad," said the Scarecrow. "What seems to be the trouble?"

"Why, one of them made a very insulting remark about my people. He said we were lacking in understanding, because we had only one leg to a person. I can't see that legs have anything to do with understanding things. The Horners each have two legs, just as you have. That's one leg too many, it seems to me."

"No," declared Dorothy, "it's just the right number."

"You don't need them," argued the Hopper, obstinately. "You've only one head, and one body, and one nose and mouth. Two legs are quite unnecessary, and they spoil one's shape."

"But how can you walk, with only one leg?" asked Ojo.

"Walk! Who wants to walk?" exclaimed the man. "Walking is a terribly awkward way to travel. I hop, and so do all my people. It's so much more graceful and agreeable than walking."

"I don't agree with you," said the Scarecrow. "But tell me, is there any way to get to the Horner Country without going through the city of the Hoppers?"

"Yes; there is another path from the rocky lowlands, outside the mountain, that leads straight to the entrance of the Horner Country. But it's a long way around, so you'd better come with me. Perhaps they will allow you to go through the gate; but we expect to conquer them this afternoon, if we get time, and then you may go and come as you please."

They thought it best to take the Hopper's advice, and asked him to lead the way. This he did in a series of hops, and he moved so swiftly in this strange manner that those with two legs had to run to keep up with him.

The JOKING HORNERS

It was not long before they left the passage and came to a great cave, so high that it must have reached nearly to the top of the mountain within which it lay. It was a magnificent cave, illumined by the soft, invisible light, so that everything in it could be plainly seen. The walls were of polished marble, white with veins of delicate colors running through it, and the roof was arched and fantastic and beautiful.

Built beneath this vast dome was a pretty village—not very large, for there seemed not more than fifty houses altogether—and the dwellings were of marble and artistically designed. No grass nor flowers nor trees grew in this cave, so the yards surrounding the houses carved in designs both were smooth and bare and had low walls around them to mark their boundaries.

In the streets and the yards of the houses were many people all having one leg growing below their bodies and all hopping here and there whenever they moved. Even the children stood firmly upon their single legs and never lost their balance.

"All hail, Champion!" cried a man in the first group of Hoppers they met; "whom have you captured?"

"No one," replied the Champion in a gloomy voice; "these strangers have captured me."

"Then," said another, "we will rescue you, and capture them, for we are greater in number."

"No," answered the Champion, "I can't allow it. I've surrendered, and it isn't polite to capture those you've surrendered to."

"Never mind that," said Dorothy. "We will give you your liberty and set you free."

"Really?" asked the Champion in joyous tones.

"Yes," said the little girl; "your people may need you to help conquer the Horners."

At this all the Hoppers looked downcast and sad. Several more had joined the group by this time and quite a crowd of curious men, women and children surrounded the strangers.

"This war with our neighbors is a terrible thing," remarked

one of the women. "Some one is almost sure to get hurt."

"Why do you say that, madam?" inquired the Scarecrow.

"Because the horns of our enemies are sharp, and in battle they will try to stick those horns into our warriors," she replied.

"How many horns do the Horners have?" asked Dorothy.

"Each has one horn in the center of his forehead," was the answer.

"Oh, then they're unicorns," declared the Scarecrow.

"No; they're Horners. We never go to war with them if we can help it, on account of their dangerous horns; but this insult was so great and so unprovoked that our brave men decided to fight, in order to be revenged," said the woman.

"What weapons do you fight with?" the Scarecrow asked.

"We have no weapons," explained the Champion. "Whenever we fight the Horners, our plan is to push them back, for our arms are longer than theirs."

"Then you are better armed," said Scraps.

"Yes; but they have those terrible horns, and unless we are careful they prick us with the points," returned the Champion with a shudder. "That makes a war with them dangerous, and a dangerous war cannot be a pleasant one."

"I see very clearly," remarked the Scarecrow, "that you are going to have trouble in conquering those Horners—unless we help you."

"Oh!" cried the Hoppers in a chorus; "can you help us?

Please do! We will be greatly obliged! It would please us very much!" and by these exclamations the Scarecrow knew that his speech had met with favor.

"How far is it to the Horner Country?" he asked.

"Why, it's just the other side of the fence," they answered, and the Champion added:

"Come with me, please, and I'll show you the Horners."

So they followed the Champion and several others through the streets and just beyond the village came to a very high picket fence, built all of marble, which seemed to divide the great cave into two equal parts.

But the part inhabited by the Horners was in no way as grand in appearance as that of the Hoppers. Instead of being marble, the walls and roof were of dull grey rock and the square houses were plainly made of the same material. But in extent the city was much larger than that of the Hoppers and the streets were thronged with numerous people who busied themselves in various ways.

Looking through the open pickets of the fence our friends watched the Horners, who did not know they were being watched by strangers, and found them very unusual in appearance. They were little folks in size and had bodies round as balls and short legs and arms. Their heads were round, too, and they had long, pointed ears and a horn set in the center of the forehead. The horns did not seem very terrible, for they were not more than six inches long; but they were ivory white and sharp pointed, and no wonder the Hoppers feared them.

The skins of the Horners were light brown, but they wore snow-white robes and were bare-footed. Dorothy thought the most striking thing about them was their hair, which grew in three distinct colors on each and every head—red, yellow and green. The red was at the bottom and sometimes hung over their eyes; then came a broad circle of yellow and the green was at the top and formed a brush-shaped top-knot.

None of the Horners was yet aware of the presence of strangers, who watched the little brown people for a time and then went to the big gate in the center of the dividing fence. It was locked on both sides and over the latch was a sign reading:

WAR IS DECLARED

"Can't we go through?" asked Dorothy.

"Not now," answered the Champion.

"I think," said the Scarecrow, "that if I could talk with those Horners they would apologize to you, and then there would be no need to fight."

"Can't you talk from this side?" asked the Champion.

"Not so well," replied the Scarecrow. "Do you suppose you could throw me over that fence? It is high, but I am very light."

"We can try it," said the Hopper. "I am perhaps the strongest man in my country, so I'll undertake to do the throwing. But I won't promise you will land on your feet."

"No matter about that," returned the Scarecrow. "Just toss me over and I'll be satisfied."

So the Champion picked up the Scarecrow and balanced him a moment, to see how much he weighed, and then with all his strength tossed him high into the air.

Perhaps if the Scarecrow had been a trifle heavier he would have been easier to throw and would have gone a greater distance; but, as it was, instead of going over the fence he landed just on top of it, and one of the sharp pickets caught him in the middle of his back and held him fast prisoner. Had he been face downward the Scarecrow might have managed to free himself, but lying on his back on the picket his hands waved in the air of the Horner Country while his feet kicked the air of the Hopper Country; so there he was.

"Are you hurt?" called the Patchwork Girl anxiously.

"Course not," said Dorothy. "But if he wiggles that way he may tear his clothes. How can we get him down, Mr. Champion?"

The Champion shook his head.

"I don't know," he confessed. "If he could scare Horners as well as he does crows, it might be a good idea to leave him there."

"This is terrible," said Ojo, almost ready to cry. "I s'pose it's because I am Ojo the Unlucky that everyone who tries to help me gets into trouble."

"You are lucky to have anyone to help you," declared Dorothy. "But don't worry. We'll rescue the Scarecrow somehow."

"I know how," announced Scraps. "Here, Mr. Champion; just throw me up to the Scarecrow. I'm nearly as light as he is, and when I'm on top the fence I'll pull our friend off the picket and toss him down to you."

"All right," said the Champion, and he picked up the Patchwork Girl and threw her in the same manner he had the Scarecrow. He must have used more strength this time, however, for Scraps sailed far over the top of the fence and, without being able to grab the Scarecrow at all, tumbled to the ground in the Horner Country, where her stuffed body knocked over two men and a woman and made a crowd that had collected there run like rabbits to get away from her.

Seeing the next moment that she was harmless, the people slowly returned and gathered around the Patchwork Girl, regarding her with astonishment. One of them wore a jeweled star in his hair, just above his horn, and this seemed a person of importance. He spoke for the rest of his people, who treated him with great respect.

"Who are you, Unknown Being?" he asked.

"Scraps," she said, rising to her feet and patting her cotton wadding smooth where it had bunched up.

"And where did you come from?" he continued.

"Over the fence. Don't be silly. There's no other place I *could* have come from," she replied.

He looked at her thoughtfully.

"You are not a Hopper," said he, "for you have two legs.

They're not very well shaped, but they are two in number. And that strange creature on top the fence—why doesn't he stop kicking?—must be your brother, or father, or son, for he also has two legs."

"You must have been to visit the Wise Donkey," said Scraps, laughing so merrily that the crowd smiled with her, in sympathy. "But that reminds me, Captain—or King—"

"I am Chief of the Horners, and my name is Jak."

"Of course; Little Jack Horner; I might have known it. But the reason I volplaned over the fence was so I could have a talk with you about the Hoppers."

"What about the Hoppers?" asked the Chief, frowning.

"You've insulted them, and you'd better beg their pardon," said Scraps. "If you don't, they'll probably hop over here and conquer you."

"We're not afraid—as long as the gate is locked," declared the Chief. "And we didn't insult them at all. One of us made a joke that the stupid Hoppers couldn't see."

The Chief smiled as he said this and the smile made his face look quite jolly.

"What was the joke?" asked Scraps.

"A Horner said they have less understanding than we, because they've only one leg. Ha, ha! You see the point, don't you? If you stand on your legs, and your legs are under you, then—ha, ha, ha!—then your legs are your under-standing. Hee, hee, hee! Ho, ho! My, but that's a fine joke. And the stupid Hoppers couldn't see it! They couldn't see that with only one leg they must have less under-standing than we who have two legs. Ha, ha, ha! Hee, hee! Ho, ho!" The Chief wiped the tears of laughter from his eyes with the bottom hem of his white robe, and all the other Horners wiped their eyes on their robes, for they had laughed just as heartily as their Chief at the absurd joke.

"Then," said Scraps, "their understanding of the under-standing you meant led to the misunderstanding."

"Exactly; and so there's no need for us to apologize," returned the Chief.

"No need for an apology, perhaps, but much need for an explanation," said Scraps decidedly. "You don't want war, do you?"

"Not if we can help it," admitted Jak Horner. "The question is, who's going to explain the joke to the Horners? You know it spoils any joke to be obliged to explain it, and this is the best joke I ever heard."

"Who made the joke?" asked Scraps.

"Diksey Horner. He is working in the mines, just now, but he'll be home before long. Suppose we wait and talk with him about it? Maybe he'll be willing to explain his joke to the Hoppers."

"All right," said Scraps. "I'll wait, if Diksey isn't too long."

"No, he's short; he's shorter than I am. Ha, ha, ha! Say! that's a better joke than Diksey's. He won't be too long, because he's short. Hee, hee, ho!"

The other Horners who were standing by roared with laughter and seemed to like their Chief's joke as much as he did. Scraps thought it was odd that they could be so easily amused, but decided there could be little harm in people who laughed so merrily.

....——◄ Chapter 23 ►——....

PEACE Is DECLARED

Come with me to my dwelling and I'll introduce you to my daughters," said the Chief. "We're bringing them up according to a book of rules that was written by one of our leading old bachelors, and everyone says they're a remarkable lot of girls."

So Scraps accompanied him along the street to a house that seemed on the outside exceptionally grimy and dingy. The streets of this city were not paved nor had any attempt been made to beautify the houses or their surroundings, and having noticed this condition Scraps was astonished when the Chief ushered her into his home.

Here was nothing grimy or faded, indeed. On the contrary,

the room was of dazzling brilliance and beauty, for it was lined throughout with an exquisite metal that resembled translucent frosted silver. The surface of this metal was highly ornamented in raised designs representing men, animals, flowers and trees, and from the metal itself was radiated the soft light which flooded the room. All the furniture was made of the same glorious metal, and Scraps asked what it was.

"That's radium," answered the Chief. "We Horners spend all our time digging radium from the mines under this mountain, and we use it to decorate our homes and make them pretty and cosy. It is a medicine, too, and no one can ever be sick who lives near radium."

"Have you plenty of it?" asked the Patchwork Girl.

"More than we can use. All the houses in this city are decorated with it, just the same as mine is."

"Why don't you use it on your streets, then, and the outside of your houses, to make them as pretty as they are within?" she inquired.

"Outside? Who cares for the outside of anything?" asked the Chief. "We Horners don't live on the outside of our homes; we live inside. Many people are like those stupid Hoppers, who love to make an outside show. I suppose you strangers thought their city more beautiful than ours, because you judged from appearances and they have handsome marble houses and marble streets; but if you entered one of their stiff dwellings you would find it bare and uncomfortable, as all their show is on the outside. They have an idea that what is not seen by others is not important, but with us the rooms we live in are our chief delight and care, and we pay no attention to outside show."

"Seems to me," said Scraps, musingly, "it would be better to make it all pretty—inside and out."

"Seems? Why, you're all seams, my girl!" said the Chief; and then he laughed heartily at his latest joke and a chorus of small voices echoed the chorus with "tee-hee-hee! ha, ha!"

Scraps turned around and found a row of girls seated in radium chairs ranged along one wall of the room. There were nineteen of them, by actual count, and they were of all sizes from a tiny child to one almost a grown woman. All were neatly dressed in spotless white robes and had brown skins, horns on their foreheads and three-colored hair.

"These," said the Chief, "are my sweet daughters. My dears, I introduce to you Miss Scraps Patchwork, a lady who is traveling in foreign parts to increase her store of wisdom."

The nineteen Horner girls all arose and made a polite curtsey, after which they resumed their seats and rearranged their robes properly.

"Why do they sit so still, and all in a row?" asked Scraps.

"Because it is ladylike and proper," replied the Chief.

"But some are just children, poor things! Don't they ever run around and play and laugh, and have a good time?"

"No, indeed," said the Chief. "That would be improper in young ladies, as well as in those who will sometime become young ladies. My daughters are being brought up according to the rules and regulations laid down by a leading bachelor who has given the subject much study and is himself a man of taste and culture. Politeness is his great hobby, and he claims that if a child is allowed to do an impolite thing one cannot expect the grown person to do anything better."

"Is it impolite to romp and shout and be jolly?" asked Scraps.

"Well, sometimes it is, and sometimes it isn't," replied the Horner, after considering the question. "By curbing such inclinations in my daughters we keep on the safe side. Once in a while I make a good joke, as you have heard, and then I permit my daughters to laugh decorously; but they are never allowed to make a joke themselves."

"That old bachelor who made the rules ought to be skinned alive!" declared Scraps, and would have said more on the subject had not the door opened to admit a little Horner man whom the Chief introduced as Diksey.

"What's up, Chief?" asked Diksey, winking nineteen times at the nineteen girls, who demurely cast down their eyes because their father was looking.

The Chief told the man that his joke had not been understood by the dull Hoppers, who had become so angry that they had declared war. So the only way to avoid a terrible battle was to explain the joke so they could understand it.

"All right," replied Diksey, who seemed a good-natured

man; "I'll go at once to the fence and explain. I don't want any war with the Hoppers, for wars between nations always cause hard feelings."

So the Chief and Diksey and Scraps left the house and went back to the marble picket fence. The Scarecrow was still stuck on the top of his picket but had now ceased to struggle. On the other side of the fence were Dorothy and Ojo, looking between the pickets; and there, also, were the Champion and many other Hoppers.

Diksey went close to the fence and said:

"My good Hoppers, I wish to explain that what I said about you was a joke. You have but one leg each, and we have two legs each. Our legs are under us, whether one or two, and we stand on them. So, when I said you had less understanding than we, I did not mean that you had less understanding, you understand, but that you had less standundering, so to speak. Do you understand that?"

The Hoppers thought it over carefully. Then one said:

"That is clear enough; but where does the joke come in?'"

Dorothy laughed, for she couldn't help it, although all the others were solemn enough.

"I'll tell you where the joke comes in," she said, and took the Hoppers away to a distance, where the Horners could not hear them. "You know," she then explained, "those neighbors of yours are not very bright, poor things, and what they think is a joke isn't a joke at all—it's true, don't you see?"

"True that we have less understanding?" asked the Champion.

"Yes; it's true because you don't understand such a poor joke; if you did, you'd be no wiser than they are."

"Ah, yes; of course," they answered, looking very wise.

"So I'll tell you what to do," continued Dorothy. "Laugh at their poor joke and tell 'em it's pretty good for a Horner. Then they won't dare say you have less understanding, because you understand as much as they do."

The Hoppers looked at one another questioningly and blinked their eyes and tried to think what it all meant; but they couldn't figure it out.

"What do you think, Champion?" asked one of them.

"I think it is dangerous to think of this thing any more than we can help," he replied. "Let us do as this girl says and laugh with the Horners, so as to make them believe we see the joke. Then there will be peace again and no need to fight."

They readily agreed to this and returned to the fence laughing as loud and as hard as they could, although they didn't feel like laughing a bit. The Horners were much surprised.

"That's a fine joke—for a Horner—and we are much pleased with it," said the Champion, speaking between the pickets. "But please don't do it again."

"I won't," promised Diksey. "If I think of another such joke I'll try to forget it."

"Good!" cried the Chief Horner. "The war is over and peace is declared."

There was much joyful shouting on both sides of the fence and the gate was unlocked and thrown wide open, so that Scraps was able to rejoin her friends.

"What about the Scarecrow?" she asked Dorothy.

"We must get him down, somehow or other," was the reply.

"Perhaps the Horners can find a way," suggested Ojo. So they all went through the gate and Dorothy asked the Chief Horner how they could get the Scarecrow off the fence. The Chief didn't know how, but Diksey said:

"A ladder's the thing."

"Have you one?" asked Dorothy.

"To be sure. We use ladders in our mines," said he. Then he ran away to get the ladder, and while he was gone the Horners gathered around and welcomed the strangers to their country, for through them a great war had been avoided.

In a little while Diksey came back with a tall ladder which he placed against the fence. Ojo at once climbed to the top of the ladder and Dorothy went about halfway up and Scraps stood at the foot of it. Toto ran around it and barked. Then Ojo pulled the Scarecrow away from the picket and passed him down to Dorothy, who in turn lowered him to the Patchwork Girl.

As soon as he was on his feet and standing on solid ground the Scarecrow said:

"Much obliged. I feel much better. I'm not stuck on that picket any more."

The Horners began to laugh, thinking this was a joke, but the Scarecrow shook himself and patted his straw a little and said to Dorothy: "Is there much of a hole in my back?"

The little girl examined him carefully.

"There's quite a hole," she said. "But I've got a needle and thread in the knapsack and I'll sew you up again."

"Do so," he begged earnestly, and again the Hoppers laughed, to the Scarecrow's great annoyance.

While Dorothy was sewing up the hole in the straw man's back Scraps examined the other parts of him.

"One of his legs is ripped, too!" she exclaimed.

"Oho!" cried little Diksey; "that's bad. Give him the needle and thread and let him mend his ways."

"Ha, ha, ha!" laughed the Chief, and the other Horners at once roared with laughter.

"What's funny?" inquired the Scarecrow sternly.

"Don't you see?" asked Diksey, who had laughed even harder than the others. "That's a joke. It's by odds the best joke I ever made. You walk with your legs, and so that's the way you walk, and your legs are the ways. See? So, when you mend your legs, you mend your ways. Ho, ho, ho! hee, hee! I'd no idea I could make such a fine joke!"

"Just wonderful!" echoed the Chief. "How do you manage to do it, Diksey?"

"I don't know," said Diksey modestly. "Perhaps it's the radium, but I rather think it's my splendid intellect."

"If you don't quit it," the Scarecrow told him, "there'll be a worse war than the one you've escaped from."

Ojo had been deep in thought, and now he asked the Chief: "Is there a dark well in any part of your country?"

"A dark well? None that ever I heard of," was the answer.

"Oh, yes," said Diksey, who overheard the boy's question. "There's a very dark well down in my radium mine."

"Is there any water in it?" Ojo eagerly asked.

"Can't say; I've never looked to see. But we can find out."

So, as soon as the Scarecrow was mended, they decided to go with Diksey to the mine. When Dorothy had patted the straw man into shape again he declared he felt as good as new and equal to further adventures.

"Still," said he, "I prefer not to do picket duty again. High life doesn't seem to agree with my constitution." And then they hurried away to escape the laughter of the Horners, who thought this was another joke.

····◄ Chapter 24 ····—··

OJO FINDS the DARK WELL

They now followed Diksey to the farther end of the great cave, beyond the Horner city, where there were several round, dark holes leading into the ground in a slanting direction. Diksey went to one of these holes and said:

"Here is the mine in which lies the dark well you are seeking. Follow me and step carefully and I'll lead you to the place."

He went in first and after him came Ojo, and then Dorothy, with the Scarecrow behind her. The Patchwork Girl entered last of all, for Toto kept close beside his little mistress.

A few steps beyond the mouth of the opening it was pitch dark. "You won't lose your way, though," said the Horner, "for there's only one way to go. The mine's mine and I know every step of the way. How's that for a joke, eh? The mine's mine." Then he chuckled gleefully as they followed him silently down the steep slant. The hole was just big enough to permit them to walk upright, although the Scarecrow, being much the taller of the party, often had to bend his head to keep from hitting the top.

The floor of the tunnel was difficult to walk upon because it had been worn smooth as glass, and pretty soon Scraps, who was some distance behind the others, slipped and fell head foremost. At once she began to slide downward, so swiftly that when she came to the Scarecrow she knocked him off his feet and sent him tumbling against Dorothy, who tripped up Ojo. The boy fell against the Horner, so that all went tumbling down the slide in a regular mix-up, unable to see where they were going because of the darkness.

Fortunately, when they reached the bottom the Scarecrow and Scraps were in front, and the others bumped against them, so that no one was hurt. They found themselves in a vast cave which was dimly lighted by the tiny grains of radium that lay scattered among the loose rocks.

"Now," said Diksey, when they had all regained their feet, "I will show you where the dark well is. This is a big place, but if we hold fast to each other we won't get lost."

They took hold of hands and the Horner led them into a dark corner, where he halted.

"Be careful," said he warningly. "The well is at your feet."

"All right," replied Ojo, and kneeling down he felt in the well with his hand and found that it contained a quantity of water. "Where's the gold flask, Dorothy?" he asked, and the little girl handed him the flask, which she had brought with her.

Ojo knelt again and by feeling carefully in the dark managed to fill the flask with the unseen water that was in the well. Then he screwed the top of the flask firmly in place and put the precious water in his pocket.

"All right!" he said again, in a glad voice; "now we can go back."

They returned to the mouth of the tunnel and began to creep cautiously up the incline. This time they made Scraps stay behind, for fear she would slip again; but they all managed to get up in safety and the Munchkin boy was very happy when he stood in the Horner city and realized that the water from the dark well, which he and his friends had traveled so far to secure, was safe in his jacket pocket.

Chapter 25

THEY BRIBE the LAZY QUADLING

N ow," said Dorothy, as they stood on the mountain path, having left behind them the cave in which dwelt the Hoppers and the Horners, "I think we must find a road into the Country of the Winkies, for there is where Ojo wants to go next."

"Is there such a road?" asked the Scarecrow.

"I don't know," she replied. "I s'pose we can go back the way we came, to Jack Pumpkinhead's house, and then turn into the Winkie Country; but that seems like running 'round a haystack, doesn't it?"

"Yes," said the Scarecrow. "What is the next thing Ojo must get?"

"A yellow butterfly," answered the boy.

"That means the Winkie Country, all right, for it's the yellow country of Oz," remarked Dorothy. "I think, Scarecrow, we ought to take him to the Tin Woodman, for he's the Emp'ror of the Winkies and will help us to find what Ojo wants."

"Of course," replied the Scarecrow, brightening at the suggestion. "The Tin Woodman will do anything we ask him, for he's one of my dearest friends. I believe we can take a crosscut into his country and so get to his castle a day sooner than if we travel back the way we came."

"I think so, too," said the girl; "and that means we must keep to the left."

They were obliged to go down the mountain before they found any path that led in the direction they wanted to go, but among the tumbled rocks at the foot of the mountain was a faint trail which they decided to follow. Two or three hours walk along this trail brought them to a clear, level country, where there were a few farms and some scattered houses. But they knew they were still in the Country of the Quadlings, because everything had a bright red color. Not that the trees and grasses were red, but the fences and houses were painted that color and all the wildflowers that bloomed by the wayside had red blossoms. This part of the Quadling Country seemed peaceful and prosperous, if rather lonely, and the road was more distinct and easier to follow.

But just as they were congratulating themselves upon the progress they had made they came upon a broad river which swept along between high banks, and here the road ended and there was no bridge of any sort to allow them to cross.

"This is queer," mused Dorothy, looking at the water reflectively. "Why should there be any road, if the river stops everyone walking along it?"

"Wow!" said Toto, gazing earnestly into her face.

"That's the best answer you'll get," declared the Scarecrow, with his comical smile, "for no one knows any more than Toto about this road."

Said Scraps:

> *"Ev'ry time I see a river,*
> *I have chills that make me shiver,*
> *For I never can forget*
> *All the water's very wet.*
> *If my patches get a soak*
> *It will be a sorry joke;*
> *So to swim I'll never try*
> *Till I find the water dry."*

"Try to control yourself, Scraps," said Ojo; "you're getting crazy again. No one intends to swim that river."

"No," decided Dorothy, "we couldn't swim it if we tried. It's too big a river, and the water moves awful fast."

"There ought to be a ferryman with a boat," said the Scarecrow; "but I don't see any."

"Couldn't we make a raft?" suggested Ojo.

"There's nothing to make one of," answered Dorothy.

"Wow!" said Toto again, and Dorothy saw he was looking along the bank of the river.

"Why, he sees a house over there!" cried the little girl. "I wonder we didn't notice it ourselves. Let's go and ask the people how to get 'cross the river."

A quarter of a mile along the bank stood a small, round house, painted bright red, and as it was on their side of the river they hurried toward it. A chubby little man, dressed all in red, came out to greet them, and with him were two children, also in red costumes. The man's eyes were big and staring as he examined the Scarecrow and the Patchwork Girl, and the children shyly hid behind him and peeked timidly at Toto.

"Do you live here, my good man?" asked the Scarecrow.

"I think I do, Most Mighty Magician," replied the Quadling, bowing low; "but whether I'm awake or dreaming I can't be positive, so I'm not sure where I live. If you'll kindly pinch me I'll find out all about it!"

"You're awake," said Dorothy, "and this is no magician, but just the Scarecrow."

"But he's alive," protested the man, "and he oughtn't to be, you know. And that other dreadful person—the girl who is all patches—seems to be alive, too."

"Very much so," declared Scraps, making a face at him. "But that isn't your affair, you know."

"I've a right to be surprised, haven't I?" asked the man meekly.

"I'm not sure; but anyhow you've no right to say I'm dreadful. The Scarecrow, who is a gentleman of great wisdom, thinks I'm beautiful," retorted Scraps.

"Never mind all that," said Dorothy. "Tell us, good Quadling, how we can get across the river."

"I don't know," replied the Quadling.

"Don't you ever cross it?" asked the girl.

"Never."

"Don't travelers cross it?"

"Not to my knowledge," said he.

They were much surprised to hear this, and the man added: "It's a pretty big river, and the current is strong. I know a man who lives on the opposite bank, for I've seen him there a good many years; but we've never spoken because neither of us has ever crossed over."

"That's queer," said the Scarecrow. "Don't you own a boat?"

The man shook his head.

"Nor a raft?"

"Where does this river go to?" asked Dorothy.

"That way," answered the man, pointing with one hand, "it goes into the Country of the Winkies, which is ruled by the Tin Emperor, who must be a mighty magician because he's all made of tin, and yet he's alive. And that way," pointing with the other hand, "the river runs between two mountains where dangerous people dwell."

The Scarecrow looked at the water before them.

"The current flows toward the Winkie Country," said he; "and so, if we had a boat, or a raft, the river would float us there more quickly and more easily than we could walk."

"That is true," agreed Dorothy; and then they all looked thoughtful and wondered what could be done.

"Why can't the man make us a raft?" asked Ojo.

"Will you?" inquired Dorothy, turning to the Quadling.

The chubby man shook his head.

"I'm too lazy," he said. "My wife says I'm the laziest man in all Oz, and she is a truthful woman. I hate work of any kind, and making a raft is hard work."

"I'll give you my em'rald ring," promised the girl.

"No; I don't care for emeralds. If it were a ruby, which is the color I like best, I might work a little while."

"I've got some Square Meal Tablets," said the Scarecrow. "Each one is the same as a dish of soup, a fried fish, a mutton pot-pie, lobster salad, charlotte russe and lemon jelly— all made into one little tablet that you can swallow without trouble."

"Without trouble!" exclaimed the Quadling, much interested; "then those tablets would be fine for a lazy man. It's such hard work to chew when you eat."

"I'll give you six of those tablets if you'll help us make a raft," promised the Scarecrow. "They're a combination of food which people who eat are very fond of. I never eat, you know, being straw; but some of my friends eat regularly. What do you say to my offer, Quadling?"

"I'll do it," decided the man. "I'll help, and you can do most of the work. But my wife has gone fishing for red eels to-day, so some of you will have to mind the children."

Scraps promised to do that, and the children were not so shy when the Patchwork Girl sat down to play with them. They grew to like Toto, too, and the little dog allowed them to pat him on his head, which gave the little ones much joy.

There were a number of fallen trees near the house and the Quadling got his axe and chopped them into logs of equal length. He took his wife's clothes-line to bind these logs together, so that they would form a raft, and Ojo found some strips of wood and nailed them along the tops of the logs, to render them more firm. The Scarecrow and Dorothy helped roll the logs together and carry the strips of wood, but it took so long to make the raft that evening came just as it was finished, and with evening the Quadling's wife returned from her fishing.

The woman proved to be cross and bad-tempered, perhaps because she had only caught one red eel during all the day. When she found that her husband had used her clothes-line, and the logs she had wanted for firewood, and the boards she had intended to mend the shed with, and a lot of gold nails, she became very angry. Scraps wanted to shake the woman, to make her behave, but Dorothy talked to her in a gentle tone and told the Quadling's wife she was a Princess of Oz and a friend of Ozma and that when she got back to the Emerald City she would send them a lot of things to repay them for the raft, including a new clothes-line. This promise pleased the woman and she soon became more pleasant, saying they could stay the night at her house and begin their voyage on the river next morning.

This they did, spending a pleasant evening with the Quadling family and being entertained with such hospitality as the poor people were able to offer them. The man groaned a good deal and said he had overworked himself by chopping the logs, but the Scarecrow gave him two more tablets than he had promised, which seemed to comfort the lazy fellow.

·····◄ Chapter 26 ►·····

The TRICK RIVER

Next morning they pushed the raft into the water and all got aboard. The Quadling man had to hold the log craft fast while they took their places, and the flow of the river was so powerful that it nearly tore the raft from his hands. As soon as they were all seated upon the logs he let go and away it floated and the adventurers had begun their voyage toward the Winkie Country.

The little house of the Quadlings was out of sight almost before they had cried their good-byes, and the Scarecrow said in a pleased voice: "It won't take us long to get to the Winkie Country, at this rate."

They had floated several miles down the stream and were enjoying the ride when suddenly the raft slowed up, stopped short, and then began to float back the way it had come.

"Why, what's wrong?" asked Dorothy, in astonishment; but they were all just as bewildered as she was and at first no one could answer the question. Soon, however, they realized the truth: that the current of the river had reversed and the water was now flowing in the opposite direction—toward the mountains.

They began to recognize the scenes they had passed, and by and by they came in sight of the little house of the Quadlings again. The man was standing on the river bank and he called to them:

"How do you do? Glad to see you again. I forgot to tell you that the river changes its direction every little while. Sometimes it flows one way, and sometimes the other."

They had no time to answer him, for the raft was swept past the house and a long distance on the other side of it.

"We're going just the way we don't want to go," said Dorothy, "and I guess the best thing we can do is to get to land before we're carried any farther."

But they could not get to land. They had no oars, nor even a pole to guide the raft with. The logs which bore them floated in the middle of the stream and were held fast in that position by the strong current.

So they sat still and waited and, even while they were

wondering what could be done, the raft slowed down, stopped, and began drifting the other way—in the direction it had first followed. After a time they repassed the Quadling house and the man was still standing on the bank. He cried out to them:

"Good day! Glad to see you again. I expect I shall see you a good many times, as you go by, unless you happen to swim ashore."

By that time they had left him behind and were headed once more straight toward the Winkie Country.

"This is pretty hard luck," said Ojo in a discouraged voice. "The Trick River keeps changing, it seems, and here we must float back and forward forever, unless we manage in some way to get ashore."

"Can you swim?" asked Dorothy.

"No; I'm Ojo the Unlucky."

"Neither can I. Toto can swim a little, but that won't help us to get to shore."

"I don't know whether I could swim, or not," remarked Scraps; "but if I tried it I'd surely ruin my lovely patches."

"My straw would get soggy in the water and I would sink," said the Scarecrow.

So there seemed no way out of their dilemma and being helpless they simply sat still. Ojo, who was on the front of the raft, looked over into the water and thought he saw some large fishes swimming about. He found a loose end of the clothes-line which fastened the logs together, and taking a gold nail from his pocket he bent it nearly double, to form a hook, and tied it to the end of the line. Having baited the hook with some bread which he broke from his loaf, he dropped the line into the water and almost instantly it was seized by a great fish.

They knew it was a great fish, because it pulled so hard on the line that it dragged the raft forward even faster than the current of the river had carried it. The fish was frightened, and it was a strong swimmer. As the other end of the clothes-line was bound around the logs he could not get it away, and as he had greedily swallowed the gold hook at the first bite he could not get rid of that, either.

When they reached the place where the current had before changed, the fish was still swimming ahead in its wild attempt to escape. The raft slowed down, yet it did not stop, because the fish would not let it. It continued to move in the same direction it had been going. As the current reversed and rushed backward on its course it failed to drag the raft with it. Slowly, inch by inch, they floated on, and the fish tugged and tugged and kept them going.

"I hope he won't give up," said Ojo anxiously. "If the fish can hold out until the current changes again, we'll be all right."

The fish did not give up, but held the raft bravely on its course, till at last the water in the river shifted again and floated them the way they wanted to go. But now the captive fish found its strength failing. Seeking a refuge, it began to drag the raft toward the shore. As they did not wish to land in this place the boy cut the rope with his pocket-knife and set the fish free, just in time to prevent the raft from grounding.

The next time the river backed up the Scarecrow managed to seize the branch of a tree that overhung the water and they all assisted him to hold fast and prevent the raft from being carried backward. While they waited here, Ojo spied a long broken branch lying upon the bank, so he leaped ashore and got it. When he had stripped off the side shoots he believed he could use the branch as a pole, to guide the raft in case of emergency.

They clung to the tree until they found the water flowing the right way, when they let go and permitted the raft to resume its voyage. In spite of these pauses they were really making good progress toward the Winkie Country and having found a way to conquer the adverse current their spirits rose considerably. They could see little of the country through which they were passing, because of the high banks, and they met with no boats or other craft upon the surface of the river.

Once more the trick river reversed its current, but this time the Scarecrow was on guard and used the pole to push the raft toward a big rock which lay in the water. He believed the rock would prevent their floating backward with the current, and so it did. They clung to this anchorage until the water resumed its proper direction, when they allowed the raft to drift on.

Floating around a bend they saw ahead a high bank of

water, extending across the entire river, and toward this they were being irresistibly carried. There being no way to arrest the progress of the raft they clung fast to the logs and let the river sweep them on. Swiftly the raft climbed the bank of water and slid down on the other side, plunging its edge deep into the water and drenching them all with spray.

As again the raft righted and drifted on, Dorothy and Ojo laughed at the ducking they had received; but Scraps was much dismayed and the Scarecrow took out his handkerchief and wiped the water off the Patchwork Girl's patches as well as he was able to. The sun soon dried her and the colors of her patches proved good, for they did not run together nor did they fade.

After passing the wall of water the current did not change or flow backward any more but continued to sweep them steadily forward. The banks of the river grew lower, too, permitting them to see more of the country, and presently they discovered yellow buttercups and dandelions growing amongst the grass, from which evidence they knew they had reached the Winkie Country.

"Don't you think we ought to land?" Dorothy asked the Scarecrow.

"Pretty soon," he replied. "The Tin Woodman's castle is in the southern part of the Winkie Country, and so it can't be a great way from here."

Fearing they might drift too far, Dorothy and Ojo now

stood up and raised the Scarecrow in their arms, as high as they could, thus allowing him a good view of the country. For a time he saw nothing he recognized, but finally he cried:

"There it is! There it is!"

"What?" asked Dorothy.

"The Tin Woodman's tin castle. I can see its turrets glittering in the sun. It's quite a way off, but we'd better land as quickly as we can."

They let him down and began to urge the raft toward the shore by means of the pole. It obeyed very well, for the current was more sluggish now, and soon they had reached the bank and landed safely.

The Winkie Country was really beautiful, and across the fields they could see afar the silvery sheen of the tin castle. With light hearts they hurried toward it, being fully rested by their long ride on the river.

By and by they began to cross an immense field of splendid yellow lilies, the delicate fragrance of which was very delightful.

"How beautiful they are!" cried Dorothy, stopping to admire the perfection of these exquisite flowers.

"Yes," said the Scarecrow, reflectively, "but we must be careful not to crush or injure any of these lilies."

"Why not?" asked Ojo.

"The Tin Woodman is very kind-hearted," was the reply, "and he hates to see any living thing hurt in any way."

"Are flowers alive?" asked Scraps.

"Yes, of course. And these flowers belong to the Tin Woodman. So, in order not to offend him, we must not tread on a single blossom."

"Once," said Dorothy, "the Tin Woodman stepped on a beetle and killed the little creature. That made him very unhappy and he cried until his tears rusted his joints, so he couldn't move 'em."

"What did he do then?" asked Ojo.

"Put oil on them, until the joints worked smooth again."

"Oh!" exclaimed the boy, as if a great discovery had flashed across his mind. But he did not tell anybody what the discovery was and kept the idea to himself.

It was a long walk, but a pleasant one, and they did not mind it a bit. Late in the afternoon they drew near to the wonderful tin castle of the Emperor of the Winkies, and Ojo and Scraps, who had never seen it before, were filled with amazement.

Tin abounded in the Winkie Country and the Winkies were said to be the most skillful tinsmiths in all the world. So the Tin Woodman had employed them in building his magnificent castle, which was all of tin, from the ground to the tallest turret, and so brightly polished that it glittered in the sun's rays more gorgeously than silver. Around the grounds of the castle ran a tin wall, with tin gates; but the gates stood wide open because the Emperor had no enemies to disturb him.

When they entered the spacious grounds our travelers found more to admire. Tin fountains sent sprays of clear water far into the air and there were many beds of tin flowers, all as perfectly formed as any natural flowers might be. There were tin trees, too, and here and there shady bowers of tin, with tin benches and chairs to sit upon. Also, on the sides of the pathway leading up to the front door of the castle, were rows of tin statuary, very cleverly executed. Among these Ojo recognized statues of Dorothy, Toto, the Scarecrow, the Wizard, the Shaggy Man, Jack Pumpkinhead and Ozma, all standing upon neat pedestals of tin.

Toto was well acquainted with the residence of the Tin Woodman and, being assured a joyful welcome, he ran ahead and barked so loudly at the front door that the Tin Woodman heard him and came out in person to see if it were really his old friend Toto. Next moment the tin man had clasped the Scarecrow in a warm embrace and then turned to hug Dorothy. But now his eye was arrested by the strange sight of the Patchwork Girl, and he gazed upon her in mingled wonder and admiration.

The TIN WOODMAN OBJECTS

The Tin Woodman was one of the most important personages in all Oz. Though Emperor of
the Winkies, he owed allegiance to Ozma, who
ruled all the land, and the girl and the tin man
were warm personal friends. He was something of a dandy and
kept his tin body brilliantly polished and his tin joints well
oiled. Also he was very courteous in manner and so kind and
gentle that everyone loved him. The Emperor greeted Ojo and
Scraps with cordial hospitality and ushered the entire party
into his handsome tin parlor, where all the furniture and pictures were made of tin. The walls were paneled with tin and
from the tin ceiling hung tin chandeliers.

The Tin Woodman wanted to know, first of all, where Dorothy had found the Patchwork Girl, so between them the visitors told the story of how Scraps was made, as well as the accident to Margolotte and Unc Nunkie and how Ojo had set out upon a journey to procure the things needed for the Crooked Magician's magic charm. Then Dorothy told of their adventures in the Quadling Country and how at last they succeeded in getting the water from a dark well.

While the little girl was relating these adventures the Tin Woodman sat in an easy chair listening with intense interest, while the others sat grouped around him. Ojo, however, had kept his eyes fixed upon the body of the tin Emperor, and now he noticed that under the joint of his left knee a tiny drop of oil was forming. He watched this drop of oil with a fast-beating heart, and feeling in his pocket brought out a tiny vial of crystal, which he held secreted in his hand.

Presently the Tin Woodman changed his position, and at once Ojo, to the astonishment of all, dropped to the floor and held his crystal vial under the Emperor's knee joint. Just then the drop of oil fell, and the boy caught it in his bottle and immediately corked it tight. Then, with a red face and embarrassed manner, he rose to confront the others.

"What in the world were you doing?" asked the Tin Woodman.

"I caught a drop of oil that fell from your knee-joint," confessed Ojo.

"A drop of oil!" exclaimed the Tin Woodman. "Dear me, how careless my valet must have been in oiling me this morning. I'm afraid I shall have to scold the fellow, for I can't be dropping oil wherever I go."

"Never mind," said Dorothy. "Ojo seems glad to have the oil, for some reason."

"Yes," declared the Munchkin boy, "I am glad. For one of the things the Crooked Magician sent me to get was a drop of oil from a live man's body. I had no idea, at first, that there was such a thing; but it's now safe in the little crystal vial."

"You are very welcome to it, indeed," said the Tin Woodman. "Have you now secured all the things you were in search of?"

"Not quite all," answered Ojo. "There were five things I had to get, and I have found four of them. I have the three hairs in the tip of a Woozy's tail, a six-leaved clover, a gill of water from a dark well and a drop of oil from a live man's body. The last thing is the easiest of all to get, and I'm sure that my dear Unc Nunkie—and good Margolotte, as well—will soon be restored to life."

The Munchkin boy said this with much pride and pleasure.

"Good!" exclaimed the Tin Woodman; "I congratulate you. But what is the fifth and last thing you need, in order to complete the magic charm?"

"The left wing of a yellow butterfly," said Ojo. "In this yellow country, and with your kind assistance, that ought to be very easy to find."

The Tin Woodman stared at him in amazement.

"Surely you are joking!" he said.

"No," replied Ojo, much surprised; "I am in earnest."

"But do you think for a moment that I would permit you, or anyone else, to pull the left wing from a yellow butterfly?" demanded the Tin Woodman sternly.

"Why not, sir?"

"Why not? You ask me why not? It would be cruel—one of the most cruel and heartless deeds I ever heard of," asserted the Tin Woodman. "The butterflies are among the prettiest of all created things, and they are very sensitive to pain. To tear a wing from one would cause it exquisite torture and it would soon die in great agony. I would not permit such a wicked deed under any circumstances!"

Ojo was astounded at hearing this. Dorothy, too, looked grave and disconcerted, but she knew in her heart that the Tin Woodman was right. The Scarecrow nodded his head in approval of his friend's speech, so it was evident that he agreed with the Emperor's decision. Scraps looked from one to another in perplexity.

"Who cares for a butterfly?" she asked.

"Don't you?" inquired the Tin Woodman.

"Not the snap of a finger, for I have no heart," said the Patchwork Girl. "But I want to help Ojo, who is my friend, to rescue the uncle whom he loves, and I'd kill a dozen useless butterflies to enable him to do that."

The Tin Woodman sighed regretfully.

"You have kind instincts," he said, "and with a heart you would indeed be a fine creature. I cannot blame you for your heartless remark, as you cannot understand the feelings of those who possess hearts. I, for instance, have a very neat and responsive heart which the wonderful Wizard of Oz once gave me, and so I shall never—never—*never* permit a poor yellow butterfly to be tortured by anyone."

"The yellow country of the Winkies," said Ojo sadly, "is the only place in Oz where a yellow butterfly can be found."

"I'm glad of that," said the Tin Woodman. "As I rule the Winkie Country, I can protect my butterflies."

"Unless I get the wing—just one left wing—" said Ojo miserably, "I can't save Unc Nunkie."

"Then he must remain a marble statue forever," declared the Tin Emperor, firmly.

Ojo wiped his eyes, for he could not hold back the tears.

"I'll tell you what to do," said Scraps. "We'll take a whole yellow butterfly, alive and well, to the Crooked Magician, and let him pull the left wing off."

"No, you won't," said the Tin Woodman. "You can't have one of my dear little butterflies to treat in that way."

"Then what in the world shall we do?" asked Dorothy.

They all became silent and thoughtful. No one spoke for a long time. Then the Tin Woodman suddenly roused himself and said:

"We must all go back to the Emerald City and ask Ozma's advice. She's a wise little girl, our Ruler, and she may find a way to help Ojo save his Unc Nunkie."

So the following morning the party started on the journey to the Emerald City, which they reached in due time without any important adventure. It was a sad journey for Ojo, for without the wing of the yellow butterfly he saw no way to save Unc Nunkie—unless he waited six years for the Crooked Magician to make a new lot of the Powder of Life. The boy was utterly discouraged, and as he walked along he groaned aloud.

"Is anything hurting you?" inquired the Tin Woodman in a kindly tone, for the Emperor was with the party.

"I'm Ojo the Unlucky," replied the boy. "I might have known I would fail in anything I tried to do."

"Why are you Ojo the Unlucky?" asked the tin man.

"Because I was born on a Friday."

"Friday is not unlucky," declared the Emperor. "It's just one of seven days. Do you suppose all the world becomes unlucky one-seventh of the time?"

"It was the thirteenth day of the month," said Ojo.

"Thirteen! Ah, that is indeed a lucky number," replied the Tin Woodman. "All my good luck seems to happen on the thirteenth. I suppose most people never notice the good luck that comes to them with the number thirteen, and yet if the least bit of bad luck falls on that day, they blame it to the number, and not to the proper cause."

"Thirteen's my lucky number, too," remarked the Scarecrow.

"And mine," said Scraps. "I've just thirteen patches on my head."

"But," continued Ojo, "I'm left-handed."

"Many of our greatest men are that way," asserted the Emperor. "To be left-handed is usually to be two-handed; the right-handed people are usually one-handed."

"And I've a wart under my right arm," said Ojo.

"How lucky!" cried the Tin Woodman. "If it were on the end of your nose it might be unlucky, but under your arm it is luckily out of the way."

"For all those reasons," said the Munchkin boy, "I have been called Ojo the Unlucky."

"Then we must turn over a new leaf and call you henceforth Ojo the Lucky," declared the tin man. "Every reason you have given is absurd. But I have noticed that those who continually dread ill luck and fear it will overtake them, have no time to take advantage of any good fortune that comes their way. Make up your mind to be Ojo the Lucky."

"How can I?" asked the boy, "when all my attempts to save my dear uncle have failed?"

"Never give up, Ojo," advised Dorothy. "No one ever knows what's going to happen next."

Ojo did not reply, but he was so dejected that even their arrival at the Emerald City failed to interest him.

The people joyfully cheered the appearance of the Tin Woodman, the Scarecrow and Dorothy, who were all three general favorites, and on entering the royal palace word came to them from Ozma that she would at once grant them an audience.

Dorothy told the girl Ruler how successful they had been in their quest until they came to the item of the yellow butterfly, which the Tin Woodman positively refused to sacrifice to the magic potion.

"He is quite right," said Ozma, who did not seem a bit surprised. "Had Ojo told me that one of the things he sought was the wing of a yellow butterfly I would have informed him, before he started out, that he could never secure it. Then you would have been saved the troubles and annoyances of your long journey."

"I didn't mind the journey at all," said Dorothy; "it was fun."

"As it has turned out," remarked Ojo, "I can never get the things the Crooked Magician sent me for; and so, unless I wait the six years for him to make the Powder of Life, Unc Nunkie cannot be saved."

Ozma smiled.

"Dr. Pipt will make no more Powder of Life, I promise you," said she. "I have sent for him and had him brought to this palace, where he now is, and his four kettles have been destroyed and his book of recipes burned up. I have also had brought here the marble statues of your uncle and of Margolotte, which are standing in the next room."

They were all greatly astonished at this announcement.

"Oh, let me see Unc Nunkie! Let me see him at once, please!" cried Ojo eagerly.

"Wait a moment," replied Ozma, "for I have something more to say. Nothing that happens in the Land of Oz escapes the notice of our wise Sorceress, Glinda the Good. She knew all about the magic-making of Dr. Pipt, and how he had brought the Glass Cat and the Patchwork Girl to life, and the accident to Unc Nunkie and Margolotte, and of Ojo's quest and his journey with Dorothy. Glinda also knew that Ojo would fail to find all the things he sought, so she sent for our Wizard and instructed him what to do. Something is going to happen in this palace, presently, and that 'something' will, I am sure, please you all. And now," continued the girl Ruler, rising from her chair, "you may follow me into the next room."

The WONDERFUL WIZARD of OZ

When Ojo entered the room he ran quickly to the statue of Unc Nunkie and kissed the marble face affectionately.

"I did my best, Unc," he said, with a sob, "but it was no use!"

Then he drew back and looked around the room, and the sight of the assembled company quite amazed him.

Aside from the marble statues of Unc Nunkie and Margolotte, the Glass Cat was there, curled up on a rug; and the Woozy was there, sitting on its square hind legs and looking on the scene with solemn interest; and there was the Shaggy Man, in a suit of shaggy pea-green satin, and at a table sat the little Wizard, looking quite important and as if he knew much more than he cared to tell.

Last of all, Dr. Pipt was there, and the Crooked Magician sat humped up in a chair, seeming very dejected but keeping his eyes fixed on the lifeless form of his wife Margolotte, whom he fondly loved but whom he now feared was lost to him forever.

Ozma took a chair which Jellia Jamb wheeled forward for the Ruler, and back of her stood the Scarecrow, the Tin Woodman and Dorothy, as well as the Cowardly Lion and the Hungry Tiger. The Wizard now arose and made a low bow to Ozma and another less deferent bow to the assembled company.

"Ladies and gentlemen and beasts," he said, "I beg to announce that our Gracious Ruler has permitted me to obey the commands of the great Sorceress, Glinda the Good, whose humble Assistant I am proud to be. We have discovered that the Crooked Magician has been indulging in his magical arts contrary to Law, and therefore, by Royal Edict, I hereby deprive him of all power to work magic in the future. He is no longer a crooked magician, but a simple Munchkin; he is no longer even crooked, but a man like other men."

As he pronounced these words the Wizard waved his hand toward Dr. Pipt and instantly every crooked limb straightened out and became perfect. The former magician, with a cry of joy, sprang to his feet, looked at himself in wonder, and then fell back in his chair and watched the Wizard with fascinated interest.

"The Glass Cat, which Dr. Pipt lawlessly made," continued the Wizard, "is a pretty cat, but its pink brains made it so conceited that it was a disagreeable companion to everyone. So the other day I took away the pink brains and replaced them with transparent ones, and now the Glass Cat is so modest and well behaved that Ozma has decided to keep her in the palace as a pet."

"I thank you," said the cat, in a soft voice.

"The Woozy has proved himself a good Woozy and a faithful friend," the Wizard went on, "so we will send him to the Royal Menagerie, where he will have good care and plenty to eat all his life."

"Much obliged," said the Woozy. "That beats being fenced up in a lonely forest and starved."

"As for the Patchwork Girl," resumed the Wizard, "she is so remarkable in appearance, and so clever and good tempered, that our Gracious Ruler intends to preserve her carefully, as one of the curiosities of the curious Land of Oz. Scraps may live in the palace, or wherever she pleases, and be nobody's servant but her own."

"That's all right," said Scraps.

"We have all been interested in Ojo," the little Wizard continued, "because his love for his unfortunate uncle has led him bravely to face all sorts of dangers, in order that he might rescue him. The Munchkin boy has a loyal and generous heart and has done his best to restore Unc Nunkie to life. He has failed, but there are others more powerful than the Crooked Magician, and there are more ways than Dr. Pipt knew of to destroy the charm of the Liquid of Petrifaction. Glinda the Good has told me of one way, and you shall now learn how great is the knowledge and power of our peerless Sorceress."

As he said this the Wizard advanced to the statue of Margolotte and made a magic pass, at the same time muttering a magic word that none could hear distinctly. At once the woman moved, turned her head wonderingly this way and that, to note all who stood before her, and seeing Dr. Pipt, ran forward and threw herself into her husband's outstretched arms.

Then the Wizard made the magic pass and spoke the magic word before the statue of Unc Nunkie. The old Munchkin immediately came to life and with a low bow to the Wizard said: "Thanks."

But now Ojo rushed up and threw his arms joyfully about his uncle, and the old man hugged his little nephew tenderly and stroked his hair and wiped away the boy's tears with a handkerchief, for Ojo was crying from pure happiness.

Ozma came forward to congratulate them.

"I have given to you, my dear Ojo and Unc Nunkie, a nice

house just outside the walls of the Emerald City," she said, "and there you shall make your future home and be under my protection."

"Didn't I say you were Ojo the Lucky?" asked the Tin Woodman, as everyone crowded around to shake Ojo's hand.

"Yes; and it is true!" replied Ojo, gratefully.

Tik-Tok

of

OZ

To Louis F. Gottschalk,
whose sweet and dainty melodies
breathe the true spirit of fairyland,
this book is affectionately dedicated

...—...< To My Readers >...—...

The very marked success of my last year's fairy book, *The Patchwork Girl of Oz*, convinces me that my readers like the Oz stories "best of all," as one little girl wrote me. So here, my dears, is a new Oz story in which is introduced Ann Soforth, the Queen of Oogaboo, whom Tik-Tok assisted in conquering our old acquaintance, the Nome King. It also tells of Betsy Bobbin and how, after many adventures, she finally reached the marvelous Land of Oz.

There is a play called *The Tik-Tok Man of Oz*, but it is not like this story of *Tik-Tok of Oz*, although some of the adventures recorded in this book, as well as those in several other Oz books, are included in the play. Those who have seen the play and those who have read the other Oz books will find in this story a lot of strange characters and adventures that they have never heard of before.

In the letters I receive from children there has been an urgent appeal for me to write a story that will take Trot and Cap'n Bill to the Land of Oz, where they will meet Dorothy and Ozma. Also they think Button-Bright ought to get acquainted with Ojo the Lucky. As you know, I am obliged to talk these matters over with Dorothy by means of the "wireless," for that is the only way I can communicate with the Land of Oz. When I asked her about this idea, she replied: "Why, haven't you heard?" I said "No." "Well," came the message over the wireless, "I'll tell you all about it, by and by, and then you can make a book of that story for the children to read."

So, if Dorothy keeps her word and I am permitted to write another Oz book, you will probably discover how all these characters came together in the famous Emerald City. Meantime, I want to tell all my little friends—whose numbers are increasing by many thousands every year—that I am very grateful for the favor they have shown my books and for the delightful little letters I am constantly receiving. I am almost sure that I have as many friends among the children of America as any story writer alive; and this, of course, makes me very proud and happy.

L. Frank Baum.

"Ozcot" at Hollywood in California, 1914

·····⋖ Chapter 1 ⋗·····

ANN'S ARMY

I won't!" cried Ann; "I won't sweep the floor. It is beneath my dignity."

"Some one must sweep it," replied Ann's younger sister, Salye; "else we shall soon be wading in dust. And you are the eldest, and the head of the family."

"I'm Queen of Oogaboo," said Ann, proudly. "But," she added with a sigh, "my kingdom is the smallest and the poorest in all the Land of Oz."

This was quite true. Away up in the mountains, in a far corner of the beautiful fairyland of Oz, lies a small valley which is named Oogaboo, and in this valley lived a few people who were usually happy and contented and never cared to wander over the mountain pass into the more settled parts of the land. They knew that all of Oz, including their own territory, was ruled by a beautiful Princess named Ozma, who lived in the splendid Emerald City; yet the simple folk of Oogaboo never visited Ozma. They had a royal family of their own—not especially to rule over them, but just as a matter of pride. Ozma permitted the various parts of her country to have their Kings and Queens and Emperors and the like, but all were ruled over by the lovely girl Queen of the Emerald City.

The King of Oogaboo used to be a man named Jol Jemkiph Soforth, who for many years did all the drudgery of deciding disputes and telling his people when to plant cabbages and pickle onions. But the King's wife had a sharp tongue and small respect for the King, her husband; therefore one night King Jol crept over the pass into the Land of Oz and disappeared from Oogaboo for good and all. The Queen waited a few years for him to return and then started in search of him, leaving her eldest daughter, Ann Soforth, to act as Queen.

Now, Ann had not forgotten when her birthday came, for that meant a party and feasting and dancing, but she had quite forgotten how many years the birthdays marked. In a land where people live always, this is not considered a cause for regret, so we may justly say that Queen Ann of Oogaboo was old enough to make jelly—and let it go at that.

But she didn't make jelly, or do any more of the housework than she could help. She was an ambitious woman and constantly resented the fact that her kingdom was so tiny and her people so stupid and unenterprising. Often she wondered what had become of her father and mother, out beyond the pass, in the wonderful Land of Oz, and the fact that they did not return to Oogaboo led Ann to suspect that they had found a better place to live. So, when Salye refused to sweep the floor of the living room in the palace, and Ann would not sweep it, either, she said to her sister:

"I'm going away. This absurd Kingdom of Oogaboo tires me."

"Go, if you want to," answered Salye; "but you are very foolish to leave this place."

"Why?" asked Ann.

"Because in the Land of Oz, which is Ozma's country, you will be a nobody, while here you are a Queen."

"Oh, yes! Queen over eighteen men, twenty-seven women and forty-four children!" returned Ann bitterly.

"Well, there are certainly more people than that in the great Land of Oz," laughed Salye. "Why don't you raise an army and conquer them, and be Queen of all Oz?" she asked, trying to taunt Ann and so to anger her. Then she made a face at her sister and went into the back yard to swing in the hammock.

Her jeering words, however, had given Queen Ann an idea. She reflected that Oz was reported to be a peaceful country and Ozma a mere girl who ruled with gentleness to all and was obeyed because her people loved her. Even in Oogaboo the story was told that Ozma's sole army consisted of twenty-seven fine officers, who wore beautiful uniforms but carried no weapons, because there was no one to fight. Once there had been a private soldier, besides the officers, but Ozma had made him a Captain-General and taken away his gun for fear it might accidentally hurt some one.

The more Ann thought about the matter the more she was convinced it would be easy to conquer the Land of Oz and set herself up as Ruler in Ozma's place, if she but had an Army to do it with. Afterward she could go out into the world and conquer other lands, and then perhaps she could find a way to the moon, and conquer that. She had a warlike spirit that preferred trouble to idleness.

It all depended on an Army, Ann decided. She carefully counted in her mind all the men of her kingdom. Yes; there were exactly eighteen of them, all told. That would not make a very big Army, but by surprising Ozma's unarmed officers her men might easily subdue them. "Gentle people are always afraid of those that bluster," Ann told herself. "I don't wish to shed any blood, for that would shock my nerves and I might faint; but if we threaten and flash our weapons I am sure the people of Oz will fall upon their knees before me and surrender."

This argument, which she repeated to herself more than once, finally determined the Queen of Oogaboo to undertake the audacious venture.

"Whatever happens," she reflected, "can make me no more unhappy than my staying shut up in this miserable valley and sweeping floors and quarreling with Sister Salye; so I will venture all, and win what I may."

That very day she started out to organize her Army.

The first man she came to was Jo Apple, so called because he had an apple orchard.

"Jo," said Ann, "I am going to conquer the world, and I want you to join my Army."

"Don't ask me to do such a fool thing, for I must politely refuse your Majesty," said Jo Apple.

"I have no intention of asking you. I shall command you, as Queen of Oogaboo, to join," said Ann.

"In that case, I suppose I must obey," the man remarked, in a sad voice. "But I pray you to consider that I am a very important citizen, and for that reason am entitled to an office of high rank."

"You shall be a General," promised Ann.

"With gold epaulets and a sword?" he asked.

"Of course," said the Queen.

Then she went to the next man, whose name was Jo Bunn, as he owned an orchard where graham-buns and wheat-buns, in great variety, both hot and cold, grew on the trees.

"Jo," said Ann, "I am going to conquer the world, and I command you to join my Army."

"Impossible!" he exclaimed. "The bun crop has to be picked."

"Let your wife and children do the picking," said Ann.

"But I'm a man of great importance, your Majesty," he protested.

"For that reason you shall be one of my Generals, and wear a cocked hat with gold braid, and curl your mustaches and clank a long sword," she promised.

So he consented, although sorely against his will, and the Queen walked on to the next cottage. Here lived Jo Cone, so called because the trees in his orchard bore crops of excellent ice-cream cones.

"Jo," said Ann, "I am going to conquer the world, and you must join my Army."

"Excuse me, please," said Jo Cone. "I am a bad fighter. My good wife conquered me years ago, for she can fight better than I. Take her, your Majesty, instead of me, and I'll bless you for the favor."

"This must be an army of men—fierce, ferocious warriors," declared Ann, looking sternly upon the mild little man.

"And you will leave my wife here in Oogaboo?" he asked.

"Yes; and make you a General."

"I'll go," said Jo Cone, and Ann went on to the cottage of Jo Clock, who had an orchard of clock-trees. This man at first insisted that he would not join the army, but Queen Ann's promise to make him a General finally won his consent.

"How many Generals are there in your army?" he asked.

"Four, so far," replied Ann.

"And how big will the army be?" was his next question.

"I intend to make every one of the eighteen men in Ooga-boo join it," she said.

"Then four Generals are enough," announced Jo Clock. "I advise you to make the rest of them Colonels."

Ann tried to follow his advice. The next four men she visited—who were Jo Plum, Jo Egg, Jo Banjo and Jo Cheese, named after the trees in their orchards—she made Colonels of her Army; but the fifth one, Jo Nails, said Colonels and Generals were getting to be altogether too common in the Army of Oogaboo and he preferred to be a Major. So Jo Nails, Jo Cake, Jo Ham and Jo Stockings were all four made Majors, while the next four—Jo Sandwich, Jo Padlocks, Jo Sundae and Jo Buttons—were appointed Captains of the Army.

But now Queen Ann was in a quandary. There remained but two other men in all Oogaboo, and if she made these two Lieutenants, while there were four Captains, four Majors, four Colonels and four Generals, there was likely to be jealousy in her army, and perhaps mutiny and desertions.

One of these men, however, was Jo Candy, and he would not go at all. No promises could tempt him, nor could threats move him. He said he must remain at home to harvest his crop of jackson-balls, lemon-drops, bonbons and chocolate-creams. Also he had large fields of crackerjack and buttered pop corn to be mowed and threshed, and he was determined not to disappoint the children of Oogaboo by going away to conquer the world and so let the candy crop spoil.

Finding Jo Candy so obstinate, Queen Ann let him have his own way and continued her journey to the house of the eighteenth and last man in Oogaboo, who was a young fellow named Jo Files. This Files had twelve trees which bore steel files of various sorts; but also he had nine book-trees, on which grew a choice selection of story-books. In case you have never seen books growing upon trees, I will explain that those in Jo Files' orchard were enclosed in broad green husks which, when fully ripe, turned to a deep red color. Then the books were picked and husked and were ready to read. If they were picked too soon, the stories were found to be confused and uninteresting and the spelling bad. However, if allowed to ripen perfectly, the stories were fine reading and the spelling and grammar excellent.

Files freely gave his books to all who wanted them, but the people of Oogaboo cared little for books and so he had to read most of them himself, before they spoiled. For, as you probably know, as soon as the books were read the words disappeared and the leaves withered and faded—which is the worst fault of all books which grow upon trees.

When Queen Ann spoke to this young man Files, who was both intelligent and ambitious, he said he thought it would be great fun to conquer the world. But he called her attention to the fact that he was far superior to the other men of her army. Therefore, he would not be one of her Generals or Colonels or Majors or Captains, but claimed the honor of being sole Private.

Ann did not like this idea at all.

"I hate to have a Private Soldier in my army," she said; "they're so common. I am told that Princess Ozma once had a private soldier, but she made him her Captain-General, which is good evidence that the private was unnecessary."

"Ozma's army doesn't fight," returned Files; "but your army must fight like fury in order to conquer the world. I have read in my books that it is always the private soldiers who do the fighting, for no officer is ever brave enough to face the foe. Also, it stands to reason that your officers must have some one to command and to issue their orders to; therefore I'll be the one. I long to slash and slay the enemy and become a hero. Then, when we return to Oogaboo, I'll take all the marbles away from the children and melt them up and make a marble statue of myself for all to look upon and admire."

Ann was much pleased with Private Files. He seemed indeed to be such a warrior as she needed in her enterprise, and her hopes of success took a sudden bound when Files told her he knew where a gun-tree grew and would go there at once and pick the ripest and biggest musket the tree bore.

...—..◄ Chapter 2 ►..—...

OUT of OOGABOO

Three days later the Grand Army of Oogaboo assembled in the square in front of the royal palace. The sixteen officers were attired in gorgeous uniforms and carried sharp, glittering swords. The Private had picked his gun and, although it was not a very big weapon, Files tried to look fierce and succeeded so well that all his commanding officers were secretly afraid of him.

The women were there, protesting that Queen Ann Soforth had no right to take their husbands and fathers from them; but Ann commanded them to keep silent, and that was the hardest order to obey they had ever received.

The Queen appeared before her Army dressed in an imposing uniform of green, covered with gold braid. She wore a green soldier-cap with a purple plume in it and looked so royal and dignified that everyone in Oogaboo except the Army was glad she was going. The Army was sorry she was not going alone.

"Form ranks!" she cried in her shrill voice.

Salye leaned out of the palace window and laughed.

"I believe your Army can run better than it can fight," she observed.

"Of course," replied General Bunn, proudly. "We're not looking for trouble, you know, but for plunder. The more plunder and the less fighting we get, the better we shall like our work."

"For my part," said Files, "I prefer war and carnage to anything. The only way to become a hero is to conquer, and the story-books all say that the easiest way to conquer is to fight."

"That's the idea, my brave man!" agreed Ann. "To fight is to conquer and to conquer is to secure plunder and to secure plunder is to become a hero. With such noble determination to back me, the world is mine! Good-bye, Salye. When we return we shall be rich and famous. Come, Generals; let us march."

At this the Generals straightened up and threw out their chests. Then they swung their glittering swords in rapid circles and cried to the Colonels:

"For—ward March!"

Then the Colonels shouted to the Majors: "For—ward March!" and the Majors yelled to the Captains: "For—ward March!" and the Captains screamed to the Private:

"For—ward March!"

So Files shouldered his gun and began to march, and all the officers followed after him. Queen Ann came last of all, rejoicing in her noble army and wondering why she had not decided long ago to conquer the world.

In this order the procession marched out of Oogaboo and took the narrow mountain pass which led into the lovely Fairyland of Oz.

....—...◄ Chapter 3 ►...—...

Magic Mystifies the Marchers

Princess Ozma was all unaware that the Army of Oogaboo, led by their ambitious Queen, was determined to conquer her Kingdom. The beautiful girl Ruler of Oz was busy with the welfare of her subjects and had no time to think of Ann Soforth and her disloyal plans. But there was one who constantly guarded the peace and happiness of the Land of Oz and this was the Official Sorceress of the Kingdom, Glinda the Good.

In her magnificent castle, which stands far north of the Emerald City where Ozma holds her court, Glinda owns a wonderful magic Record Book, in which is printed every event that takes place anywhere, just as soon as it happens.

The smallest things and the biggest things are all recorded in this book. If a child stamps its foot in anger, Glinda reads about it; if a city burns down, Glinda finds the fact noted in her book.

The Sorceress always reads her Record Book every day, and so it was she knew that Ann Soforth, Queen of Oogaboo, had foolishly assembled an army of sixteen officers and one private soldier, with which she intended to invade and conquer the Land of Oz.

There was no danger but that Ozma, supported by the magic arts of Glinda the Good and the powerful Wizard of Oz—both her firm friends—could easily defeat a far more imposing army than Ann's; but it would be a shame to have the peace of Oz interrupted by any sort of quarreling or fighting. So Glinda did not even mention the matter to Ozma, or to anyone else. She merely went into a great chamber of her castle, known as the Magic Room, where she performed a magical ceremony which caused the mountain pass that led from Oogaboo to make several turns and twists. The result was that when Ann and her army came to the end of the pass they were not in the Land of Oz at all, but in an adjoining territory that was quite distinct from Ozma's domain and separated from Oz by an invisible barrier.

As the Oogaboo people emerged into this country, the

pass they had traversed disappeared behind them and it was not likely they would ever find their way back into the valley of Oogaboo. They were greatly puzzled, indeed, by their surroundings and did not know which way to go. None of them had ever visited Oz, so it took them some time to discover they were not in Oz at all, but in an unknown country.

"Never mind," said Ann, trying to conceal her disappointment; "we have started out to conquer the world, and here is part of it. In time, as we pursue our victorious journey, we will doubtless come to Oz; but, until we get there, we may as well conquer whatever land we find ourselves in."

"Have we conquered this place, your Majesty?" anxiously inquired Major Cake.

"Most certainly," said Ann. "We have met no people, as yet, but when we do, we will inform them that they are our slaves."

"And afterward we will plunder them of all their possessions," added General Apple.

"They may not possess anything," objected Private Files; "but I hope they will fight us, just the same. A peaceful conquest wouldn't be any fun at all."

"Don't worry," said the Queen. "*We* can fight, whether our foes do or not; and perhaps we would find it more comfortable to have the enemy surrender promptly."

It was a barren country and not very pleasant to travel in. Moreover, there was little for them to eat, and as the officers became hungry they became fretful. Many would have deserted had they been able to find their way home, but as the Oogaboo people were now hopelessly lost in a strange country they considered it more safe to keep together than to separate.

Queen Ann's temper, never very agreeable, became sharp and irritable as she and her army tramped over the rocky roads without encountering either people or plunder. She scolded her officers until they became surly, and a few of them were disloyal enough to ask her to hold her tongue. Others began to reproach her for leading them into difficulties and in the space of three unhappy days every man was mourning for his orchard in the pretty valley of Oogaboo.

Files, however, proved a different sort. The more difficulties he encountered the more cheerful he became, and the sighs of the officers were answered by the merry whistle of the Private. His pleasant disposition did much to encourage Queen Ann and before long she consulted the Private Soldier more often than she did his superiors.

It was on the third day of their pilgrimage that they encountered their first adventure. Toward evening the sky was suddenly darkened and Major Nails exclaimed:

"A fog is coming toward us."

"I do not think it is a fog," replied Files, looking with interest at the approaching cloud. "It seems to me more like the breath of a Rak."

"What is a Rak?" asked Ann, looking about fearfully.

"A terrible beast with a horrible appetite," answered the Soldier, growing a little paler than usual. "I have never seen a Rak, to be sure, but I have read of them in the story-books that grew in my orchard, and if this is indeed one of those fearful monsters, we are not likely to conquer the world."

Hearing this, the officers became quite worried and gathered closer about their soldier.

"What is the thing like?" asked one.

"The only picture of a Rak that I ever saw in a book was rather blurred," said Files, "because the book was not quite ripe when it was picked. But the creature can fly in the air and run like a deer and swim like a fish. Inside its body is a glowing furnace of fire, and the Rak breathes in air and breathes out smoke, which darkens the sky for miles around, wherever it goes. It is bigger than a hundred men and feeds on any living thing."

The officers now began to groan and to tremble, but Files tried to cheer them, saying:

"It may not be a Rak, after all, that we see approaching us, and you must not forget that we people of Oogaboo, which is part of the fairyland of Oz, cannot be killed."

"Nevertheless," said Captain Buttons, "if the Rak catches us, and chews us up into small pieces, and swallows us—what will happen then?"

"Then each small piece will still be alive," declared Files.

"I cannot see how that would help us," wailed Colonel Banjo. "A hamburger steak is a hamburger steak, whether it is alive or not!"

"I tell you, this may not be a Rak," persisted Files. "We will know, when the cloud gets nearer, whether it is the breath of a Rak or not. If it has no smell at all, it is probably a fog; but if it has an odor of salt and pepper, it is a Rak and we must prepare for a desperate fight."

They all eyed the dark cloud fearfully. Before long it reached the frightened group and began to envelop them. Every nose sniffed the cloud—and every one detected in it the odor of salt and pepper.

"The Rak!" shouted Private Files, and with a howl of despair the sixteen officers fell to the ground, writhing and moaning in anguish. Queen Ann sat down upon a rock and faced the cloud more bravely, although her heart was beating fast. As for Files, he calmly loaded his gun and stood ready to fight the foe, as a soldier should.

They were now in absolute darkness, for the cloud which covered the sky and the setting sun was black as ink. Then through the gloom appeared two round, glowing balls of red, and Files at once decided these must be the monster's eyes.

He raised his gun, took aim and fired.

There were several bullets in the gun, all gathered from an excellent bullet-tree in Oogaboo, and they were big and hard. They flew toward the monster and struck it, and with a wild, weird cry the Rak came fluttering down and its huge body fell plump upon the forms of the sixteen officers, who thereupon screamed louder than before.

"Badness me!" moaned the Rak. "See what you've done with that dangerous gun of yours!"

"I can't see," replied Files, "for the cloud formed by your breath darkens my sight!"

"Don't tell me it was an accident," continued the Rak, reproachfully, as it still flapped its wings in a helpless manner. "Don't claim you didn't know the gun was loaded, I beg of you!"

"I don't intend to," replied Files. "Did the bullets hurt you very badly?"

"One has broken my jaw, so that I can't open my mouth. You will notice that my voice sounds rather harsh and husky, because I have to talk with my teeth set close together. Another bullet broke my left wing, so that I can't fly; and still another broke my right leg, so that I can't walk. It was the most careless shot I ever heard of!"

"Can't you manage to lift your body off from my commanding officers?" inquired Files. "From their cries I'm afraid your great weight is crushing them."

"I hope it is," growled the Rak. "I want to crush them, if possible, for I have a bad disposition. If only I could open my mouth, I'd eat all of you, although my appetite is poorly this warm weather."

With this the Rak began to roll its immense body sidewise, so as to crush the officers more easily; but in doing this it rolled completely off from them and the entire sixteen scrambled to their feet and made off as fast as they could run.

Private Files could not see them go but he knew from the sound of their voices that they had escaped, so he ceased to worry about them.

"Pardon me if I now bid you good-bye," he said to the Rak. "The parting is caused by our desire to continue our journey. If you die, do not blame me, for I was obliged to shoot you as a matter of self-protection."

"I shall not die," answered the monster, "for I bear a charmed life. But I beg you not to leave me!"

"Why not?" asked Files.

"Because my broken jaw will heal in about an hour, and then I shall be able to eat you. My wing will heal in a day and my leg will heal in a week, when I shall be as well as ever. Having shot me, and so caused me all this annoyance, it is only fair and just that you remain here and allow me to eat you as soon as I can open my jaws."

"I beg to differ with you," returned the Soldier firmly. "I have made an engagement with Queen Ann of Oogaboo to help her conquer the world, and I cannot break my word for the sake of being eaten by a Rak."

"Oh; that's different," said the monster. "If you've an engagement, don't let me detain you."

So Files felt around in the dark and grasped the hand of the trembling Queen, whom he led away from the flapping, sighing Rak. They stumbled over the stones for a way but presently began to see dimly the path ahead of them, as they got farther and farther away from the dreadful spot where the wounded monster lay. By and by they reached a little hill and could see the last rays of the sun flooding a pretty valley beyond, for now they had passed beyond the cloudy breath of the Rak. Here were huddled the sixteen officers, still frightened and panting from their run. They had halted only because it was impossible for them to run any farther.

Queen Ann gave them a severe scolding for their cowardice, at the same time praising Files for his courage.

"We are wiser than he, however," muttered General Clock, "for by running away we are now able to assist your Majesty in conquering the world; whereas, had Files been eaten by the Rak, he would have deserted your Army."

After a brief rest they descended into the valley, and as soon as they were out of sight of the Rak the spirits of the entire party rose quickly. Just at dusk they came to a brook, on the banks of which Queen Ann commanded them to make camp for the night.

Each officer carried in his pocket a tiny white tent. This, when placed upon the ground, quickly grew in size until it was large enough to permit the owner to enter it and sleep within its canvas walls. Files was obliged to carry a knapsack, in which was not only his own tent but an elaborate pavilion for Queen Ann, besides a bed and chair and a magic table. This table, when set upon the ground in Ann's pavilion, became of large size, and in a drawer of the table was contained the Queen's supply of extra clothing, her manicure and toilet articles and other necessary things. The royal bed was the only one in the camp, the officers and private sleeping in hammocks attached to their tent poles.

There was also in the knapsack a flag bearing the royal emblem of Oogaboo, and this flag Files flew upon its staff every night, to show that the country they were in had been conquered by the Queen of Oogaboo. So far, no one but themselves had seen the flag, but Ann was pleased to see it flutter in the breeze and considered herself already a famous conqueror.

·····‹ Chapter 4 ›·····

BETSY BRAVES the BILLOWS

The waves dashed and the lightning flashed and the thunder rolled and the ship struck a rock. Betsy Bobbin was running across the deck and the shock sent her flying through the air until she fell with a splash into the dark blue water. The same shock caught Hank, a thin little, sad-faced mule, and tumbled him also into the sea, far from the ship's side.

When Betsy came up, gasping for breath because the wet plunge had surprised her, she reached out in the dark and grabbed a bunch of hair. At first she thought it was the end of a rope, but presently she heard a dismal "Hee-haw!" and knew she was holding fast to the end of Hank's tail.

Suddenly the sea was lighted up by a vivid glare. The ship, now in the far distance, caught fire, blew up and sank beneath the waves.

Betsy shuddered at the sight, but just then her eye caught a mass of wreckage floating near her and she let go the mule's tail and seized the rude raft, pulling herself up so that she rode upon it in safety. Hank also saw the raft and swam to it, but he was so clumsy he never would have been able to climb upon it had not Betsy helped him to get aboard.

They had to crowd close together, for their support was only a hatch-cover torn from the ship's deck; but it floated them fairly well and both the girl and the mule knew it would keep them from drowning.

The storm was not over, by any means, when the ship went down. Blinding bolts of lightning shot from cloud to cloud and the clamor of deep thunderclaps echoed far over the sea. The waves tossed the little raft here and there as a child tosses a rubber ball and Betsy had a solemn feeling that for hundreds of watery miles in every direction there was no living thing besides herself and the small donkey.

Perhaps Hank had the same thought, for he gently rubbed his nose against the frightened girl and said "Hee-haw!" in his softest voice, as if to comfort her.

"You'll protect me, Hank dear, won't you?" she cried helplessly, and the mule said "Hee-haw!" again, in tones that meant a promise.

On board the ship, during the days that preceded the wreck, when the sea was calm, Betsy and Hank had become good friends; so, while the girl might have preferred a more powerful protector in this dreadful emergency, she felt that the mule would do all in a mule's power to guard her safety.

All night they floated, and when the storm had worn itself out and passed away with a few distant growls, and the waves had grown smaller and easier to ride, Betsy stretched herself out on the wet raft and fell asleep.

Hank did not sleep a wink. Perhaps he felt it his duty to guard Betsy. Anyhow, he crouched on the raft beside the tired sleeping girl and watched patiently until the first light of dawn swept over the sea.

The light wakened Betsy Bobbin. She sat up, rubbed her eyes and stared across the water.

"Oh, Hank; there's land ahead!" she exclaimed.

"Hee-haw!" answered Hank in his plaintive voice.

The raft was floating swiftly toward a very beautiful country and as they drew near Betsy could see banks of lovely flowers showing brightly between leafy trees. But no people were to be seen at all.

....—.◄ Chapter 5 ►.—....

The ROSES REPULSE the
REFUGEES

Gently the raft grated on the sandy beach.
Then Betsy easily waded ashore, the mule following closely behind her. The sun was now
shining and the air was warm and laden with
the fragrance of roses.

"I'd like some breakfast, Hank," remarked the girl, feeling
more cheerful now that she was on dry land; "but we can't eat
the flowers, although they do smell mighty good."

"Hee-haw!" replied Hank and trotted up a little pathway
to the top of the bank.

Betsy followed and from the eminence looked around
her. A little way off stood a splendid big greenhouse, its thou-

sands of crystal panes glittering in the sunlight.

"There ought to be people somewhere 'round," observed Betsy thoughtfully; "gardeners, or somebody. Let's go and see, Hank. I'm getting hungrier ev'ry minute."

So they walked toward the great greenhouse and came to its entrance without meeting with anyone at all. A door stood ajar, so Hank went in first, thinking if there was any danger he could back out and warn his companion. But Betsy was close at his heels and the moment she entered was lost in amazement at the wonderful sight she saw.

The greenhouse was filled with magnificent rosebushes, all growing in big pots. On the central stem of each bush bloomed a splendid Rose, gorgeously colored and deliciously fragrant, and in the center of each Rose was the face of a lovely girl.

As Betsy and Hank entered, the heads of the Roses were drooping and their eyelids were closed in slumber; but the mule was so amazed that he uttered a loud "Hee-haw!" and at the sound of his harsh voice the rose leaves fluttered, the Roses raised their heads and a hundred startled eyes were instantly fixed upon the intruders.

"I—I beg your pardon!" stammered Betsy, blushing and confused.

"O-o-o-h!" cried the Roses, in a sort of sighing chorus; and one of them added: "What a horrid noise!"

"Why, that was only Hank," said Betsy, and as if to prove the truth of her words the mule uttered another loud "Hee-haw!"

At this all the Roses turned on their stems as far as they were able and trembled as if some one were shaking their bushes. A dainty Moss Rose gasped: "Dear me! How dreadfully dreadful!"

"It isn't dreadful at all," said Betsy, somewhat indignant. "When you get used to Hank's voice it will put you to sleep."

The Roses now looked at the mule less fearfully and one of them asked:

"Is that savage beast named Hank?"

"Yes; Hank's my comrade, faithful and true," answered the girl, twining her arms around the little mule's neck and hugging him tight. "Aren't you, Hank?"

Hank could only say in reply: "Hee-haw!" and at his bray the Roses shivered again.

"Please go away!" begged one. "Can't you see you're frightening us out of a week's growth?"

"Go away!" echoed Betsy. "Why, we've no place to go. We've just been wrecked."

"Wrecked?" asked the Roses in a surprised chorus.

"Yes; we were on a big ship and the storm came and wrecked it," explained the girl. "But Hank and I caught hold of a raft and floated ashore to this place, and—we're tired and hungry. What country *is* this, please?"

"This is the Rose Kingdom," replied the Moss Rose, haughtily, "and it is devoted to the culture of the rarest and fairest Roses grown."

"I believe it," said Betsy, admiring the pretty blossoms.

"But only Roses are allowed here," continued a delicate Tea Rose, bending her brows in a frown; "therefore you must go away before the Royal Gardener finds you and casts you back into the sea."

"Oh! Is there a Royal Gardener, then?" inquired Betsy.

"To be sure."

"And is he a Rose, also?"

"Of course not; he's a man—a wonderful man," was the reply.

"Well, I'm not afraid of a man," declared the girl, much relieved, and even as she spoke the Royal Gardener popped into the greenhouse—a spading fork in one hand and a watering pot in the other.

He was a funny little man, dressed in a rose-colored costume, with ribbons at his knees and elbows, and a bunch of ribbons in his hair. His eyes were small and twinkling, his nose sharp and his face puckered and deeply lined.

"O-ho!" he exclaimed, astonished to find strangers in his greenhouse, and when Hank gave a loud bray the Gardener threw the watering pot over the mule's head and danced around with his fork, in such agitation that presently he fell over the handle of the implement and sprawled at full length upon the ground.

Betsy laughed and pulled the watering pot off from Hank's head. The little mule was angry at the treatment he had received and backed toward the Gardener threateningly.

"Look out for his heels!" called Betsy warningly and the Gardener scrambled to his feet and hastily hid behind the Roses.

"You are breaking the Law!" he shouted, sticking out his head to glare at the girl and the mule.

"What Law?" asked Betsy.

"The Law of the Rose Kingdom. No strangers are allowed in these domains."

"Not when they're shipwrecked?" she inquired.

"The Law doesn't except shipwrecks," replied the Royal Gardener, and he was about to say more when suddenly there was a crash of glass and a man came tumbling through the roof of the greenhouse and fell plump to the ground.

Chapter 6

SHAGGY SEEKS His STRAY BROTHER

This sudden arrival was a queer looking man, dressed all in garments so shaggy that Betsy at first thought he must be some animal. But the stranger ended his fall in a sitting position and then the girl saw it was really a man. He held an apple in his hand, which he had evidently been eating when he fell, and so little was he jarred or flustered by the accident that he continued to munch this apple as he calmly looked around him.

"Good gracious!" exclaimed Betsy, approaching him. "Who *are* you, and where did you come from?"

"Me? Oh, I'm Shaggy Man," said he, taking another bite of

the apple. "Just dropped in for a short call. Excuse my seeming haste."

"Why, I s'pose you couldn't help the haste," said Betsy.

"No. I climbed an apple tree, outside; branch gave way and—here I am."

As he spoke the Shaggy Man finished his apple, gave the core to Hank—who ate it greedily—and then stood up to bow politely to Betsy and the Roses.

The Royal Gardener had been frightened nearly into fits by the crash of glass and the fall of the shaggy stranger into the bower of Roses, but now he peeped out from behind a bush and cried in his squeaky voice:

"You're breaking the Law! You're breaking the Law!"

Shaggy stared at him solemnly.

"Is the glass the Law in this country?" he asked.

"Breaking the glass is breaking the Law," squeaked the Gardener, angrily. "Also, to intrude in any part of the Rose Kingdom is breaking the Law."

"How do you know?" asked Shaggy.

"Why, it's printed in a book," said the Gardener, coming forward and taking a small book from his pocket. "Page thirteen. Here it is: 'If any stranger enters the Rose Kingdom he shall at once be condemned by the Ruler and put to death.' So you see, strangers," he continued triumphantly, "it's death for you all and your time has come!"

But just here Hank interposed. He had been stealthily

backing toward the Royal Gardener, whom he disliked, and now the mule's heels shot out and struck the little man in the middle. He doubled up like the letter "U" and flew out of the door so swiftly—never touching the ground—that he was gone before Betsy had time to wink.

But the mule's attack frightened the girl.

"Come," she whispered, approaching the Shaggy Man and taking his hand; "let's go somewhere else. They'll surely kill us if we stay here!"

"Don't worry, my dear," replied Shaggy, patting the child's head. "I'm not afraid of anything, so long as I have the Love Magnet."

"The Love Magnet! Why, what is that?" asked Betsy.

"It's a charming little enchantment that wins the heart of everyone who looks upon it," was the reply. "The Love Magnet used to hang over the gateway to the Emerald City, in the Land of Oz; but when I started on this journey our beloved Ruler, Ozma of Oz, allowed me to take it with me."

"Oh!" cried Betsy, staring hard at him; "are you really from the wonderful Land of Oz?"

"Yes. Ever been there, my dear?"

"No; but I've heard about it. And do you know Princess Ozma?"

"Very well indeed."

"And—and Princess Dorothy?"

"Dorothy's an old chum of mine," declared Shaggy.

"Dear me!" exclaimed Betsy. "And why did you ever leave such a beautiful land as Oz?"

"On an errand," said Shaggy, looking sad and solemn. "I'm trying to find my dear little brother."

"Oh! Is he lost?" questioned Betsy, feeling very sorry for the poor man.

"Been lost these ten years," replied Shaggy, taking out a handkerchief and wiping a tear from his eye. "I didn't know it until lately, when I saw it recorded in the magic Record Book of the Sorceress Glinda, in the Land of Oz. So now I'm trying to find him."

"Where was he lost?" asked the girl sympathetically.

"Back in Colorado, where I used to live before I went to Oz. Brother was a miner, and dug gold out of a mine. One day he went into his mine and never came out. They searched for him, but he was not there. Disappeared entirely," Shaggy ended miserably.

"For goodness sake! What do you s'pose became of him?" she asked.

"There is only one explanation," replied Shaggy, taking another apple from his pocket and eating it to relieve his misery. "The Nome King probably got him."

"The Nome King! Who is he?"

"Why, he's sometimes called the Metal Monarch, and his name is Ruggedo. Lives in some underground cavern. Claims to own all the metals hidden in the earth. Don't ask me why."

"Why?"

"Cause I don't know. But this Ruggedo gets wild with anger if anyone digs gold out of the earth, and my private opinion is that he captured Brother and carried him off to his underground kingdom. No—don't ask me why. I see you're dying to ask me why. But I don't know."

"But—dear me!—in that case you will never find your lost brother!" exclaimed the girl.

"Maybe not; but it's my duty to try," answered Shaggy. "I've wandered so far without finding him, but that only proves he is not where I've been looking. What I seek now is the hidden passage to the underground cavern of the terrible Metal Monarch."

"Well," said Betsy doubtfully, "it strikes me that if you ever manage to get there the Metal Monarch will make you, too, his prisoner."

"Nonsense!" answered Shaggy, carelessly. "You mustn't forget the Love Magnet."

"What about it?" she asked.

"When the fierce Metal Monarch sees the Love Magnet, he will love me dearly and do anything I ask."

"It must be wonderful," said Betsy, with awe.

"It is," the man assured her. "Shall I show it to you?"

"Oh, do!" she cried; so Shaggy searched in his shaggy pocket and drew out a small silver magnet, shaped like a horseshoe.

The moment Betsy saw it she began to like the Shaggy Man better than before. Hank also saw the Magnet and crept up to Shaggy to rub his head lovingly against the man's knee.

But they were interrupted by the Royal Gardener, who stuck his head into the greenhouse and shouted angrily:

"You are all condemned to death! Your only chance to escape is to leave here instantly."

This startled little Betsy, but the Shaggy Man merely waved the Magnet toward the Gardener, who, seeing it, rushed forward and threw himself at Shaggy's feet, murmuring in honeyed words:

"Oh, you lovely, lovely man! How fond I am of you! Every shag and bobtail that decorates you is dear to me—all I have is yours! But for goodness' sake get out of here before you die the death."

"I'm not going to die," declared Shaggy Man.

"You must. It's the Law," exclaimed the Gardener, beginning to weep real tears. "It breaks my heart to tell you this bad news, but the Law says that all strangers must be condemned by the Ruler to die the death."

"No Ruler has condemned us yet," said Betsy.

"Of course not," added Shaggy. "We haven't even seen the Ruler of the Rose Kingdom."

"Well, to tell the truth," said the Gardener, in a perplexed tone of voice, "we haven't any real Ruler, just now. You see, all our Rulers grow on bushes in the Royal Gardens, and the last one we had got mildewed and withered before his time. So we had to plant him, and at this time there is no one growing on the Royal Bushes who is ripe enough to pick."

"How do you know?" asked Betsy.

"Why, I'm the Royal Gardener. Plenty of royalties are growing, I admit; but just now they are all green. Until one ripens, I am supposed to rule the Rose Kingdom myself, and see that its Laws are obeyed. Therefore, much as I love you, Shaggy, I must put you to death."

"Wait a minute," pleaded Betsy. "I'd like to see those Royal Gardens before I die."

"So would I," added Shaggy Man. "Take us there, Gardener."

"Oh, I can't do that," objected the Gardener. But Shaggy again showed him the Love Magnet and after one glance at it the Gardener could no longer resist.

He led Shaggy, Betsy and Hank to the end of the great greenhouse and carefully unlocked a small door. Passing through this they came into the splendid Royal Garden of the Rose Kingdom.

It was all surrounded by a tall hedge and within the enclosure grew several enormous rosebushes having thick green leaves of the texture of velvet. Upon these bushes grew the members of the Royal Family of the Rose Kingdom—men, women and children in all stages of maturity. They all seemed to have a light green hue, as if unripe or not fully developed, their flesh and clothing being alike green. They stood perfectly lifeless upon their branches, which swayed softly in the breeze, and their wide open eyes stared straight ahead, unseeing and unintelligent.

While examining these curious growing people, Betsy passed behind a big central bush and at once uttered an exclamation of surprise and pleasure. For there, blooming in perfect color and shape, stood a Royal Princess, whose beauty was amazing.

"Why, she's ripe!" cried Betsy, pushing aside some of the broad leaves to observe her more clearly.

"Well, perhaps so," admitted the Gardener, who had come to the girl's side; "but she's a girl, and so we can't use her for a Ruler."

"No, indeed!" came a chorus of soft voices, and looking around Betsy discovered that all the Roses had followed them from the greenhouse and were now grouped before the entrance.

"You see," explained the Gardener, "the subjects of Rose Kingdom don't want a girl Ruler. They want a King."

"A King! We want a King!" repeated the chorus of Roses.

"Isn't she Royal?" inquired Shaggy, admiring the lovely Princess.

"Of course, for she grows on a Royal Bush. This Princess is named Ozga, as she is a distant cousin of Ozma of Oz; and, were she but a man, we would joyfully hail her as our Ruler."

The Gardener then turned away to talk with his Roses and

Betsy whispered to her companion: "Let's pick her, Shaggy."

"All right," said he. "If she's royal, she has the right to rule this Kingdom, and if we pick her she will surely protect us and prevent our being hurt, or driven away."

So Betsy and Shaggy each took an arm of the beautiful Rose Princess and a little twist of her feet set her free of the branch upon which she grew. Very gracefully she stepped down from the bush to the ground, where she bowed low to Betsy and Shaggy and said in a delightfully sweet voice: "I thank you."

But at the sound of these words the Gardener and the Roses turned and discovered that the Princess had been picked, and was now alive. Over every face flashed an expression of resentment and anger, and one of the Roses cried aloud.

"Audacious mortals! What have you done?"

"Picked a Princess for you, that's all," replied Betsy, cheerfully.

"But we won't have her! We want a King!" exclaimed a Jacque Rose, and another added with a voice of scorn: "No girl shall rule over us!"

The newly-picked Princess looked from one to another of her rebellious subjects in astonishment. A grieved look came over her exquisite features.

"Have I no welcome here, pretty subjects?" she asked gently. "Have I not come from my Royal Bush to be your Ruler?"

"You were picked by mortals, without our consent," replied

the Moss Rose, coldly; "so we refuse to allow you to rule us."

"Turn her out, Gardener, with the others!" cried the Tea Rose.

"Just a second, please!" called Shaggy, taking the Love Magnet from his pocket. "I guess this will win their love, Princess. Here—take it in your hand and let the roses see it."

Princess Ozga took the Magnet and held it poised before the eyes of her subjects; but the Roses regarded it with calm disdain.

"Why, what's the matter?" demanded Shaggy in surprise. "The Magnet never failed to work before!"

"I know," said Betsy, nodding her head wisely. "These Roses have no hearts."

"That's it," agreed the Gardener. "They're pretty, and sweet, and alive; but still they are Roses. Their stems have thorns, but no hearts."

The Princess sighed and handed the Magnet to the Shaggy Man.

"What shall I do?" she asked sorrowfully.

"Turn her out, Gardener, with the others!" commanded the Roses. "We will have no Ruler until a man-rose—a King—is ripe enough to pick."

"Very well," said the Gardener meekly. "You must excuse me, my dear Shaggy, for opposing your wishes, but you and the others, including Ozga, must get out of Rose Kingdom immediately, if not before."

"Don't you love me, Gardy?" asked Shaggy, carelessly displaying the Magnet.

"I do. I dote on thee!" answered the Gardener earnestly; "but no true man will neglect his duty for the sake of love. My duty is to drive you out, so—out you go!"

With this he seized a garden fork and began jabbing it at the strangers, in order to force them to leave. Hank the mule was not afraid of the fork and when he got his heels near to the Gardener the man fell back to avoid a kick.

But now the Roses crowded around the outcasts and it was soon discovered that beneath their draperies of green leaves were many sharp thorns which were more dangerous than Hank's heels. Neither Betsy nor Ozga nor Shaggy nor the mule cared to brave those thorns and when they pressed away from them they found themselves slowly driven through the garden door into the greenhouse. From there they were forced out at the entrance and so through the territory of the flower-strewn Rose Kingdom, which was not of very great extent.

The Rose Princess was sobbing bitterly; Betsy was indignant and angry; Hank uttered defiant "Hee-haws" and the Shaggy Man whistled softly to himself.

The boundary of the Rose Kingdom was a deep gulf, but there was a drawbridge in one place and this the Royal Gardener let down until the outcasts had passed over it. Then he drew it up again and returned with his Roses to the greenhouse, leaving the four queerly assorted comrades to wander into the bleak and unknown country that lay beyond.

"I don't mind, much," remarked Shaggy, as he led the way over the stony, barren ground. "I've got to search for my long-lost little brother, anyhow, so it won't matter where I go."

"Hank and I will help you find your brother," said Betsy in her most cheerful voice. "I'm so far away from home now that I don't s'pose I'll ever find my way back; and, to tell the truth, it's more fun traveling around and having adventures than sticking at home. Don't you think so, Hank?"

"Hee-haw!" said Hank, and the Shaggy Man thanked them both.

"For my part," said Princess Ozga of Roseland, with a gentle sigh, "I must remain forever exiled from my Kingdom. So I, too, will be glad to help the Shaggy Man find his lost brother."

"That's very kind of you, ma'am," said Shaggy. "But unless I can find the underground cavern of Ruggedo,[1] the Metal Monarch, I shall never find poor brother."

"Doesn't anyone know where it is?" inquired Betsy.

"*Some* one must know, of course," was Shaggy's reply. "But we are not the ones. The only way to succeed is for us to keep going until we find a person who can direct us to Ruggedo's cavern."

"We may find it ourselves, without any help," suggested Betsy. "Who knows?"

[1] This King was formerly named "Roquat," but after he drank of the "Waters of Oblivion" he forgot his own name and had to take another.

"No one knows that, except the person who's writing this story," said Shaggy. "But we won't find anything—not even supper—unless we travel on. Here's a path. Let's take it and see where it leads to."

Chapter 7

POLYCHROME'S PITIFUL PLIGHT

The Rain King got too much water in his basin and spilled some over the brim. That made it rain in a certain part of the country—a real hard shower, for a time—and sent the Rainbow scampering to the place to show the gorgeous colors of his glorious bow as soon as the mist of rain had passed and the sky was clear.

The coming of the Rainbow is always a joyous event to earth folk, yet few have ever seen it close by. Usually the Rainbow is so far distant that you can observe its splendid hues but dimly, and that is why we seldom catch sight of the dancing Daughters of the Rainbow.

In the barren country where the rain had just fallen there appeared to be no human beings at all; but the Rainbow appeared, just the same, and dancing gayly upon its arch were the Rainbow's Daughters, led by the fairylike Polychrome, who is so dainty and beautiful that no girl has ever quite equalled her in loveliness.

Polychrome was in a merry mood and danced down the arch of the bow to the ground, daring her sisters to follow her. Laughing and gleeful, they also touched the ground with their twinkling feet; but all the Daughters of the Rainbow knew that this was a dangerous pastime, so they quickly climbed upon their bow again.

All but Polychrome. Though the sweetest and merriest of them all, she was likewise the most reckless. Moreover, it was an unusual sensation to pat the cold, damp earth with her rosy toes. Before she realized it the bow had lifted and disappeared in the billowy blue sky, and here was Polychrome standing helpless upon a rock, her gauzy draperies floating about her like brilliant cobwebs and not a soul—fairy or mortal—to help her regain her lost bow!

"Dear me!" she exclaimed, a frown passing across her pretty face, "I'm caught again. This is the second time my carelessness has left me on earth while my sisters returned to our Sky Palaces. The first time I enjoyed some pleasant adventures, but this is a lonely, forsaken country and I shall be very unhappy until my Rainbow comes again and I can climb aboard. Let me think what is best to be done."

She crouched low upon the flat rock, drew her draperies about her and bowed her head.

It was in this position that Betsy Bobbin spied Polychrome as she came along the stony path, followed by Hank, the Princess and Shaggy. At once the girl ran up to the radiant Daughter of the Rainbow and exclaimed:

"Oh, what a lovely, lovely creature!"

Polychrome raised her golden head. There were tears in her blue eyes.

"I'm the most miserable girl in the whole world!" she sobbed.

The others gathered around her.

"Tell us your troubles, pretty one," urged the Princess.

"I—I've lost my bow!" wailed Polychrome.

"Take me, my dear," said Shaggy Man in a sympathetic tone, thinking she meant "beau" instead of "bow."

"I don't want you!" cried Polychrome, stamping her foot imperiously; "I want my *Rain*bow."

"Oh; that's different," said Shaggy. "But try to forget it. When I was young I used to cry for the Rainbow myself, but I couldn't have it. Looks as if *you* couldn't have it, either; so please don't cry."

Polychrome looked at him reproachfully.

"I don't like you," she said.

"No?" replied Shaggy, drawing the Love Magnet from his

pocket; "not a little bit?—just a wee speck of a like?"

"Yes, yes!" said Polychrome, clasping her hands in ecstasy as she gazed at the enchanted talisman; "I love you, Shaggy Man!"

"Of course you do," said he calmly; "but I don't take any credit for it. It's the Love Magnet's powerful charm. But you seem quite alone and friendless, little Rainbow. Don't you want to join our party until you find your father and sisters again?"

"Where are you going?" she asked.

"We don't just know that," said Betsy, taking her hand; "but we're trying to find Shaggy's long-lost brother, who has been captured by the terrible Metal Monarch. Won't you come with us, and help us?"

Polychrome looked from one to another of the queer party of travelers and a bewitching smile suddenly lighted her face.

"A donkey, a mortal maid, a Rose Princess and a Shaggy Man!" she exclaimed. "Surely you need help, if you intend to face Ruggedo."

"Do you know him, then?" inquired Betsy.

"No, indeed. Ruggedo's caverns are beneath the earth's surface, where no Rainbow can ever penetrate. But I've heard of the Metal Monarch. He is also called the Nome King, you know, and he has made trouble for a good many people— mortals and fairies—in his time," said Polychrome.

"Do you fear him, then?" asked the Princess, anxiously.

"No one can harm a Daughter of the Rainbow," said Polychrome proudly. "I'm a sky fairy."

"Then," said Betsy, quickly, "you will be able to tell us the way to Ruggedo's cavern."

"No," returned Polychrome, shaking her head, "that is one thing I cannot do. But I will gladly go with you and help you search for the place."

This promise delighted all the wanderers and after the Shaggy Man had found the path again they began moving along it in a more happy mood. The Rainbow's Daughter danced lightly over the rocky trail, no longer sad, but with her beautiful features wreathed in smiles. Shaggy came next, walking steadily and now and then supporting the Rose Princess, who followed him. Betsy and Hank brought up the rear, and if she tired with walking the girl got upon Hank's back and let the stout little donkey carry her for a while.

At nightfall they came to some trees that grew beside a tiny brook and here they made camp and rested until morning. Then away they tramped, finding berries and fruits here and there which satisfied the hunger of Betsy, Shaggy and Hank, so that they were well content with their lot.

It surprised Betsy to see the Rose Princess partake of their food, for she considered her a fairy; but when she mentioned this to Polychrome, the Rainbow's Daughter explained that when Ozga was driven out of her Rose Kingdom she ceased to be a fairy and would never again be more than a mere mortal.

Polychrome, however, was a fairy wherever she happened to be, and if she sipped a few dewdrops by moonlight for refreshment no one ever saw her do it.

As they continued their wandering journey, direction meant very little to them, for they were hopelessly lost in this strange country. Shaggy said it would be best to go toward the mountains, as the natural entrance to Ruggedo's underground cavern was likely to be hidden in some rocky, deserted place; but mountains seemed all around them except in the one direction that they had come from, which led to the Rose Kingdom and the sea. Therefore it mattered little which way they traveled.

By and by they espied a faint trail that looked like a path and after following this for some time they reached a crossroads. Here were many paths, leading in various directions, and there was a signpost so old that there were now no words upon the sign. At one side was an old well, with a chain windlass for drawing water, yet there was no house or other building anywhere in sight.

While the party halted, puzzled which way to proceed, the mule approached the well and tried to look into it.

"He's thirsty," said Betsy.

"It's a dry well," remarked Shaggy. "Probably there has been no water in it for many years. But, come; let us decide which way to travel."

No one seemed able to decide that. They sat down in a

group and tried to consider which road might be the best to take. Hank, however, could not keep away from the well and finally he reared up on his hind legs, got his head over the edge and uttered a loud "Hee-haw!" Betsy watched her animal friend curiously.

"I wonder if he sees anything down there?" she said.

At this, Shaggy rose and went over to the well to investigate, and Betsy went with him. The Princess and Polychrome, who had become fast friends, linked arms and sauntered down one of the roads, to find an easy path.

"Really," said Shaggy, "there does seem to be something at the bottom of this old well."

"Can't we pull it up, and see what it is?" asked the girl.

There was no bucket at the end of the windlass chain, but there was a big hook that at one time was used to hold a bucket. Shaggy let down this hook, dragged it around on the bottom and then pulled it up. An old hoopskirt came with it, and Betsy laughed and threw it away. The thing frightened Hank, who had never seen a hoopskirt before, and he kept a good distance away from it.

Several other objects the Shaggy Man captured with the hook and drew up, but none of these was important.

"This well seems to have been the dump for all the old rubbish in the country," he said, letting down the hook once more. "I guess I've captured everything now. No—the hook has caught again. Help me, Betsy! Whatever this thing is, it's heavy."

She ran up and helped him turn the windlass and after much effort a confused mass of copper came in sight.

"Good gracious!" exclaimed Shaggy. "Here is a surprise, indeed!"

"What is it?" inquired Betsy, clinging to the windlass and panting for breath.

For answer the Shaggy Man grasped the bundle of copper and dumped it upon the ground, free of the well. Then he turned it over with his foot, spread it out, and to Betsy's astonishment the thing proved to be a copper man.

"Just as I thought," said Shaggy, looking hard at the object. "But unless there are two copper men in the world this is the most astonishing thing I ever came across."

At this moment the Rainbow's Daughter and the Rose Princess approached them, and Polychrome said:

"What have you found, Shaggy One?"

"Either an old friend, or a stranger," he replied.

"Oh, here's a sign on his back!" cried Betsy, who had knelt down to examine the man. "Dear me; how funny! Listen to this."

Then she read the following words, engraved upon the copper plates of the man's body:

SMITH & TINKER'S

Patent Double-Action, Extra-Responsive,

Thought-Creating, Perfect-Talking

L. Frank Baum

MECHANICAL MAN

Fitted with our Special Clockwork Attachment.

Thinks, Speaks, Acts, and Does Everything but Live.

"Isn't he wonderful!" exclaimed the Princess.

"Yes; but here's more," said Betsy, reading from another engraved plate:

DIRECTIONS FOR USING:

For THINKING—Wind the Clockwork

Man under his left arm, (marked No. 1).

For SPEAKING—Wind the Clockwork

Man under his right arm, (marked No. 2).

For WALKING and ACTION—Wind Clockwork Man

in the middle of his back, (marked No. 3).

N. B.—This Mechanism is guaranteed to

work perfectly for a thousand years.

"If he's guaranteed for a thousand years," said Poly-chrome, "he ought to work yet."

"Of course," replied Shaggy. "Let's wind him up."

In order to do this they were obliged to set the copper man upon his feet, in an upright position, and this was no easy task. He was inclined to topple over, and had to be propped again and again. The girls assisted Shaggy, and at last Tik-Tok seemed to be balanced and stood alone upon his broad feet.

"Yes," said Shaggy, looking at the copper man carefully, "this must be, indeed, my old friend Tik-Tok, whom I left ticking merrily in the Land of Oz. But how he came to this lonely place, and got into that old well, is surely a mystery."

"If we wind him, perhaps he will tell us," suggested Betsy. "Here's the key, hanging to a hook on his back. What part of him shall I wind up first?"

"His thoughts, of course," said Polychrome, "for it requires thought to speak or move intelligently."

So Betsy wound him under his left arm, and at once little flashes of light began to show in the top of his head, which was proof that he had begun to think.

"Now, then," said Shaggy, "wind up his phonograph."

"What's that?" she asked.

"Why, his talking-machine. His thoughts may be interesting, but they don't tell us anything."

So Betsy wound the copper man under his right arm, and then from the interior of his copper body came in jerky tones the words: "Ma-ny thanks!"

"Hurrah!" cried Shaggy, joyfully, and he slapped Tik-Tok upon the back in such a hearty manner that the copper man lost his balance and tumbled to the ground in a heap. But the clockwork that enabled him to speak had been wound up and he kept saying: "Pick-me-up! Pick-me-up! Pick-me-up!" until they had again raised him and balanced him upon his feet, when he added politely: "Ma-ny thanks!"

"He won't be self-supporting until we wind up his action," remarked Shaggy; so Betsy wound it, as tight as she could—for the key turned rather hard—and then Tik-Tok lifted his feet, marched around in a circle and ended by stopping before the group and making them all a low bow.

"How in the world did you happen to be in that well, when I left you safe in Oz?" inquired Shaggy.

"It is a long sto-ry," replied Tik-Tok, "but I'll tell it in a few words. Af-ter you had gone in search of your broth-er, Oz-ma saw you wan-der-ing in strange lands when-ev-er she looked in her mag-ic pic-ture, and she also saw your broth-er in the Nome King's cavern; so she sent me to tell you where to find your broth-er and told me to help you if I could. The Sor-cer-ess, Glin-da the Good, trans-port-ed me to this place in the wink of an eye; but here I met the Nome King him-self—old Rug-ge-do, who is called in these parts the Met-al Mon-arch. Rug-ge-do knew what I had come for, and he was so an-gry that he threw me down the well. Af-ter my works ran down I was help-less un-til you came a-long and pulled me out a-gain. Ma-ny thanks."

"This is, indeed, good news," said Shaggy. "I suspected that my brother was the prisoner of Ruggedo; but now I know it. Tell us, Tik-Tok, how shall we get to the Nome King's underground cavern?"

"The best way is to walk," said Tik-Tok. "We might crawl, or jump, or roll o-ver and o-ver until we get there; but the best way is to walk."

"I know; but which road shall we take?"

"My ma-chin-er-y is-n't made to tell that," replied Tik-Tok.

"There is more than one entrance to the underground cavern," said Polychrome; "but old Ruggedo has cleverly concealed every opening, so that earth dwellers can not intrude in his domain. If we find our way underground at all, it will be by chance."

"Then," said Betsy, "let us select any road, haphazard, and see where it leads us."

"That seems sensible," declared the Princess. "It may require a lot of time for us to find Ruggedo, but we have more time than anything else."

"If you keep me wound up," said Tik-Tok, "I will last a thou-sand years."

"Then the only question to decide is which way to go," added Shaggy, looking first at one road and then at another.

But while they stood hesitating, a peculiar sound reached their ears—a sound like the tramping of many feet.

"What's coming?" cried Betsy; and then she ran to the left-hand road and glanced along the path. "Why, it's an army!" she exclaimed. "What shall we do, hide or run?"

"Stand still," commanded Shaggy. "I'm not afraid of an army. If they prove to be friendly, they can help us; if they are enemies, I'll show them the Love Magnet."

Chapter 8

TIK-TOK TACKLES a TOUGH TASK

While Shaggy and his companions stood huddled in a group at one side, the Army of Oogaboo was approaching along the pathway, the tramp of their feet being now and then accompanied by a dismal groan as one of the officers stepped on a sharp stone or knocked his funnybone against his neighbor's sword-handle.

Then out from among the trees marched Private Files, bearing the banner of Oogaboo, which fluttered from a long pole. This pole he stuck in the ground just in front of the well and then he cried in a loud voice:

"I hereby conquer this territory in the name of Queen Ann Soforth of Oogaboo, and all the inhabitants of the land I proclaim her slaves!"

Some of the officers now stuck their heads out of the bushes and asked:

"Is the coast clear, Private Files?"

"There is no coast here," was the reply, "but all's well."

"I hope there's water in it," said General Cone, mustering courage to advance to the well; but just then he caught a glimpse of Tik-Tok and Shaggy and at once fell upon his knees, trembling and frightened and cried out:

"Mercy, kind enemies! Mercy! Spare us, and we will be your slaves forever!"

The other officers, who had now advanced into the clearing, likewise fell upon their knees and begged for mercy.

Files turned around and, seeing the strangers for the first time, examined them with much curiosity. Then, discovering that three of the party were girls, he lifted his cap and made a polite bow.

"What's all this?" demanded a harsh voice, as Queen Ann reached the place and beheld her kneeling army.

"Permit us to introduce ourselves," replied Shaggy, stepping forward. "This is Tik-Tok, the Clockwork Man—who works better than some meat people. And here is Princess Ozga of Roseland, just now unfortunately exiled from her

Kingdom of Roses. I next present Polychrome, a sky fairy, who lost her Bow by an accident and can't find her way home. The small girl here is Betsy Bobbin, from some unknown earthly paradise called Oklahoma, and with her you see Mr. Hank, a mule with a long tail and a short temper."

"Puh!" said Ann, scornfully; "a pretty lot of vagabonds you are, indeed; all lost or strayed, I suppose, and not worth a Queen's plundering. I'm sorry I've conquered you."

"But you haven't conquered us yet," called Betsy indignantly.

"No," agreed Files, "that is a fact. But if my officers will kindly command me to conquer you, I will do so at once, after which we can stop arguing and converse more at our ease."

The officers had by this time risen from their knees and brushed the dust from their trousers. To them the enemy did not look very fierce, so the Generals and Colonels and Majors and Captains gained courage to face them and began strutting in their most haughty manner.

"You must understand," said Ann, "that I am the Queen of Oogaboo, and this is my invincible Army. We are busy conquering the world, and since you seem to be a part of the world, and are obstructing our journey, it is necessary for us to conquer you—unworthy though you may be of such high honor."

"That's all right," replied Shaggy. "Conquer us as often as you like. We don't mind."

"But we won't be anybody's slaves," added Betsy, positively.

"We'll see about that," retorted the Queen, angrily. "Advance, Private Files, and bind the enemy hand and foot!"

But Private Files looked at pretty Betsy and fascinating Polychrome and the beautiful Rose Princess and shook his head.

"It would be impolite, and I won't do it," he asserted.

"You must!" cried Ann. "It is your duty to obey orders."

"I haven't received any orders from my officers," objected the Private.

But the Generals now shouted: "Forward, and bind the prisoners!" and the Colonels and Majors and Captains repeated the command, yelling it as loud as they could.

All this noise annoyed Hank, who had been eyeing the Army of Oogaboo with strong disfavor. The mule now dashed forward and began backing upon the officers and kicking fierce and dangerous heels at them. The attack was so sudden that the officers scattered like dust in a whirlwind, dropping their swords as they ran and trying to seek refuge behind the trees and bushes.

Betsy laughed joyously at the comical rout of the "noble army," and Polychrome danced with glee. But Ann was furious at this ignoble defeat of her gallant forces by one small mule.

"Private Files, I command you to do your duty!" she cried again, and then she herself ducked to escape the mule's heels—for Hank made no distinction in favor of a lady who was an open enemy. Betsy grabbed her champion by the forelock, however, and so held him fast, and when the officers saw that the mule was restrained from further attacks they crept fearfully back and picked up their discarded swords.

"Private Files, seize and bind these prisoners!" screamed the Queen.

"No," said Files, throwing down his gun and removing the knapsack which was strapped to his back, "I resign my position as the Army of Oogaboo. I enlisted to fight the enemy and become a hero, but if you want some one to bind harmless girls you will have to hire another Private."

Then he walked over to the others and shook hands with Shaggy and Tik-Tok.

"Treason!" shrieked Ann, and all the officers echoed her cry.

"Nonsense," said Files. "I've the right to resign if I want to."

"Indeed you haven't!" retorted the Queen. "If you resign it will break up my Army, and then I cannot conquer the world." She now turned to the officers and said: "I must ask you to do me a favor. I know it is undignified in officers to fight, but unless you immediately capture Private Files and force him to obey my orders there will be no plunder for any of us. Also it is likely you will all suffer the pangs of hunger, and when we meet a powerful foe you are liable to be captured and made slaves."

The prospect of this awful fate so frightened the officers that they drew their swords and rushed upon Files, who stood beside Shaggy, in a truly ferocious manner. The next instant, however, they halted and again fell upon their knees; for there, before them, was the glistening Love Magnet, held in the hand of the smiling Shaggy Man, and the sight of this magic talisman at once won the heart of every Oogabooite. Even Ann saw the Love Magnet, and forgetting all enmity and anger threw herself upon Shaggy and embraced him lovingly.

Quite disconcerted by this unexpected effect of the Magnet, Shaggy disengaged himself from the Queen's encircling arms and quickly hid the talisman in his pocket. The adventurers from Oogaboo were now his firm friends, and there was no more talk about conquering and binding any of his party.

"If you insist on conquering anyone," said Shaggy, "you may march with me to the underground Kingdom of Ruggedo. To conquer the world, as you have set out to do, you must conquer everyone under its surface as well as those upon its surface, and no one in all the world needs conquering so much as Ruggedo."

"Who is he?" asked Ann.

"The Metal Monarch, King of the Nomes."

"Is he rich?" inquired Major Stockings in an anxious voice.

"Of course," answered Shaggy. "He owns all the metal that lies underground—gold, silver, copper, brass and tin. He has an idea he also owns all the metals above ground, for he says all metal was once a part of his kingdom. So, by conquering the Metal Monarch, you will win all the riches in the world."

"Ah!" exclaimed General Apple, heaving a deep sigh, "that would be plunder worth our while. Let's conquer him, your Majesty."

The Queen looked reproachfully at Files, who was sitting next to the lovely Princess and whispering in her ear.

"Alas," said Ann, "I have no longer an Army. I have plenty of brave officers, indeed, but no private soldier for them to command. Therefore I cannot conquer Ruggedo and win all his wealth."

"Why don't you make one of your officers the Private?" asked Shaggy; but at once every officer began to protest and the Queen of Oogaboo shook her head as she replied:

"That is impossible. A private soldier must be a terrible fighter, and my officers are unable to fight. They are exceptionally brave in commanding others to fight, but could not themselves meet the enemy and conquer."

"Very true, your Majesty," said Colonel Plum, eagerly. "There are many kinds of bravery and one cannot be expected to possess them all. I myself am brave as a lion in all ways until it comes to fighting, but then my nature revolts. Fighting is unkind and liable to be injurious to others; so, being a gentleman, I never fight."

"Nor I!" shouted each of the other officers.

"You see," said Ann, "how helpless I am. Had not Private

Files proved himself a traitor and a deserter, I would gladly have conquered this Ruggedo; but an Army without a private soldier is like a bee without a stinger."

"I am not a traitor, your Majesty," protested Files. "I resigned in a proper manner, not liking the job. But there are plenty of people to take my place. Why not make Shaggy Man the private soldier?"

"He might be killed," said Ann, looking tenderly at Shaggy, "for he is mortal, and able to die. If anything happened to him, it would break my heart."

"It would hurt me worse than that," declared Shaggy. "You must admit, your Majesty, that I am commander of this expedition, for it is my brother we are seeking, rather than plunder. But I and my companions would like the assistance of your Army, and if you help us to conquer Ruggedo and to rescue my brother from captivity we will allow you to keep all the gold and jewels and other plunder you may find."

This prospect was so tempting that the officers began whispering together and presently Colonel Cheese said: "Your Majesty, by combining our brains we have just evolved a most brilliant idea. We will make the Clockwork Man the private soldier!"

"Who? Me?" asked Tik-Tok. "Not for a sin-gle sec-ond! I can-not fight, and you must not for-get that it was Rug-ge-do who threw me in the well."

"At that time you had no gun," said Polychrome. "But if

you join the Army of Oogaboo you will carry the gun that Mr. Files used."

"A sol-dier must be a-ble to run as well as to fight," protested Tik-Tok, "and if my works run down, as they of-ten do, I could nei-ther run nor fight."

"I'll keep you wound up, Tik-Tok," promised Betsy.

"Why, it isn't a bad idea," said Shaggy. "Tik-Tok will make an ideal soldier, for nothing can injure him except a sledge hammer. And, since a private soldier seems to be necessary to this Army, Tik-Tok is the only one of our party fitted to undertake the job."

"What must I do?" asked Tik-Tok.

"Obey orders," replied Ann. "When the officers command you to do anything, you must do it; that is all."

"And that's enough, too," said Files.

"Do I get a salary?" inquired Tik-Tok.

"You get your share of the plunder," answered the Queen.

"Yes," remarked Files, "one-half of the plunder goes to Queen Ann, the other half is divided among the officers, and the Private gets the rest."

"That will be sat-is-fac-tor-y," said Tik-Tok, picking up the gun and examining it wonderingly, for he had never before seen such a weapon.

Then Ann strapped the knapsack to Tik-Tok's copper back and said: "Now we are ready to march to Ruggedo's Kingdom and conquer it. Officers, give the command to march."

"Fall—in!" yelled the Generals, drawing their swords.

"Fall—in!" cried the Colonels, drawing their swords.

"Fall—in!" shouted the Majors, drawing their swords.

"Fall—in!" bawled the Captains, drawing their swords.

Tik-Tok looked at them and then around him in surprise.

"Fall in what? The well?" he asked.

"No," said Queen Ann, "you must fall in marching order."

"Can-not I march without fall-ing in-to it?" asked the Clockwork Man.

"Shoulder your gun and stand ready to march," advised Files; so Tik-Tok held the gun straight and stood still.

"What next?" he asked.

The Queen turned to Shaggy.

"Which road leads to the Metal Monarch's cavern?"

"We don't know, your Majesty," was the reply.

"But this is absurd!" said Ann with a frown. "If we can't get to Ruggedo, it is certain that we can't conquer him."

"You are right," admitted Shaggy; "but I did not say we could not get to him. We have only to discover the way, and that was the matter we were considering when you and your magnificent Army arrived here."

"Well, then, get busy and discover it," snapped the Queen.

That was no easy task. They all stood looking from one road to another in perplexity. The paths radiated from the little clearing like the rays of the midday sun, and each path seemed like all the others.

Files and the Rose Princess, who had by this time become good friends, advanced a little way along one of the roads and found that it was bordered by pretty wild flowers.

"Why don't you ask the flowers to tell you the way?" he said to his companion.

"The flowers?" returned the Princess, surprised at the question.

"Of course," said Files. "The field-flowers must be second-cousins to a Rose Princess, and I believe if you ask them they will tell you."

She looked more closely at the flowers. There were hundreds of white daisies, golden buttercups, bluebells and daffodils growing by the roadside, and each flower-head was firmly set upon its slender but stout stem. There were even a few wild roses scattered here and there and perhaps it was the sight of these that gave the Princess courage to ask the important question.

She dropped to her knees, facing the flowers, and extended both her arms pleadingly toward them.

"Tell me, pretty cousins," she said in her sweet, gentle voice, "which way will lead us to the Kingdom of Ruggedo, the Nome King?"

At once all the stems bent gracefully to the right and the flower heads nodded once—twice—thrice in that direction.

"That's it!" cried Files joyfully. "Now we know the way."

Ozga rose to her feet and looked wonderingly at the

field-flowers, which had now resumed their upright position.

"Was it the wind, do you think?" she asked in a low whisper.

"No, indeed," replied Files. "There is not a breath of wind stirring. But these lovely blossoms are indeed your cousins and answered your question at once, as I knew they would."

RUGGEDO'S RAGE Is RASH and RECKLESS

The way taken by the adventurers led up hill and down dale and wound here and there in a fashion that seemed aimless. But always it drew nearer to a range of low mountains and Files said more than once that he was certain the entrance to Ruggedo's cavern would be found among these rugged hills.

In this he was quite correct. Far underneath the nearest mountain was a gorgeous chamber hollowed from the solid rock, the walls and roof of which glittered with thousands of magnificent jewels. Here, on a throne of virgin gold, sat the famous Nome King, dressed in splendid robes and wearing a superb crown cut from a single blood-red ruby.

Ruggedo, the Monarch of all the Metals and Precious Stones of the Underground World, was a round little man with a flowing white beard, a red face, bright eyes and a scowl that covered all his forehead. One would think, to look at him, that he ought to be jolly; one might think, considering his enormous wealth, that he ought to be happy; but this was not the case. The Metal Monarch was surly and cross because mortals had dug so much treasure out of the earth and kept it above ground, where all the power of Ruggedo and his nomes was unable to recover it. He hated not only the mortals but also the fairies who live upon the earth or above it, and instead of being content with the riches he still possessed he was unhappy because he did not own all the gold and jewels in the world.

Ruggedo had been nodding, half asleep, in his chair when suddenly he sat upright, uttered a roar of rage and began pounding upon a huge gong that stood beside him.

The sound filled the vast cavern and penetrated to many caverns beyond, where countless thousands of nomes were working at their unending tasks, hammering out gold and silver and other metals, or melting ores in great furnaces, or polishing glittering gems. The nomes trembled at the sound of the King's gong and whispered fearfully to one another that something unpleasant was sure to happen; but none dared pause in his task.

The heavy curtains of cloth-of-gold were pushed aside

and Kaliko, the King's High Chamberlain, entered the royal presence.

"What's up, your Majesty?" he asked, with a wide yawn, for he had just wakened.

"Up?" roared Ruggedo, stamping his foot viciously. "Those foolish mortals are up, that's what! And they want to come down."

"Down here?" inquired Kaliko.

"Yes!"

"How do you know?" continued the Chamberlain, yawning again.

"I feel it in my bones," said Ruggedo. "I can always feel it when those hateful earth-crawlers draw near to my Kingdom. I am positive, Kaliko, that mortals are this very minute on their way here to annoy me—and I hate mortals more than I do catnip tea!"

"Well, what's to be done?" demanded the nome.

"Look through your spyglass, and see where the invaders are," commanded the King.

So Kaliko went to a tube in the wall of rock and put his eye to it. The tube ran from the cavern up to the side of the mountain and turned several curves and corners, but as it was a magic spyglass Kaliko was able to see through it just as easily as if it had been straight.

"Ho—hum," said he. "I see 'em, your Majesty."

"What do they look like?" inquired the Monarch.

"That's a hard question to answer, for a queerer assortment of creatures I never yet beheld," replied the nome. "However, such a collection of curiosities may prove dangerous. There's a copper man, worked by machinery—"

"Bah! that's only Tik-Tok," said Ruggedo. "I'm not afraid of him. Why, only the other day I met the fellow and threw him down a well."

"Then some one must have pulled him out again," said Kaliko. "And there's a little girl—"

"Dorothy?" asked Ruggedo, jumping up in fear.

"No; some other girl. In fact, there are several girls, of various sizes; but Dorothy is not with them, nor is Ozma."

"That's good!" exclaimed the King, sighing in relief.

Kaliko still had his eye to the spyglass.

"I see," said he, "an army of men from Oogaboo. They are all officers and carry swords. And there is a Shaggy Man—who seems very harmless—and a little donkey with big ears."

"Pooh!" cried Ruggedo, snapping his fingers in scorn. "I've no fear of such a mob as that. A dozen of my nomes can destroy them all in a jiffy."

"I'm not so sure of that," said Kaliko. "The people of Oogaboo are hard to destroy, and I believe the Rose Princess is a fairy. As for Polychrome, you know very well that the Rainbow's Daughter cannot be injured by a nome."

"Polychrome! Is she among them?" asked the King.

"Yes; I have just recognized her."

"Then these people are coming here on no peaceful errand," declared Ruggedo, scowling fiercely. "In fact, no one ever comes here on a peaceful errand. I hate everybody, and everybody hates me!"

"Very true," said Kaliko.

"I must in some way prevent these people from reaching my dominions. Where are they now?"

"Just now they are crossing the Rubber Country, your Majesty."

"Good! Are your magnetic rubber wires in working order?"

"I think so," replied Kaliko. "Is it your Royal Will that we have some fun with these invaders?"

"It is," answered Ruggedo. "I want to teach them a lesson they will never forget."

Now, Shaggy had no idea that he was in a Rubber Country, nor had any of his companions. They noticed that everything around them was of a dull grey color and that the path upon which they walked was soft and springy, yet they had no suspicion that the rocks and trees were rubber and even the path they trod was made of rubber.

Presently they came to a brook where sparkling water dashed through a deep channel and rushed away between high rocks far down the mountain-side. Across the brook were stepping-stones, so placed that travelers might easily leap from one to another and in that manner cross the water to the farther bank.

Tik-Tok was marching ahead, followed by his officers and Queen Ann. After them came Betsy Bobbin and Hank, Polychrome and Shaggy, and last of all the Rose Princess with Files. The Clockwork Man saw the stream and the stepping stones and, without making a pause, placed his foot upon the first stone.

The result was astonishing. First he sank down in the soft rubber, which then rebounded and sent Tik-Tok soaring high in the air, where he turned a succession of flip-flops and alighted upon a rubber rock far in the rear of the party.

General Apple did not see Tik-Tok bound, so quickly had he disappeared; therefore he also stepped upon the stone (which you will guess was connected with Kaliko's magnetic rubber wire) and instantly shot upward like an arrow. General Cone came next and met with a like fate, but the others now noticed that something was wrong and with one accord they halted the column and looked back along the path.

There was Tik-Tok, still bounding from one rubber rock to another, each time rising a less distance from the ground. And there was General Apple, bounding away in another direction, his three-cornered hat jammed over his eyes and his long sword thumping him upon the arms and head as it swung this way and that. And there, also, appeared General Cone, who had struck a rubber rock headforemost and was so crumpled up that his round body looked more like a bouncing-ball than the form of a man.

Betsy laughed merrily at the strange sight and Polychrome echoed her laughter. But Ozga was grave and wondering, while Queen Ann became angry at seeing the chief officers of the Army of Oogaboo bounding around in so undignified a manner. She shouted to them to stop, but they were unable to obey, even though they would have been glad to do so. Finally, however, they all ceased bounding and managed to get upon their feet and rejoin the Army.

"Why did you do that?" demanded Ann, who seemed greatly provoked.

"Don't ask them why," said Shaggy earnestly. "I knew you would ask them why, but you ought not to do it. The reason is plain. Those stones are rubber; therefore they are not stones. Those rocks around us are rubber, and therefore they are not rocks. Even this path is not a path; it's rubber. Unless we are very careful, your Majesty, we are all likely to get the bounce, just as your poor officers and Tik-Tok did."

"Then let's be careful," remarked Files, who was full of wisdom; but Polychrome wanted to test the quality of the rubber, so she began dancing. Every step sent her higher and higher into the air, so that she resembled a big butterfly fluttering lightly. Presently she made a great bound and bounded way across the stream, landing lightly and steadily on the other side.

"There is no rubber over here," she called to them. "Suppose you all try to bound over the stream, without touching the stepping-stones."

Ann and her officers were reluctant to undertake such a risky adventure, but Betsy at once grasped the value of the suggestion and began jumping up and down until she found herself bounding almost as high as Polychrome had done. Then she suddenly leaned forward and the next bound took her easily across the brook, where she alighted by the side of the Rainbow's Daughter.

"Come on, Hank!" called the girl, and the donkey tried to obey. He managed to bound pretty high but when he tried to bound across the stream he misjudged the distance and fell with a splash into the middle of the water.

"Hee-haw!" he wailed, struggling toward the far bank. Betsy rushed forward to help him out, but when the mule stood safely beside her she was amazed to find he was not wet at all.

"It's dry water," said Polychrome, dipping her hand into the stream and showing how the water fell from it and left it perfectly dry.

"In that case," returned Betsy, "they can all walk through the water."

She called to Ozga and Shaggy to wade across, assuring them the water was shallow and would not wet them. At once they followed her advice, avoiding the rubber stepping stones, and made the crossing with ease. This encouraged the entire party to wade through the dry water, and in a few minutes all had assembled on the bank and renewed their journey along the path that led to the Nome King's dominions.

When Kaliko again looked through his magic spyglass he exclaimed:

"Bad luck, your Majesty! All the invaders have passed the Rubber Country and now are fast approaching the entrance to your caverns."

Ruggedo raved and stormed at the news and his anger was so great that several times, as he strode up and down his jeweled cavern, he paused to kick Kaliko upon his shins, which were so sensitive that the poor nome howled with pain. Finally the King said:

"There's no help for it; we must drop these audacious invaders down the Hollow Tube."

Kaliko gave a jump, at this, and looked at his master wonderingly.

"If you do that, your Majesty," he said, "you will make Tititi-Hoochoo very angry."

"Never mind that," retorted Ruggedo. "Tititi-Hoochoo lives on the other side of the world, so what do I care for his anger?"

Kaliko shuddered and uttered a little groan.

"Remember his terrible powers," he pleaded, "and remember that he warned you, the last time you slid people through the Hollow Tube, that if you did it again he would take vengeance upon you."

The Metal Monarch walked up and down in silence, thinking deeply.

"Of two dangers," said he, "it is wise to choose the least. What do you suppose these invaders want?"

"Let the Long-Eared Hearer listen to them," suggested Kaliko.

"Call him here at once!" commanded Ruggedo eagerly.

So in a few minutes there entered the cavern a nome with enormous ears, who bowed low before the King.

"Strangers are approaching," said Ruggedo, "and I wish to know their errand. Listen carefully to their talk and tell me why they are coming here, and what for."

The nome bowed again and spread out his great ears, swaying them gently up and down and back and forth. For half an hour he stood silent, in an attitude of listening, while both the King and Kaliko grew impatient at the delay. At last the Long-Eared Hearer spoke:

"Shaggy Man is coming here to rescue his brother from captivity," said he.

"Ha, the Ugly One!" exclaimed Ruggedo. "Well, Shaggy Man may have his ugly brother, for all I care. He's too lazy to work and is always getting in my way. Where is the Ugly One now, Kaliko?"

"The last time your Majesty stumbled over the prisoner you commanded me to send him to the Metal Forest, which I did. I suppose he is still there."

"Very good. The invaders will have a hard time finding the Metal Forest," said the King, with a grin of malicious delight, "for half the time I can't find it myself. Yet I created the forest and made every tree, out of gold and silver, so as to keep the precious metals in a safe place and out of the reach of mortals. But tell me, Hearer, do the strangers want anything else?"

"Yes, indeed they do!" returned the nome. "The Army of Oogaboo is determined to capture all the rich metals and rare jewels in your kingdom, and the officers and their Queen have arranged to divide the spoils and carry them away."

When he heard this Ruggedo uttered a bellow of rage and began dancing up and down, rolling his eyes, clicking his teeth together and swinging his arms furiously. Then, in an ecstasy of anger he seized the long ears of the Hearer and pulled and twisted them cruelly; but Kaliko grabbed up the King's sceptre and rapped him over the knuckles with it, so that Ruggedo let go the ears and began to chase his Royal Chamberlain around the throne.

The Hearer took advantage of this opportunity to slip away from the cavern and escape, and after the King had tired himself out chasing Kaliko he threw himself into his throne and panted for breath, while he glared wickedly at his defiant subject.

"You'd better save your strength to fight the enemy," suggested Kaliko. "There will be a terrible battle when the Army of Oogaboo gets here."

"The Army won't get here," said the King, still coughing

and panting. "I'll drop 'em down the Hollow Tube—every man Jack and every girl Jill of 'em!"

"And defy Tititi-Hoochoo?" asked Kaliko.

"Yes. Go at once to my Chief Magician and order him to turn the path toward the Hollow Tube, and to make the tip of the Tube invisible, so they'll all fall into it."

Kaliko went away shaking his head, for he thought Ruggedo was making a great mistake. He found the Magician and had the path twisted so that it led directly to the opening of the Hollow Tube, and this opening he made invisible.

Having obeyed the orders of his master, the Royal Chamberlain went to his private room and began to write letters of recommendation of himself, stating that he was an honest man, a good servant and a small eater.

"Pretty soon," he said to himself, "I shall have to look for another job, for it is certain that Ruggedo has ruined himself by this reckless defiance of the mighty Tititi-Hoochoo. And in seeking a job nothing is so effective as a letter of recommendation."

A TERRIBLE TUMBLE
THROUGH a TUBE

I suppose that Polychrome, and perhaps Queen Ann and her Army, might have been able to dispel the enchantment of Ruggedo's Chief Magician had they known that danger lay in their pathway; for the Rainbow's Daughter was a fairy and as Oogaboo is a part of the Land of Oz its inhabitants cannot easily be deceived by such common magic as the Nome King could command. But no one suspected any especial danger until after they had entered Ruggedo's cavern, and so they were journeying along in quite a contented manner when Tik-Tok, who marched ahead, suddenly disappeared.

The officers thought he must have turned a corner, so they

kept on their way and all of them likewise disappeared—one after another. Queen Ann was rather surprised at this, and in hastening forward to learn the reason she also vanished from sight.

Betsy Bobbin had tired her feet by walking, so she was now riding upon the back of the stout little mule, facing backward and talking to Shaggy and Polychrome, who were just behind. Suddenly Hank pitched forward and began falling and Betsy would have tumbled over his head had she not grabbed the mule's shaggy neck with both arms and held on for dear life.

All around was darkness, and they were not falling directly downward but seemed to be sliding along a steep incline. Hank's hoofs were resting upon some smooth substance over which he slid with the swiftness of the wind. Once Betsy's heels flew up and struck a similar substance overhead. They were, indeed, descending the "Hollow Tube" that led to the other side of the world.

"Stop, Hank—stop!" cried the girl; but Hank only uttered a plaintive "Hee-haw!" for it was impossible for him to obey.

After several minutes had passed and no harm had befallen them, Betsy gained courage. She could see nothing at all, nor could she hear anything except the rush of air past her ears as they plunged downward along the Tube. Whether she and Hank were alone, or the others were with them, she could not tell. But had some one been able to take a flash-light photograph of the Tube at that time a most curious picture would have resulted. There was Tik-Tok, flat upon his back and sliding headforemost down the incline. And there were the Officers of the Army of Oogaboo, all tangled up in a confused crowd, flapping their arms and trying to shield their faces from the clanking swords, which swung back and forth during the swift journey and pommeled everyone within their reach. Now followed Queen Ann, who had struck the Tube in a sitting position and went flying along with a dash and abandon that thoroughly bewildered the poor lady, who had no idea what had happened to her. Then, a little distance away, but unseen by the others in the inky darkness, slid Betsy and Hank, while behind them were Shaggy and Polychrome and finally Files and the Princess.

When first they tumbled into the Tube all were too dazed to think clearly, but the trip was a long one, because the cavity led straight through the earth to a place just opposite the Nome King's dominions, and long before the adventurers got to the end they had begun to recover their wits.

"This is awful, Hank!" cried Betsy in a loud voice, and Queen Ann heard her and called out: "Are you safe, Betsy?"

"Mercy, no!" answered the little girl. "How could anyone be safe when she's going about sixty miles a minute?" Then, after a pause, she added: "But where do you s'pose we're going to, your Maj'sty?"

"Don't ask her that, please don't!" said Shaggy, who was not too far away to overhear them. "And please don't ask me why, either."

"Why?" said Betsy.

"No one can tell where we are going until we get there," replied Shaggy, and then he yelled "Ouch!" for Polychrome had overtaken him and was now sitting on his head.

The Rainbow's Daughter laughed merrily, and so infectious was this joyous laugh that Betsy echoed it and Hank said "Hee haw!" in a mild and sympathetic tone of voice.

"I'd like to know where and when we'll arrive, just the same," exclaimed the little girl.

"Be patient and you'll find out, my dear," said Polychrome. "But isn't this an odd experience? Here am I, whose home is in the skies, making a journey through the center of the earth— where I never expected to be!"

"How do you know we're in the center of the earth?" asked Betsy, her voice trembling a little through nervousness.

"Why, we can't be anywhere else," replied Polychrome. "I have often heard of this passage, which was once built by a Magician who was a great traveler. He thought it would save him the bother of going around the earth's surface, but he tumbled through the Tube so fast that he shot out at the other end and hit a star in the sky, which at once exploded."

"The star exploded?" asked Betsy wonderingly.

"Yes; the Magician hit it so hard."

"And what became of the Magician?" inquired the girl.

"No one knows that," answered Polychrome. "But I don't think it matters much."

"It matters a good deal, if we also hit the stars when we come out," said Queen Ann, with a moan.

"Don't worry," advised Polychrome. "I believe the Magician was going the other way, and probably he went much faster than we are going."

"It's fast enough to suit me," remarked Shaggy, gently removing Polychrome's heel from his left eye. "Couldn't you manage to fall all by yourself, my dear?"

"I'll try," laughed the Rainbow's Daughter.

All this time they were swiftly falling through the Tube, and it was not so easy for them to talk as you may imagine when you read their words. But although they were so helpless and altogether in the dark as to their fate, the fact that they were able to converse at all cheered them, considerably.

Files and Ozga were also conversing as they clung tightly to one another, and the young fellow bravely strove to reassure the Princess, although he was terribly frightened, both on her account and on his own.

An hour, under such trying circumstances, is a very long time, and for more than an hour they continued their fearful journey. Then, just as they began to fear the Tube would never end, Tik-Tok popped out into broad daylight and, after making a graceful circle in the air, fell with a splash into a great marble fountain.

Out came the officers, in quick succession, tumbling heels over head and striking the ground in many undignified attitudes.

"For the love of sassafras!" exclaimed a Peculiar Person who was hoeing pink violets in a garden. "What can all this mean?"

For answer, Queen Ann sailed up from the Tube, took a ride through the air as high as the treetops, and alighted squarely on top of the Peculiar Person's head, smashing a jeweled crown over his eyes and tumbling him to the ground.

The mule was heavier and had Betsy clinging to his back, so he did not go so high up. Fortunately for his little rider he struck the ground upon his four feet. Betsy was jarred a trifle but not hurt and when she looked around her she saw the Queen and the Peculiar Person struggling together upon the ground, where the man was trying to choke Ann and she had both hands in his bushy hair and was pulling with all her might. Some of the officers, when they got upon their feet, hastened to separate the combatants and sought to restrain the Peculiar Person so that he could not attack their Queen again.

By this time, Shaggy, Polychrome, Ozga and Files had all arrived and were curiously examining the strange country in which they found themselves and which they knew to be exactly on the opposite side of the world from the place where they had fallen into the Tube. It was a lovely place, indeed, and seemed to be the garden of some great Prince, for through the vistas of trees and shrubbery could be seen the towers of an immense castle. But as yet the only inhabitant to greet them was the Peculiar Person just mentioned, who had shaken off the grasp of the officers without effort and was now trying to pull the battered crown from off his eyes.

Shaggy, who was always polite, helped him to do this and when the man was free and could see again he looked at his visitors with evident amazement.

"Well, well, well!" he exclaimed. "Where did you come from and how did you get here?"

Betsy tried to answer him, for Queen Ann was surly and silent.

"I can't say, exac'ly where we came from, cause I don't know the name of the place," said the girl, "but the way we got here was through the Hollow Tube."

"Don't call it a 'hollow' Tube, please," exclaimed the Peculiar Person in an irritated tone of voice. "If it's a tube, it's sure to be hollow."

"Why?" asked Betsy.

"Because all tubes are made that way. But this Tube is private property and everyone is forbidden to fall into it."

"We didn't do it on purpose," explained Betsy, and Polychrome added: "I am quite sure that Ruggedo, the Nome King, pushed us down that Tube."

"Ha! Ruggedo! Did you say Ruggedo?" cried the man, becoming much excited.

"That is what she said," replied Shaggy, "and I believe she is right. We were on our way to conquer the Nome King when suddenly we fell into the Tube."

"Then you are enemies of Ruggedo?" inquired the Peculiar Person.

"Not exac'ly enemies," said Betsy, a little puzzled by the question, "'cause we don't know him at all; but we started out to conquer him, which isn't as friendly as it might be."

"True," agreed the man. He looked thoughtfully from one to another of them for a while and then he turned his head over his shoulder and said: "Never mind the fire and pincers, my good brothers. It will be best to take these strangers to the Private Citizen."

"Very well, Tubekins," responded a Voice, deep and powerful, that seemed to come out of the air, for the speaker was invisible.

All our friends gave a jump, at this. Even Polychrome was so startled that her gauze draperies fluttered like a banner in a breeze. Shaggy shook his head and sighed; Queen Ann looked very unhappy; the officers clung to each other, trembling violently.

But soon they gained courage to look more closely at the Peculiar Person. As he was a type of all the inhabitants of this extraordinary land whom they afterward met, I will try to tell you what he looked like.

His face was beautiful, but lacked expression. His eyes were large and blue in color and his teeth finely formed and white as snow. His hair was black and bushy and seemed inclined to curl at the ends. So far no one could find any fault with his appearance. He wore a robe of scarlet, which did not cover his arms and extended no lower than his bare knees. On the bosom of the robe was embroidered a terrible dragon's head, as horrible to look at as the man was beautiful. His arms and legs were left bare and the skin of one arm was bright yellow and the skin of the other arm a vivid green. He had one blue leg and one pink one, while both his feet—which showed through the open sandals he wore—were jet black.

Betsy could not decide whether these gorgeous colors were dyes or the natural tints of the skin, but while she was thinking it over the man who had been called "Tubekins" said:

"Follow me to the Residence—all of you!"

But just then a Voice exclaimed: "Here's another of them, Tubekins, lying in the water of the fountain."

"Gracious!" cried Betsy; "it must be Tik-Tok, and he'll drown."

"Water is a bad thing for his clockworks, anyway," agreed Shaggy, as with one accord they all started for the fountain. But before they could reach it, invisible hands raised Tik-Tok from the marble basin and set him upon his feet beside it, water dripping from every joint of his copper body.

"Ma—ny tha—tha—tha—thanks!" he said; and then his copper jaws clicked together and he could say no more. He next made an attempt to walk but after several awkward trials found he could not move his joints.

Peals of jeering laughter from persons unseen greeted

Tik-Tok's failure, and the new arrivals in this strange land found it very uncomfortable to realize that there were many creatures around them who were invisible, yet could be heard plainly.

"Shall I wind him up?" asked Betsy, feeling very sorry for Tik-Tok.

"I think his machinery is wound; but he needs oiling," replied Shaggy.

At once an oil-can appeared before him, held on a level with his eyes by some unseen hand. Shaggy took the can and tried to oil Tik-Tok's joints. As if to assist him, a strong current of warm air was directed against the copper man which quickly dried him. Soon he was able to say "Ma-ny thanks!" quite smoothly and his joints worked fairly well.

"Come!" commanded Tubekins, and turning his back upon them he walked up the path toward the castle.

"Shall we go?" asked Queen Ann, uncertainly; but just then she received a shove that almost pitched her forward on her head; so she decided to go. The officers who hesitated received several energetic kicks, but could not see who delivered them; therefore they also decided—very wisely—to go. The others followed willingly enough, for unless they ventured upon another terrible journey through the Tube they must make the best of the unknown country they were in, and the best seemed to be to obey orders.

Chapter 11

The FAMOUS FELLOWSHIP of FAIRIES

fter a short walk through very beautiful gardens they came to the castle and followed Tubekins through the entrance and into a great domed chamber, where he commanded them to be seated.

From the crown which he wore, Betsy had thought this man must be the King of the country they were in, yet after he had seated all the strangers upon benches that were ranged in a semicircle before a high throne, Tubekins bowed humbly before the vacant throne and in a flash became invisible and disappeared.

The hall was an immense place, but there seemed to be

no one in it beside themselves. Presently, however, they heard a low cough near them, and here and there was the faint rustling of a robe and a slight patter as of footsteps. Then suddenly there rang out the clear tone of a bell and at the sound all was changed.

Gazing around the hall in bewilderment they saw that it was filled with hundreds of men and women, all with beautiful faces and staring blue eyes and all wearing scarlet robes and jeweled crowns upon their heads. In fact, these people seemed exact duplicates of Tubekins and it was difficult to find any mark by which to tell them apart.

"My! what a lot of Kings and Queens!" whispered Betsy to Polychrome, who sat beside her and appeared much interested in the scene but not a bit worried.

"It is certainly a strange sight," was Polychrome's reply; "but I cannot see how there can be more than one King, or Queen, in any one country, for were these all Rulers, no one could tell who was Master."

One of the Kings who stood near and overheard this remark turned to her and said: "One who is Master of himself is always a King, if only to himself. In this favored land all Kings and Queens are equal, and it is our privilege to bow before one supreme Ruler—the Private Citizen."

"Who's he?" inquired Betsy.

As if to answer her, the clear tones of the bell again rang out and instantly there appeared seated in the throne the man who was lord and master of all these royal ones. This fact was evident when with one accord they fell upon their knees and touched their foreheads to the floor.

The Private Citizen was not unlike the others, except that his eyes were black instead of blue and in the centers of the black irises glowed red sparks that seemed like coals of fire. But his features were very beautiful and dignified and his manner composed and stately. Instead of the prevalent scarlet robe, he wore one of white, and the same dragon's head that decorated the others was embroidered upon its bosom.

"What charge lies against these people, Tubekins?" he asked in quiet, even tones.

"They came through the forbidden Tube, O Mighty Citizen," was the reply.

"You see, it was this way," said Betsy. "We were marching to the Nome King, to conquer him and set Shaggy's brother free, when on a sudden—"

"Who are you?" demanded the Private Citizen sternly.

"Me? Oh, I'm Betsy Bobbin, and—"

"Who is the leader of this party?" asked the Citizen.

"Sir, I am Queen Ann of Oogaboo, and—"

"Then keep quiet," said the Citizen. "Who is the leader?"

No one answered for a moment. Then General Bunn stood up.

"Sit down!" commanded the Citizen. "I can see that sixteen of you are merely officers, and of no account."

"But we have an Army," said General Clock, blusteringly, for he didn't like to be told he was of no account.

"Where is your Army?" asked the Citizen.

"It's me," said Tik-Tok, his voice sounding a little rusty. "I'm the on-ly Pri-vate Sol-dier in the par-ty."

Hearing this, the Citizen rose and bowed respectfully to the Clockwork Man.

"Pardon me for not realizing your importance before," said he. "Will you oblige me by taking a seat beside me on my throne?"

Tik-Tok rose and walked over to the throne, all the Kings and Queens making way for him. Then with clanking steps he mounted the platform and sat on the broad seat beside the Citizen.

Ann was greatly provoked at this mark of favor shown to the humble Clockwork Man, but Shaggy seemed much pleased that his old friend's importance had been recognized by the Ruler of this remarkable country. The Citizen now began to question Tik-Tok, who told in his mechanical voice about Shaggy's quest of his lost brother, and how Ozma of Oz had sent the Clockwork Man to assist him, and how they had fallen in with Queen Ann and her people from Oogaboo. Also he told how Betsy and Hank and Polychrome and the Rose Princess had happened to join their party.

"And you intended to conquer Ruggedo, the Metal Monarch and King of the Nomes?" asked the Citizen.

"Yes. That seemed the on-ly thing for us to do," was Tik-Tok's reply. "But he was too cle-ver for us. When we got close to his cav-ern he made our path lead to the Tube, and made the op-en-ing in-vis-i-ble, so that we all fell in-to it be-fore we knew it was there. It was an eas-y way to get rid of us and now Rug-gedo is safe and we are far a-way in a strange land."

The Citizen was silent a moment and seemed to be think-ing. Then he said:

"Most noble Private Soldier, I must inform you that by the Laws of our country anyone who comes through the Forbidden Tube must be tortured for nine days and ten nights and then thrown back into the Tube. But it is wise to disregard Laws when they conflict with justice, and it seems that you and your followers did not disobey our Laws willingly, being forced into the Tube by Ruggedo. Therefore the Nome King is alone to blame, and he alone must be punished."

"That suits me," said Tik-Tok. "But Rug-ge-do is on the o-ther side of the world where he is a-way out of your reach."

The Citizen drew himself up proudly.

"Do you imagine anything in the world or upon it can be out of the reach of the Great Jinjin?" he asked.

"Oh! Are you, then, the Great Jinjin?" inquired Tik-Tok.

"I am."

"Then your name is Ti-ti-ti-Hoo-choo?"

"It is."

Queen Ann gave a scream and began to tremble. Shaggy

was so disturbed that he took out a handkerchief and wiped the perspiration from his brow. Polychrome looked sober and uneasy for the first time, while Files put his arms around the Rose Princess as if to protect her. As for the officers, the name of the great Jinjin set them moaning and weeping at a great rate and every one fell upon his knees before the throne, begging for mercy. Betsy was worried at seeing her companions so disturbed, but did not know what it was all about. Only Tik-Tok was unmoved at the discovery.

"Then," said he, "if you are Ti-ti-ti-Hoo-choo, and think Rug-ge-do is to blame, I am sure that some-thing queer will hap-pen to the King of the Nomes."

"I wonder what 'twill be," said Betsy.

The Private Citizen—otherwise known as Tititi-Hoochoo, the Great Jinjin—looked at the little girl steadily.

"I will presently decide what is to happen to Ruggedo," said he in a hard, stern voice. Then, turning to the throng of Kings and Queens, he continued: "Tik-Tok has spoken truly, for his machinery will not allow him to lie, nor will it allow his thoughts to think falsely. Therefore these people are not our enemies and must be treated with consideration and justice. Take them to your palaces and entertain them as guests until to-morrow, when I command that they be brought again to my Residence. By then I shall have formed my plans."

No sooner had Tititi-Hoochoo spoken than he disappeared from sight. Immediately after, most of the Kings and Queens likewise disappeared. But several of them remained visible and approached the strangers with great respect. One of the lovely Queens said to Betsy:

"I trust you will honor me by being my guest. I am Erma, Queen of Light."

"May Hank come with me?" asked the girl.

"The King of Animals will care for your mule," was the reply. "But do not fear for him, for he will be treated royally. All of your party will be reunited on the morrow."

"I—I'd like to have *some* one with me," said Betsy, pleadingly.

Queen Erma looked around and smiled upon Polychrome.

"Will the Rainbow's Daughter be an agreeable companion?" she asked.

"Oh, yes!" exclaimed the girl.

So Polychrome and Betsy became guests of the Queen of Light, while other beautiful Kings and Queens took charge of the others of the party.

The two girls followed Erma out of the hall and through the gardens of the Residence to a village of pretty dwellings. None of these was so large or imposing as the castle of the Private Citizen, but all were handsome enough to be called palaces—as, in fact, they really were.

Chapter 12

The LOVELY LADY of LIGHT

The palace of the Queen of Light stood on a little eminence and was a mass of crystal windows, surmounted by a vast crystal dome. When they entered the portals Erma was greeted by six lovely maidens, evidently of high degree, who at once aroused Betsy's admiration. Each bore a wand in her hand, tipped with an emblem of light, and their costumes were also emblematic of the lights they represented. Erma introduced them to her guests and each made a graceful and courteous acknowledgment.

First was Sunlight, radiantly beautiful and very fair; the second was Moonlight, a soft, dreamy damsel with nut-brown hair; next came Starlight, equally lovely but inclined to be retiring and shy. These three were dressed in shimmering robes of silvery white. The fourth was Daylight, a brilliant damsel with laughing eyes and frank manners, who wore a variety of colors. Then came Firelight, clothed in a fleecy flame-colored robe that wavered around her shapely form in a very attractive manner. The sixth maiden, Electra, was the most beautiful of all, and Betsy thought from the first that both Sunlight and Daylight regarded Electra with envy and were a little jealous of her.

But all were cordial in their greetings to the strangers and seemed to regard the Queen of Light with much affection, for they fluttered around her in a flashing, radiant group as she led the way to her regal drawing-room.

This apartment was richly and cosily furnished, the upholstery being of many tints, and both Betsy and Polychrome enjoyed resting themselves upon the downy divans after their strenuous adventures of the day.

The Queen sat down to chat with her guests, who noticed that Daylight was the only maiden now seated beside Erma. The others had retired to another part of the room, where they sat modestly with entwined arms and did not intrude themselves at all.

The Queen told the strangers all about this beautiful land, which is one of the chief residences of fairies who minister to the needs of mankind. So many important fairies lived there that, to avoid rivalry, they had elected as their Ruler the only important personage in the country who had no duties to mankind to perform and was, in effect, a Private Citizen. This Ruler, or Jinjin, as was his title, bore the name of Tititi-Hoochoo, and the most singular thing about him was that he had no heart. But instead of this he possessed a high degree of Reason and Justice and while he showed no mercy in his judgments he never punished unjustly or without reason. To wrong-doers Tititi-Hoochoo was as terrible as he was heartless, but those who were innocent of evil had nothing to fear from him.

All the Kings and Queens of this fairyland paid reverence to Jinjin, for as they expected to be obeyed by others they were willing to obey the one in authority over them.

The inhabitants of the Land of Oz had heard many tales of this fearfully just Jinjin, whose punishments were always equal to the faults committed. Polychrome also knew of him, although this was the first time she had ever seen him face to face. But to Betsy the story was all new, and she was greatly interested in Tititi-Hoochoo, whom she no longer feared.

Time sped swiftly during their talk and suddenly Betsy noticed that Moonlight was sitting beside the Queen of Light, instead of Daylight.

"But tell me, please," she pleaded, "why do you all wear a dragon's head embroidered on your gowns?"

Erma's pleasant face became grave as she answered:

"The Dragon, as you must know, was the first living creature ever made; therefore the Dragon is the oldest and wisest of living things. By good fortune the Original Dragon, who still lives, is a resident of this land and supplies us with wisdom whenever we are in need of it. He is old as the world and remembers everything that has happened since the world was created."

"Did he ever have any children?" inquired the girl.

"Yes, many of them. Some wandered into other lands, where men, not understanding them, made war upon them; but many still reside in this country. None, however, is as wise as the Original Dragon, for whom we have great respect. As he was the first resident here, we wear the emblem of the dragon's head to show that we are the favored people who alone have the right to inhabit this fairyland, which in beauty almost equals the Fairyland of Oz, and in power quite surpasses it."

"I understand about the dragon, now," said Polychrome, nodding her lovely head. Betsy did not quite understand, but she was at present interested in observing the changing lights. As Daylight had given way to Moonlight, so now Starlight sat at the right hand of Erma the Queen, and with her coming a spirit of peace and content seemed to fill the room. Polychrome, being herself a fairy, had many questions to ask about the various Kings and Queens who lived in this far-away, secluded place, and before Erma had finished answering them a rosy glow filled the room and Firelight took her place beside the Queen.

Betsy liked Firelight, but to gaze upon her warm and glowing features made the little girl sleepy, and presently she began to nod. Thereupon Erma rose and took Betsy's hand gently in her own.

"Come," said she; "the feast time has arrived and the feast is spread."

"That's nice," exclaimed the small mortal. "Now that I think of it, I'm awful hungry. But p'raps I can't eat your fairy food."

The Queen smiled and led her to a doorway. As she pushed aside a heavy drapery a flood of silvery light greeted them, and Betsy saw before her a splendid banquet hall, with a table spread with snowy linen and crystal and silver. At one side was a broad, throne-like seat for Erma and beside her now sat the brilliant maid Electra. Polychrome was placed on the Queen's right hand and Betsy upon her left. The other five messengers of light now waited upon them, and each person was supplied with just the food she liked best. Polychrome found her dish of dewdrops, all fresh and sparkling, while Betsy was so lavishly served that she decided she had never in her life eaten a dinner half so good.

"I s'pose," she said to the Queen, "that Miss Electra is the youngest of all these girls."

"Why do you suppose that?" inquired Erma, with a smile.

"'Cause electric'ty is the newest light we know of. Didn't Mr. Edison discover it?"

"Perhaps he was the first mortal to discover it," replied the Queen. "But electricity was a part of the world from its creation, and therefore my Electra is as old as Daylight or Moonlight, and equally beneficent to mortals and fairies alike."

Betsy was thoughtful for a time. Then she remarked, as she looked at the six messengers of light:

"We couldn't very well do without any of 'em; could we?"

Erma laughed softly. "*I* couldn't, I'm sure," she replied, "and I think mortals would miss any one of my maidens, as well. Daylight cannot take the place of Sunlight, which gives us strength and energy. Moonlight is of value when Daylight, worn out with her long watch, retires to rest. If the moon in its course is hidden behind the earth's rim, and my sweet Moonlight cannot cheer us, Starlight takes her place, for the skies always lend her power. Without Firelight we should miss much of our warmth and comfort, as well as much cheer when the walls of houses encompass us. But always, when other lights forsake us, our glorious Electra is ready to flood us with bright rays. As Queen of Light, I love all my maidens, for I know them to be faithful and true."

"I love 'em too!" declared Betsy. "But sometimes, when I'm *real* sleepy, I can get along without any light at all."

"Are you sleepy now?" inquired Erma, for the feast had ended.

"A little," admitted the girl.

So Electra showed her to a pretty chamber where there

was a soft, white bed, and waited patiently until Betsy had undressed and put on a shimmery silken nightrobe that lay beside her pillow. Then the light-maid bade her good night and opened the door.

When she closed it after her Betsy was in darkness. In six winks the little girl was fast asleep.

⟶⟶⟶⋅⟨ Chapter 13 ⟩⋅⟶⟶⟶

The JINJIN'S JUST JUDGMENT

ll the adventurers were reunited next morning
when they were brought from various palaces
to the Residence of Tititi-Hoochoo and ushered into the great Hall of State.

As before, no one was visible except our friends and their
escorts until the first bell sounded. Then in a flash the room
was seen to be filled with the beautiful Kings and Queens
of the land. The second bell marked the appearance in the
throne of the mighty Jinjin, whose handsome countenance
was as composed and expressionless as ever.

All bowed low to the Ruler. Their voices softly murmured: "We greet the Private Citizen, mightiest of Rulers, whose word is Law and whose Law is just."

Tititi-Hoochoo bowed in acknowledgment. Then, looking around the brilliant assemblage, and at the little group of adventurers before him, he said:

"An unusual thing has happened. Inhabitants of other lands than ours, who are different from ourselves in many ways, have been thrust upon us through the Forbidden Tube, which one of our people foolishly made years ago and was properly punished for his folly. But these strangers had no desire to come here and were wickedly thrust into the Tube by a cruel King on the other side of the world, named Ruggedo. This King is an immortal, but he is not good. His magic powers hurt mankind more than they benefit them. Because he had unjustly kept the Shaggy Man's brother a prisoner, this little band of honest people, consisting of both mortals and immortals, determined to conquer Ruggedo and to punish him. Fearing they might succeed in this, the Nome King misled them so that they fell into the Tube.

"Now, this same Ruggedo has been warned by me, many times, that if ever he used this Forbidden Tube in any way he would be severely punished. I find, by referring to the Fairy Records, that this King's servant, a nome named Kaliko, begged his master not to do such a wrong act as to drop these people into the Tube and send them tumbling into our country. But Ruggedo defied me and my orders.

"Therefore these strangers are innocent of any wrong. It is only Ruggedo who deserves punishment, and I will punish him." He paused a moment and then continued in the same cold, merciless voice:

"These strangers must return through the Tube to their own side of the world; but I will make their fall more easy and pleasant than it was before. Also I shall send with them an Instrument of Vengeance, who in my name will drive Ruggedo from his underground caverns, take away his magic powers and make him a homeless wanderer on the face of the earth—a place he detests."

There was a little murmur of horror from the Kings and Queens at the severity of this punishment, but no one uttered a protest, for all realized that the sentence was just.

"In selecting my Instrument of Vengeance," went on Tititi-Hoochoo, "I have realized that this will be an unpleasant mission. Therefore no one of us who is blameless should be forced to undertake it. In this wonderful land it is seldom one is guilty of wrong, even in the slightest degree, and on examining the Records I found no King or Queen had erred. Nor had any among their followers or servants done any wrong. But finally I came to the Dragon Family, which we highly respect, and then it was that I discovered the error of Quox.

"Quox, as you well know, is a young dragon who has not yet acquired the wisdom of his race. Because of this lack, he has been disrespectful toward his most ancient ancestor, the Original Dragon, telling him once to mind his own business and again saying that the Ancient One had grown foolish with age. We are aware that dragons are not the same as fairies and cannot be altogether guided by our Laws, yet such disrespect as Quox has shown should not be unnoticed by us. Therefore I have selected Quox as my royal Instrument of Vengeance and he shall go through the Tube with these people and inflict upon Ruggedo the punishment I have decreed."

All had listened quietly to this speech and now the Kings and Queens bowed gravely to signify their approval of the Jinjin's judgment.

Tititi-Hoochoo turned to Tubekins.

"I command you," said he, "to escort these strangers to the Tube and see that they all enter it."

The King of the Tube, who had first discovered our friends and brought them to the Private Citizen, stepped forward and bowed. As he did so, the Jinjin and all the Kings and Queens suddenly disappeared and only Tubekins remained visible.

"All right," said Betsy, with a sigh; "I don't mind going back so *very* much, 'cause the Jinjin promised to make it easy for us."

Indeed, Queen Ann and her officers were the only ones who looked solemn and seemed to fear the return journey. One thing that bothered Ann was her failure to conquer this land of Tititi-Hoochoo. As they followed their guide through the gardens to the mouth of the Tube she said to Shaggy:

"How can I conquer the world, if I go away and leave this rich country unconquered?"

"You can't," he replied. "Don't ask me why, please, for if you don't know I can't inform you."

"Why not?" said Ann; but Shaggy paid no attention to the question.

This end of the Tube had a silver rim and around it was a gold railing to which was attached a sign that read:

IF YOU ARE OUT, STAY THERE.
IF YOU ARE IN, DON'T COME OUT.

On a little silver plate just inside the Tube was engraved the words:

Burrowed and built by
Hiergargo the Magician,
In the Year of the World
1 9 6 2 5 4 7 8
For his own exclusive uses.

"He was some builder, I must say," remarked Betsy, when she had read the inscription; "but if he had known about that star I guess he'd have spent his time playing solitaire."

"Well, what are we waiting for?" inquired Shaggy, who was impatient to start.

"Quox," replied Tubekins. "But I think I hear him coming."

"Is the young dragon invisible?" asked Ann, who had never seen a live dragon and was a little fearful of meeting one.

"No, indeed," replied the King of the Tube. "You'll see him in a minute; but before you part company I'm sure you'll wish he *was* invisible."

"Is he dangerous, then?" questioned Files.

"Not at all. But Quox tires me dreadfully," said Tubekins, "and I prefer his room to his company."

At that instant a scraping sound was heard, drawing nearer and nearer until from between two big bushes appeared a huge dragon, who approached the party, nodded his head and said: "Good morning."

Had Quox been at all bashful I am sure he would have felt uncomfortable at the astonished stare of every eye in the group—except Tubekins, of course, who was not astonished because he had seen Quox so often.

Betsy had thought a "young" dragon must be a small dragon, yet here was one so enormous that the girl decided he must be full grown, if not overgrown. His body was a lovely sky-blue in color and it was thickly set with glittering silver scales, each one as big as a serving-tray. Around his neck was a pink ribbon with a bow just under his left ear, and below the ribbon appeared a chain of pearls to which was attached a golden locket about as large around as the end of a bass drum.

This locket was set with many large and beautiful jewels.

The head and face of Quox were not especially ugly, when you consider that he was a dragon; but his eyes were so large that it took him a long time to wink and his teeth seemed very sharp and terrible when they showed, which they did whenever the beast smiled. Also his nostrils were quite large and wide, and those who stood near him were liable to smell brimstone—especially when he breathed out fire, as it is the nature of dragons to do. To the end of his long tail was attached a big electric light.

Perhaps the most singular thing about the dragon's appearance at this time was the fact that he had a row of seats attached to his back, one seat for each member of the party. These seats were double, with curved backs, so that two could sit in them, and there were twelve of these double seats, all strapped firmly around the dragon's thick body and placed one behind the other, in a row that extended from his shoulders nearly to his tail.

"Aha!" exclaimed Tubekins; "I see that Tititi-Hoochoo has transformed Quox into a carryall."

"I'm glad of that," said Betsy. "I hope, Mr. Dragon, you won't mind our riding on your back."

"Not a bit," replied Quox. "I'm in disgrace just now, you know, and the only way to redeem my good name is to obey the orders of the Jinjin. If he makes me a beast of burden, it is only a part of my punishment, and I must bear it like a dragon. I don't blame you people at all, and I hope you'll enjoy the ride. Hop on, please. All aboard for the other side of the world!"

Silently they took their places. Hank sat in the front seat with Betsy, so that he could rest his front hoofs upon the dragon's head. Behind them were Shaggy and Polychrome, then Files and the Princess, and Queen Ann and Tik-Tok. The officers rode in the rear seats. When all had mounted to their places the dragon looked very like one of those sightseeing wagons so common in big cities—only he had legs instead of wheels.

"All ready?" asked Quox, and when they said they were he crawled to the mouth of the Tube and put his head in.

"Good-bye, and good luck to you!" called Tubekins; but no one thought to reply, because just then the dragon slid his great body into the Tube and the journey to the other side of the world had begun.

At first they went so fast that they could scarcely catch their breaths, but presently Quox slowed up and said with a sort of cackling laugh:

"My scales! but that is some tumble. I think I shall take it easy and fall slower, or I'm likely to get dizzy. Is it very far to the other side of the world?"

"Haven't you ever been through this Tube before?" inquired Shaggy.

"Never. Nor has anyone else in our country; at least, not since I was born."

"How long ago was that?" asked Betsy.

"That I was born? Oh, not very long ago. I'm only a mere child. If I had not been sent on this journey, I would have celebrated my three thousand and fifty-sixth birthday next Thursday. Mother was going to make me a birthday cake with three thousand and fifty-six candles on it; but now, of course, there will be no celebration, for I fear I shall not get home in time for it."

"Three thousand and fifty-six years!" cried Betsy. "Why, I had no idea anything could live that long!"

"My respected Ancestor, whom I would call a stupid old humbug if I had not reformed, is so old that I am a mere baby compared with him," said Quox. "He dates from the beginning of the world, and insists on telling us stories of things that happened fifty thousand years ago, which are of no interest at all to youngsters like me. In fact, Grandpa isn't up to date. He lives altogether in the past, so I can't see any good reason for his being alive to-day. . . . Are you people able to see your way, or shall I turn on more light?"

"Oh, we can see very nicely, thank you; only there's nothing to see but ourselves," answered Betsy.

This was true. The dragon's big eyes were like headlights on an automobile and illuminated the Tube far ahead of them. Also he curled his tail upward so that the electric light on the end of it enabled them to see one another quite clearly. But the Tube itself was only dark metal, smooth as glass but exactly the same from one of its ends to the other. Therefore there was no scenery of interest to beguile the journey.

They were now falling so gently that the trip was proving entirely comfortable, as the Jinjin had promised it would be; but this meant a longer journey and the only way they could make time pass was to engage in conversation. The dragon seemed a willing and persistent talker and he was of so much interest to them that they encouraged him to chatter. His voice was a little gruff but not unpleasant when one became used to it.

"My only fear," said he presently, "is that this constant sliding over the surface of the Tube will dull my claws. You see, this hole isn't straight down, but on a steep slant, and so instead of tumbling freely through the air I must skate along the Tube. Fortunately, there is a file in my tool-kit, and if my claws get dull they can be sharpened again."

"Why do you want sharp claws?" asked Betsy.

"They are my natural weapons, and you must not forget that I have been sent to conquer Ruggedo."

"Oh, you needn't mind about that," remarked Queen Ann, in her most haughty manner; "for when we get to Ruggedo I and my invincible Army can conquer him without your assistance."

"Very good," returned the dragon, cheerfully. "That will save me a lot of bother—if you succeed. But I think I shall file my claws, just the same."

He gave a long sigh, as he said this, and a sheet of flame, several feet in length, shot from his mouth. Betsy shuddered and Hank said "Hee-haw!" while some of the officers screamed in terror. But the dragon did not notice that he had done anything unusual.

"Is there fire inside of you?" asked Shaggy.

"Of course," answered Quox. "What sort of a dragon would I be if my fire went out?"

"What keeps it going?" Betsy inquired.

"I've no idea. I only know it's there," said Quox. "The fire keeps me alive and enables me to move; also to think and speak."

"Ah! You are ver-y much like my-self," said Tik-Tok. "The on-ly dif-fer-ence is that I move by clock-work, while you move by fire."

"I don't see a particle of likeness between us, I must confess," retorted Quox, gruffly. "You are not a live thing; you're a dummy."

"But I can do things, you must ad-mit," said Tik-Tok.

"Yes, when you are wound up," sneered the dragon. "But if you run down, you are helpless."

"What would happen to you, Quox, if you ran out of gasoline?" inquired Shaggy, who did not like this attack upon his friend.

"I don't use gasoline."

"Well, suppose you ran out of fire."

"What's the use of supposing that?" asked Quox. "My great-great-great-grandfather has lived since the world began, and he has never once run out of fire to keep him going. But I will confide to you that as he gets older he shows more smoke and less fire. As for Tik-Tok, he's well enough in his way, but he's merely copper. And the Metal Monarch knows copper through and through. I wouldn't be surprised if Ruggedo melted Tik-Tok in one of his furnaces and made copper pennies of him."

"In that case, I would still keep going," remarked Tik-Tok, calmly.

"Pennies do," said Betsy regretfully.

"This is all nonsense," said the Queen, with irritation. "Tik-Tok is my great Army—all but the officers—and I believe he will be able to conquer Ruggedo with ease. What do you think, Polychrome?"

"You might let him try," answered the Rainbow's Daughter, with her sweet ringing laugh, that sounded like the tinkling of tiny bells. "And if Tik-Tok fails, you have still the big fire-breathing dragon to fall back on."

"Ah!" said the dragon, another sheet of flame gushing from his mouth and nostrils; "it's a wise little girl, this Polychrome. Anyone would know she is a fairy."

Chapter 14

The LONG-EARED HEARER
LEARNS by LISTENING

During this time Ruggedo, the Metal Monarch and King of the Nomes, was trying to amuse himself in his splendid jeweled cavern. It was hard work for Ruggedo to find amusement to-day, for all the nomes were behaving well and there was no one to scold or to punish. The King had thrown his sceptre at Kaliko six times, without hitting him once. Not that Kaliko had done anything wrong. On the contrary, he had obeyed the King in every way but one: he would not stand still, when commanded to do so, and let the heavy sceptre strike him.

We can hardly blame Kaliko for this, and even the cruel Ruggedo forgave him; for he knew very well that if he mashed his Royal Chamberlain he could never find another so intelligent and obedient. Kaliko could make the nomes work when their King could not, for the nomes hated Ruggedo and there were so many thousands of the quaint little underground people that they could easily have rebelled and defied the King had they dared to do so. Sometimes, when Ruggedo abused them worse than usual, they grew sullen and threw down their hammers and picks. Then, however hard the King scolded or whipped them, they would not work until Kaliko came and begged them to. For Kaliko was one of themselves and was as much abused by the King as any nome in the vast series of caverns.

But to-day all the little people were working industriously at their tasks and Ruggedo, having nothing to do, was greatly bored. He sent for the Long-Eared Hearer and asked him to listen carefully and report what was going on in the big world.

"It seems," said the Hearer, after listening for awhile, "that the women in America have clubs."

"Are there spikes in them?" asked Ruggedo, yawning.

"I cannot hear any spikes, your Majesty," was the reply.

"Then their clubs are not as good as my sceptre. What else do you hear?'

"There's a war.

"Bah! there's always a war. What else?"

For a time the Hearer was silent, bending forward and spreading out his big ears to catch the slightest sound. Then suddenly he said:

"Here is an interesting thing, your Majesty. These people are arguing as to who shall conquer the Metal Monarch, seize his treasure and drive him from his dominions."

"What people?" demanded Ruggedo, sitting up straight in his throne.

"The ones you threw down the Hollow Tube."

"Where are they now?"

"In the same Tube, and coming back this way," said the Hearer.

Ruggedo got out of his throne and began to pace up and down the cavern.

"I wonder what can be done to stop them," he mused.

"Well," said the Hearer, "if you could turn the Tube upside down, they would be falling the other way, your Majesty."

Ruggedo glared at him wickedly, for it was impossible to turn the Tube upside down and he believed the Hearer was slyly poking fun at him. Presently he asked:

"How far away are those people now?"

"About nine thousand three hundred and six miles, seventeen furlongs, eight feet and four inches—as nearly as I can judge from the sound of their voices," replied the Hearer.

"Aha! Then it will be some time before they arrive," said Ruggedo, "and when they get here I shall be ready to receive them."

He rushed to his gong and pounded upon it so fiercely that Kaliko came bounding into the cavern with one shoe off and one shoe on, for he was just dressing himself after a swim in the hot bubbling lake of the Underground Kingdom.

"Kaliko, those invaders whom we threw down the Tube are coming back again!" he exclaimed.

"I thought they would," said the Royal Chamberlain, pulling on the other shoe. "Tititi-Hoochoo would not allow them to remain in his kingdom, of course, and so I've been expecting them back for some time. That was a very foolish action of yours, Rug."

"What, to throw them down the Tube?"

"Yes. Tititi-Hoochoo has forbidden us to throw even rubbish into the Tube."

"Pooh! what do I care for the Jinjin?" asked Ruggedo scornfully. "He never leaves his own kingdom, which is on the other side of the world."

"True; but he might send some one through the Tube to punish you," suggested Kaliko.

"I'd like to see him do it! Who could conquer my thousands of nomes?"

"Why, they've been conquered before, if I remember aright," answered Kaliko with a grin. "Once I saw you running from a little girl named Dorothy, and her friends, as if you were really afraid."

"Well, I *was* afraid, that time," admitted the Nome King, with a deep sigh, "for Dorothy had a Yellow Hen that laid eggs!"

The King shuddered as he said "eggs," and Kaliko also

shuddered, and so did the Long-Eared Hearer; for eggs are the only things that the nomes greatly dread. The reason for this is that eggs belong on the earth's surface, where birds and fowl of all sorts live, and there is something about a hen's egg, especially, that fills a nome with horror. If by chance the inside of an egg touches one of these underground people, he withers up and blows away and that is the end of him—unless he manages quickly to speak a magical word which only a few of the nomes know. Therefore Ruggedo and his followers had very good cause to shudder at the mere mention of eggs.

"But Dorothy," said the King, "is not with this band of invaders; nor is the Yellow Hen. As for Tititi-Hoochoo, he has no means of knowing that we are afraid of eggs."

"You mustn't be too sure of that," Kaliko warned him. "Tititi-Hoochoo knows a great many things, being a fairy, and his powers are far superior to any we can boast."

Ruggedo shrugged impatiently and turned to the Hearer.

"Listen," said he, "and tell me if you hear any eggs coming through the Tube."

The Long-Eared one listened and then shook his head. But Kaliko laughed at the King.

"No one can hear an egg, your Majesty," said he. "The only way to discover the truth is to look through the Magic Spyglass."

"That's it!" cried the King. "Why didn't I think of it before? Look at once, Kaliko!"

So Kaliko went to the Spyglass and by uttering a mumbled charm he caused the other end of it to twist around, so that it pointed down the opening of the Tube. Then he put his eye to the glass and was able to gaze along all the turns and windings of the Magic Spyglass and then deep into the Tube, to where our friends were at that time falling.

"Dear me!" he exclaimed. "Here comes a dragon."

"A big one?" asked Ruggedo.

"A monster. He has an electric light on the end of his tail, so I can see him very plainly. And the other people are all riding upon his back."

"How about the eggs?" inquired the King.

Kaliko looked again.

"I can see no eggs at all," said he; "but I imagine that the dragon is as dangerous as eggs. Probably Tititi-Hoochoo has sent him here to punish you for dropping those strangers into the Forbidden Tube. I warned you not to do it, your Majesty."

This news made the Nome King anxious. For a few minutes he paced up and down, stroking his long beard and thinking with all his might. After this he turned to Kaliko and said:

"All the harm a dragon can do is to scratch with his claws and bite with his teeth."

"That is not all, but it's quite enough," returned Kaliko earnestly. "On the other hand, no one can hurt a dragon, because he's the toughest creature alive. One flop of his huge tail could smash a hundred nomes to pancakes, and with teeth and claws he could tear even you or me into small bits, so that it would be almost impossible to put us together again. Once, a few hundred years ago, while wandering through some deserted caverns, I came upon a small piece of a nome lying on the rocky floor. I asked the piece of nome what had happened to it. Fortunately the mouth was a part of this piece—the mouth and the left eye—so it was able to tell me that a fierce dragon was the cause. It had attacked the poor nome and scattered him in every direction, and as there was no friend near to collect his pieces and put him together, they had been separated for a great many years. So you see, your Majesty, it is not in good taste to sneer at a dragon."

The King had listened attentively to Kaliko. Said he:

"It will only be necessary to chain this dragon which Tititi-Hoochoo has sent here, in order to prevent his reaching us with his claws and teeth."

"He also breathes flames," Kaliko reminded him.

"My nomes are not afraid of fire, nor am I," said Ruggedo.

"Well, how about the Army of Oogaboo?"

"Sixteen cowardly officers and Tik-Tok! Why, I could defeat them single-handed; but I won't try to. I'll summon my army of nomes to drive the invaders out of my territory, and if we catch any of them I intend to stick needles into them until they hop with pain."

"I hope you won't hurt any of the girls," said Kaliko.

"I'll hurt 'em all!" roared the angry Metal Monarch. "And

that braying Mule I'll make into hoof-soup, and feed it to my nomes, that it may add to their strength."

"Why not be good to the strangers and release your prisoner, the Shaggy Man's brother?" suggested Kaliko.

"Never!"

"It may save you a lot of annoyance. And you don't want the Ugly One."

"I don't want him; that's true. But I won't allow anybody to order me around. I'm King of the Nomes and I'm the Metal Monarch, and I shall do as I please and what I please and when I please!"

With this speech Ruggedo threw his sceptre at Kaliko's head, aiming it so well that the Royal Chamberlain had to fall flat upon the floor in order to escape it. But the Hearer did not see the sceptre coming and it swept past his head so closely that it broke off the tip of one of his long ears. He gave a dreadful yell that quite startled Ruggedo, and the King was sorry for the accident because those long ears of the Hearer were really valuable to him.

So the Nome King forgot to be angry with Kaliko and ordered his Chamberlain to summon General Guph and the army of nomes and have them properly armed. They were then to march to the mouth of the Tube, where they could seize the travelers as soon as they appeared.

·····◄ Chapter 15 ►·····

The DRAGON DEFIES DANGER

Although the journey through the Tube was longer, this time, than before, it was so much more comfortable that none of our friends minded it at all. They talked together most of the time and as they found the dragon good-natured and fond of the sound of his own voice they soon became well acquainted with him and accepted him as a companion.

"You see," said Shaggy, in his frank way, "Quox is on our side, and therefore the dragon is a good fellow. If he happened to be an enemy, instead of a friend, I am sure I should dislike him very much, for his breath smells of brimstone, he is very conceited and he is so strong and fierce that he would prove a dangerous foe."

"Yes, indeed," returned Quox, who had listened to this speech with pleasure; "I suppose I am about as terrible as any living thing. I am glad you find me conceited, for that proves I know my good qualities. As for my breath smelling of brimstone, I really can't help it, and I once met a man whose breath smelled of onions, which I consider far worse."

"I don't," said Betsy; "I love onions.

"And I love brimstone," declared the dragon, "so don't let us quarrel over one another's peculiarities."

Saying this, he breathed a long breath and shot a flame fifty feet from his mouth. The brimstone made Betsy cough, but she remembered about the onions and said nothing.

They had no idea how far they had gone through the center of the earth, nor when to expect the trip to end. At one time the little girl remarked:

"I wonder when we'll reach the bottom of this hole. And isn't it funny, Shaggy Man, that what is the bottom to us now, was the top when we fell the other way?"

"What puzzles me," said Files, "is that we are able to fall both ways."

"That," announced Tik-Tok, "is be-cause the world is round."

"Exactly," responded Shaggy. "The machinery in your

head is in fine working order, Tik-Tok. You know, Betsy, that there is such a thing as the Attraction of Gravitation, which draws everything toward the center of the earth. That is why we fall out of bed, and why everything clings to the surface of the earth."

"Then why doesn't everyone go on down to the center of the earth?" inquired the little girl.

"I was afraid you were going to ask me that," replied Shaggy in a sad tone. "The reason, my dear, is that the earth is so solid that other solid things can't get through it. But when there's a hole, as there is in this case, we drop right down to the center of the world."

"Why don't we stop there?" asked Betsy.

"Because we go so fast that we acquire speed enough to carry us right up to the other end."

"I don't understand that, and it makes my head ache to try to figure it out," she said after some thought. "One thing draws us to the center and another thing pushes us away from it. But—"

"Don't ask me why, please," interrupted the Shaggy Man. "If you can't understand it, let it go at that."

"Do *you* understand it?" she inquired.

"All the magic isn't in fairyland," he said gravely. "There's lots of magic in all Nature, and you may see it as well in the United States, where you and I once lived, as you can here."

"I never did," she replied.

"Because you were so used to it all that you didn't realize it was magic. Is anything more wonderful than to see a flower grow and blossom, or to get light out of the electricity in the air? The cows that manufacture milk for us must have machinery fully as remarkable as that in Tik-Tok's copper body, and perhaps you've noticed that—"

And then, before Shaggy could finish his speech, the strong light of day suddenly broke upon them, grew brighter, and completely enveloped them. The dragon's claws no longer scraped against the metal Tube, for he shot into the open air a hundred feet or more and sailed so far away from the slanting hole that when he landed it was on the peak of a mountain and just over the entrance to the many underground caverns of the Nome King.

Some of the officers tumbled off their seats when Quox struck the ground, but most of the dragon's passengers only felt a slight jar. All were glad to be on solid earth again and they at once dismounted and began to look about them. Queerly enough, as soon as they had left the dragon, the seats that were strapped to the monster's back disappeared, and this probably happened because there was no further use for them and because Quox looked far more dignified in just his silver scales. Of course he still wore the forty yards of ribbon around his neck, as well as the great locket, but these only made him look "dressed up," as Betsy remarked.

Now the army of nomes had gathered thickly around the

mouth of the Tube, in order to be ready to capture the band of invaders as soon as they popped out. There were, indeed, hundreds of nomes assembled, and they were led by Guph, their most famous General. But they did not expect the dragon to fly so high, and he shot out of the Tube so suddenly that it took them by surprise. When the nomes had rubbed the astonishment out of their eyes and regained their wits, they discovered the dragon quietly seated on the mountainside far above their heads, while the other strangers were standing in a group and calmly looking down upon them.

General Guph was very angry at the escape, which was no one's fault but his own.

"Come down here and be captured!" he shouted, waving his sword at them.

"Come up here and capture us—if you dare!" replied Queen Ann, who was winding up the clockwork of her Private Soldier, so he could fight more briskly.

Guph's first answer was a roar of rage at the defiance; then he turned and issued a command to his nomes. These were all armed with sharp spears and with one accord they raised these spears and threw them straight at their foes, so that they rushed through the air in a perfect cloud of flying weapons.

Some damage might have been done had not the dragon quickly crawled before the others, his body being so big that it shielded every one of them, including Hank. The spears rattled against the silver scales of Quox and then fell harmlessly to the ground. They were magic spears, of course, and all straightway bounded back into the hands of those who had thrown them, but even Guph could see that it was useless to repeat the attack.

It was now Queen Ann's turn to attack, so the Generals yelled "For—ward march!" and the Colonels and Majors and Captains repeated the command and the valiant Army of Oogaboo, which seemed to be composed mainly of Tik-Tok, marched forward in single column toward the nomes, while Betsy and Polychrome cheered and Hank gave a loud "Hee-haw!" and Shaggy shouted "Hooray!" and Queen Ann screamed: "At 'em, Tik-Tok—at 'em!"

The nomes did not await the Clockwork Man's attack but in a twinkling disappeared into the underground caverns. They made a great mistake in being so hasty, for Tik-Tok had not taken a dozen steps before he stubbed his copper toe on a rock and fell flat to the ground, where he cried: "Pick me up! Pick me up! Pick me up!" until Shaggy and Files ran forward and raised him to his feet again.

The dragon chuckled softly to himself as he scratched his left ear with his hind claw, but no one was paying much attention to Quox just then.

It was evident to Ann and her officers that there could be no fighting unless the enemy was present, and in order to find the enemy they must boldly enter the underground Kingdom of the Nomes. So bold a step demanded a council of war.

"Don't you think I'd better drop in on Ruggedo and obey the orders of the Jinjin?" asked Quox.

"By no means!" returned Queen Ann. "We have already put the army of nomes to flight and all that yet remains is to force our way into those caverns, and conquer the Nome King and all his people."

"That seems to me something of a job," said the dragon, closing his eyes sleepily. "But go ahead, if you like, and I'll wait here for you. Don't be in any hurry on my account. To one who lives thousands of years the delay of a few days means nothing at all, and I shall probably sleep until the time comes for me to act."

Ann was provoked at this speech.

"You may as well go back to Tititi-Hoochoo now," she said, "for the Nome King is as good as conquered already."

But Quox shook his head. "No," said he; "I'll wait."

·····—·< Chapter 16 >·—····

The NAUGHTY NOME

Shaggy Man had said nothing during the conversation between Queen Ann and Quox, for the simple reason that he did not consider the matter worth an argument. Safe within his pocket reposed the Love Magnet, which had never failed to win every heart. The nomes, he knew, were not like the heartless Roses and therefore could be won to his side as soon as he exhibited the magic talisman.

Shaggy's chief anxiety had been to reach Ruggedo's Kingdom and now that the entrance lay before him he was confident he would be able to rescue his lost brother. Let Ann and the dragon quarrel as to who should conquer the nomes, if they liked; Shaggy would let them try, and if they failed he had the means of conquest in his own pocket.

But Ann was positive she could not fail, for she thought her Army could do anything. So she called the officers together and told them how to act, and she also instructed Tik-Tok what to do and what to say.

"Please do not shoot your gun except as a last resort," she added, "for I do not wish to be cruel or to shed any blood— unless it is absolutely necessary."

"All right," replied Tik-Tok; "but I do not think Rug-ge-do would bleed if I filled him full of holes and put him in a ci-der press."

Then the officers fell in line, the four Generals abreast and then the four Colonels and the four Majors and the four Captains. They drew their glittering swords and commanded Tik-Tok to march, which he did. Twice he fell down, being tripped by the rough rocks, but when he struck the smooth path he got along better. Into the gloomy mouth of the cavern entrance he stepped without hesitation, and after him proudly pranced the officers and Queen Ann. The others held back a little, waiting to see what would happen.

Of course the Nome King knew they were coming and was prepared to receive them. Just within the rocky passage that led to the jeweled throne-room was a deep pit, which was usually covered. Ruggedo had ordered the cover removed and it now stood open, scarcely visible in the gloom.

The pit was so large around that it nearly filled the passage and there was barely room for one to walk around it by pressing close to the rock walls. This Tik-Tok did, for his copper eyes saw the pit clearly and he avoided it; but the officers marched straight into the hole and tumbled in a heap on the bottom. An instant later Queen Ann also walked into the pit, for she had her chin in the air and was careless where she placed her feet. Then one of the nomes pulled a lever which replaced the cover on the pit and made the officers of Oogaboo and their Queen fast prisoners.

As for Tik-Tok, he kept straight on to the cavern where Ruggedo sat in his throne and there he faced the Nome King and said:

"I here-by con-quer you in the name of Queen Ann So-forth of Oo-ga-boo, whose Ar-my I am, and I de-clare that you are her pris-on-er!"

Ruggedo laughed at him.

"Where is this famous Queen?" he asked.

"She'll be here in a min-ute," said Tik-Tok. "Per-haps she stopped to tie her shoe-string."

"Now, see here, Tik-Tok," began the Nome King, in a stern voice, "I've had enough of this nonsense. Your Queen and her officers are all prisoners, having fallen into my power, so perhaps you'll tell me what you mean to do."

"My or-ders were to con-quer you," replied Tik-Tok, "and my ma-chin-er-y has done the best it knows how to car-ry out those or-ders."

Ruggedo pounded on his gong and Kaliko appeared, followed closely by General Guph.

"Take this copper man into the shops and set him to work hammering gold," commanded the King. "Being run by machinery he ought to be a steady worker. He ought never to have been made, but since he exists I shall hereafter put him to good use."

"If you try to cap-ture me," said Tik-Tok, "I shall fight."

"Don't do that!" exclaimed General Guph, earnestly, "for it will be useless to resist and you might hurt some one."

But Tik-Tok raised his gun and took aim and not knowing what damage the gun might do the nomes were afraid to face it.

While he was thus defying the Nome King and his high officials, Betsy Bobbin rode calmly into the royal cavern, seated upon the back of Hank the mule. The little girl had grown tired of waiting for "something to happen" and so had come to see if Ruggedo had been conquered.

"Nails and nuggets!" roared the King; "how dare you bring that beast here and enter my presence unannounced?"

"There wasn't anybody to announce me," replied Betsy. "I guess your folks were all busy. Are you conquered yet?"

"No!" shouted the King, almost beside himself with rage.

"Then please give me something to eat, for I'm awful hungry," said the girl. "You see, this conquering business is a good deal like waiting for a circus parade; it takes a long time to get around and don't amount to much anyhow."

The nomes were so much astonished at this speech that for a time they could only glare at her silently, not finding words to reply. The King finally recovered the use of his tongue and said:

"Earth-crawler! this insolence to my majesty shall be your death-warrant. You are an ordinary mortal, and to stop a mortal from living is so easy a thing to do that I will not keep you waiting half so long as you did for my conquest."

"I'd rather you wouldn't stop me from living," remarked Betsy, getting off Hank's back and standing beside him. "And it would be a pretty cheap King who killed a visitor while she was hungry. If you'll give me something to eat, I'll talk this killing business over with you afterward; only, I warn you now that I don't approve of it, and never will."

Her coolness and lack of fear impressed the Nome King, although he bore an intense hatred toward all mortals.

"What do you wish to eat?" he asked gruffly.

"Oh, a ham-sandwich would do, or perhaps a couple of hard-boiled eggs—"

"Eggs!" shrieked the three nomes who were present, shuddering till their teeth chattered.

"What's the matter?" asked Betsy wonderingly. "Are eggs as high here as they are at home?"

"Guph," said the King in an agitated voice, turning to his General, "let us destroy this rash mortal at once! Seize her and take her to the Slimy Cave and lock her in."

Guph glanced at Tik-Tok, whose gun was still pointed, but just then Kaliko stole softly behind the copper man and kicked his knee-joints so that they suddenly bent forward and tumbled Tik-Tok to the floor, his gun falling from his grasp.

Then Guph, seeing Tik-Tok helpless, made a grab at Betsy. At the same time Hank's heels shot out and caught the General just where his belt was buckled. He rose into the air swift as a cannon-ball, struck the Nome King fairly and flattened his Majesty against the wall of rock on the opposite side of the cavern. Together they fell to the floor in a dazed and crumpled condition, seeing which Kaliko whispered to Betsy:

"Come with me—quick!—and I will save you."

She looked into Kaliko's face inquiringly and thought he seemed honest and good-natured, so she decided to follow him. He led her and the mule through several passages and into a small cavern very nicely and comfortably furnished.

"This is my own room," said he, "but you are quite welcome to use it. Wait here a minute and I'll get you something to eat."

When Kaliko returned he brought a tray containing some broiled mushrooms, a loaf of mineral bread and some petroleum-butter. The butter Betsy could not eat, but the bread was good and the mushrooms delicious.

"Here's the door key," said Kaliko, "and you'd better lock yourself in."

"Won't you let Polychrome and the Rose Princess come here, too?" she asked.

"I'll see. Where are they?"

"I don't know. I left them outside," said Betsy.

"Well, if you hear three raps on the door, open it," said Kaliko; "but don't let anyone in unless they give the three raps."

"All right," promised Betsy, and when Kaliko left the cosy cavern she closed and locked the door.

In the meantime Ann and her officers, finding themselves prisoners in the pit, had shouted and screamed until they were tired out, but no one had come to their assistance. It was very dark and damp in the pit and they could not climb out because the walls were higher than their heads and the cover was on. The Queen was first angry and then annoyed and then discouraged; but the officers were only afraid. Every one of the poor fellows heartily wished he was back in Oogaboo caring for his orchard, and some were so unhappy that they began to reproach Ann for causing them all this trouble and danger.

Finally the Queen sat down on the bottom of the pit and leaned her back against the wall. By good luck her sharp elbow touched a secret spring in the wall and a big flat rock swung inward. Ann fell over backward, but the next instant she jumped up and cried to the others:

"A passage! A passage! Follow me, my brave men, and we may yet escape."

Then she began to crawl through the passage, which was as dark and dank as the pit, and the officers followed her in single file. They crawled, and they crawled, and they kept on crawling, for the passage was not big enough to allow them to stand upright. It turned this way and twisted that, sometimes like a corkscrew and sometimes zigzag, but seldom ran for long in a straight line.

"It will never end—never!" moaned the officers, who were rubbing all the skin off their knees on the rough rocks.

"It *must* end," retorted Ann courageously, "or it never would have been made. We don't know where it will lead us to, but any place is better than that loathsome pit."

So she crawled on, and the officers crawled on, and while they were crawling through this awful underground passage Polychrome and Shaggy and Files and the Rose Princess, who were standing outside the entrance to Ruggedo's domains, were wondering what had become of them.

A TRAGIC TRANSFORMATION

D on't let us worry," said Shaggy to his companions, "for it may take the Queen some time to conquer the Metal Monarch, as Tik-Tok has to do everything in his slow, mechanical way."

"Do you suppose they are likely to fail?" asked the Rose Princess.

"I do, indeed," replied Shaggy. "This Nome King is really a powerful fellow and has a legion of nomes to assist him, whereas our bold Queen commands a Clockwork Man and a band of faint-hearted officers."

"She ought to have let Quox do the conquering," said Polychrome, dancing lightly upon a point of rock and fluttering her beautiful draperies. "But perhaps the dragon was wise to let her go first, for when she fails to conquer Ruggedo she may become more modest in her ambitions."

"Where is the dragon now?" inquired Ozga.

"Up there on the rocks," replied Files. "Look, my dear; you may see him from here. He said he would take a little nap while we were mixing up with Ruggedo, and he added that after we had gotten into trouble he would wake up and conquer the Nome King in a jiffy, as his master the Jinjin has ordered him to do."

"Quox means well," said Shaggy, "but I do not think we shall need his services; for just as soon as I am satisfied that Queen Ann and her army have failed to conquer Ruggedo, I shall enter the caverns and show the King my Love Magnet. That he cannot resist; therefore the conquest will be made with ease."

This speech of Shaggy Man's was overheard by the Long-Eared Hearer, who was at that moment standing by Ruggedo's side. For when the King and Guph had recovered from Hank's kick and had picked themselves up, their first act was to turn Tik-Tok on his back and put a heavy diamond on top of him, so that he could not get up again. Then they carefully put his gun in a corner of the cavern and the King sent Guph to fetch the Long-Eared Hearer.

The Hearer was still angry at Ruggedo for breaking his ear, but he acknowledged the Nome King to be his master and was ready to obey his commands. Therefore he repeated Shaggy's speech to the King, who at once realized that his Kingdom was in grave danger. For Ruggedo knew of the Love Magnet and its powers and was horrified at the thought that Shaggy might show him the magic talisman and turn all the hatred in his heart into love. Ruggedo was proud of his hatred and abhorred love of any sort.

"Really," said he, "I'd rather be conquered and lose my wealth and my Kingdom than gaze at that awful Love Magnet. What can I do to prevent the Shaggy Man from taking it out of his pocket?"

Kaliko returned to the cavern in time to overhear this question, and being a loyal nome and eager to serve his King, he answered by saying:

"If we can manage to bind the Shaggy Man's arms, tight to his body, he could not get the Love Magnet out of his pocket."

"True!" cried the King in delight at this easy solution of the problem. "Get at once a dozen nomes, with ropes, and place them in the passage where they can seize and bind Shaggy as soon as he enters."

This Kaliko did, and meanwhile the watchers outside the entrance were growing more and more uneasy about their friends.

"I don't worry so much about the Oogaboo people," said Polychrome, who had grown sober with waiting, and perhaps a little nervous, "for they could not be killed, even though

Ruggedo might cause them much suffering and perhaps destroy them utterly. But we should not have allowed Betsy and Hank to go alone into the caverns. The little girl is mortal and possesses no magic powers whatever, so if Ruggedo captures her she will be wholly at his mercy."

"That is indeed true," replied Shaggy. "I wouldn't like to have anything happen to dear little Betsy, so I believe I'll go in right away and put an end to all this worry."

"We may as well go with you," asserted Files, "for by means of the Love Magnet, you can soon bring the Nome King to reason."

So it was decided to wait no longer. Shaggy walked through the entrance first, and after him came the others. They had no thought of danger to themselves, and Shaggy, who was going along with his hands thrust into his pockets, was much surprised when a rope shot out from the darkness and twined around his body, pinning down his arms so securely that he could not even withdraw his hands from the pockets. Then appeared several grinning nomes, who speedily tied knots in the ropes and then led the prisoner along the passage to the cavern. No attention was paid to the others, but Files and the Princess followed on after Shaggy, determined not to desert their friend and hoping that an opportunity might arise to rescue him.

As for Polychrome, as soon as she saw that trouble had overtaken Shaggy she turned and ran lightly back through the passage and out of the entrance. Then she easily leaped from rock to rock until she paused beside the great dragon, who lay fast asleep.

"Wake up, Quox!" she cried. "It is time for you to act."

But Quox did not wake up. He lay as one in a trance, absolutely motionless, with his enormous eyes tight closed. The eyelids had big silver scales on them, like all the rest of his body.

Polychrome might have thought Quox was dead had she not known that dragons do not die easily or had she not observed his huge body swelling as he breathed. She picked up a piece of rock and pounded against his eyelids with it, saying:

"Wake up, Quox—wake up!" But he would not waken.

"Dear me, how unfortunate!" sighed the lovely Rainbow's Daughter. "I wonder what is the best and surest way to waken a dragon. All our friends may be captured and destroyed while this great beast lies asleep."

She walked around Quox two or three times, trying to discover some tender place on his body where a thump or a punch might be felt; but he lay extended along the rocks with his chin flat upon the ground and his legs drawn underneath his body, and all that one could see was his thick sky-blue skin— thicker than that of a rhinoceros—and his silver scales.

Then, despairing at last of wakening the beast, and worried over the fate of her friends, Polychrome again ran down to the entrance and hurried along the passage into the Nome King's cavern.

Here she found Ruggedo lolling in his throne and smoking a long pipe. Beside him stood General Guph and Kaliko, and ranged before the King were the Rose Princess, Files and the Shaggy Man. Tik-Tok still lay upon the floor, weighted down by the big diamond.

Ruggedo was now in a more contented frame of mind. One by one he had met the invaders and easily captured them. The dreaded Love Magnet was indeed in Shaggy's pocket, only a few feet away from the King, but Shaggy was powerless to show it and unless Ruggedo's eyes beheld the talisman it could not affect him. As for Betsy Bobbin and her mule, he believed Kaliko had placed them in the Slimy Cave, while Ann and her officers he thought safely imprisoned in the pit. Ruggedo had no fear of Files or Ozga, but to be on the safe side he had ordered golden handcuffs placed upon their wrists. These did not cause them any great annoyance but prevented them from making an attack, had they been inclined to do so.

The Nome King, thinking himself wholly master of the situation, was laughing and jeering at his prisoners when Poly-chrome, exquisitely beautiful and dancing like a ray of light, entered the cavern.

"Oho!" cried the King; "a Rainbow under ground, eh?" and then he stared hard at Polychrome, and still harder, and then he sat up and pulled the wrinkles out of his robe and arranged his whiskers. "On my word," said he, "you are a very captivating creature; moreover, I perceive you are a fairy."

"I am Polychrome, the Rainbow's Daughter," she said proudly.

"Well," replied Ruggedo, "I like you. The others I hate. I hate everybody—but you! Wouldn't you like to live always in this beautiful cavern, Polychrome? See! the jewels that stud the walls have every tint and color of your Rainbow—and they are not so elusive. I'll have fresh dewdrops gathered for your feasting every day and you shall be Queen of all my nomes and pull Kaliko's nose whenever you like."

"No, thank you," laughed Polychrome. "My home is in the sky, and I'm only on a visit to this solid, sordid earth. But tell me, Ruggedo, why my friends have been wound with cords and bound with chains?"

"They threatened me," answered Ruggedo. "The fools did not know how powerful I am."

"Then, since they are now helpless, why not release them and send them back to the earth's surface?"

"Because I hate 'em and mean to make 'em suffer for their invasion. But I'll make a bargain with you, sweet Polly. Remain here and live with me and I'll set all these people free. You shall be my daughter or my wife or my aunt or grandmother—whichever you like—only stay here to brighten my gloomy kingdom and make me happy!"

Polychrome looked at him wonderingly. Then she turned to Shaggy and asked:

"Are you sure he hasn't seen the Love Magnet?"

"I'm positive," answered Shaggy. "But you seem to be something of a Love Magnet yourself, Polychrome."

She laughed again and said to Ruggedo: "Not even to rescue my friends would I live in your kingdom. Nor could I endure for long the society of such a wicked monster as you."

"You forget," retorted the King, scowling darkly, "that you also are in my power."

"Not so, Ruggedo. The Rainbow's Daughter is beyond the reach of your spite or malice."

"Seize her!" suddenly shouted the King, and General Guph sprang forward to obey. Polychrome stood quite still, yet when Guph attempted to clutch her his hands met in air, and now the Rainbow's Daughter was in another part of the room, as smiling and composed as before.

Several times Guph endeavored to capture her and Ruggedo even came down from his throne to assist his General; but never could they lay hands upon the lovely sky fairy, who flitted here and there with the swiftness of light and constantly defied them with her merry laughter as she evaded their efforts.

So after a time they abandoned the chase and Ruggedo returned to his throne and wiped the perspiration from his face with a finely-woven handkerchief of cloth-of-gold.

"Well," said Polychrome, "what do you intend to do now?"

"I'm going to have some fun, to repay me for all my bother," replied the Nome King. Then he said to Kaliko: "Summon the executioners."

Kaliko at once withdrew and presently returned with a score of nomes, all of whom were nearly as evil looking as their hated master. They bore great golden pincers, and prods of silver, and clamps and chains and various wicked-looking instruments, all made of precious metals and set with diamonds and rubies.

"Now, Pang," said Ruggedo, addressing the leader of the executioners, "fetch the Army of Oogaboo and their Queen from the pit and torture them here in my presence—as well as in the presence of their friends. It will be great sport."

"I hear your Majesty, and I obey your Majesty," answered Pang, and went with his nomes into the passage. In a few minutes he returned and bowed to Ruggedo.

"They're all gone," said he.

"Gone!" exclaimed the Nome King. "Gone where?"

"They left no address, your Majesty; but they are not in the pit."

"Picks and puddles!" roared the King; "who took the cover off?"

"No one," said Pang. "The cover was there, but the prisoners were not under it."

"In that case," snarled the King, trying to control his disappointment, "go to the Slimy Cave and fetch hither the girl and the donkey. And while we are torturing them Kaliko must take a hundred nomes and search for the escaped prisoners— the Queen of Oogaboo and her officers. If he does not find them, I will torture Kaliko."

Kaliko went away looking sad and disturbed, for he knew the King was cruel and unjust enough to carry out this threat. Pang and the executioners also went away, in another direction, but when they came back Betsy Bobbin was not with them, nor was Hank.

"There is no one in the Slimy Cave, your Majesty," reported Pang.

"Jumping jellycakes!" screamed the King. "Another escape? Are you sure you found the right cave?"

"There is but one Slimy Cave, and there is no one in it," returned Pang positively.

Ruggedo was beginning to be alarmed as well as angry. However, these disappointments but made him the more vindictive and he cast an evil look at the other prisoners and said:

"Never mind the girl and the donkey. Here are four, at least, who cannot escape my vengeance. Let me see; I believe I'll change my mind about Tik-Tok. Have the gold crucible heated to a white, seething heat, and then we'll dump the copper man into it and melt him up."

"But, your Majesty," protested Kaliko, who had returned to the room after sending a hundred nomes to search for the Oogaboo people, "you must remember that Tik-Tok is a very curious and interesting machine. It would be a shame to deprive the world of such a clever contrivance."

"Say another word, and you'll go into the furnace with him!" roared the King. "I'm getting tired of you, Kaliko, and the first thing you know I'll turn you into a potato and make Saratoga-chips of you! The next to consider," he added more mildly, "is the Shaggy Man. As he owns the Love Magnet, I think I'll transform him into a dove, and then we can practice shooting at him with Tik-Tok's gun. Now, this is a very interesting ceremony and I beg you all to watch me closely and see that I've nothing up my sleeve."

He came out of his throne to stand before the Shaggy Man, and then he waved his hands, palms downward, in seven semicircles over his victim's head, saying in a low but clear tone of voice the magic wugwa:

"*Adi, edi, idi, odi, udi, oo-i-oo!*
Idu, ido, idi, ide, ida, woo!"

The effect of this well-known sorcery was instantaneous. Instead of the Shaggy Man, a pretty dove lay fluttering upon the floor, its wings confined by tiny cords wound around them. Ruggedo gave an order to Pang, who cut the cords with a pair of scissors. Being freed, the dove quickly flew upward and alighted on the shoulder of the Rose Princess, who stroked it tenderly.

"Very good! Very good!" cried Ruggedo, rubbing his hands gleefully together. "One enemy is out of my way, and now for the others."

(Perhaps my readers should be warned not to attempt the

above transformation; for, although the exact magical formula
has been described, it is unlawful in all civilized countries for
anyone to transform a person into a dove by muttering the
words Ruggedo used. There were no Laws to prevent the Nome
King from performing this transformation, but if it should be
attempted in any other country, and the magic worked, the
magician would be severely punished.)

When Polychrome saw Shaggy Man transformed into a
dove and realized that Ruggedo was about do something as
dreadful to the Princess and Files, and that Tik-Tok would
soon be melted in a crucible, she turned and ran from the cavern, through the passage and back to the place where Quox
lay asleep.

----◄ Chapter 18 ►----

A CLEVER CONQUEST

The great dragon still had his eyes closed and was even snoring in a manner that resembled distant thunder; but Polychrome was now desperate, because any further delay meant the destruction of her friends. She seized the pearl necklace, to which was attached the great locket, and jerked it with all her strength.

The result was encouraging. Quox stopped snoring and his eyelids flickered. So Polychrome jerked again—and again— till slowly the great lids raised and the dragon looked at her steadily. Said he, in a sleepy tone:

"What's the matter, little Rainbow?"

"Come quick!" exclaimed Polychrome. "Ruggedo has

captured all our friends and is about to destroy them."

"Well, well," said Quox, "I suspected that would happen. Step a little out of my path, my dear, and I'll make a rush for the Nome King's cavern."

She fell back a few steps and Quox raised himself on his stout legs, whisked his long tail and in an instant had slid down the rocks and made a dive through the entrance.

Along the passage he swept, nearly filling it with his immense body, and now he poked his head into the jeweled cavern of Ruggedo.

But the King had long since made arrangements to capture the dragon, whenever he might appear. No sooner did Quox stick his head into the room than a thick chain fell from above and encircled his neck. Then the ends of the chain were drawn tight—for in an adjoining cavern a thousand nomes were pulling on them—and so the dragon could advance no further toward the King. He could not use his teeth or his claws and as his body was still in the passage he had not even room to strike his foes with his terrible tail.

Ruggedo was delighted with the success of his stratagem. He had just transformed the Rose Princess into a fiddle and was about to transform Files into a fiddle bow, when the dragon appeared to interrupt him. So he called out:

"Welcome, my dear Quox, to my royal entertainment. Since you are here, you shall witness some very neat magic, and after I have finished with Files and Tik-Tok I mean to transform you into a tiny lizard—one of the chameleon sort—and you shall live in my cavern and amuse me."

"Pardon me for contradicting your Majesty," returned Quox in a quiet voice, "but I don't believe you'll perform any more magic."

"Eh? Why not?" asked the King in surprise.

"There's a reason," said Quox. "Do you see this ribbon around my neck?"

"Yes; and I'm astonished that a dignified dragon should wear such a silly thing."

"Do you see it plainly?" persisted the dragon, with a little chuckle of amusement.

"I do," declared Ruggedo.

"Then you no longer possess any magical powers, and are as helpless as a clam," asserted Quox. "My great master, Tititi-Hoochoo, the Jinjin, enchanted this ribbon in such a way that whenever your Majesty looked upon it all knowledge of magic would desert you instantly, nor will any magical formula you can remember ever perform your bidding."

"Pooh! I don't believe a word of it!" cried Ruggedo, half frightened, nevertheless. Then he turned toward Files and tried to transform him into a fiddle bow. But he could not remember the right words or the right pass of the hands and after several trials he finally gave up the attempt.

By this time the Nome King was so alarmed that he was secretly shaking in his shoes.

"I told you not to anger Tititi-Hoochoo," grumbled Kaliko, "and now you see the result of your disobedience."

Ruggedo promptly threw his sceptre at his Royal Chamberlain, who dodged it with his usual cleverness, and then he said with an attempt to swagger:

"Never mind; I don't need magic to enable me to destroy these invaders; fire and the sword will do the business and I am still King of the Nomes and lord and master of my Underground Kingdom!"

"Again I beg to differ with your Majesty," said Quox. "The Great Jinjin commands you to depart instantly from this Kingdom and seek the earth's surface, where you will wander for all time to come, without a home or country, without a friend or follower, and without any more riches than you can carry with you in your pockets. The Great Jinjin is so generous that he will allow you to fill your pockets with jewels or gold, but you must take nothing more."

Ruggedo now stared at the dragon in amazement.

"Does Tititi-Hoochoo condemn me to such a fate?" he asked in a hoarse voice.

"He does," said Quox.

"And just for throwing a few strangers down the Forbidden Tube?"

"Just for that," repeated Quox in a stern, gruff voice.

"Well, I won't do it. And your crazy old Jinjin can't make me do it, either!" declared Ruggedo. "I intend to remain here,

King of the Nomes, until the end of the world, and I defy your Tititi-Hoochoo and all his fairies—as well as his clumsy messenger, whom I have been obliged to chain up!"

The dragon smiled again, but it was not the sort of smile that made Ruggedo feel very happy. Instead, there was something so cold and merciless in the dragon's expression that the condemned Nome King trembled and was sick at heart.

There was little comfort for Ruggedo in the fact that the dragon was now chained, although he had boasted of it. He glared at the immense head of Quox as if fascinated and there was fear in the old King's eyes as he watched his enemy's movements.

For the dragon was now moving; not abruptly, but as if he had something to do and was about to do it. Very deliberately he raised one claw, touched the catch of the great jeweled locket that was suspended around his neck, and at once it opened wide.

Nothing much happened at first; half a dozen hen's eggs rolled out upon the floor and then the locket closed with a sharp click. But the effect upon the nomes of this simple thing was astounding. General Guph, Kaliko, Pang and his band of executioners were all standing close to the door that led to the vast series of underground caverns which constituted the dominions of the nomes, and as soon as they saw the eggs they raised a chorus of frantic screams and rushed through the door, slamming it in Ruggedo's face and placing a heavy bronze bar across it.

Ruggedo, dancing with terror and uttering loud cries, now leaped upon the seat of his throne to escape the eggs, which had rolled steadily toward him. Perhaps these eggs, sent by the wise and crafty Tititi-Hoochoo, were in some way enchanted, for they all rolled directly after Ruggedo and when they reached the throne where he had taken refuge they began rolling up the legs to the seat.

This was too much for the King to bear. His horror of eggs was real and absolute and he made a leap from the throne to the center of the room and then ran to a far corner.

The eggs followed, rolling slowly but steadily in his direction. Ruggedo threw his sceptre at them, and then his ruby crown, and then he drew off his heavy golden sandals and hurled these at the advancing eggs. But the eggs dodged every missile and continued to draw nearer. The King stood trembling, his eyes staring in terror, until they were but half a yard distant; then with an agile leap he jumped clear over them and made a rush for the passage that led to the outer entrance.

Of course the dragon was in his way, being chained in the passage with his head in the cavern, but when he saw the King making toward him he crouched as low as he could and dropped his chin to the floor, leaving a small space between his body and the roof of the passage.

Ruggedo did not hesitate an instant. Impelled by fear, he leaped to the dragon's nose and then scrambled to his back, where he succeeded in squeezing himself through the opening. After the head was passed there was more room and he slid along the dragon's scales to his tail and then ran as fast as his legs would carry him to the entrance. Not pausing here, so great was his fright, the King dashed on down the mountain path, but before he had gone very far he stumbled and fell.

When he picked himself up he observed that no one was following him, and while he recovered his breath he happened to think of the decree of the Jinjin—that he should be driven from his Kingdom and made a wanderer on the face of the earth. Well, here he was, driven from his cavern in truth; driven by those dreadful eggs; but he would go back and defy them; he would not submit to losing his precious Kingdom and his tyrannical powers, all because Tititi-Hoochoo had said he must.

So, although still afraid, Ruggedo nerved himself to creep back along the path to the entrance, and when he arrived there he saw the six eggs lying in a row just before the arched opening.

At first he paused a safe distance away to consider the case, for the eggs were now motionless. While he was wondering what could be done, he remembered there was a magical charm which would destroy eggs and render them harmless to nomes. There were nine passes to be made and six verses of incantation to be recited; but Ruggedo knew them all. Now that he had ample time to be exact, he carefully went through the entire ceremony.

L. Frank Baum

But nothing happened. The eggs did not disappear, as he had expected; so he repeated the charm a second time. When that also failed, he remembered, with a moan of despair, that his magic power had been taken away from him and in the future he could do no more than any common mortal.

And there were the eggs, forever barring him from the Kingdom which he had ruled so long with absolute sway! He threw rocks at them, but could not hit a single egg. He raved and scolded and tore his hair and beard, and danced in helpless passion, but that did nothing to avert the just judgment of the Jinjin, which Ruggedo's own evil deeds had brought upon him.

From this time on he was an outcast—a wanderer upon the face of the earth—and he had even forgotten to fill his pockets with gold and jewels before he fled from his former Kingdom!

····◄ Chapter 19 ►····

KING KALIKO

After the King had made good his escape Files said to the dragon, in a sad voice:

"Alas! why did you not come before? Because you were sleeping instead of conquering, the lovely Rose Princess has become a fiddle without a bow, while poor Shaggy sits there a cooing dove!"

"Don't worry," replied Quox. "Tititi-Hoochoo knows his business, and I have my orders from the Great Jinjin himself. Bring the fiddle here and touch it lightly to my pink ribbon."

Files obeyed and at the moment of contact with the ribbon the Nome King's charm was broken and the Rose Princess herself stood before them as sweet and smiling as ever.

The dove, perched on the back of the throne, had seen and heard all this, so without being told what to do it flew straight to the dragon and alighted on the ribbon. Next instant Shaggy was himself again and Quox said to him grumblingly:

"Please get off my left toe, Shaggy Man, and be more particular where you step."

"I beg your pardon!" replied Shaggy, very glad to resume his natural form. Then he ran to lift the heavy diamond off Tik-Tok's chest and to assist the Clockwork Man to his feet.

"Ma-ny thanks!" said Tik-Tok. "Where is the wicked King who want-ed to melt me in a cru-ci-ble?"

"He has gone, and gone for good," answered Polychrome, who had managed to squeeze into the room beside the dragon and had witnessed the occurrences with much interest. "But I wonder where Betsy Bobbin and Hank can be, and if any harm has befallen them."

"We must search the cavern until we find them," declared Shaggy; but when he went to the door leading to the other caverns he found it shut and barred.

"I've a pretty strong push in my forehead," said Quox, "and I believe I can break down that door, even though it's made of solid gold."

"But you are a prisoner, and the chains that hold you are fastened in some other room, so that we cannot release you," Files said anxiously.

"Oh, never mind that," returned the dragon. "I have

remained a prisoner only because I wished to be one," and with this he stepped forward and burst the stout chains as easily as if they had been threads.

But when he tried to push in the heavy metal door, even his mighty strength failed, and after several attempts he gave it up and squatted himself in a corner to think of a better way.

"I'll o-pen the door," asserted Tik-Tok, and going to the King's big gong he pounded upon it until the noise was almost deafening.

Kaliko, in the next cavern, was wondering what had happened to Ruggedo and if he had escaped the eggs and outwitted the dragon. But when he heard the sound of the gong, which had so often called him into the King's presence, he decided that Ruggedo had been victorious; so he took away the bar, threw open the door and entered the royal cavern.

Great was his astonishment to find the King gone and the enchantments removed from the Princess and Shaggy. But the eggs were also gone and so Kaliko advanced to the dragon, whom he knew to be Tititi-Hoochoo's messenger, and bowed humbly before the beast.

"What is your will?" he inquired.

"Where is Betsy?" demanded the dragon.

"Safe in my own private room," said Kaliko.

"Go and get her!" commanded Quox.

So Kaliko went to Betsy's room and gave three raps upon

the door. The little girl had been asleep, but she heard the raps and opened the door.

"You may come out now," said Kaliko. "The King has fled in disgrace and your friends are asking for you."

So Betsy and Hank returned with the Royal Chamberlain to the throne cavern, where she was received with great joy by her friends. They told her what had happened to Ruggedo and she told them how kind Kaliko had been to her. Quox did not have much to say until the conversation was ended, but then he turned to Kaliko and asked:

"Do you suppose you could rule your nomes better than Ruggedo has done?"

"Me?" stammered the Chamberlain, greatly surprised by the question. "Well, I couldn't be a worse King, I'm sure."

"Would the nomes obey you?" inquired the dragon.

"Of course," said Kaliko. "They like me better than ever they did Ruggedo."

"Then hereafter you shall be the Metal Monarch, King of the Nomes, and Tititi-Hoochoo expects you to rule your Kingdom wisely and well," said Quox.

"Hooray!" cried Betsy; "I'm glad of that. King Kaliko, I salute your Majesty and wish you joy in your gloomy old Kingdom!"

"We all wish him joy," said Polychrome; and then the others made haste to congratulate the new King.

"Will you release my dear brother?" asked Shaggy.

"The Ugly One? Very willingly," replied Kaliko. "I begged Ruggedo long ago to send him away, but he would not do so. I also offered to help your brother to escape, but he would not go."

"He's so conscientious!" said Shaggy, highly pleased. "All of our family have noble natures. But is my dear brother well?" he added anxiously.

"He eats and sleeps very steadily," replied the new King.

"I hope he doesn't work too hard," said Shaggy.

"He doesn't work at all. In fact, there is nothing he can do in these dominions as well as our nomes, whose numbers are so great that it worries us to keep them all busy. So your brother has only to amuse himself."

"Why, it's more like visiting, than being a prisoner," asserted Betsy.

"Not exactly," returned Kaliko. "A prisoner cannot go where or when he pleases, and is not his own master."

"Where is my brother now?" inquired Shaggy.

"In the Metal Forest."

"Where is that?"

"The Metal Forest is in the Great Domed Cavern, the largest in all our dominions," replied Kaliko. "It is almost like being out of doors, it is so big, and Ruggedo made the wonderful forest to amuse himself, as well as to tire out his hard-working nomes. All the trees are gold and silver and the ground is strewn with precious stones, so it is a sort of treasury."

"Let us go there at once and rescue my dear brother," pleaded Shaggy earnestly.

Kaliko hesitated.

"I don't believe I can find the way," said he. "Ruggedo made three secret passages to the Metal Forest, but he changes the location of these passages every week, so that no one can get to the Metal Forest without his permission. However, if we look sharp, we may be able to discover one of these secret ways."

"That reminds me to ask what has become of Queen Ann and the Officers of Oogaboo," said Files.

"I'm sure I can't say," replied Kaliko.

"Do you suppose Ruggedo destroyed them?"

"Oh, no; I'm quite sure he didn't. They fell into the big pit in the passage, and we put the cover on to keep them there; but when the executioners went to look for them they had all disappeared from the pit and we could find no trace of them."

"That's funny," remarked Betsy thoughtfully. "I don't believe Ann knew any magic, or she'd have worked it before. But to disappear like that *seems* like magic; now, doesn't it?"

They agreed that it did, but no one could explain the mystery.

"However," said Shaggy, "they are gone, that is certain, so we cannot help them or be helped by them. And the important thing just now is to rescue my dear brother from captivity."

"Why do they call him the Ugly One?" asked Betsy.

"I do not know," confessed Shaggy. "I can not remember his looks very well, it is so long since I have seen him; but all of our family are noted for their handsome faces."

Betsy laughed and Shaggy seemed rather hurt; but Polychrome relieved his embarrassment by saying softly: "One can be ugly in looks, but lovely in disposition."

"Our first task," said Shaggy, a little comforted by this remark, "is to find one of those secret passages to the Metal Forest."

"True," agreed Kaliko. "So I think I will assemble the chief nomes of my kingdom in this throne room and tell them that I am their new King. Then I can ask them to assist us in searching for the secret passages.

"That's a good idea," said the dragon, who seemed to be getting sleepy again.

Kaliko went to the big gong and pounded on it just as Ruggedo used to do; but no one answered the summons.

"Of course not," said he, jumping up from the throne, where he had seated himself. "That is my call, and I am still the Royal Chamberlain, and will be until I appoint another in my place."

So he ran out of the room and found Guph and told him to answer the summons of the King's gong. Having returned to the royal cavern, Kaliko first pounded the gong and then sat in the throne, wearing Ruggedo's discarded ruby crown and holding in his hand the sceptre which Ruggedo had so often thrown at his head.

When Guph entered he was amazed.

"Better get out of that throne before old Ruggedo comes back," he said warningly.

"He isn't coming back, and I am now the King of the Nomes, in his stead," announced Kaliko.

"All of which is quite true," asserted the dragon, and all of those who stood around the throne bowed respectfully to the new King.

Seeing this, Guph also bowed, for he was glad to be rid of such a hard master as Ruggedo. Then Kaliko, in quite a kingly way, informed Guph that he was appointed the Royal Chamberlain, and promised not to throw the sceptre at his head unless he deserved it.

All this being pleasantly arranged, the new Chamberlain went away to tell the news to all the nomes of the underground Kingdom, every one of whom would be delighted with the change in Kings.

..——·◁ Chapter 20 ▷···——··

QUOX QUIETLY QUITS

When the chief nomes assembled before their new King they joyfully saluted him and promised to obey his commands. But, when Kaliko questioned them, none knew the way to the Metal Forest, although all had assisted in its making. So the King instructed them to search carefully for one of the passages and to bring him the news as soon as they had found it.

Meantime Quox had managed to back out of the rocky corridor and so regain the open air and his old station on the mountain-side, and there he lay upon the rocks, sound asleep, until the next day. The others of the party were all given as good rooms as the caverns of the nomes afforded, for King Kaliko felt that he was indebted to them for his promotion and was anxious to be as hospitable as he could.

Much wonderment had been caused by the absolute disappearance of the sixteen officers of Oogaboo and their Queen. Not a nome had seen them, nor were they discovered during the search for the passages leading to the Metal Forest. Perhaps no one was unhappy over their loss, but all were curious to know what had become of them.

On the next day, when our friends went to visit the dragon, Quox said to them: "I must now bid you good-bye, for my mission here is finished and I must depart for the other side of the world, where I belong."

"Will you go through the Tube again?" asked Betsy.

"To be sure. But it will be a lonely trip this time, with no one to talk to, and I cannot invite any of you to go with me. Therefore, as soon as I slide into the hole I shall go to sleep, and when I pop out at the other end I will wake up at home."

They thanked the dragon for befriending them and wished him a pleasant journey. Also they sent their thanks to the great Jinjin, whose just condemnation of Ruggedo had served their interests so well. Then Quox yawned and stretched himself and ambled over to the Tube, into which he slid headforemost and disappeared.

They really felt as if they had lost a friend, for the dragon had been both kind and sociable during their brief acquaintance with him; but they knew it was his duty to return to his own country. So they went back to the caverns to renew the search for the hidden passages that led to the forest, but for three days all efforts to find them proved in vain.

It was Polychrome's custom to go every day to the mountain and watch for her father, the Rainbow, for she was growing tired with wandering upon the earth and longed to rejoin her sisters in their sky palaces. And on the third day, while she sat motionless upon a point of rock, whom should she see slyly creeping up the mountain but Ruggedo!

The former King looked very forlorn. His clothes were soiled and torn and he had no sandals upon his feet or hat upon his head. Having left his crown and sceptre behind when he fled, the old nome no longer seemed kingly, but more like a beggerman.

Several times had Ruggedo crept up to the mouth of the caverns, only to find the six eggs still on guard. He knew quite well that he must accept his fate and become a homeless wanderer, but his chief regret now was that he had neglected to fill his pockets with gold and jewels. He was aware that a wanderer with wealth at his command would fare much better than one who was a pauper, so he still loitered around the caverns wherein he knew so much treasure was stored, hoping for a chance to fill his pockets.

That was how he came to recollect the Metal Forest.

"Aha!" said he to himself, "I alone know the way to that

Forest, and once there I can fill my pockets with the finest jewels in all the world."

He glanced at his pockets and was grieved to find them so small. Perhaps they might be enlarged, so that they would hold more. He knew of a poor woman who lived in a cottage at the foot of the mountain, so he went to her and begged her to sew pockets all over his robe, paying her with the gift of a diamond ring which he had worn upon his finger. The woman was delighted to possess so valuable a ring and she sewed as many pockets on Ruggedo's robe as she possibly could.

Then he returned up the mountain and, after gazing cautiously around to make sure he was not observed, he touched a spring in a rock and it swung slowly backward, disclosing a broad passageway. This he entered, swinging the rock in place behind him.

However, Ruggedo had failed to look as carefully as he might have done, for Polychrome was seated only a little distance off and her clear eyes marked exactly the manner in which Ruggedo had released the hidden spring. So she rose and hurried into the cavern, where she told Kaliko and her friends of her discovery.

"I've no doubt that that is a way to the Metal Forest," exclaimed Shaggy. "Come, let us follow Ruggedo at once and rescue my poor brother!"

They agreed to this and King Kaliko called together a band of nomes to assist them by carrying torches to light their way.

"The Metal Forest has a brilliant light of its own," said he, "but the passage across the valley is likely to be dark."

Polychrome easily found the rock and touched the spring, so in less than an hour after Ruggedo had entered they were all in the passage and following swiftly after the former King.

"He means to rob the Forest, I'm sure," said Kaliko; "but he will find he is no longer of any account in this Kingdom and I will have my nomes throw him out."

"Then please throw him as hard as you can," said Betsy, "for he deserves it. I don't mind an honest, out-an'-out enemy, who fights square; but changing girls into fiddles and ordering 'em put into Slimy Caves is mean and tricky, and Ruggedo doesn't deserve any sympathy. But you'll have to let him take as much treasure as he can get in his pockets, Kaliko."

"Yes, the Jinjin said so; but we won't miss it much. There is more treasure in the Metal Forest than a million nomes could carry in their pockets."

It was not difficult to walk through this passage, especially when the torches lighted the way, so they made good progress. But it proved to be a long distance and Betsy had tired herself with walking and was seated upon the back of the mule when the passage made a sharp turn and a wonderful and glorious light burst upon them. The next moment they were all standing upon the edge of the marvelous Metal Forest.

It lay under another mountain and occupied a great domed cavern, the roof of which was higher than a church steeple. In this space the industrious nomes had built, during many years of labor, the most beautiful forest in the world. The trees—trunks, branches and leaves—were all of solid gold, while the bushes and underbrush were formed of filigree silver, virgin pure. The trees towered as high as natural live oaks do and were of exquisite workmanship.

On the ground were thickly strewn precious gems of every hue and size, while here and there among the trees were paths pebbled with cut diamonds of the clearest water. Taken all together, more treasure was gathered in this Metal Forest than is contained in all the rest of the world—if we except the Land of Oz, where perhaps its value is equalled in the famous Emerald City.

Our friends were so amazed at the sight that for a while they stood gazing in silent wonder. Then Shaggy exclaimed.

"My brother! My dear lost brother! Is he indeed a prisoner in this place?"

"Yes," replied Kaliko. "The Ugly One has been here for two or three years, to my positive knowledge."

"But what could he find to eat?" inquired Betsy. "It's an awfully swell place to live in, but one can't breakfast on rubies and di'monds, or even gold."

"One doesn't need to, my dear," Kaliko assured her. "The Metal Forest does not fill all of this great cavern, by any means. Beyond these gold and silver trees are other trees of the real sort, which bear foods very nice to eat. Let us walk in that direction, for I am quite sure we will find Shaggy's brother in that part of the cavern, rather than in this."

So they began to tramp over the diamond-pebbled paths, and at every step they were more and more bewildered by the wondrous beauty of the golden trees with their glittering foliage.

Suddenly they heard a scream. Jewels scattered in every direction as some one hidden among the bushes scampered away before them. Then a loud voice cried: "Halt!" and there was the sound of a struggle.

Chapter 21

A BASHFUL BROTHER

With fast beating hearts they all rushed forward and, beyond a group of stately metal trees, came full upon a most astonishing scene.

There was Ruggedo in the hands of the officers of Oogaboo, a dozen of whom were clinging to the old nome and holding him fast in spite of his efforts to escape. There also was Queen Ann, looking grimly upon the scene of strife; but when she observed her former companions approaching she turned away in a shamefaced manner.

For Ann and her officers were indeed a sight to behold. Her Majesty's clothing, once so rich and gorgeous, was now worn and torn into shreds by her long crawl through the tunnel, which, by the way, had led her directly into the Metal Forest. It was, indeed, one of the three secret passages, and by far the most difficult of the three. Ann had not only torn her pretty skirt and jacket, but her crown had become bent and battered and even her shoes were so cut and slashed that they were ready to fall from her feet.

The officers had fared somewhat worse than their leader, for holes were worn in the knees of their trousers, while sharp points of rock in the roof and sides of the tunnel had made rags of every inch of their once brilliant uniforms. A more tattered and woeful army never came out of a battle, than these harmless victims of the rocky passage. But it had seemed their only means of escape from the cruel Nome King; so they had crawled on, regardless of their sufferings.

When they reached the Metal Forest their eyes beheld more plunder than they had ever dreamed of; yet they were prisoners in this huge dome and could not escape with the riches heaped about them. Perhaps a more unhappy and homesick lot of "conquerors" never existed than this band from Oogaboo.

After several days of wandering in their marvelous prison they were frightened by the discovery that Ruggedo had come among them. Rendered desperate by their sad condition, the officers exhibited courage for the first time since they left home and, ignorant of the fact that Ruggedo was no longer

King of the nomes, they threw themselves upon him and had just succeeded in capturing him when their fellow adventurers reached the spot.

"Goodness gracious!" cried Betsy. "What has happened to you all?"

Ann came forward to greet them, sorrowful and indignant.

"We were obliged to escape from the pit through a small tunnel, which was lined with sharp and jagged rocks," said she, "and not only was our clothing torn to rags but our flesh is so bruised and sore that we are stiff and lame in every joint. To add to our troubles we find we are still prisoners; but now that we have succeeded in capturing the wicked Metal Monarch we shall force him to grant us our liberty."

"Ruggedo is no longer Metal Monarch, or King of the nomes," Files informed her. "He has been deposed and cast out of his kingdom by Quox; but here is the new King, whose name is Kaliko, and I am pleased to assure your Majesty that he is our friend."

"Glad to meet your Majesty, I'm sure," said Kaliko, bowing as courteously as if the Queen still wore splendid raiment.

The officers, having heard this explanation, now set Ruggedo free; but, as he had no place to go, he stood by and faced his former servant, who was now King in his place, in a humble and pleading manner.

"What are you doing here?" asked Kaliko sternly.

"Why, I was promised as much treasure as I could carry in

my pockets," replied Ruggedo; "so I came here to get it, not wishing to disturb your Majesty."

"You were commanded to leave the country of the nomes forever!" declared Kaliko.

"I know; and I'll go as soon as I have filled my pockets," said Ruggedo, meekly.

"Then fill them, and be gone," returned the new King.

Ruggedo obeyed. Stooping down, he began gathering up jewels by the handful and stuffing them into his many pockets. They were heavy things, these diamonds and rubies and emeralds and amethysts and the like, so before long Ruggedo was staggering with the weight he bore, while the pockets were not yet filled. When he could no longer stoop over without falling, Betsy and Polychrome and the Rose Princess came to his assistance, picking up the finest gems and tucking them into his pockets.

At last these were all filled and Ruggedo presented a comical sight, for surely no man ever before had so many pockets, or any at all filled with such a choice collection of precious stones. He neglected to thank the young ladies for their kindness, but gave them a surly nod of farewell and staggered down the path by the way he had come. They let him depart in silence, for with all he had taken, the masses of jewels upon the ground seemed scarcely to have been disturbed, so numerous were they. Also they hoped they had seen the last of the degraded King.

"I'm awful glad he's gone," said Betsy, sighing deeply. "If

he doesn't get reckless and spend his wealth foolishly, he's got enough to start a bank when he gets to Oklahoma."

"But my brother—my dear brother! Where is he?" inquired Shaggy anxiously. "Have you seen him, Queen Ann?"

"What does your brother look like?" asked the Queen.

Shaggy hesitated to reply, but Betsy said: "He's called the Ugly One. Perhaps you'll know him by that."

"The only person we have seen in this cavern," said Ann, "has run away from us whenever we approached him. He hides over yonder, among the trees that are not gold, and we have never been able to catch sight of his face. So I can not tell whether he is ugly or not."

"That must be my dear brother!" exclaimed Shaggy.

"Yes, it must be," assented Kaliko. "No one else inhabits this splendid dome, so there can be no mistake."

"But why does he hide among those green trees, instead of enjoying all these glittery golden ones?" asked Betsy.

"Because he finds food among the natural trees," replied Kaliko, "and I remember that he has built a little house there, to sleep in. As for these glittery golden trees, I will admit they are very pretty at first sight. One cannot fail to admire them, as well as the rich jewels scattered beneath them; but if one has to look at them always, they become pretty tame."

"I believe that is true," declared Shaggy. "My dear brother is very wise to prefer real trees to the imitation ones. But come; let us go there and find him."

Shaggy started for the green grove at once, and the others followed him, being curious to witness the final rescue of his long-sought, long-lost brother.

Not far from the edge of the grove they came upon a small hut, cleverly made of twigs and golden branches woven together. As they approached the place they caught a glimpse of a form that darted into the hut and slammed the door tight shut after him.

Shaggy Man ran to the door and cried aloud:

"Brother! Brother!"

"Who calls," demanded a sad, hollow voice from within.

"It is Shaggy—your own loving brother—who has been searching for you a long time and has now come to rescue you."

"Too late!" replied the gloomy voice. "No one can rescue me now."

"Oh, but you are mistaken about that," said Shaggy. "There is a new King of the nomes, named Kaliko, in Ruggedo's place, and he has promised you shall go free."

"Free! I dare not go free!" said the Ugly One, in a voice of despair.

"Why not, Brother?" asked Shaggy, anxiously.

"Do you know what they have done to me?" came the answer through the closed door.

"No. Tell me, Brother, what have they done?"

"When Ruggedo first captured me I was very handsome. Don't you remember, Shaggy?"

"Not very well, Brother; you were so young when I left home. But I remember that mother thought you were beautiful."

"She was right! I am sure she was right," wailed the prisoner. "But Ruggedo wanted to injure me—to make me ugly in the eyes of all the world—so he performed a wicked enchantment. I went to bed beautiful—or you might say handsome—to be very modest I will merely claim that I was good-looking—and I wakened the next morning the homeliest man in all the world! I am so repulsive that when I look in a mirror I frighten myself."

"Poor Brother!" said Shaggy softly, and all the others were silent from sympathy.

"I was so ashamed of my looks," continued the voice of Shaggy's brother, "that I tried to hide; but the cruel King Ruggedo forced me to appear before all the legion of nomes, to whom he said: 'Behold the Ugly One!' But when the nomes saw my face they all fell to laughing and jeering, which prevented them from working at their tasks. Seeing this, Ruggedo became angry and pushed me into a tunnel, closing the rock entrance so that I could not get out. I followed the length of the tunnel until I reached this huge dome, where the marvelous Metal Forest stands, and here I have remained ever since."

"Poor Brother!" repeated Shaggy. "But I beg you now to come forth and face us, who are your friends. None here will laugh or jeer, however unhandsome you may be."

"No, indeed," they all added pleadingly.

But the Ugly One refused the invitation.

"I cannot," said he; "indeed, I cannot face strangers, ugly as I am."

Shaggy Man turned to the group surrounding him.

"What shall I do?" he asked in sorrowful tones. "I cannot leave my dear brother here, and he refuses to come out of that house and face us."

"I'll tell you," replied Betsy. "Let him put on a mask."

"The very idea I was seeking!" exclaimed Shaggy joyfully; and then he called out: "Brother, put a mask over your face, and then none of us can see what your features are like."

"I have no mask," answered the Ugly One.

"Look here," said Betsy; "he can use my handkerchief."

Shaggy looked at the little square of cloth and shook his head.

"It isn't big enough," he objected; "I'm sure it isn't big enough to hide a man's face. But he can use mine."

Saying this he took from his pocket his own handkerchief and went to the door of the hut.

"Here, my Brother," he called, "take this handkerchief and make a mask of it. I will also pass you my knife, so that you may cut holes for the eyes, and then you must tie it over your face."

The door slowly opened, just far enough for the Ugly One to thrust out his hand and take the handkerchief and the knife. Then it closed again.

"Don't forget a hole for your nose," cried Betsy. "You must breathe, you know."

For a time there was silence. Queen Ann and her army sat down upon the ground to rest. Betsy sat on Hank's back. Polychrome danced lightly up and down the jeweled paths while Files and the Princess wandered through the groves arm in arm. Tik-Tok, who never tired, stood motionless.

By and by a noise sounded from within the hut.

"Are you ready?" asked Shaggy.

"Yes, Brother," came the reply and the door was thrown open to allow the Ugly One to step forth.

Betsy might have laughed aloud had she not remembered how sensitive to ridicule Shaggy's brother was, for the handkerchief with which he had masked his features was a red one covered with big white polka dots. In this two holes had been cut—in front of the eyes—while two smaller ones before the nostrils allowed the man to breathe freely. The cloth was then tightly drawn over the Ugly One's face and knotted at the back of his neck.

He was dressed in clothes that had once been good, but now were sadly worn and frayed. His silk stockings had holes in them, and his shoes were stub-toed and needed blackening. "But what can you expect," whispered Betsy, "when the poor man has been a prisoner for so many years?"

Shaggy had darted forward, and embraced his newly found brother with both his arms. The brother also embraced

Shaggy, who then led him forward and introduced him to all the assembled company.

"This is the new Nome King," he said when he came to Kaliko. "He is our friend, and has granted you your freedom."

"That is a kindly deed," replied Ugly in a sad voice, "but I dread to go back to the world in this direful condition. Unless I remain forever masked, my dreadful face would curdle all the milk and stop all the clocks."

"Can't the enchantment be broken in some way?" inquired Betsy.

Shaggy looked anxiously at Kaliko, who shook his head.

"I am sure *I* can't break the enchantment," he said. "Ruggedo was fond of magic, and learned a good many enchantments that we nomes know nothing of."

"Perhaps Ruggedo himself might break his own enchantment," suggested Ann; "but unfortunately we have allowed the old King to escape."

"Never mind, my dear Brother," said Shaggy consolingly; "I am very happy to have found you again, although I may never see your face. So let us make the most of this joyful reunion."

The Ugly One was affected to tears by this tender speech, and the tears began to wet the red handkerchief; so Shaggy gently wiped them away with his coat sleeve.

KINDLY KISSES

"Won't you be dreadful sorry to leave this lovely place?" Betsy asked the Ugly One.

"No, indeed," said he. "Jewels and gold are cold and heartless things, and I am sure I would presently have died of loneliness had I not found the natural forest at the edge of the artificial one. Anyhow, without these real trees I should soon have starved to death."

Betsy looked around at the quaint trees.

"I don't just understand that," she admitted. "What could you find to eat here."

"The best food in the world," Ugly answered. "Do you see that grove at your left?" he added, pointing it out; "well, such trees as those do not grow in your country, or in any other place but this cavern. I have named them 'Hotel Trees,' because they bear a certain kind of table d'hote fruit called 'Three-Course Nuts.'"

"That's funny!" said Betsy. "What are the 'Three-Course Nuts' like?"

"Something like cocoanuts, to look at," explained the Ugly One. "All you have to do is to pick one of them and then sit down and eat your dinner. You first unscrew the top part and find a cupfull of good soup. After you've eaten that, you unscrew the middle part and find a hollow filled with meat and potatoes, vegetables and a fine salad. Eat that, and unscrew the next section, and you come to the dessert in the bottom of the nut. That is, pie and cake, cheese and crackers, and nuts and raisins. The Three-Course Nuts are not all exactly alike in flavor or in contents, but they are all good and in each one may be found a complete three-course dinner."

"But how about breakfasts?" inquired Betsy.

"Why, there are Breakfast Trees for that, which grow over there at the right. They bear nuts, like the others, only the nuts contain coffee or chocolate, instead of soup; oatmeal instead of meat-and-potatoes, and fruits instead of dessert. Sad as has been my life in this wonderful prison, I must admit that no one could live more luxuriously in the best hotel in the world than I have lived here; but I will be glad to get into the open air again and see the good old sun and the silvery moon and the soft green grass and the flowers that are kissed by the morning dew. Ah, how much more lovely are those blessed things than the glitter of gems or the cold gleam of gold!"

"Of course," said Betsy. "I once knew a little boy who wanted to catch the measles, because all the little boys in his neighborhood but him had 'em, and he was really unhappy 'cause he couldn't catch 'em, try as he would. So I'm pretty certain that the things we want, and can't have, are not good for us. Isn't that true, Shaggy?"

"Not always, my dear," he gravely replied. "If we didn't want anything, we would never get anything, good or bad. I think our longings are natural, and if we act as nature prompts us we can't go far wrong."

"For my part," said Queen Ann, "I think the world would be a dreary place without the gold and jewels."

"All things are good in their way," said Shaggy; "but we may have too much of any good thing. And I have noticed that the value of anything depends upon how scarce it is, and how difficult it is to obtain."

"Pardon me for interrupting you," said King Kaliko, coming to their side, "but now that we have rescued Shaggy's brother I would like to return to my royal cavern. Being the King of the Nomes, it is my duty to look after my restless subjects and see that they behave themselves."

So they all turned and began walking through the Metal

Forest to the other side of the great domed cave, where they had first entered it. Shaggy and his brother walked side by side and both seemed rejoiced that they were together after their long separation. Betsy didn't dare look at the polka dot handkerchief, for fear she would laugh aloud; so she walked behind the two brothers and led Hank by holding fast to his left ear.

When at last they reached the place where the passage led to the outer world, Queen Ann said, in a hesitating way that was unusual with her:

"I have not conquered this Nome Country, nor do I expect to do so; but I would like to gather a few of these pretty jewels before I leave this place."

"Help yourself, ma'am," said King Kaliko, and at once the officers of the Army took advantage of his royal permission and began filling their pockets, while Ann tied a lot of diamonds in a big handkerchief.

This accomplished, they all entered the passage, the nomes going first to light the way with their torches. They had not proceeded far when Betsy exclaimed:

"Why, there are jewels here, too!"

All eyes were turned upon the ground and they found a regular trail of jewels strewn along the rock floor.

"This is queer!" said Kaliko, much surprised. "I must send some of my nomes to gather up these gems and replace them in the Metal Forest, where they belong. I wonder how they came to be here?"

All the way along the passage they found this trail of jewels, but when they neared the end the mystery was explained. For there, squatted upon the floor with his back to the rock wall, sat old Ruggedo, puffing and blowing as if he was all tired out. Then they realized it was he who had scattered the jewels, from his many pockets, which one by one had burst with the weight of their contents as he had stumbled along the passage.

"But I don't mind," said Ruggedo, with a deep sigh. "I now realize that I could not have carried such a weighty load very far, even had I managed to escape from this passage with it. The woman who sewed the pockets on my robe used poor thread, for which I shall thank her."

"Have you any jewels left?" inquired Betsy.

He glanced into some of the remaining pockets.

"A few," said he, "but they will be sufficient to supply my wants, and I no longer have any desire to be rich. If some of you will kindly help me to rise, I'll get out of here and leave you, for I know you all despise me and prefer my room to my company."

Shaggy and Kaliko raised the old King to his feet, when he was confronted by Shaggy's brother, whom he now noticed for the first time. The queer and unexpected appearance of the Ugly One so startled Ruggedo that he gave a wild cry and began to tremble, as if he had seen a ghost.

"Wh—wh—who is this?" he faltered.

"I am that helpless prisoner whom your cruel magic transformed from a handsome man into an ugly one!" answered Shaggy's brother, in a voice of stern reproach.

"Really, Ruggedo," said Betsy, "you ought to be ashamed of that mean trick."

"I am, my dear," admitted Ruggedo, who was now as meek and humble as formerly he had been cruel and vindictive.

"Then," returned the girl, "you'd better do some more magic and give the poor man his own face again."

"I wish I could," answered the old King; "but you must remember that Tititi-Hoochoo has deprived me of all my magic powers. However, I never took the trouble to learn just how to break the charm I cast over Shaggy's brother, for I intended he should always remain ugly."

"Every charm," remarked pretty Polychrome, "has its antidote; and, if you knew this charm of ugliness, Ruggedo, you must have known how to dispel it."

He shook his head.

"If I did, I—I've forgotten," he stammered regretfully.

"Try to think!" pleaded Shaggy, anxiously. "*Please* try to think!"

Ruggedo ruffled his hair with both hands, sighed, slapped his chest, rubbed his ear, and stared stupidly around the group.

"I've a faint recollection that there was one thing that would break the charm," said he; "but misfortune has so addled my brain that I can't remember what it was."

"See here, Ruggedo," said Betsy, sharply, "we've treated you pretty well, so far, but we won't stand for any nonsense, and if you know what's good for yourself you'll think of that charm!"

"Why?" he demanded, turning to look wonderingly at the little girl.

"Because it means so much to Shaggy's brother. He's dreadfully ashamed of himself, the way he is now, and you're to blame for it. Fact is, Ruggedo, you've done so much wickedness in your life that it won't hurt you to do a kind act now."

Ruggedo blinked at her, and sighed again, and then tried very hard to think.

"I seem to remember, dimly," said he, "that a certain kind of a kiss will break the charm of ugliness."

"What kind of a kiss?"

"What kind? Why, it was—it was—it was either the kiss of a Mortal Maid; or—or—the kiss of a Mortal Maid who had once been a Fairy; or—or the kiss of one who is still a Fairy. I can't remember which. But of course no maid, mortal or fairy, would ever consent to kiss a person so ugly—so dreadfully, fearfully, terribly ugly—as Shaggy's brother."

"I'm not so sure of that," said Betsy, with admirable courage; "I'm a Mortal Maid, and if it is my kiss that will break this awful charm, I—I'll do it!"

"Oh, you really couldn't," protested Ugly. "I would be obliged to remove my mask, and when you saw my face, nothing could induce you to kiss me, generous as you are."

"Well, as for that," said the little girl, "I needn't see your face at all. Here's my plan: You stay in this dark passage, and we'll send away the nomes with their torches. Then you'll take off the handkerchief, and I—I'll kiss you."

"This is awfully kind of you, Betsy!" said Shaggy, gratefully.

"Well, it surely won't kill me," she replied; "and, if it makes you and your brother happy, I'm willing to take some chances."

So Kaliko ordered the torch-bearers to leave the passage, which they did by going through the rock opening. Queen Ann and her army also went out; but the others were so interested in Betsy's experiment that they remained grouped at the mouth of the passageway. When the big rock swung into place, closing tight the opening, they were left in total darkness.

"Now, then," called Betsy in a cheerful voice, "have you got that handkerchief off your face, Ugly?"

"Yes," he replied.

"Well, where are you, then?" she asked, reaching out her arms.

"Here," said he.

"You'll have to stoop down, you know."

He found her hands and clasping them in his own stooped until his face was near to that of the little girl. The others heard a clear, smacking kiss, and then Betsy exclaimed:

"There! I've done it, and it didn't hurt a bit!"

"Tell me, dear brother; is the charm broken?" asked Shaggy.

"I do not know," was the reply. "It may be, or it may not be. I cannot tell."

"Has anyone a match?" inquired Betsy.

"I have several," said Shaggy.

"Then let Ruggedo strike one of them and look at your brother's face, while we all turn our backs. Ruggedo made your brother ugly, so I guess he can stand the horror of looking at him, if the charm isn't broken."

Agreeing to this, Ruggedo took the match and lighted it. He gave one look and then blew out the match.

"Ugly as ever!" he said with a shudder. "So it wasn't the kiss of a Mortal Maid, after all."

"Let me try," proposed the Rose Princess, in her sweet voice. "I am a Mortal Maid who was once a Fairy. Perhaps my kiss will break the charm."

Files did not wholly approve of this, but he was too generous to interfere. So the Rose Princess felt her way through the darkness to Shaggy's brother and kissed him.

Ruggedo struck another match, while they all turned away.

"No," announced the former King; "that didn't break the charm, either. It must be the kiss of a Fairy that is required—or else my memory has failed me altogether."

"Polly," said Betsy, pleadingly, "won't *you* try?"

"Of course I will!" answered Polychrome, with a merry laugh. "I've never kissed a mortal man in all the thousands of years I have existed, but I'll do it to please our faithful Shaggy Man, whose unselfish affection for his ugly brother deserves to be rewarded."

Even as Polychrome was speaking she tripped lightly to the side of the Ugly One and quickly touched his cheek with her lips.

"Oh, thank you—thank you!" he fervently cried. "I've changed, this time, I know. I can feel it! I'm different. Shaggy—dear Shaggy—I am myself again!"

Files, who was near the opening, touched the spring that released the big rock and it suddenly swung backward and let in a flood of daylight.

Everyone stood motionless, staring hard at Shaggy's brother, who, no longer masked by the polka-dot handkerchief, met their gaze with a glad smile.

"Well," said Shaggy Man, breaking the silence at last and drawing a long, deep breath of satisfaction, "you are no longer the Ugly One, my dear brother; but, to be entirely frank with you, the face that belongs to you is no more handsome than it ought to be."

"I think he's rather good looking," remarked Betsy, gazing at the man critically.

"In comparison with what he was," said King Kaliko, "he is really beautiful. You, who never beheld his ugliness, may not understand that; but it was my misfortune to look at the Ugly One many times, and I say again that, in comparison with what he was, the man is now beautiful."

"All right," returned Betsy, briskly, "we'll take your word for it, Kaliko. And now let us get out of this tunnel and into the world again."

Chapter 23

RUGGEDO REFORMS

It did not take them long to regain the royal cavern of the Nome King, where Kaliko ordered served to them the nicest refreshments the place afforded.

Ruggedo had come trailing along after the rest of the party and while no one paid any attention to the old King they did not offer any objection to his presence or command him to leave them. He looked fearfully to see if the eggs were still guarding the entrance, but they had now disappeared; so he crept into the cavern after the others and humbly squatted down in a corner of the room.

There Betsy discovered him. All of the little girl's companions were now so happy at the success of Shaggy's quest for his brother, and the laughter and merriment seemed so general, that Betsy's heart softened toward the friendless old man who had once been their bitter enemy, and she carried to him some of the food and drink. Ruggedo's eyes filled with tears at this unexpected kindness. He took the child's hand in his own and pressed it gratefully.

"Look here, Kaliko," said Betsy, addressing the new King, "what's the use of being hard on Ruggedo? All his magic power is gone, so he can't do any more harm, and I'm sure he's sorry he acted so badly to everybody."

"Are you?" asked Kaliko, looking down at his former master.

"I am," said Ruggedo. "The girl speaks truly. I'm sorry and I'm harmless. I don't want to wander through the wide world, on top of the ground, for I'm a nome. No nome can ever be happy any place but underground."

"That being the case," said Kaliko, "I will let you stay here as long as you behave yourself; but, if you try to act badly again, I shall drive you out, as Tititi-Hoochoo has commanded, and you'll have to wander."

"Never fear. I'll behave," promised Ruggedo. "It is hard work being a King, and harder still to be a good King. But now that I am a common nome I am sure I can lead a blameless life."

They were all pleased to hear this and to know that Ruggedo had really reformed.

"I hope he'll keep his word," whispered Betsy to Shaggy;

"but if he gets bad again we will be far away from the Nome Kingdom and Kaliko will have to 'tend to the old nome himself."

Polychrome had been a little restless during the last hour or two. The lovely Daughter of the Rainbow knew that she had now done all in her power to assist her earth friends, and so she began to long for her sky home.

"I think," she said, after listening intently, "that it is beginning to rain. The Rain King is my uncle, you know, and perhaps he has read my thoughts and is going to help me. Anyway I must take a look at the sky and make sure."

So she jumped up and ran through the passage to the outer entrance, and they all followed after her and grouped themselves on a ledge of the mountain-side. Sure enough, dark clouds had filled the sky and a slow, drizzling rain had set in.

"It can't last for long," said Shaggy, looking upward, "and when it stops we shall lose the sweet little fairy we have learned to love. Alas," he continued, after a moment, "the clouds are already breaking in the west, and—see!—isn't that the Rainbow coming?"

Betsy didn't look at the sky; she looked at Polychrome, whose happy, smiling face surely foretold the coming of her father to take her to the Cloud Palaces. A moment later a gleam of sunshine flooded the mountain and a gorgeous Rainbow appeared.

With a cry of gladness Polychrome sprang upon a point of rock and held out her arms. Straightway the Rainbow descended until its end was at her very feet, when with a graceful leap she sprang upon it and was at once clasped in the arms of her radiant sisters, the Daughters of the Rainbow. But Polychrome released herself to lean over the edge of the glowing arch and nod, and smile and throw a dozen kisses to her late comrades.

"Good-bye!" she called, and they all shouted "Good-bye!" in return and waved their hands to their pretty friend.

Slowly the magnificent bow lifted and melted into the sky, until the eyes of the earnest watchers saw only fleecy clouds flitting across the blue.

"I'm dreadful sorry to see Polychrome go," said Betsy, who felt like crying; "but I s'pose she'll be a good deal happier with her sisters in the sky palaces."

"To be sure," returned Shaggy, nodding gravely. "It's her home, you know, and those poor wanderers who, like ourselves, have no home, can realize what that means to her."

"Once," said Betsy, "I, too, had a home. Now, I've only—only—dear old Hank!"

She twined her arms around her shaggy friend who was not human, and he said: "Hee-haw!" in a tone that showed he understood her mood. And the shaggy friend who was human stroked the child's head tenderly and said: "You're wrong about that, Betsy, dear. I will never desert you."

"Nor I!" exclaimed Shaggy's brother, in earnest tones.

The little girl looked up at them gratefully, and her eyes smiled through their tears.

"All right," she said. "It's raining again, so let's go back into the cavern."

Rather soberly, for all loved Polychrome and would miss her, they reentered the dominions of the Nome King.

······· *Chapter 24* ·······

DOROTHY Is DELIGHTED

W ell," said Queen Ann, when all were again seated in Kaliko's royal cavern, "I wonder what we shall do next. If I could find my way back to Oogaboo I'd take my army home at once, for I'm sick and tired of these dreadful hardships."

"Don't you want to conquer the world?" asked Betsy.

"No; I've changed my mind about that," admitted the Queen. "The world is too big for one person to conquer and I was happier with my own people in Oogaboo. I wish—Oh, how earnestly I wish—that I was back there this minute!"

"So do I!" yelled every officer in a fervent tone.

Now, it is time for the reader to know that in the far-away

Land of Oz the lovely Ruler, Ozma, had been following the adventures of her Shaggy Man, and Tik-Tok, and all the others they had met. Day by day Ozma, with the wonderful Wizard of Oz seated beside her, had gazed upon a Magic Picture in a radium frame, which occupied one side of the Ruler's cosy boudoir in the palace of the Emerald City. The singular thing about this Magic Picture was that it showed whatever scene Ozma wished to see, with the figures all in motion, just as it was taking place. So Ozma and the Wizard had watched every action of the adventurers from the time Shaggy had met ship-wrecked Betsy and Hank in the Rose Kingdom, at which time the Rose Princess, a distant cousin of Ozma, had been exiled by her heartless subjects.

When Ann and her people so earnestly wished to return to Oogaboo, Ozma was sorry for them and remembered that Oogaboo was a corner of the Land of Oz. She turned to her attendant and asked:

"Can not your magic take these unhappy people to their old home, Wizard?"

"It can, your Highness," replied the little Wizard.

"I think the poor Queen has suffered enough in her mis-guided effort to conquer the world," said Ozma, smiling at the absurdity of the undertaking, "so no doubt she will here-after be contented in her own little Kingdom. Please send her there, Wizard, and with her the officers and Files."

"How about the Rose Princess?" asked the Wizard.

"Send her to Oogaboo with Files," answered Ozma. "They have become such good friends that I am sure it would make them unhappy to separate them."

"Very well," said the Wizard, and without any fuss or mystery whatever he performed a magical rite that was simple and effective. Therefore those seated in the Nome King's cavern were both startled and amazed when all the people of Oogaboo suddenly disappeared from the room, and with them the Rose Princess. At first they could not understand it at all; but presently Shaggy suspected the truth, and believing that Ozma was now taking an interest in the party he drew from his pocket a tiny instrument which he placed against his ear.

Ozma, observing this action in her Magic Picture, at once caught up a similar instrument from a table beside her and held it to her own ear. The two instruments recorded the same delicate vibrations of sound and formed a wireless telephone, an invention of the Wizard. Those separated by any distance were thus enabled to converse together with perfect ease and without any wire connection.

"Do you hear me, Shaggy Man?" asked Ozma.

"Yes, your Highness," he replied.

"I have sent the people of Oogaboo back to their own little valley," announced the Ruler of Oz; "so do not worry over their disappearance."

"That was very kind of you," said Shaggy. "But your Highness must permit me to report that my own mission here is now ended. I have found my lost brother, and he is now beside me, freed from the enchantment of ugliness which Ruggedo cast upon him. Tik-Tok has served me and my comrades faithfully, as you requested him to do, and I hope you will now transport the Clockwork Man back to your fairyland of Oz."

"I will do that," replied Ozma. "But how about yourself, Shaggy?"

"I have been very happy in Oz," he said, "but my duty to others forces me to exile myself from that delightful land. I must take care of my new-found brother, for one thing, and I have a new comrade in a dear little girl named Betsy Bobbin, who has no home to go to, and no other friends but me and a small donkey named Hank. I have promised Betsy never to desert her as long as she needs a friend, and so I must give up the delights of the Land of Oz forever."

He said this with a sigh of regret, and Ozma made no reply but laid the tiny instrument on her table, thus cutting off all further communication with the Shaggy Man. But the lovely Ruler of Oz still watched her magic picture, with a thoughtful expression upon her face, and the little Wizard of Oz watched Ozma and smiled softly to himself.

In the cavern of the Nome King Shaggy replaced the wireless telephone in his pocket and turning to Betsy said in as cheerful a voice as he could muster:

"Well, little comrade, what shall we do next?"

"I don't know, I'm sure," she answered with a puzzled

face. "I'm kind of sorry our adventures are over, for I enjoyed them, and now that Queen Ann and her people are gone, and Polychrome is gone, and—dear me!—where's Tik-Tok, Shaggy?"

"He also has disappeared," said Shaggy, looking around the cavern and nodding wisely. "By this time he is in Ozma's palace in the Land of Oz, which is his home."

"Isn't it your home, too?" asked Betsy.

"It used to be, my dear; but now my home is wherever you and my brother are. We are wanderers, you know, but if we stick together I am sure we shall have a good time."

"Then," said the girl, "let us get out of this stuffy, underground cavern and go in search of new adventures. I'm sure it has stopped raining."

"I'm ready," said Shaggy, and then they bade good-bye to King Kaliko, and thanked him for his assistance, and went out to the mouth of the passage.

The sky was now clear and a brilliant blue in color; the sun shone brightly and even this rugged, rocky country seemed delightful after their confinement underground. There were but four of them now—Betsy and Hank, and Shaggy and his brother—and the little party made their way down the mountain and followed a faint path that led toward the southwest.

During this time Ozma had been holding a conference with the Wizard, and later with Tik-Tok, whom the magic of the Wizard had quickly transported to Ozma's palace. Tik-

Tok had only words of praise for Betsy Bobbin, "who," he said, "is al-most as nice as Dor-o-thy her-self."

"Let us send for Dorothy," said Ozma, and summoning her favorite maid, who was named Jellia Jamb, she asked her to request Princess Dorothy to attend her at once. So a few moments later Dorothy entered Ozma's room and greeted her and the Wizard and Tik-Tok with the same gentle smile and simple manner that had won for the little girl the love of everyone she met.

"Did you want to see me, Ozma?" she asked.

"Yes, dear. I am puzzled how to act, and I want your advice."

"I don't b'lieve it's worth much," replied Dorothy, "but I'll do the best I can. What is it all about, Ozma?"

"You all know," said the girl Ruler, addressing her three friends, "what a serious thing it is to admit any mortals into this fairyland of Oz. It is true I have invited several mortals to make their home here, and all of them have proved true and loyal subjects. Indeed, no one of you three was a native of Oz. Dorothy and the Wizard came here from the United States, and Tik-Tok came from the Land of Ev. But of course he is not a mortal. Shaggy is another American, and he is the cause of all my worry, for our dear Shaggy will not return here and desert the new friends he has found in his recent adventures, because he believes they need his services."

"Shaggy Man was always kind-hearted," remarked Dorothy.

"But who are these new friends he has found?"

"One is his brother, who for many years has been a prisoner of the Nome King, our old enemy Ruggedo. This brother seems a kindly, honest fellow, but he has done nothing to entitle him to a home in the Land of Oz."

"Who else?" asked Dorothy.

"I have told you about Betsy Bobbin, the little girl who was shipwrecked—in much the same way you once were—and has since been following the Shaggy Man in his search for his lost brother. You remember her, do you not?"

"Oh, yes!" exclaimed Dorothy. "I've often watched her and Hank in the Magic Picture, you know. She's a dear little girl, and old Hank is a darling! Where are they now?"

"Look and see," replied Ozma with a smile at her friend's enthusiasm.

Dorothy turned to the Picture, which showed Betsy and Hank, with Shaggy and his brother, trudging along the rocky paths of a barren country.

"Seems to me," she said, musingly, "that they're a good way from any place to sleep, or any nice things to eat."

"You are right," said Tik-Tok. "I have been in that country, and it is a wil-der-ness."

"It is the country of the nomes," explained the Wizard, "who are so mischievous that no one cares to live near them. I'm afraid Shaggy and his friends will endure many hardships before they get out of that rocky place, unless—"

He turned to Ozma and smiled.

"Unless I ask you to transport them all here?" she asked.

"Yes, your Highness."

"Could your magic do that?" inquired Dorothy.

"I think so," said the Wizard.

"Well," said Dorothy, "as far as Betsy and Hank are concerned, I'd like to have them here in Oz. It would be such fun to have a girl playmate of my own age, you see. And Hank is such a dear little mule!"

Ozma laughed at the wistful expression in the girl's eyes, and then she drew Dorothy to her and kissed her.

"Am I not your friend and playmate?" she asked.

Dorothy flushed.

"You know how dearly I love you, Ozma!" she cried. "But you're so busy ruling all this Land of Oz that we can't always be together."

"I know, dear. My first duty is to my subjects, and I think it would be a delight to us all to have Betsy with us. There's a pretty suite of rooms just opposite your own where she can live, and I'll build a golden stall for Hank in the stable where the Sawhorse lives. Then we'll introduce the mule to the Cowardly Lion and the Hungry Tiger, and I'm sure they will soon become firm friends. But I cannot very well admit Betsy and Hank into Oz unless I also admit Shaggy's brother."

"And, unless you admit Shaggy's brother, you will keep out poor Shaggy, whom we are all very fond of," said the Wizard.

"Well, why not ad-mit him?" demanded Tik-Tok.

"The Land of Oz is not a refuge for all mortals in distress," explained Ozma. "I do not wish to be unkind to Shaggy Man, but his brother has no claim on me."

"The Land of Oz isn't crowded," suggested Dorothy.

"Then you advise me to admit Shaggy's brother?" inquired Ozma.

"Well, we can't afford to lose our Shaggy Man, can we?"

"No, indeed!" returned Ozma. "What do you say, Wizard?"

"I'm getting my magic ready to transport them all."

"And you, Tik-Tok?"

"Shag-gy's broth-er is a good fel-low, and we can't spare Shag-gy."

"So, then; the question is settled," decided Ozma. "Perform your magic, Wizard!"

He did so, placing a silver plate upon a small standard and pouring upon the plate a small quantity of pink powder which was contained in a crystal vial. Then he muttered a rather difficult incantation which the sorceress Glinda the Good had taught him, and it all ended in a puff of perfumed smoke from the silver plate. This smoke was so pungent that it made both Ozma and Dorothy rub their eyes for a moment.

"You must pardon these disagreeable fumes," said the Wizard. "I assure you the smoke is a very necessary part of my wizardry."

"Look!" cried Dorothy, pointing to the Magic Picture; "they're gone! All of them are gone."

Indeed, the picture now showed the same rocky landscape as before, but the three people and the mule had disappeared from it.

"They are gone," said the Wizard, polishing the silver plate and wrapping it in a fine cloth, "because they are here."

At that moment Jellia Jamb entered the room.

"Your Highness," she said to Ozma, "the Shaggy Man and another man are in the waiting room and ask to pay their respects to you. Shaggy is crying like a baby, but he says they are tears of joy."

"Send them here at once, Jellia!" commanded Ozma.

"Also," continued the maid, "a girl and a small-sized mule have mysteriously arrived, but they don't seem to know where they are or how they came here. Shall I send them here, too?"

"Oh, no!" exclaimed Dorothy, eagerly jumping up from her chair; "I'll go to meet Betsy myself, for she'll feel awful strange in this big palace."

And she ran down the stairs two at a time to greet her new friend, Betsy Bobbin.

·····◄ Chapter 25 ►·····

The LAND of LOVE

"Well, is 'hee-haw' all you are able to say?" inquired the Sawhorse, as he examined Hank with his knot eyes and slowly wagged the branch that served him for a tail.

They were in a beautiful stable in the rear of Ozma's palace, where the wooden Sawhorse—very much alive—lived in a gold-paneled stall, and where there were rooms for the Cowardly Lion and the Hungry Tiger, which were filled with soft cushions for them to lie upon and golden troughs for them to eat from.

Beside the stall of the Sawhorse had been placed another for Hank, the mule. This was not quite so beautiful as the other, for the Sawhorse was Ozma's favorite steed; but Hank had a supply of cushions for a bed (which the Sawhorse did not need because he never slept) and all this luxury was so strange to the little mule that he could only stand still and regard his surroundings and his queer companions with wonder and amazement.

The Cowardly Lion, looking very dignified, was stretched out upon the marble floor of the stable, eyeing Hank with a calm and critical gaze, while near by crouched the huge Hungry Tiger, who seemed equally interested in the new animal that had just arrived. The Sawhorse, standing stiffly before Hank, repeated his question:

"Is 'hee-haw' all you are able to say?"

Hank moved his ears in an embarrassed manner.

"I have never said anything else, until now," he replied; and then he began to tremble with fright to hear himself talk.

"I can well understand that," remarked the Lion, wagging his great head with a swaying motion. "Strange things happen in this Land of Oz, as they do everywhere else. I believe you came here from the cold, civilized, outside world, did you not?"

"I did," replied Hank. "One minute I was outside of Oz— and the next minute I was inside! That was enough to give me a nervous shock, as you may guess; but to find myself able to talk, as Betsy does, is a marvel that staggers me."

"That is because you are in the Land of Oz," said the Sawhorse. "All animals talk, in this favored country, and you must admit it is more sociable than to bray your dreadful 'hee-haw,' which nobody can understand."

"Mules understand it very well," declared Hank.

"Oh, indeed! Then there must be other mules in your outside world," said the Tiger, yawning sleepily.

"There are a great many in America," said Hank. "Are you the only Tiger in Oz?"

"No," acknowledged the Tiger, "I have many relatives living in the Jungle Country; but I am the only Tiger living in the Emerald City."

"There are other Lions, too," said the Sawhorse; "but I am the only horse, of any description, in this favored Land."

"That is why this Land is favored," said the Tiger. "You must understand, friend Hank, that the Sawhorse puts on airs because he is shod with plates of gold, and because our beloved Ruler, Ozma of Oz, likes to ride upon his back."

"Betsy rides upon *my* back," declared Hank proudly.

"Who is Betsy?"

"The dearest, sweetest girl in all the world!"

The Sawhorse gave an angry snort and stamped his golden feet. The Tiger crouched and growled. Slowly the great Lion rose to his feet, his mane bristling.

"Friend Hank," said he, "either you are mistaken in judgment or you are willfully trying to deceive us. The dearest, sweetest girl in the world is our Dorothy, and I will fight anyone—animal or human—who dares to deny it!"

"So will I!" snarled the Tiger, showing two rows of enormous white teeth.

"You are all wrong!" asserted the Sawhorse in a voice of scorn. "No girl living can compare with my mistress, Ozma of Oz!"

Hank slowly turned around until his heels were toward the others. Then he said stubbornly:

"I am not mistaken in my statement, nor will I admit there can be a sweeter girl alive than Betsy Bobbin. If you want to fight, come on—I'm ready for you!"

While they hesitated, eyeing Hank's heels doubtfully, a merry peal of laughter startled the animals and turning their heads they beheld three lovely girls standing just within the richly carved entrance to the stable. In the center was Ozma, her arms encircling the waists of Dorothy and Betsy, who stood on either side of her. Ozma was nearly half a head taller than the two other girls, who were almost of one size. Unobserved, they had listened to the talk of the animals, which was a very strange experience indeed to little Betsy Bobbin.

"You foolish beasts!" exclaimed the Ruler of Oz, in a gentle but chiding voice. "Why should you fight to defend us, who are all three loving friends and in no sense rivals? Answer me!" she continued, as they bowed their heads sheepishly.

"I have the right to express my opinion, your Highness," pleaded the Lion.

"And so have the others," replied Ozma. "I am glad you and the Hungry Tiger love Dorothy best, for she was your first friend and companion. Also I am pleased that my Sawhorse loves me best, for together we have endured both joy and sorrow. Hank has proved his faith and loyalty by defending his own little mistress; and so you are all right in one way, but wrong in another. Our Land of Oz is a Land of Love, and here friendship outranks every other quality. Unless you can all be friends, you cannot retain our love."

They accepted this rebuke very meekly.

"All right," said the Sawhorse, quite cheerfully; "shake hoofs, friend Mule."

Hank touched his hoof to that of the wooden horse.

"Let us be friends and rub noses," said the Tiger. So Hank modestly rubbed noses with the big beast.

The Lion merely nodded and said, as he crouched before the mule:

"Any friend of a friend of our beloved Ruler is a friend of the Cowardly Lion. That seems to cover your case. If ever you need help or advice, friend Hank, call on me."

"Why, this is as it should be," said Ozma, highly pleased to see them so fully reconciled. Then she turned to her companions: "Come, my dears, let us resume our walk."

As they turned away Betsy said wonderingly:

"Do all the animals in Oz talk as we do?"

"Almost all," answered Dorothy. "There's a Yellow Hen

here, and she can talk, and so can her chickens; and there's a Pink Kitten upstairs in my room who talks very nicely; but I've a little fuzzy black dog, named Toto, who has been with me in Oz a long time, and he's never said a single word but 'Bow-wow!'"

"Do you know why?" asked Ozma.

"Why, he's a Kansas dog; so I s'pose he's different from these fairy animals," replied Dorothy.

"Hank isn't a fairy animal, any more than Toto," said Ozma, "yet as soon as he came under the spell of our fairyland he found he could talk. It was the same way with Billina, the Yellow Hen whom you brought here at one time. The same spell has affected Toto, I assure you; but he's a wise little dog and while he knows everything that is said to him he prefers not to talk."

"Goodness me!" exclaimed Dorothy. "I never s'pected Toto was fooling me all this time." Then she drew a small silver whistle from her pocket and blew a shrill note upon it. A moment later there was a sound of scurrying footsteps, and a shaggy black dog came running up the path.

Dorothy knelt down before him and shaking her finger just above his nose she said:

"Toto, haven't I always been good to you?"

Toto looked up at her with his bright black eyes and wagged his tail.

"Bow-wow!" he said, and Betsy knew at once that meant

yes, as well as Dorothy and Ozma knew it, for there was no mistaking the tone of Toto's voice.

"That's a dog answer," said Dorothy. "How would you like it, Toto, if I said nothing to you but 'bow-wow'?"

Toto's tail was wagging furiously now, but otherwise he was silent.

"Really, Dorothy," said Betsy, "he can talk with his bark and his tail just as well as we can. Don't you understand such dog language?"

"Of course I do," replied Dorothy. "But Toto's got to be more sociable. See here, sir!" she continued, addressing the dog, "I've just learned, for the first time, that you can say words—if you want to. Don't you want to, Toto?"

"Woof!" said Toto, and that meant "no."

"Not just one word, Toto, to prove you're as any other animal in Oz?"

"Woof!"

"Just one word, Toto—and then you may run away."

He looked at her steadily a moment.

"All right. Here I go!" he said, and darted away as swift as an arrow.

Dorothy clapped her hands in delight, while Betsy and Ozma both laughed heartily at her pleasure and the success of her experiment. Arm in arm they sauntered away through the beautiful gardens of the palace, where magnificent flowers bloomed in abundance and fountains shot their silvery sprays far into the air. And by and by, as they turned a corner, they came upon Shaggy Man and his brother, who were seated together upon a golden bench.

The two arose to bow respectfully as the Ruler of Oz approached them.

"How are you enjoying our Land of Oz?" Ozma asked the stranger.

"I am very happy here, your Highness," replied Shaggy's brother. "Also I am very grateful to you for permitting me to live in this delightful place."

"You must thank Shaggy for that," said Ozma. "Being his brother, I have made you welcome here."

"When you know Brother better," said Shaggy earnestly, "you will be glad he has become one of your loyal subjects. I am just getting acquainted with him myself and I find much in his character to admire."

Leaving the brothers, Ozma and the girls continued their walk. Presently Betsy exclaimed:

"Shaggy's brother can't ever be as happy in Oz as I am. Do you know, Dorothy, I didn't believe any girl could ever have such a good time—anywhere—as I'm having now?"

"I know," answered Dorothy. "I've felt that way myself, lots of times."

"I wish," continued Betsy, dreamily, "that every little girl in the world could live in the Land of Oz; and every little boy, too!"

Ozma laughed at this.

"It is quite fortunate for us, Betsy, that your wish cannot be granted," said she, "for all that army of girls and boys would crowd us so that we would have to move away."

"Yes," agreed Betsy, after a little thought, "I guess that's true."

The
Scarecrow
of
Oz

Dedicated to
"The Uplifters" of Los Angeles, California, in
grateful appreciation of the pleasure I have derived
from association with them, and in recognition of
their sincere endeavor to uplift humanity through
kindness, consideration and good-fellowship. They are
big men—all of them—and all with the generous
hearts of little children.

......·◄ 'Twixt You and Me ►·······

The Army of Children which besieged the Post-
office, conquered the Postmen and delivered to
me its imperious Commands, insisted that Trot
and Cap'n Bill be admitted to the Land of Oz,
where Trot could enjoy the society of Dorothy, Betsy Bobbin
and Ozma, while the one-legged sailor-man might become a
comrade of the Tin Woodman, the Shaggy Man, Tik-Tok and
all the other quaint people who inhabit this wonderful fairyland.

It was no easy task to obey this order and land Trot and
Cap'n Bill safely in Oz, as you will discover by reading this book.
Indeed, it required the best efforts of our dear old friend, the
Scarecrow, to save them from a dreadful fate on the journey;
but the story leaves them happily located in Ozma's splendid
palace and Dorothy has promised me that Button-Bright and
the three girls are sure to encounter, in the near future, some

marvelous adventures in the Land of Oz, which I hope to be permitted to relate to you in the next Oz Book.

Meantime, I am deeply grateful to my little readers for their continued enthusiasm over the Oz stories, as evinced in the many letters they send me, all of which are lovingly cherished. It takes more and more Oz Books every year to satisfy the demands of old and new readers, and there have been formed many "Oz Reading Societies," where the Oz Books owned by different members are read aloud. All this is very gratifying to me and encourages me to write more stories. When the children have had enough of them, I hope they will let me know, and then I'll try to write something different.

L. Frank Baum, Royal Historian of Oz

"Ozcot" at Hollywood in California, 1915

... — .. Chapter 1 ... — ..

Chapter 1

The GREAT WHIRLPOOL

Seems to me," said Cap'n Bill, as he sat beside Trot under the big acacia tree, looking out over the blue ocean, "seems to me, Trot, as how the more we know, the more we find we don't know."

"I can't quite make that out, Cap'n Bill," answered the little girl in a serious voice, after a moment's thought, during which her eyes followed those of the old sailor-man across the glassy surface of the sea. "Seems to me that all we learn is jus' so much gained."

"I know; it looks that way at first sight," said the sailor, nodding his head; "but those as knows the least have a habit of thinkin' they know all there is to know, while them as knows the most admits what a turr'ble big world this is. It's the knowing ones that realize one lifetime ain't long enough to git more'n a few dips o' the oars of knowledge."

Trot didn't answer. She was a very little girl, with big, solemn eyes and an earnest, simple manner. Cap'n Bill had been her faithful companion for years and had taught her almost everything she knew.

He was a wonderful man, this Cap'n Bill. Not so very old, although his hair was grizzled—what there was of it. Most of his head was bald as an egg and as shiny as oilcloth, and this made his big ears stick out in a funny way. His eyes had a gentle look and were pale blue in color, and his round face was rugged and bronzed. Cap'n Bill's left leg was missing, from the knee down, and that was why the sailor no longer sailed the seas. The wooden leg he wore was good enough to stump around with on land, or even to take Trot out for a row or a sail on the ocean, but when it came to "runnin' up aloft" or performing active duties on shipboard, the old sailor was not equal to the task. The loss of his leg had ruined his career and the old sailor found comfort in devoting himself to the education and companionship of the little girl.

The accident to Cap'n Bill's leg had happened at about the time Trot was born, and ever since that he had lived with Trot's mother as "a star boarder," having enough money saved up to pay for his weekly "keep." He loved the baby and often held her on his lap; her first ride was on Cap'n Bill's shoulders, for she had no baby-carriage; and when she began to toddle around, the child and the sailor became close comrades and enjoyed many strange adventures together. It is said the fairies had been present at Trot's birth and had marked her forehead with their invisible mystic signs, so that she was able to see and do many wonderful things.

The acacia tree was on top of a high bluff, but a path ran down the bank in a zigzag way to the water's edge, where Cap'n Bill's boat was moored to a rock by means of a stout cable. It had been a hot, sultry afternoon, with scarcely a breath of air stirring, so Cap'n Bill and Trot had been quietly sitting beneath the shade of the tree, waiting for the sun to get low enough for them to take a row.

They had decided to visit one of the great caves which the waves had washed out of the rocky coast during many years of steady effort. The caves were a source of continual delight to both the girl and the sailor, who loved to explore their awesome depths.

"I b'lieve, Cap'n," remarked Trot, at last, "that it's time for us to start."

The old man cast a shrewd glance at the sky, the sea and the motionless boat. Then he shook his head.

"Mebbe it's time, Trot," he answered, "but I don't jes' like the looks o' things this afternoon."

"What's wrong?" she asked wonderingly.

"Can't say as to that. Things is too quiet to suit me, that's all. No breeze, not a ripple a-top the water, nary a gull a-flyin' anywhere, an' the end o' the hottest day o' the year. I ain't no weather-prophet, Trot, but any sailor would know the signs is ominous."

"There's nothing wrong that I can see," said Trot. "If there was a cloud in the sky even as big as my thumb, we might worry about it; but—look, Cap'n!—the sky is as clear as can be."

He looked again and nodded.

"P'r'aps we can make the cave, all right," he agreed, not wishing to disappoint her. "It's only a little way out, an' we'll be on the watch; so come along, Trot."

Together they descended the winding path to the beach. It was no trouble for the girl to keep her footing on the steep way, but Cap'n Bill, because of his wooden leg, had to hold on to rocks and roots now and then to save himself from tumbling. On a level path he was as spry as anyone, but to climb up hill or down required some care.

They reached the boat safely and while Trot was untying the rope Cap'n Bill reached into a crevice of the rock and drew out several tallow candles and a box of wax matches, which he thrust into the capacious pockets of his "sou'wester." This sou'wester was a short coat of oilskin which the old sailor wore on all occasions—when he wore a coat at all—and the pockets always contained a variety of objects, useful and ornamental, which made even Trot wonder where they all came from and why Cap'n Bill should treasure them. The jackknives—a big one and a little one—the bits of cord, the fishhooks, the nails: these were handy to have on certain occasions. But bits of shell, and tin boxes with unknown contents, buttons, pincers, bottles of curious stones and the like, seemed quite unnecessary to carry around. That was Cap'n Bill's business, however, and now that he added the candles and the matches to his collection Trot made no comment, for she knew these last were to light their way through the caves.

The sailor always rowed the boat, for he handled the oars with strength and skill. Trot sat in the stern and steered. The place where they embarked was a little bight or circular bay, and the boat cut across a much larger bay toward a distant headland where the caves were located, right at the water's edge. They were nearly a mile from shore and about half-way across the bay when Trot suddenly sat up straight and exclaimed: "What's that, Cap'n?"

He stopped rowing and turned half around to look.

"That, Trot," he slowly replied, "looks to me mighty like a whirlpool."

"What makes it, Cap'n?"

"A whirl in the air makes the whirl in the water. I was afraid as we'd meet with trouble, Trot. Things didn't look right. The air was too still."

"It's coming closer," said the girl.

The old man grabbed the oars and began rowing with all his strength.

"'Tain't comin' closer to us, Trot," he gasped; "it's we that are comin' closer to the whirlpool. The thing is drawin' us to it like a magnet!"

Trot's sun-bronzed face was a little paler as she grasped the tiller firmly and tried to steer the boat away; but she said not a word to indicate fear.

The swirl of the water as they came nearer made a roaring sound that was fearful to listen to. So fierce and powerful was the whirlpool that it drew the surface of the sea into the form of a great basin, slanting downward toward the center, where a big hole had been made in the ocean—a hole with walls of water that were kept in place by the rapid whirling of the air.

The boat in which Trot and Cap'n Bill were riding was just on the outer edge of this saucer-like slant, and the old sailor knew very well that unless he could quickly force the little craft away from the rushing current they would soon be drawn into the great black hole that yawned in the middle. So he exerted all his might and pulled as he had never pulled before. He pulled so hard that the left oar snapped in two and sent Cap'n Bill sprawling upon the bottom of the boat.

He scrambled up quickly enough and glanced over the side. Then he looked at Trot, who sat quite still, with a serious, far-away look in her sweet eyes. The boat was now speeding swiftly of its own accord, following the line of the circular basin round and round and gradually drawing nearer to the great hole in the center. Any further effort to escape the whirlpool was useless, and realizing this fact Cap'n Bill turned toward Trot and put an arm around her, as if to shield her from the awful fate before them. He did not try to speak, because the roar of the waters would have drowned the sound of his voice.

These two faithful comrades had faced dangers before, but nothing to equal that which now faced them. Yet Cap'n Bill, noting the look in Trot's eyes and remembering how often she had been protected by unseen powers, did not quite give way to despair.

The great hole in the dark water—now growing nearer and nearer—looked very terrifying; but they were both brave enough to face it and await the result of the adventure.

The CAVERN UNDER the SEA

The circles were so much smaller at the bottom of the basin, and the boat moved so much more swiftly, that Trot was beginning to get dizzy with the motion, when suddenly the boat made a leap and dived headlong into the murky depths of the hole. Whirling like tops, but still clinging together, the sailor and the girl were separated from their boat and plunged down—down—down— into the farthermost recesses of the great ocean.

At first their fall was swift as an arrow, but presently they seemed to be going more moderately and Trot was almost sure that unseen arms were about her, supporting her and protecting her. She could see nothing, because the water filled her eyes and blurred her vision, but she clung fast to Cap'n Bill's sou'wester, while other arms clung fast to her, and so they gradually sank down and down until a full stop was made, when they began to ascend again.

But it seemed to Trot that they were not rising straight to the surface from where they had come. The water was no longer whirling them and they seemed to be drawn in a slanting direction through still, cool ocean depths. And then—in much quicker time than I have told it—up they popped to the surface and were cast at full length upon a sandy beach, where they lay choking and gasping for breath and wondering what had happened to them.

Trot was the first to recover. Disengaging herself from Cap'n Bill's wet embrace and sitting up, she rubbed the water from her eyes and then looked around her. A soft, bluish-green glow lighted the place, which seemed to be a sort of cavern, for above and on either side of her were rugged rocks. They had been cast upon a beach of clear sand, which slanted upward from the pool of water at their feet—a pool which doubtless led into the big ocean that fed it. Above the reach of the waves of the pool were more rocks, and still more and more, into the dim windings and recesses of which the glowing light from the water did not penetrate.

The place looked grim and lonely, but Trot was thankful that she was still alive and had suffered no severe injury during her trying adventure under water. At her side Cap'n

Bill was sputtering and coughing, trying to get rid of the water he had swallowed. Both of them were soaked through, yet the cavern was warm and comfortable and a wetting did not dismay the little girl in the least.

She crawled up the slant of sand and gathered in her hand a bunch of dried seaweed, with which she mopped the face of Cap'n Bill and cleared the water from his eyes and ears. Presently the old man sat up and stared at her intently. Then he nodded his bald head three times and said in a gurgling voice:

"Mighty good, Trot; mighty good! We didn't reach Davy Jones's locker that time, did we? Though why we didn't, an' why we're here, is more'n I kin make out."

"Take it easy, Cap'n," she replied. "We're safe enough, I guess, at least for the time being."

He squeezed the water out of the bottoms of his loose trousers and felt of his wooden leg and arms and head, and finding he had brought all of his person with him he gathered courage to examine closely their surroundings.

"Where d'ye think we are, Trot?" he presently asked.

"Can't say, Cap'n. P'r'aps in one of our caves."

He shook his head. "No," said he, "I don't think that, at all. The distance we came up didn't seem half as far as the distance we went down; an' you'll notice there ain't any outside entrance to this cavern whatever. It's a reg'lar dome over this pool o' water, and unless there's some passage at the back, up yonder, we're fast pris'ners."

Trot looked thoughtfully over her shoulder.

"When we're rested," she said, "we will crawl up there and see if there's a way to get out."

Cap'n Bill reached in the pocket of his oilskin coat and took out his pipe. It was still dry, for he kept it in an oilskin pouch with his tobacco. His matches were in a tight tin box, so in a few moments the old sailor was smoking contentedly. Trot knew it helped him to think when he was in any difficulty. Also, the pipe did much to restore the old sailor's composure, after his long ducking and his terrible fright—a fright that was more on Trot's account than his own.

The sand was dry where they sat, and soaked up the water that dripped from their clothing. When Trot had squeezed the wet out of her hair she began to feel much like her old self again. By and by they got upon their feet and crept up the incline to the scattered boulders above. Some of these were of huge size, but by passing between some and around others, they were able to reach the extreme rear of the cavern.

"Yes," said Trot, with interest, "here's a round hole."

"And it's black as night inside it," remarked Cap'n Bill.

"Just the same," answered the girl, "we ought to explore it, and see where it goes, 'cause it's the only poss'ble way we can get out of this place."

Cap'n Bill eyed the hole doubtfully

"It may be a way out o' here, Trot," he said, "but it may be a way into a far worse place than this. I'm not sure but our best plan is to stay right here."

Trot wasn't sure, either, when she thought of it in that light. After awhile she made her way back to the sands again, and Cap'n Bill followed her. As they sat down, the child looked thoughtfully at the sailor's bulging pockets.

"How much food have we got, Cap'n?" she asked.

"Half a dozen ship's biscuits an' a hunk o' cheese," he replied. "Want some now, Trot?"

She shook her head, saying:

"That ought to keep us alive 'bout three days if we're careful of it."

"Longer'n that, Trot," said Cap'n Bill, but his voice was a little troubled and unsteady.

"But if we stay here we're bound to starve in time," continued the girl, "while if we go into the dark hole—"

"Some things are more hard to face than starvation," said the sailor-man, gravely. "We don't know what's inside that dark hole: Trot, nor where it might lead us to."

"There's a way to find that out," she persisted.

Instead of replying, Cap'n Bill began searching in his pockets. He soon drew out a little package of fish-hooks and a long line. Trot watched him join them together. Then he crept a little way up the slope and turned over a big rock. Two or three small crabs began scurrying away over the sands and the old sailor caught them and put one on his hook and the others in his pocket. Coming back to the pool he swung the hook over his shoulder and circled it around his head and cast it nearly into the center of the water, where he allowed it to sink gradually, paying out the line as far as it would go. When the end was reached, he began drawing it in again, until the crab bait was floating on the surface.

Trot watched him cast the line a second time, and a third. She decided that either there were no fishes in the pool or they would not bite the crab bait. But Cap'n Bill was an old fisherman and not easily discouraged. When the crab got away he put another on the hook. When the crabs were all gone he climbed up the rocks and found some more.

Meantime Trot tired of watching him and lay down upon the sands, where she fell fast asleep. During the next two hours her clothing dried completely, as did that of the old sailor. They were both so used to salt water that there was no danger of taking cold.

Finally the little girl was wakened by a splash beside her and a grunt of satisfaction from Cap'n Bill. She opened her eyes to find that the Cap'n had landed a silver-scaled fish weighing about two pounds. This cheered her considerably and she hurried to scrape together a heap of seaweed, while Cap'n Bill cut up the fish with his jackknife and got it ready for cooking.

They had cooked fish with seaweed before. Cap'n Bill wrapped his fish in some of the weed and dipped it in the water to dampen it. Then he lighted a match and set fire to Trot's heap, which speedily burned down to a glowing bed of ashes. Then they laid the wrapped fish on the ashes, covered it with more seaweed, and allowed this to catch fire and burn to embers. After feeding the fire with seaweed for some time, the sailor finally decided that their supper was ready, so he scattered the ashes and drew out the bits of fish, still encased in their smoking wrappings.

When these wrappings were removed, the fish was found thoroughly cooked and both Trot and Cap'n Bill ate of it freely. It had a slight flavor of seaweed and would have been better with a sprinkling of salt.

The soft glow which until now had lighted the cavern, began to grow dim, but there was a great quantity of seaweed in the place, so after they had eaten their fish they kept the fire alive for a time by giving it a handful of fuel now and then.

From an inner pocket the sailor drew a small flask of battered metal and unscrewing the cap handed it to Trot. She took but one swallow of the water although she wanted more, and she noticed that Cap'n Bill merely wet his lips with it.

"S'pose," said she, staring at the glowing seaweed fire and speaking slowly, "that we can catch all the fish we need; how 'bout the drinking-water, Cap'n?"

He moved uneasily but did not reply. Both of them were thinking about the dark hole, but while Trot had little fear of it the old man could not overcome his dislike to enter the place. He knew that Trot was right, though. To remain in the cavern, where they now were, could only result in slow but sure death.

It was nighttime up on the earth's surface, so the little girl became drowsy and soon fell asleep. After a time the old sailor slumbered on the sands beside her. It was very still and nothing disturbed them for hours. When at last they awoke the cavern was light again.

They had divided one of the biscuits and were munching it for breakfast when they were startled by a sudden splash in the pool. Looking toward it they saw emerging from the water the most curious creature either of them had ever beheld. It wasn't a fish, Trot decided, nor was it a beast. It had wings, though, and queer wings they were: shaped like an inverted chopping-bowl and covered with tough skin instead of feathers. It had four legs—much like the legs of a stork, only double the number—and its head was shaped a good deal like that of a poll parrot, with a beak that curved downward in front and upward at the edges, and was half bill and half mouth. But to call it a bird was out of the question, because it had no feathers whatever except a crest of wavy plumes of a scarlet color on the very top of its head. The strange creature must have weighed as much as Cap'n Bill, and as it floundered and struggled to get out of the water to the sandy beach it was so big and unusual that both Trot and her companion stared at it in wonder—in wonder that was not unmixed with fear.

RAINBOW

·——·◄ Chapter 3 ►·——·

The ORK

The eyes that regarded them, as the creature stood dripping before them, were bright and mild in expression, and the queer addition to their party made no attempt to attack them and seemed quite as surprised by the meeting as they were.

"I wonder," whispered Trot, "what it is."

"Who, me?" exclaimed the creature in a shrill, high-pitched voice. "Why, I'm an Ork."

"Oh!" said the girl. "But what is an Ork?"

"I am," he repeated, a little proudly, as he shook the water from his funny wings; "and if ever an Ork was glad to be out of the water and on dry land again, you can be mighty sure that I'm that especial, individual Ork!"

"Have you been in the water long?" inquired Cap'n Bill, thinking it only polite to show an interest in the strange creature.

"Why, this last ducking was about ten minutes, I believe, and that's about nine minutes and sixty seconds too long for comfort," was the reply. "But last night I was in an awful pickle, I assure you. The whirlpool caught me, and—"

"Oh, were you in the whirlpool, too?" asked Trot eagerly.

He gave her a glance that was somewhat reproachful.

"I believe I was mentioning the fact, young lady, when your desire to talk interrupted me," said the Ork. "I am not usually careless in my actions, but that whirlpool was so busy yesterday that I thought I'd see what mischief it was up to. So I flew a little too near it and the suction of the air drew me down into the depths of the ocean. Water and I are natural enemies, and it would have conquered me this time had not a bevy of pretty mermaids come to my assistance and dragged me away from the whirling water and far up into a cavern, where they deserted me."

"Why, that's about the same thing that happened to us," cried Trot. "Was your cavern like this one?"

"I haven't examined this one yet," answered the Ork; "but if they happen to be alike I shudder at our fate, for the other one was a prison, with no outlet except by means of the water. I stayed there all night, however, and this morning I plunged into the pool, as far down as I could go, and then swam as hard and as far as I could. The rocks scraped my back, now and then, and I barely escaped the clutches of an ugly sea-monster; but by and by I came to the surface to catch my breath, and found myself here. That's the whole story, and as I see you have something to eat I entreat you to give me a share of it. The truth is, I'm half starved."

With these words the Ork squatted down beside them. Very reluctantly Cap'n Bill drew another biscuit from his pocket and held it out. The Ork promptly seized it in one of its front claws and began to nibble the biscuit in much the same manner a parrot might have done.

"We haven't much grub," said the sailor-man, "but we're willin' to share it with a comrade in distress."

"That's right," returned the Ork, cocking its head side-wise in a cheerful manner, and then for a few minutes there was silence while they all ate of the biscuits. After a while Trot said:

"I've never seen or heard of an Ork before. Are there many of you?"

"We are rather few and exclusive, I believe," was the reply. "In the country where I was born we are the absolute Rulers of all living things, from ants to elephants."

"What country is that?" asked Cap'n Bill.

"Orkland."

"Where does it lie?"

"I don't know, exactly. You see, I have a restless nature, for some reason, while all the rest of my race are quiet and contented Orks and seldom stray far from home. From childhood days I loved to fly long distances away, although father often warned me that I would get into trouble by so doing.

"'It's a big world, Flipper, my son,' he would say, 'and I've heard that in parts of it live queer two-legged creatures called Men, who war upon all other living things and would have little respect for even an Ork.'

"This naturally aroused my curiosity and after I had completed my education and left school I decided to fly out into the world and try to get a glimpse of the creatures called Men. So I left home without saying good-bye, an act I shall always regret. Adventures were many, I found. I sighted men several times, but have never before been so close to them as now. Also I had to fight my way through the air, for I met gigantic birds, with fluffy feathers all over them, which attacked me fiercely. Besides, it kept me busy escaping from floating airships. In my rambling I had lost all track of distance or direction, so that when I wanted to go home I had no idea where my country was located. I've now been trying to find it for several months and it was during one of my flights over the ocean that I met the whirlpool and became its victim."

Trot and Cap'n Bill listened to this recital with much

interest, and from the friendly tone and harmless appearance of the Ork they judged he was not likely to prove so disagreeable a companion as at first they had feared he might be.

The Ork sat upon its haunches much as a cat does, but used the finger-like claws of its front legs almost as cleverly as if they were hands. Perhaps the most curious thing about the creature was its tail, or what ought to have been its tail. This queer arrangement of skin, bones and muscle was shaped like the propellers used on boats and airships, having fan-like surfaces and being pivoted to its body. Cap'n Bill knew something of mechanics, and observing the propeller-like tail of the Ork he said:

"I s'pose you're a pretty swift flyer?"

"Yes, indeed; the Orks are admitted to be Kings of the Air."

"Your wings don't seem to amount to much," remarked Trot.

"Well, they are not very big," admitted the Ork, waving the four hollow skins gently to and fro, "but they serve to support my body in the air while I speed along by means of my tail. Still, taken altogether, I'm very handsomely formed, don't you think?"

Trot did not like to reply, but Cap'n Bill nodded gravely. "For an Ork," said he, "you're a wonder. I've never seen one afore, but I can imagine you're as good as any."

That seemed to please the creature and it began walking around the cavern, making its way easily up the slope. While it was gone, Trot and Cap'n Bill each took another sip from the water-flask, to wash down their breakfast.

"Why, here's a hole—an exit—an outlet!" exclaimed the Ork from above.

"We know," said Trot. "We found it last night."

"Well, then, let's be off," continued the Ork, after sticking its head into the black hole and sniffing once or twice. "The air seems fresh and sweet, and it can't lead us to any worse place than this."

The girl and the sailor-man got up and climbed to the side of the Ork.

"We'd about decided to explore this hole before you came," explained Cap'n Bill; "but it's a dangerous place to navigate in the dark, so wait till I light a candle."

"What is a candle?" inquired the Ork.

"You'll see in a minute," said Trot.

The old sailor drew one of the candles from his right-side pocket and the tin matchbox from his left-side pocket. When he lighted the match the Ork gave a startled jump and eyed the flame suspiciously; but Cap'n Bill proceeded to light the candle and the action interested the Ork very much.

"Light," it said, somewhat nervously, "is valuable in a hole of this sort. The candle is not dangerous, I hope?"

"Sometimes it burns your fingers," answered Trot, "but that's about the worst it can do—'cept to blow out when you don't want it to."

Cap'n Bill shielded the flame with his hand and crept into the hole. It wasn't any too big for a grown man, but after he had crawled a few feet it grew larger. Trot came close behind him and then the Ork followed.

"Seems like a reg'lar tunnel," muttered the sailor-man, who was creeping along awkwardly because of his wooden leg. The rocks, too, hurt his knees.

For nearly half an hour the three moved slowly along the tunnel, which made many twists and turns and sometimes slanted downward and sometimes upward. Finally Cap'n Bill stopped short, with an exclamation of disappointment, and held the flickering candle far ahead to light the scene.

"What's wrong?" demanded Trot, who could see nothing because the sailor's form completely filled the hole.

"Why, we've come to the end of our travels, I guess," he replied.

"Is the hole blocked?" inquired the Ork.

"No; it's wuss nor that," replied Cap'n Bill sadly. "I'm on the edge of a precipice. Wait a minute an' I'll move along and let you see for yourselves. Be careful, Trot, not to fall."

Then he crept forward a little and moved to one side, holding the candle so that the girl could see to follow him. The Ork came next and now all three knelt on a narrow ledge of rock which dropped straight away and left a huge black space which the tiny flame of the candle could not illuminate.

"H-m!" said the Ork, peering over the edge; "this doesn't

look very promising, I'll admit. But let me take your candle, and I'll fly down and see what's below us."

"Aren't you afraid?" asked Trot.

"Certainly I'm afraid," responded the Ork. "But if we intend to escape we can't stay on this shelf forever. So, as I notice you poor creatures cannot fly, it is my duty to explore the place for you."

Cap'n Bill handed the Ork the candle, which had now burned to about half its length. The Ork took it in one claw rather cautiously and then tipped its body forward and slipped over the edge. They heard a queer buzzing sound, as the tail revolved, and a brisk flapping of the peculiar wings, but they were more interested just then in following with their eyes the tiny speck of light which marked the location of the candle. This light first made a great circle, then dropped slowly downward and suddenly was extinguished, leaving everything before them black as ink.

"Hi, there! How did that happen?" cried the Ork.

"It blew out, I guess," shouted Cap'n Bill. "Fetch it here."

"I can't see where you are," said the Ork.

So Cap'n Bill got out another candle and lighted it, and its flame enabled the Ork to fly back to them. It alighted on the edge and held out the bit of candle.

"What made it stop burning?" asked the creature.

"The wind," said Trot. "You must be more careful, this time."

"What's the place like?" inquired Cap'n Bill.

"I don't know, yet; but there must be a bottom to it, so I'll try to find it."

With this the Ork started out again and this time sank downward more slowly. Down, down, down it went, till the candle was a mere spark, and then it headed away to the left and Trot and Cap'n Bill lost all sight of it.

In a few minutes, however, they saw the spark of light again, and as the sailor still held the second lighted candle the Ork made straight toward them. It was only a few yards distant when suddenly it dropped the candle with a cry of pain and next moment alighted, fluttering wildly, upon the rocky ledge.

"What's the matter?" asked Trot.

"It bit me!" wailed the Ork. "I don't like your candles. The thing began to disappear slowly as soon as I took it in my claw, and it grew smaller and smaller until just now it turned and bit me—a most unfriendly thing to do. Oh—oh! Ouch, what a bite!"

"That's the nature of candles, I'm sorry to say," explained Cap'n Bill, with a grin. "You have to handle 'em mighty keerful. But tell us, what did you find down there?"

"I found a way to continue our journey," said the Ork, nursing tenderly the claw which had been burned. "Just below us is a great lake of black water, which looked so cold and wicked that it made me shudder; but away at the left there's a big tunnel, which we can easily walk through. I don't know where it leads to, of course, but we must follow it and find out."

"Why, we can't get to it," protested the little girl. "We can't fly, as you do, you must remember."

"No, that's true," replied the Ork musingly. "Your bodies are built very poorly, it seems to me, since all you can do is crawl upon the earth's surface. But you may ride upon my back, and in that way I can promise you a safe journey to the tunnel."

"Are you strong enough to carry us?" asked Cap'n Bill, doubtfully.

"Yes, indeed; I'm strong enough to carry a dozen of you, if you could find a place to sit," was the reply; "but there's only room between my wings for one at a time, so I'll have to make two trips."

"All right; I'll go first," decided Cap'n Bill.

He lit another candle for Trot to hold while they were gone and to light the Ork on his return to her, and then the old sailor got upon the Ork's back, where he sat with his wooden leg sticking straight out sidewise.

"If you start to fall, clasp your arms around my neck," advised the creature.

"If I start to fall, it's good night an' pleasant dreams," said Cap'n Bill.

"All ready?" asked the Ork.

"Start the buzz-tail," said Cap'n Bill, with a tremble in his voice. But the Ork flew away so gently that the old man never even tottered in his seat.

Trot watched the light of Cap'n Bill's candle till it disappeared in the far distance. She didn't like to be left alone on this dangerous ledge, with a lake of black water hundreds of feet below her; but she was a brave little girl and waited patiently for the return of the Ork. It came even sooner than she had expected and the creature said to her:

"Your friend is safe in the tunnel. Now, then, get aboard and I'll carry you to him in a jiffy."

I'm sure not many little girls would have cared to take that awful ride through the huge black cavern on the back of a skinny Ork. Trot didn't care for it, herself, but it just had to be done and so she did it as courageously as possible. Her heart beat fast and she was so nervous she could scarcely hold the candle in her fingers as the Ork sped swiftly through the darkness.

It seemed like a long ride to her, yet in reality the Ork covered the distance in a wonderfully brief period of time and soon Trot stood safely beside Cap'n Bill on the level floor of a big arched tunnel. The sailor-man was very glad to greet his little comrade again and both were grateful to the Ork for his assistance.

"I dunno where this tunnel leads to," remarked Cap'n Bill, "but it surely looks more promisin' than that other hole we crept through."

"When the Ork is rested," said Trot, "we'll travel on and see what happens."

"Rested!" cried the Ork, as scornfully as his shrill voice would allow. "That bit of flying didn't tire me at all. I'm used to flying days at a time, without ever once stopping."

"Then let's move on," proposed Cap'n Bill. He still held in his hand one lighted candle, so Trot blew out the other flame and placed her candle in the sailor's big pocket. She knew it was not wise to burn two candles at once.

The tunnel was straight and smooth and very easy to walk through, so they made good progress. Trot thought that the tunnel began about two miles from the cavern where they had been cast by the whirlpool, but now it was impossible to guess the miles traveled, for they walked steadily for hours and hours without any change in their surroundings.

Finally Cap'n Bill stopped to rest.

"There's somethin' queer about this 'ere tunnel, I'm certain," he declared, wagging his head dolefully. "Here's three candles gone a'ready, an' only three more left us, yet the tunnel's the same as it was when we started. An' how long it's goin' to keep up, no one knows."

"Couldn't we walk without a light?" asked Trot. "The way seems safe enough."

"It does right now," was the reply, "but we can't tell when we are likely to come to another gulf, or somethin' jes' as dangerous. In that case we'd be killed afore we knew it."

"Suppose I go ahead?" suggested the Ork. "I don't fear a fall, you know, and if anything happens I'll call out and warn you."

"That's a good idea," declared Trot, and Cap'n Bill thought so, too. So the Ork started off ahead, quite in the dark, and hand in hand the two followed him.

When they had walked in this way for a good long time the Ork halted and demanded food. Cap'n Bill had not mentioned food because there was so little left—only three biscuits and a lump of cheese about as big as his two fingers—but he gave the Ork half of a biscuit, sighing as he did so. The creature didn't care for the cheese, so the sailor divided it between himself and Trot. They lighted a candle and sat down in the tunnel while they ate.

"My feet hurt me," grumbled the Ork. "I'm not used to walking and this rocky passage is so uneven and lumpy that it hurts me to walk upon it."

"Can't you fly along?" asked Trot.

"No; the roof is too low," said the Ork.

After the meal they resumed their journey, which Trot began to fear would never end. When Cap'n Bill noticed how tired the little girl was, he paused and lighted a match and looked at his big silver watch.

"Why, it's night!" he exclaimed. "We've tramped all day, an' still we're in this awful passage, which mebbe goes straight through the middle of the world, an' mebbe is a circle—in which case we can keep walkin' till doomsday. Not knowin' what's before us so well as we know what's behind us, I propose we make a stop, now, an' try to sleep till mornin'."

"That will suit me," asserted the Ork, with a groan. "My feet are hurting me dreadfully and for the last few miles I've been limping with pain."

"My foot hurts, too," said the sailor, looking for a smooth place on the rocky floor to sit down.

"*Your* foot!" cried the Ork. "why, you've only one to hurt you, while I have four. So I suffer four times as much as you possibly can. Here; hold the candle while I look at the bottoms of my claws. I declare," he said, examining them by the flickering light, "there are bunches of pain all over them!"

"P'r'aps," said Trot, who was very glad to sit down beside her companions, "you've got corns."

"Corns? Nonsense! Orks never have corns," protested the creature, rubbing its sore feet tenderly.

"Then mebbe they're—they're— What do you call 'em, Cap'n Bill? Something 'bout the Pilgrim's Progress, you know."

"Bunions," said Cap'n Bill.

"Oh, yes; mebbe you've got bunions."

"It is possible," moaned the Ork. "But whatever they are, another day of such walking on them would drive me crazy."

"I'm sure they'll feel better by mornin'," said Cap'n Bill, encouragingly. "Go to sleep an' try to forget your sore feet."

The Ork cast a reproachful look at the sailor-man, who didn't see it. Then the creature asked plaintively: "Do we eat now, or do we starve?"

"There's only half a biscuit left for you," answered Cap'n

Bill. "No one knows how long we'll have to stay in this dark tunnel, where there's nothing whatever to eat; so I advise you to save that morsel o' food till later."

"Give it me now!" demanded the Ork. "If I'm going to starve, I'll do it all at once—not by degrees."

Cap'n Bill produced the biscuit and the creature ate it in a trice. Trot was rather hungry and whispered to Cap'n Bill that she'd take part of her share; but the old man secretly broke his own half-biscuit in two, saving Trot's share for a time of greater need.

He was beginning to be worried over the little girl's plight and long after she was asleep and the Ork was snoring in a rather disagreeable manner, Cap'n Bill sat with his back to a rock and smoked his pipe and tried to think of some way to escape from this seemingly endless tunnel. But after a time he also slept, for hobbling on a wooden leg all day was tiresome, and there in the dark slumbered the three adventurers for many hours, until the Ork roused itself and kicked the old sailor with one foot.

"It must be another day," said he.

···•◄ Chapter 4 ►•···

DAYLIGHT at LAST

Cap'n Bill rubbed his eyes, lit a match and consulted his watch.

"Nine o'clock. Yes, I guess it's another day, sure enough. Shall we go on?" he asked.

"Of course," replied the Ork. "Unless this tunnel is different from everything else in the world, and has no end, we'll find a way out of it sooner or later."

The sailor gently wakened Trot. She felt much rested by her long sleep and sprang to her feet eagerly.

"Let's start, Cap'n," was all she said.

They resumed the journey and had only taken a few steps when the Ork cried "Wow!" and made a great fluttering of its wings and whirling of its tail. The others, who were following a short distance behind, stopped abruptly.

"What's the matter?" asked Cap'n Bill.

"Give us a light," was the reply. "I think we've come to the end of the tunnel." Then, while Cap'n Bill lighted a candle, the creature added: "If that is true, we needn't have wakened so soon, for we were almost at the end of this place when we went to sleep."

The sailor-man and Trot came forward with a light. A wall of rock really faced the tunnel, but now they saw that the opening made a sharp turn to the left. So they followed on, by a narrower passage, and then made another sharp turn this time to the right.

"Blow out the light, Cap'n," said the Ork, in a pleased voice. "We've struck daylight."

Daylight at last! A shaft of mellow light fell almost at their feet as Trot and the sailor turned the corner of the passage, but it came from above, and raising their eyes they found they were at the bottom of a deep, rocky well, with the top far, far above their heads. And here the passage ended.

For a while they gazed in silence, at least two of them being filled with dismay at the sight. But the Ork merely whistled softly and said cheerfully:

"That was the toughest journey I ever had the misfortune to undertake, and I'm glad it's over. Yet, unless I can manage to fly to the top of this pit, we are entombed here forever."

"Do you think there is room enough for you to fly in?" asked the little girl anxiously; and Cap'n Bill added:

"It's a straight-up shaft, so I don't see how you'll ever manage it."

"Were I an ordinary bird—one of those horrid feathered things—I wouldn't even make the attempt to fly out," said the Ork. "But my mechanical propeller tail can accomplish wonders, and whenever you're ready I'll show you a trick that is worth while."

"Oh!" exclaimed Trot; "do you intend to take us up, too?"

"Why not?"

"I thought," said Cap'n Bill, "as you'd go first, an' then send somebody to help us by lettin' down a rope."

"Ropes are dangerous," replied the Ork, "and I might not be able to find one to reach all this distance. Besides, it stands to reason that if I can get out myself I can also carry you two with me."

"Well, I'm not afraid," said Trot, who longed to be on the earth's surface again.

"S'pose we fall?" suggested Cap'n Bill, doubtfully.

"Why, in that case we would all fall together," returned the Ork. "Get aboard, little girl; sit across my shoulders and put both your arms around my neck."

Trot obeyed and when she was seated on the Ork, Cap'n Bill inquired:

"How 'bout me, Mr. Ork?"

"Why, I think you'd best grab hold of my rear legs and let me carry you up in that manner," was the reply.

Cap'n Bill looked way up at the top of the well, and then he looked at the Ork's slender, skinny legs and heaved a deep sigh.

"It's goin' to be some dangle, I guess; but if you don't waste too much time on the way up, I may be able to hang on," said he.

"All ready, then!" cried the Ork, and at once his whirling tail began to revolve. Trot felt herself rising into the air; when the creature's legs left the ground Cap'n Bill grasped two of them firmly and held on for dear life. The Ork's body was tipped straight upward, and Trot had to embrace the neck very tightly to keep from sliding off. Even in this position the Ork had trouble in escaping the rough sides of the well. Several times it exclaimed "Wow!" as it bumped its back, or a wing hit against some jagged projection; but the tail kept whirling with remarkable swiftness and the daylight grew brighter and brighter. It was, indeed, a long journey from the bottom to the top, yet almost before Trot realized they had come so far, they popped out of the hole into the clear air and sunshine and a moment later the Ork alighted gently upon the ground.

The release was so sudden that even with the creature's care for its passengers Cap'n Bill struck the earth with a shock that sent him rolling heel over head; but by the time Trot had slid down from her seat the old sailor-man was sitting up and looking around him with much satisfaction.

"It's sort o' pretty here," said he.

"Earth is a beautiful place!" cried Trot.

"I wonder where on earth we are?" pondered the Ork, turning first one bright eye and then the other to this side and that. Trees there were, in plenty, and shrubs and flowers and green turf. But there were no houses; there were no paths; there was no sign of civilization whatever.

"Just before I settled down on the ground I thought I caught a view of the ocean," said the Ork. "Let's see if I was right." Then he flew to a little hill, near by, and Trot and Cap'n Bill followed him more slowly. When they stood on the top of the hill they could see the blue waves of the ocean in front of them, to the right of them, and at the left of them. Behind the hill was a forest that shut out the view.

"I hope it ain't an island, Trot," said Cap'n Bill gravely.

"If it is, I s'pose we're prisoners," she replied.

"Ezzackly so, Trot."

"But, even so, it's better than those terr'ble underground tunnels and caverns," declared the girl.

"You are right, little one," agreed the Ork. "Anything above ground is better than the best that lies under ground. So let's not quarrel with our fate but be thankful we've escaped."

"We are, indeed!" she replied. "But I wonder if we can find something to eat in this place?"

"Let's explore an' find out," proposed Cap'n Bill. "Those trees over at the left look like cherry-trees."

On the way to them the explorers had to walk through a tangle of vines and Cap'n Bill, who went first, stumbled and pitched forward on his face.

"Why, it's a melon!" cried Trot delightedly, as she saw what had caused the sailor to fall.

Cap'n Bill rose to his foot, for he was not at all hurt, and examined the melon. Then he took his big jackknife from his pocket and cut the melon open. It was quite ripe and looked delicious; but the old man tasted it before he permitted Trot to eat any. Deciding it was good he gave her a big slice and then offered the Ork some. The creature looked at the fruit somewhat disdainfully, at first, but once he had tasted its flavor he ate of it as heartily as did the others. Among the vines they discovered many other melons, and Trot said gratefully: "Well, there's no danger of our starving, even if this is an island."

"Melons," remarked Cap'n Bill, "are both food an' water. We couldn't have struck anything better."

Farther on they came to the cherry trees, where they obtained some of the fruit, and at the edge of the little forest were wild plums. The forest itself consisted entirely of nut trees—walnuts, filberts, almonds and chestnuts—so there would be plenty of wholesome food for them while they remained there.

Cap'n Bill and Trot decided to walk through the forest, to discover what was on the other side of it, but the Ork's feet were still so sore and "lumpy" from walking on the rocks that the creature said he preferred to fly over the tree-tops and meet them on the other side. The forest was not large, so by walking briskly for fifteen minutes they reached its farthest edge and saw before them the shore of the ocean.

"It's an island, all right," said Trot, with a sigh.

"Yes, and a pretty island, too," said Cap'n Bill, trying to conceal his disappointment on Trot's account. "I guess, partner, if the wuss comes to the wuss, I could build a raft—or even a boat—from those trees, so's we could sail away in it."

The little girl brightened at this suggestion. "I don't see the Ork anywhere," she remarked, looking around. Then her eyes lighted upon something and she exclaimed: "Oh, Cap'n Bill! Isn't that a house, over there to the left?"

Cap'n Bill, looking closely, saw a shed-like structure built at one edge of the forest.

"Seems like it, Trot. Not that I'd call it much of a house, but it's a buildin', all right. Let's go over an' see if it's occupied."

The LITTLE OLD MAN
of the ISLAND

A few steps brought them to the shed, which was merely a roof of boughs built over a square space, with some branches of trees fastened to the sides to keep off the wind. The front was quite open and faced the sea, and as our friends came nearer they observed a little man, with a long pointed beard, sitting motionless on a stool and staring thoughtfully out over the water.

"Get out of the way, please," he called in a fretful voice. "Can't you see you are obstructing my view?"

"Good morning," said Cap'n Bill, politely.

"It isn't a good morning!" snapped the little man. "I've

seen plenty of mornings better than this. Do you call it a good morning when I'm pestered with such a crowd as you?"

Trot was astonished to hear such words from a stranger whom they had greeted quite properly, and Cap'n Bill grew red at the little man's rudeness. But the sailor said, in a quiet tone of voice:

"Are you the only one as lives on this 'ere island?"

"Your grammar's bad," was the reply. "But this is my own exclusive island, and I'll thank you to get off it as soon as possible."

"We'd like to do that," said Trot, and then she and Cap'n Bill turned away and walked down to the shore, to see if any other land was in sight.

The little man rose and followed them, although both were now too provoked to pay any attention to him.

"Nothin' in sight, partner," reported Cap'n Bill, shading his eyes with his hand; "so we'll have to stay here for a time, anyhow. It isn't a bad place, Trot, by any means."

"That's all you know about it!" broke in the little man. "The trees are altogether too green and the rocks are harder than they ought to be. I find the sand very grainy and the water dreadfully wet. Every breeze makes a draught and the sun shines in the daytime, when there's no need of it, and disappears just as soon as it begins to get dark. If you remain here you'll find the island very unsatisfactory."

Trot turned to look at him, and her sweet face was grave and curious.

"I wonder who you are," she said.

"My name is Pessim," said he, with an air of pride. "I'm called the Observer."

"Oh. What do you observe?" asked the little girl.

"Everything I see," was the reply, in a more surly tone. Then Pessim drew back with a startled exclamation and looked at some footprints in the sand. "Why, good gracious me!" he cried in distress.

"What's the matter now?" asked Cap'n Bill.

"Someone has pushed the earth in! Don't you see it?

"It isn't pushed in far enough to hurt anything," said Trot, examining the footprints.

"Everything hurts that isn't right," insisted the man. "If the earth were pushed in a mile, it would be a great calamity, wouldn't it?"

"I s'pose so," admitted the little girl.

"Well, here it is pushed in a full inch! That's a twelfth of a foot, or a little more than a millionth part of a mile. Therefore it is one-millionth part of a calamity—Oh, dear! How dreadful!" said Pessim in a wailing voice.

"Try to forget it, sir," advised Cap'n Bill, soothingly. "It's beginning to rain. Let's get under your shed and keep dry."

"Raining! Is it really raining?" asked Pessim, beginning to weep.

"It is," answered Cap'n Bill, as the drops began to descend, "and I don't see any way to stop it—although I'm some observer myself."

"No; we can't stop it, I fear," said the man. "Are you very busy just now?"

"I won't be after I get to the shed," replied the sailor-man.

"Then do me a favor, please," begged Pessim, walking briskly along behind them, for they were hastening to the shed.

"Depends on what it is," said Cap'n Bill.

"I wish you would take my umbrella down to the shore and hold it over the poor fishes till it stops raining. I'm afraid they'll get wet," said Pessim.

Trot laughed, but Cap'n Bill thought the little man was poking fun at him and so he scowled upon Pessim in a way that showed he was angry.

They reached the shed before getting very wet, although the rain was now coming down in big drops. The roof of the shed protected them and while they stood watching the rainstorm something buzzed in and circled around Pessim's head. At once the Observer began beating it away with his hands, crying out:

"A bumblebee! A bumblebee! The queerest bumblebee I ever saw!"

Cap'n Bill and Trot both looked at it and the little girl said in surprise:

"Dear me! It's a wee little Ork!"

"That's what it is, sure enough," exclaimed Cap'n Bill.

Really, it wasn't much bigger than a big bumblebee, and when it came toward Trot she allowed it to alight on her shoulder.

"It's me, all right," said a very small voice in her ear; "but I'm in an awful pickle, just the same!"

"What, are you *our* Ork, then?" demanded the girl, much amazed.

"No, I'm my own Ork. But I'm the only Ork you know," replied the tiny creature.

"What's happened to you?" asked the sailor, putting his head close to Trot's shoulder in order to hear the reply better. Pessim also put his head close, and the Ork said:

"You will remember that when I left you I started to fly over the trees, and just as I got to this side of the forest I saw a bush that was loaded down with the most luscious fruit you can imagine. The fruit was about the size of a gooseberry and of a lovely lavender color. So I swooped down and picked off one in my bill and ate it. At once I began to grow small. I could feel myself shrinking, shrinking away, and it frightened me terribly, so that I lighted on the ground to think over what was happening. In a few seconds I had shrunk to the size you now see me; but there I remained, getting no smaller, indeed, but no larger. It is certainly a dreadful affliction! After I had recovered somewhat from the shock I began to search for you.

It is not so easy to find one's way when a creature is so small, but fortunately I spied you here in this shed and came to you at once."

Cap'n Bill and Trot were much astonished at this story and felt grieved for the poor Ork, but the little man Pessim seemed to think it a good joke. He began laughing when he heard the story and laughed until he choked, after which he lay down on the ground and rolled and laughed again, while the tears of merriment coursed down his wrinkled cheeks.

"Oh, dear! Oh, dear!" he finally gasped, sitting up and wiping his eyes. "This is too rich! It's almost too joyful to be true."

"I don't see anything funny about it," remarked Trot indignantly.

"You would if you'd had my experience," said Pessim, getting upon his feet and gradually resuming his solemn and dissatisfied expression of countenance. "The same thing happened to me."

"Oh, did it? And how did you happen to come to this island?" asked the girl.

"I didn't come; the neighbors brought me," replied the little man, with a frown at the recollection. "They said I was quarrelsome and fault-finding and blamed me because I told them all the things that went wrong, or never were right, and because I told them how things ought to be. So they brought me here and left me all alone, saying that if I quarreled with myself, no one else would be made unhappy. Absurd, wasn't it?"

"Seems to me," said Cap'n Bill, "those neighbors did the proper thing."

"Well," resumed Pessim, "when I found myself King of this island I was obliged to live upon fruits, and I found many fruits growing here that I had never seen before. I tasted several and found them good and wholesome. But one day I ate a lavender berry—as the Ork did—and immediately I grew so small that I was scarcely two inches high. It was a very unpleasant condition and like the Ork I became frightened. I could not walk very well nor very far, for every lump of earth in my way seemed a mountain, every blade of grass a tree and every grain of sand a rocky boulder. For several days I stumbled around in an agony of fear. Once a tree toad nearly gobbled me up, and if I ran out from the shelter of the bushes the gulls and cormorants swooped down upon me. Finally I decided to eat another berry and become nothing at all, since life, to one as small as I was, had become a dreary nightmare.

"At last I found a small tree that I thought bore the same fruit as that I had eaten. The berry was dark purple instead of light lavender, but otherwise it was quite similar. Being unable to climb the tree, I was obliged to wait underneath it until a sharp breeze arose and shook the limbs so that a berry fell. Instantly I seized it and taking a last view of the world— as I then thought—I ate the berry in a twinkling. Then, to my surprise, I began to grow big again, until I became of my former stature, and so I have since remained. Needless to say, I have never eaten again of the lavender fruit, nor do any of the beasts or birds that live upon this island eat it."

They had all three listened eagerly to this amazing tale, and when it was finished the Ork exclaimed:

"Do you think, then, that the deep purple berry is the antidote for the lavender one?"

"I'm sure of it," answered Pessim.

"Then lead me to the tree at once!" begged the Ork, "for this tiny form I now have terrifies me greatly."

Pessim examined the Ork closely

"You are ugly enough as you are," said he. "Were you any larger you might be dangerous."

"Oh, no," Trot assured him; "the Ork has been our good friend. Please take us to the tree."

Then Pessim consented, although rather reluctantly. He led them to the right, which was the east side of the island, and in a few minutes brought them near to the edge of the grove which faced the shore of the ocean. Here stood a small tree bearing berries of a deep purple color. The fruit looked very enticing and Cap'n Bill reached up and selected one that seemed especially plump and ripe.

The Ork had remained perched upon Trot's shoulder but now it flew down to the ground. It was so difficult for Cap'n Bill to kneel down, with his wooden leg, that the little girl took the berry from him and held it close to the Ork's head.

"It's too big to go into my mouth," said the little creature, looking at the fruit sidewise.

"You'll have to make sev'ral mouthfuls of it, I guess," said Trot; and that is what the Ork did. He pecked at the soft, ripe fruit with his bill and ate it up very quickly, because it was good.

Even before he had finished the berry they could see the Ork begin to grow. In a few minutes he had regained his natural size and was strutting before them, quite delighted with his transformation.

"Well, well! What do you think of me now?" he asked proudly.

"You are very skinny and remarkably ugly," declared Pessim.

"You are a poor judge of Orks," was the reply. "Anyone can see that I'm much handsomer than those dreadful things called birds, which are all fluff and feathers."

"Their feathers make soft beds," asserted Pessim.

"And my skin would make excellent drumheads," retorted the Ork. "Nevertheless, a plucked bird or a skinned Ork would be of no value to himself, so we needn't brag of our usefulness after we are dead. But for the sake of argument, friend Pessim, I'd like to know what good *you* would be, were you not alive?"

"Never mind that," said Cap'n Bill. "He isn't much good as he is."

"I am King of this Island, allow me to say, and you're intruding on my property," declared the little man, scowling upon them. "If you don't like me—and I'm sure you don't, for no one else does—why don't you go away and leave me to myself?"

"Well, the Ork can fly, but we can't," explained Trot, in answer. "We don't want to stay here a bit, but I don't see how we can get away."

"You can go back into the hole you came from."

Cap'n Bill shook his head; Trot shuddered at the thought; the Ork laughed aloud.

"You may be King here," the creature said to Pessim, "but we intend to run this island to suit ourselves, for we are three and you are one, and the balance of power lies with us."

The little man made no reply to this, although as they walked back to the shed his face wore its fiercest scowl. Cap'n Bill gathered a lot of leaves and, assisted by Trot, prepared two nice beds in opposite corners of the shed. Pessim slept in a hammock which he swung between two trees.

They required no dishes, as all their food consisted of fruits and nuts picked from the trees; they made no fire, for the weather was warm and there was nothing to cook; the shed had no furniture other than the rude stool which the little man was accustomed to sit upon. He called it his "throne" and they let him keep it.

So they lived upon the island for three days, and rested and ate to their hearts' content. Still, they were not at all happy in this life because of Pessim. He continually found fault with them, and all that they did, and all their surroundings. He could see nothing good or admirable in all the world and Trot soon came to understand why the little man's former neighbors had brought him to this island and left him there, all alone, so he could not annoy anyone. It was their misfortune that they had been led to this place by their adventures, for often they would have preferred the company of a wild beast to that of Pessim.

On the fourth day a happy thought came to the Ork. They had all been racking their brains for a possible way to leave the island, and discussing this or that method, without finding a plan that was practical. Cap'n Bill had said he could make a raft of the trees, big enough to float them all, but he had no tools except those two pocketknives and it was not possible to chop down tree with such small blades.

"And s'pose we got afloat on the ocean," said Trot, "where would we drift to, and how long would it take us to get there?"

Cap'n Bill was forced to admit he didn't know. The Ork could fly away from the island any time it wished to, but the queer creature was loyal to his new friends and refused to leave them in such a lonely, forsaken place.

It was when Trot urged him to go, on this fourth morning, that the Ork had his happy thought.

"I will go," said he, "if you two will agree to ride upon my back."

"We are too heavy; you might drop us," objected Cap'n Bill.

"Yes, you are rather heavy for a long journey," acknowledged the Ork, "but you might eat of those lavender berries and become so small that I could carry you with ease."

This quaint suggestion startled Trot and she looked gravely at the speaker while she considered it, but Cap'n Bill gave a scornful snort and asked:

"What would become of us afterward? We wouldn't be much good if we were some two or three inches high. No, Mr. Ork, I'd rather stay here, as I am, than be a hop-o'-my-thumb somewhere else."

"Why couldn't you take some of the dark purple berries along with you, to eat after we had reached our destination?" inquired the Ork. "Then you could grow big again whenever you pleased."

Trot clapped her hands with delight.

"That's it!" she exclaimed. "Let's do it, Cap'n Bill."

The old sailor did not like the idea at first, but he thought it over carefully and the more he thought the better it seemed.

"How could you manage to carry us, if we were so small?" he asked.

"I could put you in a paper bag, and tie the bag around my neck."

"But we haven't a paper bag," objected Trot.

The Ork looked at her.

"There's your sunbonnet," it said presently, "which is hollow in the middle and has two strings that you could tie around my neck."

Trot took off her sunbonnet and regarded it critically. Yes, it might easily hold both her and Cap'n Bill, after they had eaten the lavender berries and been reduced in size. She tied the strings around the Ork's neck and the sunbonnet made a bag in which two tiny people might ride without danger of falling out. So she said:

"I b'lieve we'll do it that way, Cap'n."

Cap'n Bill groaned but could make no logical objection except that the plan seemed to him quite dangerous—and dangerous in more ways than one.

"I think so, myself," said Trot soberly. "But nobody can stay alive without getting into danger sometimes, and danger doesn't mean getting hurt, Cap'n; it only means we *might* get hurt. So I guess we'll have to take the risk."

"Let's go and find the berries," said the Ork.

They said nothing to Pessim, who was sitting on his stool and scowling dismally as he stared at the ocean, but started at once to seek the trees that bore the magic fruits. The Ork remembered very well where the lavender berries grew and led his companions quickly to the spot.

Cap'n Bill gathered two berries and placed them carefully in his pocket. Then they went around to the east side of the island and found the tree that bore the dark purple berries.

"I guess I'll take four of these," said the sailor-man, "so in case one doesn't make us grow big we can eat another."

"Better take six," advised the Ork. "It's well to be on the safe side, and I'm sure these trees grow nowhere else in all the world."

So Cap'n Bill gathered six of the purple berries and with their precious fruit they returned to the shed to bid good-bye to Pessim. Perhaps they would not have granted the surly little man this courtesy had they not wished to use him to tie the sunbonnet around the Ork's neck.

When Pessim learned they were about to leave him he at first looked greatly pleased, but he suddenly recollected that nothing ought to please him and so began to grumble about being left alone.

"We knew it wouldn't suit you," remarked Cap'n Bill. "It didn't suit you to have us here, and it won't suit you to have us go away."

"That is quite true," admitted Pessim. "I haven't been suited since I can remember; so it doesn't matter to me in the least whether you go or stay."

He was interested in their experiment, however, and willingly agreed to assist, although he prophesied they would fall out of the sunbonnet on their way and be either drowned in the ocean or crushed upon some rocky shore. This uncheerful prospect did not daunt Trot, but it made Cap'n Bill quite nervous.

"I will eat my berry first," said Trot, as she placed her

L. Frank Baum

sunbonnet on the ground, in such manner that they could get into it.

Then she ate the lavender berry and in a few seconds became so small that Cap'n Bill picked her up gently with his thumb and one finger and placed her in the middle of the sun-bonnet. Then he placed beside her the six purple berries—each one being about as big as the tiny Trot's head—and all preparations being now made the old sailor ate his lavender berry and became very small—wooden leg and all!

Cap'n Bill stumbled sadly in trying to climb over the edge of the sunbonnet and pitched in beside Trot headfirst, which caused the unhappy Pessim to laugh with glee. Then the King of the Island picked up the sunbonnet—so rudely that he shook its occupants like peas in a pod—and tied it, by means of its strings, securely around the Ork's neck.

"I hope, Trot, you sewed those strings on tight," said Cap'n Bill anxiously.

"Why, we are not very heavy, you know," she replied, "so I think the stitches will hold. But be careful and not crush the berries, Cap'n."

"One is jammed already," he said, looking at them.

"All ready?" asked the Ork.

"Yes!" they cried together, and Pessim came close to the sunbonnet and called out to them: "You'll be smashed or drowned, I'm sure you will! But farewell, and good riddance to you."

The Ork was provoked by this unkind speech, so he turned his tail toward the little man and made it revolve so fast that the rush of air tumbled Pessim over backward and he rolled several times upon the ground before he could stop himself and sit up. By that time the Ork was high in the air and speeding swiftly over the ocean.

The FLIGHT of the MIDGETS

C ap'n Bill and Trot rode very comfortably in the sunbonnet. The motion was quite steady, for they weighed so little that the Ork flew without effort. Yet they were both somewhat nervous about their future fate and could not help wishing they were safe on land and their natural size again.

"You're terr'ble small, Trot," remarked Cap'n Bill, looking at his companion.

"Same to you, Cap'n," she said with a laugh; "but as long as we have the purple berries we needn't worry about our size."

"In a circus," mused the old man, "we'd be curiosities.

But in a sunbonnet—high up in the air—sailin' over a big, unknown ocean—they ain't no word in any booktionary to describe us."

"Why, we're tiny, that's all," said the little girl. The Ork flew silently for a long time. The slight swaying of the sunbonnet made Cap'n Bill drowsy, and he began to doze. Trot, however, was wide awake, and after enduring the monotonous journey as long as she was able she called out:

"Don't you see land anywhere, Mr. Ork?"

"Not yet," he answered. "This is a big ocean and I've no idea in which direction the nearest land to that island lies; but if I keep flying in a straight line I'm sure to reach some place some time."

That seemed reasonable, so the little people in the sunbonnet remained as patient as possible; that is, Cap'n Bill dozed and Trot tried to remember her geography lessons so she could figure out what land they were likely to arrive at.

For hours and hours the Ork flew steadily, keeping to the straight line and searching with his eyes the horizon of the ocean for land. Cap'n Bill was fast asleep and snoring and Trot had laid her head on his shoulder to rest it when suddenly the Ork exclaimed:

"There! I've caught a glimpse of land, at last."

At this announcement they roused themselves. Cap'n Bill stood up and tried to peek over the edge of the sunbonnet.

"What does it look like?" he inquired.

"Looks like another island," said the Ork; "but I can judge it better in a minute or two."

"I don't care much for islands, since we visited that other one," declared Trot.

Soon the Ork made another announcement.

"It is surely an island, and a little one, too," said he. "But I won't stop, because I see a much bigger land straight ahead of it."

"That's right," approved Cap'n Bill. "The bigger the land, the better it will suit us."

"It's almost a continent," continued the Ork after a brief silence, during which he did not decrease the speed of his flight. "I wonder if it can be Orkland, the place I have been seeking so long?"

"I hope not," whispered Trot to Cap'n Bill—so softly that the Ork could not hear her—"for I shouldn't like to be in a country where only Orks live. This one Ork isn't a bad companion, but a lot of him wouldn't be much fun."

After a few more minutes of flying the Ork called out in a sad voice:

"No! this is not my country. It's a place I have never seen before, although I have wandered far and wide. It seems to be all mountains and deserts and green valleys and queer cities and lakes and rivers—mixed up in a very puzzling way."

"Most countries are like that," commented Cap'n Bill. "Are you going to land?"

"Pretty soon," was the reply. "There is a mountain peak just ahead of me. What do you say to our landing on that?"

"All right," agreed the sailor-man, for both he and Trot were getting tired of riding in the sunbonnet and longed to set foot on solid ground again.

So in a few minutes the Ork slowed down his speed and then came to a stop so easily that they were scarcely jarred at all. Then the creature squatted down until the sunbonnet rested on the ground, and began trying to unfasten with its claws the knotted strings.

This proved a very clumsy task, because the strings were tied at the back of the Ork's neck, just where his claws would not easily reach. After much fumbling he said:

"I'm afraid I can't let you out, and there is no one near to help me."

This was at first discouraging, but after a little thought Cap'n Bill said:

"If you don't mind, Trot, I can cut a slit in your sunbonnet with my knife."

"Do," she replied. "The slit won't matter, 'cause I can sew it up again afterward, when I am big."

So Cap'n Bill got out his knife, which was just as small, in proportion, as he was, and after considerable trouble managed to cut a long slit in the sunbonnet. First he squeezed through the opening himself and then helped Trot to get out.

When they stood on firm ground again their first act was to begin eating the dark purple berries which they had brought with them. Two of these Trot had guarded carefully during the long journey, by holding them in her lap, for their safety meant much to the tiny people.

"I'm not very hungry," said the little girl as she handed a berry to Cap'n Bill, "but hunger doesn't count, in this case. It's like taking medicine to make you well, so we must manage to eat 'em, somehow or other."

But the berries proved quite pleasant to taste and as Cap'n Bill and Trot nibbled at their edges their forms began to grow in size—slowly but steadily. The bigger they grew the easier it was for them to eat the berries, which of course became smaller to them, and by the time the fruit was eaten our friends had regained their natural size.

The little girl was greatly relieved when she found herself as large as she had ever been, and Cap'n Bill shared her satisfaction; for, although they had seen the effect of the berries on the Ork, they had not been sure the magic fruit would have the same effect on human beings, or that the magic would work in any other country than that in which the berries grew.

"What shall we do with the other four berries?" asked Trot, as she picked up her sunbonnet, marveling that she had ever been small enough to ride in it. "They're no good to us now, are they, Cap'n?"

"I'm not sure as to that," he replied. "If they were eaten by one who had never eaten the lavender berries, they might have no effect at all; but then, contrariwise, they might. One of 'em has got badly jammed, so I'll throw it away, but the other three I b'lieve I'll carry with me. They're magic things, you know, and may come handy to us some time."

He now searched in his big pockets and drew out a small wooden box with a sliding cover. The sailor had kept an assortment of nails, of various sizes, in this box, but those he now dumped loosely into his pocket and in the box placed the three sound purple berries.

When this important matter was attended to they found time to look about them and see what sort of place the Ork had landed them in.

The BUMPY MAN

The mountain on which they had alighted was not a barren waste, but had on its sides patches of green grass, some bushes, a few slender trees and here and there masses of tumbled rocks. The sides of the slope seemed rather steep, but with care one could climb up or down them with ease and safety. The view from where they now stood showed pleasant valleys and fertile hills lying below the heights. Trot thought she saw some houses of queer shapes scattered about the lower landscape, and there were moving dots that might be people or animals, yet were too far away for her to see them clearly.

Not far from the place where they stood was the top of the

mountain, which seemed to be flat, so the Ork proposed to his companions that he would fly up and see what was there.

"That's a good idea," said Trot, "'cause it's getting toward evening and we'll have to find a place to sleep."

The Ork had not been gone more than a few minutes when they saw him appear on the edge of the top which was nearest them.

"Come on up!" he called.

So Trot and Cap'n Bill began to ascend the steep slope and it did not take them long to reach the place where the Ork awaited them.

Their first view of the mountain top pleased them very much. It was a level space of wider extent than they had guessed and upon it grew grass of a brilliant green color. In the very center stood a house built of stone and very neatly constructed. No one was in sight, but smoke was coming from the chimney, so with one accord all three began walking toward the house.

"I wonder," said Trot, "in what country we are, and if it's very far from my home in California."

"Can't say as to that, partner," answered Cap'n Bill, "but I'm mighty certain we've come a long way since we struck that whirlpool."

"Yes," she agreed, with a sigh, "it must be miles and miles!"

"Distance means nothing," said the Ork. "I have flown pretty much all over the world, trying to find my home, and it is astonishing how many little countries there are, hidden away in the cracks and corners of this big globe of Earth. If one travels, he may find some new country at every turn, and a good many of them have never yet been put upon the maps."

"P'raps this is one of them," suggested Trot.

They reached the house after a brisk walk and Cap'n Bill knocked upon the door. It was at once opened by a rugged looking man who had "bumps all over him," as Trot afterward declared. There were bumps on his head, bumps on his body and bumps on his arms and legs and hands. Even his fingers had bumps on the ends of them. For dress he wore an old grey suit of fantastic design, which fitted him very badly because of the bumps it covered but could not conceal.

But the Bumpy Man's eyes were kind and twinkling in expression and as soon as he saw his visitors he bowed low and said in a rather bumpy voice:

"Happy day! Come in and shut the door, for it grows cool when the sun goes down. Winter is now upon us."

"Why, it isn't cold a bit, outside," said Trot, "so it can't be winter yet."

"You will change your mind about that in a little while," declared the Bumpy Man. "My bumps always tell me the state of the weather, and they feel just now as if a snowstorm was coming this way. But make yourselves at home, strangers. Supper is nearly ready and there is food enough for all."

Inside the house there was but one large room, simply but comfortably furnished. It had benches, a table and a fireplace, all made of stone. On the hearth a pot was bubbling and steaming, and Trot thought it had a rather nice smell. The visitors seated themselves upon the benches—except the Ork. which squatted by the fireplace—and the Bumpy Man began stirring the kettle briskly.

"May I ask what country this is, sir?" inquired Cap'n Bill.

"Goodness me—fruit-cake and apple-sauce!—don't you know where you are?" asked the Bumpy Man, as he stopped stirring and looked at the speaker in surprise.

"No," admitted Cap'n Bill. "We've just arrived."

"Lost your way?" questioned the Bumpy Man.

"Not exactly," said Cap'n Bill. "We didn't have any way to lose."

"Ah!" said the Bumpy Man, nodding his bumpy head. "This," he announced, in a solemn, impressive voice, "is the famous Land of Mo."

"Oh!" exclaimed the sailor and the girl, both in one breath. But, never having heard of the Land of Mo, they were no wiser than before.

"I thought that would startle you," remarked the Bumpy Man, well pleased, as he resumed his stirring. The Ork watched him a while in silence and then asked:

"Who may *you* be?"

"Me?" answered the Bumpy Man. "Haven't you heard of me? Gingerbread and lemon-juice! I'm known, far and wide, as the Mountain Ear."

They all received this information in silence at first, for they were trying to think what he could mean. Finally Trot mustered up courage to ask:

"What is a Mountain Ear, please?"

For answer the man turned around and faced them, waving the spoon with which he had been stirring the kettle, as he recited the following verses in a singsong tone of voice:

> *"Here's a mountain, hard of hearing,*
> *That's sad-hearted and needs cheering,*
> *So my duty is to listen to all sounds that Nature makes,*
> *So the hill won't get uneasy—*
> *Get to coughing, or get sneezy—*
> *For this monster bump, when frightened, is quite liable to*
> > *quakes.*
>
> *"You can hear a bell that's ringing;*
> *I can feel some people's singing;*
> *But a mountain isn't sensible of what goes on, and so*
> *When I hear a blizzard blowing*
> *Or it's raining hard, or snowing,*
> *I tell it to the mountain and the mountain seems to know.*
>
> *"Thus I benefit all people*
> *While I'm living on this steeple,*
> *For I keep the mountain steady so my neighbors all may thrive.*

> *With my list'ning and my shouting*
> *I prevent this mount from spouting,*
> *And that makes me so important that I'm glad that I'm*
>   *alive."*

When he had finished these lines of verse the Bumpy Man turned again to resume his stirring. The Ork laughed softly and Cap'n Bill whistled to himself and Trot made up her mind that the Mountain Ear must be a little crazy. But the Bumpy Man seemed satisfied that he had explained his position fully and presently he placed four stone plates upon the table and then lifted the kettle from the fire and poured some of its contents on each of the plates. Cap'n Bill and Trot at once approached the table, for they were hungry, but when she examined her plate the little girl exclaimed:

"Why, it's molasses candy!"

"To be sure," returned the Bumpy Man, with a pleasant smile. "Eat it quick, while it's hot, for it cools very quickly this winter weather."

With this he seized a stone spoon and began putting the hot molasses candy into his mouth, while the others watched him in astonishment.

"Doesn't it burn you?" asked the girl.

"No indeed," said he. "Why don't you eat? Aren't you hungry?"

"Yes," she replied, "I am hungry. But we usually eat our

candy when it is cold and hard. We always pull molasses candy before we eat it."

"Ha, ha, ha!" laughed the Mountain Ear. "What a funny idea! Where in the world did you come from?"

"California," she said.

"California! Pooh! there isn't any such place. I've heard of every place in the Land of Mo, but I never before heard of California."

"It isn't in the Land of Mo," she explained.

"Then it isn't worth talking about," declared the Bumpy Man, helping himself again from the steaming kettle, for he had been eating all the time he talked.

"For my part," sighed Cap'n Bill, "I'd like a decent square meal, once more, just by way of variety. In the last place there was nothing but fruit to eat, and here it's worse, for there's nothing but candy."

"Molasses candy isn't so bad," said Trot. "Mine's nearly cool enough to pull, already. Wait a bit, Cap'n, and you can eat it."

A little later she was able to gather the candy from the stone plate and begin to work it back and forth with her hands. The Mountain Ear was greatly amazed at this and watched her closely. It was really good candy and pulled beautifully, so that Trot was soon ready to cut it into chunks for eating.

Cap'n Bill condescended to eat one or two pieces and the Ork ate several, but the Bumpy Man refused to try it. Trot finished the plate of candy herself and then asked for a drink of water.

"Water?" said the Mountain Ear wonderingly. "What is that?"

"Something to drink. Don't you have water in Mo?"

"None that ever I heard of," said he. "But I can give you some fresh lemonade. I caught it in a jar the last time it rained, which was only day before yesterday."

"Oh, does it rain lemonade here?" she inquired.

"Always; and it is very refreshing and healthful."

With this he brought from a cupboard a stone jar and a dipper, and the girl found it very nice lemonade, indeed. Cap'n Bill liked it, too; but the Ork would not touch it.

"If there is no water in this country, I cannot stay here for long," the creature declared. "Water means life to man and beast and bird."

"There must be water in lemonade," said Trot.

"Yes," answered the Ork, "I suppose so; but there are other things in it, too, and they spoil the good water."

The day's adventures had made our wanderers tired, so the Bumpy Man brought them some blankets in which they rolled themselves and then lay down before the fire, which their host kept alive with fuel all through the night. Trot wakened several times and found the Mountain Ear always alert and listening intently for the slightest sound. But the little girl could hear no sound at all except the snores of Cap'n Bill.

···—·◄ Chapter 8 ►·—···

BUTTON-BRIGHT Is LOST and FOUND AGAIN

"Wake up—wake up!" called the voice of the Bumpy Man. "Didn't I tell you winter was coming? I could hear it coming with my left ear, and the proof is that it is now snowing hard outside."

"Is it?" said Trot, rubbing her eyes and creeping out of her blanket. "Where I live, in California, I have never seen snow, except far away on the tops of high mountains."

"Well, this is the top of a high mountain," returned the bumpy one, "and for that reason we get our heaviest snowfalls right here."

The little girl went to the window and looked out. The

air was filled with falling white flakes, so large in size and so queer in form that she was puzzled.

"Are you certain this is snow?" she asked.

"To be sure. I must get my snow-shovel and turn out to shovel a path. Would you like to come with me?"

"Yes," she said, and followed the Bumpy Man out when he opened the door. Then she exclaimed: "Why, it isn't cold a bit!"

"Of course not," replied the man. "It was cold last night, before the snowstorm; but snow, when it falls, is always crisp and warm."

Trot gathered a handful of it.

"Why, it's popcorn?" she cried.

"Certainly; all snow is popcorn. What did you expect it to be?"

"Popcorn is not snow in my country."

"Well, it is the only snow we have in the Land of Mo, so you may as well make the best of it," said he, a little impatiently. "I'm not responsible for the absurd things that happen in your country, and when you're in Mo you must do as the Momen do. Eat some of our snow, and you will find it is good. The only fault I find with our snow is that we get too much of it at times."

With this the Bumpy Man set to work shoveling a path and he was so quick and industrious that he piled up the popcorn in great banks on either side of the trail that led to the mountain-top from the plains below. While he worked, Trot ate popcorn and found it crisp and slightly warm, as well as nicely salted and buttered. Presently Cap'n Bill came out of the house and joined her.

"What's this?" he asked.

"Mo snow," said she. "But it isn't real snow, although it falls from the sky. It's popcorn."

Cap'n Bill tasted it; then he sat down in the path and began to eat. The Ork came out and pecked away with its bill as fast as it could. They all liked popcorn and they all were hungry this morning.

Meantime the flakes of "Mo snow" came down so fast that the number of them almost darkened the air. The Bumpy Man was now shoveling quite a distance down the mountain-side, while the path behind him rapidly filled up with fresh-fallen popcorn. Suddenly Trot heard him call out:

"Goodness gracious—mince pie and pancakes!—here is some one buried in the snow."

She ran toward him at once and the others followed, wading through the corn and crunching it underneath their feet. The Mo snow was pretty deep where the Bumpy Man was shoveling and from beneath a great bank of it he had uncovered a pair of feet.

"Dear me! Someone has been lost in the storm," said Cap'n Bill. "I hope he is still alive. Let's pull him out and see."

He took hold of one foot and the Bumpy Man took hold

of the other. Then they both pulled and out from the heap of popcorn came a little boy. He was dressed in a brown velvet jacket and knickerbockers, with brown stockings, buckled shoes and a blue shirt-waist that had frills down its front. When drawn from the heap the boy was chewing a mouthful of popcorn and both his hands were full of it. So at first he couldn't speak to his rescuers but lay quite still and eyed them calmly until he had swallowed his mouthful. Then he said:

"Get my cap," and stuffed more popcorn into his mouth.

While the Bumpy Man began shoveling into the corn-bank to find the boy's cap, Trot was laughing joyfully and Cap'n Bill had a broad grin on his face. The Ork looked from one to another and asked:

"Who is this stranger?"

"Why, it's Button-Bright, of course," answered Trot. "If anyone ever finds a lost boy, he can make up his mind it's Button-Bright. But how he ever came to be lost in this faraway country is more'n I can make out."

"Where does he belong?" inquired the Ork.

"His home used to be in Philadelphia, I think; but I'm quite sure Button-Bright doesn't belong anywhere."

"That's right," said the boy, nodding his head as he swallowed the second mouthful.

"Everyone belongs somewhere," remarked the Ork.

"Not me," insisted Button-Bright. "I'm half way round the

world from Philadelphia, and I've lost my Magic Umbrella, that used to carry me anywhere. Stands to reason that if I can't get back I haven't any home. But I don't care much. This is a pretty good country, Trot. I've had lots of fun here."

By this time the Mountain Ear had secured the boy's cap and was listening to the conversation with much interest.

"It seems you know this poor, snow-covered cast-away," he said.

"Yes, indeed," answered Trot. "We made a journey together to Sky Island, once, and were good friends."

"Well, then I'm glad I saved his life," said the Bumpy Man.

"Much obliged, Mr. Knobs," said Button-Bright, sitting up and staring at him, "but I don't believe you've saved anything except some popcorn that I might have eaten had you not disturbed me. It was nice and warm in that bank of popcorn, and there was plenty to eat. What made you dig me out? And what makes you so bumpy everywhere?"

"As for the bumps," replied the man, looking at himself with much pride, "I was born with them and I suspect they were a gift from the fairies. They make me look rugged and big, like the mountain I serve."

"All right," said Button-Bright and began eating popcorn again.

It had stopped snowing, now, and great flocks of birds were gathering around the mountain-side, eating the popcorn with much eagerness and scarcely noticing the people at all.

There were birds of every size and color, most of them having gorgeous feathers and plumes.

"Just look at them!" exclaimed the Ork scornfully. "Aren't they dreadful creatures, all covered with feathers?"

"I think they're beautiful," said Trot, and this made the Ork so indignant that he went back into the house and sulked.

Button-Bright reached out his hand and caught a big bird by the leg. At once it rose into the air and it was so strong that it nearly carried the little boy with it. He let go the leg in a hurry and the bird flew down again and began to eat of the popcorn, not being frightened in the least.

This gave Cap'n Bill an idea. He felt in his pocket and drew out several pieces of stout string. Moving very quietly, so as to not alarm the birds, he crept up to several of the biggest ones and tied cords around their legs, thus making them prisoners. The birds were so intent on their eating that they did not notice what had happened to them, and when about twenty had been captured in this manner Cap'n Bill tied the ends of all the strings together and fastened them to a huge stone, so they could not escape.

The Bumpy Man watched the old sailor's actions with much curiosity.

"The birds will be quiet until they've eaten up all the snow," he said, "but then they will want to fly away to their homes. Tell me, sir, what will the poor things do when they find they can't fly?"

"It may worry 'em a little," replied Cap'n Bill, "but they're not going to be hurt if they take it easy and behave themselves."

Our friends had all made a good breakfast of the delicious popcorn and now they walked toward the house again. Button-Bright walked beside Trot and held her hand in his, because they were old friends and he liked the little girl very much. The boy was not so old as Trot, and small as she was he was half a head shorter in height. The most remarkable thing about Button-Bright was that he was always quiet and composed, whatever happened, and nothing was ever able to astonish him. Trot liked him because he was not rude and never tried to plague her. Cap'n Bill liked him because he had found the boy cheerful and brave at all times, and willing to do anything he was asked to do.

When they came to the house Trot sniffed the air and asked "Don't I smell perfume?"

"I think you do," said the Bumpy Man. "You smell violets, and that proves there is a breeze springing up from the south. All our winds and breezes are perfumed and for that reason we are glad to have them blow in our direction. The south breeze always has a violet odor; the north breeze has the fragrance of wild roses; the east breeze is perfumed with lilies-of-the-valley and the west wind with lilac blossoms. So we need no weathervane to tell us which way the wind is blowing. We have only to smell the perfume and it informs us at once."

Inside the house they found the Ork, and Button-Bright regarded the strange, birdlike creature with curious interest. After examining it closely for a time he asked:

"Which way does your tail whirl?"

"Either way," said the Ork.

Button-Bright put out his hand and tried to spin it.

"Don't do that!" exclaimed the Ork.

"Why not?" inquired the boy.

"Because it happens to be my tail, and I reserve the right to whirl it myself," explained the Ork.

"Let's go out and fly somewhere," proposed Button-Bright. "I want to see how the tail works."

"Not now," said the Ork. "I appreciate your interest in me, which I fully deserve; but I only fly when I am going somewhere, and if I got started I might not stop."

"That reminds me," remarked Cap'n Bill, "to ask you, friend Ork, how we are going to get away from here?"

"Get away!" exclaimed the Bumpy Man. "Why don't you stay here? You won't find any nicer place than Mo."

"Have you been anywhere else, sir?"

"No; I can't say that I have," admitted the Mountain Ear.

"Then permit me to say you're no judge," declared Cap'n Bill. "But you haven't answered my question, friend Ork. How are we to get away from this mountain?"

The Ork reflected a while before he answered.

"I might carry one of you—the boy or the girl—upon my

back," said he, "but three big people are more than I can manage, although I have carried two of you for a short distance. You ought not to have eaten those purple berries so soon."

"P'r'aps we did make a mistake," Cap'n Bill acknowledged.

"Or we might have brought some of those lavender berries with us, instead of so many purple ones," suggested Trot regretfully.

Cap'n Bill made no reply to this statement, which showed he did not fully agree with the little girl; but he fell into deep thought, with wrinkled brows, and finally he said:

"If those purple berries would make anything grow bigger, whether it'd eaten the lavender ones or not, I could find a way out of our troubles."

They did not understand this speech and looked at the old sailor as if expecting him to explain what he meant. But just then a chorus of shrill cries rose from outside.

"Here! Let me go—let me go!" the voices seemed to say. "Why are we insulted in this way? Mountain Ear, come and help us!"

Trot ran to the window and looked out.

"It's the birds you caught, Cap'n," she said. "I didn't know they could talk."

"Oh, yes; all the birds in Mo are educated to talk," said the Bumpy Man. Then he looked at Cap'n Bill uneasily and added: "Won't you let the poor things go?"

"I'll see," replied the sailor, and walked out to where the birds were fluttering and complaining because the strings would not allow them to fly away.

"Listen to me!" he cried, and at once they became still. "We three people who are strangers in your land want to go to some other country, and we want three of you birds to carry us there. We know we are asking a great favor, but it's the only way we can think of—excep' walkin', an' I'm not much good at that because I've a wooden leg. Besides, Trot an' Button-Bright are too small to undertake a long and tiresome journey. Now, tell me: Which three of you birds will consent to carry us?"

The birds looked at one another as if greatly astonished. Then one of them replied:

"You must be crazy, old man. Not one of us is big enough to fly with even the smallest of your party."

"I'll fix the matter of size," promised Cap'n Bill. "If three of you will agree to carry us, I'll make you big an' strong enough to do it, so it won't worry you a bit."

The birds considered this gravely. Living in a magic country, they had no doubt but that the strange one-legged man could do what he said. After a little, one of them asked:

"If you make us big, would we stay big always?"

"I think so," replied Cap'n Bill.

They chattered a while among themselves and then the bird that had first spoken said: "I'll go, for one."

"So will I," said another; and after a pause a third said: "I'll go, too."

Perhaps more would have volunteered, for it seemed that for some reason they all longed to be bigger than they were; but three were enough for Cap'n Bill's purpose and so he promptly released all the others, who immediately flew away.

The three that remained were cousins, and all were of the same brilliant plumage and in size about as large as eagles. When Trot questioned them she found they were quite young, having only abandoned their nests a few weeks before. They were strong young birds, with clear, brave eyes, and the little girl decided they were the most beautiful of all the feathered creatures she had ever seen.

Cap'n Bill now took from his pocket the wooden box with the sliding cover and removed the three purple berries, which were still in good condition.

"Eat these," he said, and gave one to each of the birds. They obeyed, finding the fruit very pleasant to taste. In a few seconds they began to grow in size and grew so fast that Trot feared they would never stop. But they finally did stop growing, and then they were much larger than the Ork, and nearly the size of full-grown ostriches.

Cap'n Bill was much pleased by this result.

"You can carry us now, all right," said he.

The birds strutted around with pride, highly pleased with their immense size.

"I don't see, though," said Trot doubtfully, "how we're going to ride on their backs without falling off."

"We're not going to ride on their backs," answered Cap'n Bill. "I'm going to make swings for us to ride in."

He then asked the Bumpy Man for some rope, but the man had no rope. He had, however, an old suit of grey clothes which he gladly presented to Cap'n Bill, who cut the cloth into strips and twisted it so that it was almost as strong as rope. With this material he attached to each bird a swing that dangled below its feet, and Button-Bright made a trial flight in one of them to prove that it was safe and comfortable. When all this had been arranged one of the birds asked:

"Where do you wish us to take you?"

"Why, just follow the Ork," said Cap'n Bill. "He will be our leader, and wherever the Ork flies you are to fly, and wherever the Ork lands you are to land. Is that satisfactory?"

The birds declared it was quite satisfactory, so Cap'n Bill took counsel with the Ork.

"On our way here," said that peculiar creature, "I noticed a broad, sandy desert at the left of me, on which was no living thing."

"Then we'd better keep away from it," replied the sailor.

"Not so," insisted the Ork. "I have found, on my travels, that the most pleasant countries often lie in the midst of deserts; so I think it would be wise for us to fly over this desert and discover what lies beyond it. For in the direction we came from lies the ocean, as we well know, and beyond here is this strange Land of Mo, which we do not care to explore. On one side, as we can see from this mountain, is a broad expanse of plain, and on the other the desert. For my part, I vote for the desert."

"What do you say, Trot?" inquired Cap'n Bill.

"It's all the same to me," she replied.

No one thought of asking Button-Bright's opinion, so it was decided to fly over the desert. They bade good-bye to the Bumpy Man and thanked him for his kindness and hospitality. Then they seated themselves in the swings—one for each bird—and told the Ork to start away and they would follow.

The whirl of the Ork's tail astonished the birds at first, but after he had gone a short distance they rose in the air, carrying their passengers easily, and flew with strong, regular strokes of their great wings in the wake of their leader.

······◄ Chapter 9 ►·······

The KINGDOM of JINXLAND

Trot rode with more comfort than she had expected, although the swing swayed so much that she had to hold on tight with both hands. Cap'n Bill's bird followed the Ork, and Trot came next, with Button-Bright trailing behind her. It was quite an imposing procession, but unfortunately there was no one to see it, for the Ork had headed straight for the great sandy desert and in a few minutes after starting they were flying high over the broad waste, where no living thing could exist.

The little girl thought this would be a bad place for the birds to lose strength, or for the cloth ropes to give way; but although she could not help feeling a trifle nervous and fidgety she had confidence in the huge and brilliantly plumaged bird that bore her, as well as in Cap'n Bill's knowledge of how to twist and fasten a rope so it would hold.

That was a remarkably big desert. There was nothing to relieve the monotony of view and every minute seemed an hour and every hour a day. Disagreeable fumes and gases rose from the sands, which would have been deadly to the travelers had they not been so high in the air. As it was, Trot was beginning to feel sick, when a breath of fresher air filled her nostrils and on looking ahead she saw a great cloud of pink-tinted mist. Even while she wondered what it could be, the Ork plunged boldly into the mist and the other birds followed. She could see nothing for a time, nor could the bird which carried her see where the Ork had gone, but it kept flying as sturdily as ever and in a few moments the mist was passed and the girl saw a most beautiful landscape spread out below her, extending as far as her eye could reach.

She saw bits of forest, verdure clothed hills, fields of waving grain, fountains, rivers and lakes; and throughout the scene were scattered groups of pretty houses and a few grand castles and palaces.

Over all this delightful landscape—which from Trot's high perch seemed like a magnificent painted picture—was a rosy glow such as we sometimes see in the west at sunset. In this case, however, it was not in the west only, but everywhere.

No wonder the Ork paused to circle slowly over this lovely

country. The other birds followed his action, all eyeing the place with equal delight. Then, as with one accord, the four formed a group and slowly sailed downward. This brought them to that part of the newly-discovered land which bordered on the desert's edge; but it was just as pretty here as anywhere, so the Ork and the birds alighted and the three passengers at once got out of their swings.

"Oh, Cap'n Bill, isn't this fine an' dandy?" exclaimed Trot rapturously. "How lucky we were to discover this beautiful country!"

"The country seems rather high class, I'll admit, Trot," replied the old sailor-man, looking around him, "but we don't know, as yet, what its people are like."

"No one could live in such a country without being happy and good—I'm sure of that," she said earnestly. "Don't you think so, Button-Bright?"

"I'm not thinking, just now," answered the little boy. "It tires me to think, and I never seem to gain anything by it. When we see the people who live here we will know what they are like, and no 'mount of thinking will make them any different."

"That's true enough," said the Ork. "But now I want to make a proposal. While you are getting acquainted with this new country, which looks as if it contains everything to make one happy, I would like to fly along—all by myself—and see if I can find my home on the other side of the great desert. If

I do, I will stay there, of course. But if I fail to find Orkland I will return to you in a week, to see if I can do anything more to assist you."

They were sorry to lose their queer companion, but could offer no objection to the plan; so the Ork bade them good-bye and rising swiftly in the air, he flew over the country and was soon lost to view in the distance.

The three birds which had carried our friends now begged permission to return by the way they had come, to their own homes, saying they were anxious to show their families how big they had become. So Cap'n Bill and Trot and Button-Bright all thanked them gratefully for their assistance and soon the birds began their long flight toward the Land of Mo.

Being now left to themselves in this strange land, the three comrades selected a pretty pathway and began walking along it. They believed this path would lead them to a splendid castle which they espied in the distance, the turrets of which towered far above the tops of the trees which surrounded it. It did not seem very far away, so they sauntered on slowly, admiring the beautiful ferns and flowers that lined the pathway and listening to the singing of the birds and the soft chirping of the grasshoppers.

Presently the path wound over a little hill. In a valley that lay beyond the hill was a tiny cottage surrounded by flower beds and fruit trees. On the shady porch of the cottage they saw, as they approached, a pleasant faced woman sitting amidst a group of children, to whom she was telling stories. The children quickly discovered the strangers and ran toward them with exclamations of astonishment, so that Trot and her friends became the center of a curious group, all chattering excitedly. Cap'n Bill's wooden leg seemed to arouse the wonder of the children, as they could not understand why he had not two meat legs. This attention seemed to please the old sailor, who patted the heads of the children kindly and then, raising his hat to the woman, he inquired:

"Can you tell us, madam, just what country this is?"

She stared hard at all three of the strangers as she replied briefly: "Jinxland."

"Oh!" exclaimed Cap'n Bill, with a puzzled look. "And where is Jinxland, please?"

"In the Quadling Country," said she.

"What!" cried Trot, in sudden excitement. "Do you mean to say this is the Quadling Country of the Land of Oz?"

"To be sure I do," the woman answered. "Every bit of land that is surrounded by the great desert is the Land of Oz, as you ought to know as well as I do; but I'm sorry to say that Jinxland is separated from the rest of the Quadling Country by that row of high mountains you see yonder, which have such steep sides that no one can cross them. So we live here all by ourselves, and are ruled by our own King, instead of by Ozma of Oz."

"I've been to the Land of Oz before," said Button-Bright, "but I've never been here."

"Did you ever hear of Jinxland before?" asked Trot.

"No," said Button-Bright.

"It is on the Map of Oz, though," asserted the woman, "and it's a fine country, I assure you. If only," she added, and then paused to look around her with a frightened expression. "If only—" here she stopped again, as if not daring to go on with her speech.

"If only what, ma'am?" asked Cap'n Bill.

The woman sent the children into the house. Then she came closer to the strangers and whispered: "If only we had a different King, we would be very happy and contented."

"What's the matter with your King?" asked Trot, curiously. But the woman seemed frightened to have said so much. She retreated to her porch, merely saying:

"The King punishes severely any treason on the part of his subjects."

"What's treason?" asked Button-Bright.

"In this case," replied Cap'n Bill, "treason seems to consist of knockin' the King; but I guess we know his disposition now as well as if the lady had said more."

"I wonder," said Trot, going up to the woman, "if you could spare us something to eat. We haven't had anything but popcorn and lemonade for a long time."

"Bless your heart! Of course I can spare you some food," the woman answered, and entering her cottage she soon returned with a tray loaded with sandwiches, cakes and cheese. One of the children drew a bucket of clear, cold water from a spring and the three wanderers ate heartily and enjoyed the good things immensely.

When Button-Bright could eat no more he filled the pockets of his jacket with cakes and cheese, and not even the children objected to this. Indeed they all seemed pleased to see the strangers eat, so Cap'n Bill decided that no matter what the King of Jinxland was like, the people would prove friendly and hospitable.

"Whose castle is that, yonder, ma'am?" he asked, waving his hand toward the towers that rose above the trees.

"It belongs to his Majesty, King Krewl," she said.

"Oh, indeed; and does he live there?"

"When he is not out hunting with his fierce courtiers and war captains," she replied.

"Is he hunting now?" Trot inquired.

"I do not know, my dear. The less we know about the King's actions the safer we are."

It was evident the woman did not like to talk about King Krewl and so, having finished their meal, they said good-bye and continued along the pathway.

"Don't you think we'd better keep away from that King's castle, Cap'n?" asked Trot.

"Well," said he, "King Krewl would find out, sooner or later, that we are in his country, so we may as well face the music now. Perhaps he isn't quite so bad as that woman thinks he is. Kings aren't always popular with their people, you know, even if they do the best they know how."

"Ozma is pop'lar," said Button-Bright.

"Ozma is diff'rent from any other Ruler, from all I've heard," remarked Trot musingly, as she walked beside the boy. "And, after all, we are really in the Land of Oz, where Ozma rules ev'ry King and ev'rybody else. I never heard of anybody getting hurt in her dominions, did you, Button-Bright?"

"Not when she knows about it," he replied. "But those birds landed us in just the wrong place, seems to me. They might have carried us right on, over that row of mountains, to the Em'rald City."

"True enough," said Cap'n Bill; "but they didn't, an' so we must make the best of Jinxland. Let's try not to be afraid."

"Oh, I'm not very scared," said Button-Bright, pausing to look at a pink rabbit that popped its head out of a hole in the field near by.

"Nor am I," added Trot. "Really, Cap'n, I'm so glad to be anywhere at all in the wonderful fairyland of Oz that I think I'm the luckiest girl in all the world. Dorothy lives in the Em'rald City, you know, and so does the Scarecrow and the Tin Wood-man and Tik-Tok and the Shaggy Man—and all the rest of 'em that we've heard so much about—not to mention Ozma, who must be the sweetest and loveliest girl in all the world!"

"Take your time, Trot," advised Button-Bright. "You don't have to say it all in one breath, you know. And you haven't mentioned half of the curious people in the Em'rald City."

"That 'ere Em'rald City," said Cap'n Bill impressively, "happens to be on the other side o' those mountains, that we're told no one is able to cross. I don't want to discourage of you, Trot, but we're a'most as much separated from your Ozma an' Dorothy as we were when we lived in Californy."

There was so much truth in this statement that they all walked on in silence for some time. Finally they reached the grove of stately trees that bordered the grounds of the King's castle. They had gone halfway through it when the sound of sobbing, as of someone in bitter distress, reached their ears and caused them to halt abruptly.

PON, the GARDENER'S BOY

It was Button-Bright who first discovered, lying on his face beneath a broad spreading tree near the pathway, a young man whose body shook with the force of his sobs. He was dressed in a long brown smock and had sandals on his feet, betokening one in humble life. His head was bare and showed a shock of brown, curly hair. Button-Bright looked down on the young man and said:

"Who cares, anyhow?"

"I do!" cried the young man, interrupting his sobs to roll over, face upward, that he might see who had spoken. "I care, for my heart is broken!"

"Can't you get another one?" asked the little boy.

"I don't want another!" wailed the young man.

By this time Trot and Cap'n Bill arrived at the spot and the girl leaned over and said in a sympathetic voice:

"Tell us your troubles and perhaps we may help you."

The youth sat up, then, and bowed politely. Afterward he got upon his feet, but still kept wringing his hands as he tried to choke down his sobs. Trot thought he was very brave to control such awful agony so well.

"My name is Pon," he began. "I'm the gardener's boy."

"Then the gardener of the King is your father, I suppose," said Trot.

"Not my father, but my master," was the reply

"I do the work and the gardener gives the orders. And it was not my fault, in the least, that the Princess Gloria fell in love with me."

"Did she, really?" asked the little girl.

"I don't see why," remarked Button-Bright, staring at the youth.

"And who may the Princess Gloria be?" inquired Cap'n Bill.

"She is the niece of King Krewl, who is her guardian. The Princess lives in the castle and is the loveliest and sweetest maiden in all Jinxland. She is fond of flowers and used to walk in the gardens with her attendants. At such times, if I was working at my tasks, I used to cast down my eyes as Gloria passed me; but one day I glanced up and found her gazing at me with a very tender look in her eyes. The next day she dismissed her attendants and, coming to my side, began to talk with me. She said I had touched her heart as no other young man had ever done. I kissed her hand. Just then the King came around a bend in the walk. He struck me with his fist and kicked me with his foot. Then he seized the arm of the Princess and rudely dragged her into the castle."

"Wasn't he awful!" gasped Trot indignantly.

"He is a very abrupt King," said Pon, "so it was the least I could expect. Up to that time I had not thought of loving Princess Gloria, but realizing it would be impolite not to return her love, I did so. We met at evening, now and then, and she told me the King wanted her to marry a rich courtier named Googly-Goo, who is old enough to be Gloria's father. She has refused Googly-Goo thirty-nine times, but he still persists and has brought many rich presents to bribe the King. On that account King Krewl has commanded his niece to marry the old man, but the Princess has assured me, time and again, that she will wed only me. This morning we happened to meet in the grape arbor and as I was respectfully saluting the cheek of the Princess, two of the King's guards seized me and beat me terribly before the very eyes of Gloria, whom the King himself held back so she could not interfere."

"Why, this King must be a monster!" cried Trot.

"He is far worse than that," said Pon, mournfully.

"But, see here," interrupted Cap'n Bill, who had listened

carefully to Pon. "This King may not be so much to blame, after all. Kings are proud folks, because they're so high an' mighty, an' it isn't reasonable for a royal Princess to marry a common gardener's boy."

"It isn't right," declared Button-Bright. "A Princess should marry a Prince."

"I'm not a common gardener's boy," protested Pon. "If I had my rights I would be the King instead of Krewl. As it is, I'm a Prince, and as royal as any man in Jinxland."

"How does that come?" asked Cap'n Bill.

"My father used to be the King and Krewl was his Prime Minister. But one day while out hunting, King Phearse—that was my father's name—had a quarrel with Krewl and tapped him gently on the nose with the knuckles of his closed hand. This so provoked the wicked Krewl that he tripped my father backward, so that he fell into a deep pond. At once Krewl threw in a mass of heavy stones, which so weighted down my poor father that his body could not rise again to the surface. It is impossible to kill anyone in this land, as perhaps you know, but when my father was pressed down into the mud at the bottom of the deep pool and the stones held him so he could never escape, he was of no more use to himself or the world than if he had died. Knowing this, Krewl proclaimed himself King, taking possession of the royal castle and driving all my father's people out. I was a small boy, then, but when I grew up I became a gardener. I have served King Krewl without his knowing that I am the son of the same King Phearse whom he so cruelly made away with."

"My, but that's a terr'bly exciting story!" said Trot, drawing a long breath. "But tell us, Pon, who was Gloria's father?"

"Oh, he was the King before my father," replied Pon. "Father was Prime Minister for King Kynd, who was Gloria's father. She was only a baby when King Kynd fell into the Great Gulf that lies just this side of the mountains—the same mountains that separate Jinxland from the rest of the Land of Oz. It is said the Great Gulf has no bottom; but, however that may be, King Kynd has never been seen again and my father became King in his place."

"Seems to me," said Trot, "that if Gloria had her rights she would be Queen of Jinxland."

"Well, her father was a King," admitted Pon, "and so was my father; so we are of equal rank, although she's a great lady and I'm a humble gardener's boy. I can't see why we should not marry if we want to except that King Krewl won't let us."

"It's a sort of mixed-up mess, taken altogether," remarked Cap'n Bill. "But we are on our way to visit King Krewl, and if we get a chance, young man, we'll put in a good word for you."

"Do, please!" begged Pon.

"Was it the flogging you got that broke your heart?" inquired Button-Bright.

"Why, it helped to break it, of course," said Pon.

"I'd get it fixed up, if I were you," advised the boy, tossing a pebble at a chipmunk in a tree. "You ought to give Gloria just as good a heart as she gives you."

"That's common sense," agreed Cap'n Bill. So they left the gardener's boy standing beside the path, and resumed their journey toward the castle.

·····◄ Chapter 11 ►····

The WICKED KING and GOOGLY-GOO

When our friends approached the great doorway of the castle they found it guarded by several soldiers dressed in splendid uniforms. They were armed with swords and lances. Cap'n Bill walked straight up to them and asked:

"Does the King happen to be at home?"

"His Magnificent and Glorious Majesty, King Krewl, is at present inhabiting his Royal Castle," was the stiff reply.

"Then I guess we'll go in an' say how-d'ye-do," continued Cap'n Bill, attempting to enter the doorway. But a soldier barred his way with a lance.

"Who are you, what are your names, and where do you come from?" demanded the Soldier.

"You wouldn't know if we told you," returned the sailor, "seein' as we're strangers in a strange land."

"Oh, if you are strangers you will be permitted to enter," said the Soldier, lowering his lance. "His Majesty is very fond of strangers."

"Do many strangers come here?" asked Trot.

"You are the first that ever came to our country," said the man. "But his Majesty has often said that if strangers ever arrived in Jinxland he would see that they had a very exciting time."

Cap'n Bill scratched his chin thoughtfully. He wasn't very favorably impressed by this last remark. But he decided that as there was no way of escape from Jinxland it would be wise to confront the King boldly and try to win his favor. So they entered the castle, escorted by one of the soldiers.

It was certainly a fine castle, with many large rooms, all beautifully furnished. The passages were winding and handsomely decorated, and after following several of these the Soldier led them into an open court that occupied the very center of the huge building. It was surrounded on every side by high turreted walls, and contained beds of flowers, fountains and walks of many colored marbles which were matched together in quaint designs. In an open space near the middle of the court they saw a group of courtiers and their ladies, who surrounded a lean man who wore upon his head a jeweled crown. His face was hard and sullen and through the slits of his half-closed eyelids the eyes glowed like coals of fire. He was dressed in brilliant satins and velvets and was seated in a golden throne-chair.

This personage was King Krewl, and as soon as Cap'n Bill saw him the old sailor knew at once that he was not going to like the King of Jinxland.

"Hello! who's here?" said his Majesty, with a deep scowl.

"Strangers, Sire," answered the Soldier, bowing so low that his forehead touched the marble tiles.

"Strangers, eh? Well, well; what an unexpected visit! Advance, strangers, and give an account of yourselves."

The King's voice was as harsh as his features. Trot shuddered a little but Cap'n Bill calmly replied:

"There ain't much for us to say, 'cept as we've arrived to look over your country an' see how we like it. Judgin' from the way you speak, you don't know who we are, or you'd be jumpin' up to shake hands an' offer us seats. Kings usually treat us pretty well, in the great big Outside World where we come from, but in this little kingdom—which don't amount to much, anyhow—folks don't seem to 'a' got much culchure."

The King listened with amazement to this bold speech, first with a frown and then gazing at the two children and the old sailor with evident curiosity. The courtiers were dumb with fear, for no one had ever dared speak in such a manner to their self-willed, cruel King before. His Majesty, however, was somewhat frightened, for cruel people are always cowards, and he feared these mysterious strangers might possess magic powers that would destroy him unless he treated them well. So he commanded his people to give the new arrivals seats, and they obeyed with trembling haste.

After being seated, Cap'n Bill lighted his pipe and began puffing smoke from it, a sight so strange to them that it filled them all with wonder. Presently the King asked:

"How did you penetrate to this hidden country? Did you cross the desert or the mountains?"

"Desert," answered Cap'n Bill, as if the task were too easy to be worth talking about.

"Indeed! No one has ever been able to do that before," said the King.

"Well, it's easy enough, if you know how," asserted Cap'n Bill, so carelessly that it greatly impressed his hearers. The King shifted in his throne uneasily. He was more afraid of these strangers than before.

"Do you intend to stay long in Jinxland?" was his next anxious question.

"Depends on how we like it," said Cap'n Bill. "Just now I might suggest to your Majesty to order some rooms got ready for us in your dinky little castle here. And a royal banquet, with some fried onions an' pickled tripe, would set easy on our stomicks an' make us a bit happier than we are now."

"Your wishes shall be attended to," said King Krewl, but

his eyes flashed from between their slits in a wicked way that made Trot hope the food wouldn't be poisoned. At the King's command several of his attendants hastened away to give the proper orders to the castle servants and no sooner were they gone than a skinny old man entered the courtyard and bowed before the King.

This disagreeable person was dressed in rich velvets, with many furbelows and laces. He was covered with golden chains, finely wrought rings and jeweled ornaments. He walked with mincing steps and glared at all the courtiers as if he considered himself far superior to any or all of them.

"Well, well, your Majesty; what news—what news?" he demanded, in a shrill, cracked voice.

The King gave him a surly look.

"No news, Lord Googly-Goo, except that strangers have arrived," he said.

Googly-Goo cast a contemptuous glance at Cap'n Bill and a disdainful one at Trot and Button-Bright. Then he said:

"Strangers do not interest me, your Majesty. But the Princess Gloria is very interesting—very interesting, indeed! What does she say, Sire? Will she marry me?"

"Ask her," retorted the King.

"I have, many times; and every time she has refused."

"Well?" said the King harshly.

"Well," said Googly-Goo in a jaunty tone, "a bird that can sing, and won't sing, must be made to sing."

"Huh!" sneered the King. "That's easy, with a bird; but a girl is harder to manage."

"Still," persisted Googly-Goo, "we must overcome difficulties. The chief trouble is that Gloria fancies she loves that miserable gardener's boy, Pon. Suppose we throw Pon into the Great Gulf, your Majesty?"

"It would do you no good," returned the King. "She would still love him."

"Too bad, too bad!" sighed Googly-Goo. "I have laid aside more than a bushel of precious gems—each worth a King's ransom—to present to your Majesty on the day I wed Gloria."

The King's eyes sparkled, for he loved wealth above everything; but the next moment he frowned deeply again.

"It won't help us to kill Pon," he muttered. "What we must do is kill Gloria's love for Pon."

"That is better, if you can find a way to do it," agreed Googly-Goo. "Everything would come right if you could kill Gloria's love for that gardener's boy. Really, Sire, now that I come to think of it, there must be fully a bushel and a half of those jewels!"

Just then a messenger entered the court to say that the banquet was prepared for the strangers. So Cap'n Bill, Trot and Button-Bright entered the castle and were taken to a room where a fine feast was spread upon the table.

"I don't like that Lord Googly-Goo," remarked Trot as she was busily eating.

"Nor I," said Cap'n Bill. "But from the talk we heard I

guess the gardener's boy won't get the Princess."

"Perhaps not," returned the girl; "but I hope old Googly doesn't get her, either."

"The King means to sell her for all those jewels," observed Button-Bright, his mouth half full of cake and jam.

"Poor Princess!" sighed Trot. "I'm sorry for her, although I've never seen her. But if she says no to Googly-Goo, and means it, what can they do?"

"Don't let us worry about a strange Princess," advised Cap'n Bill. "I've a notion we're not too safe, ourselves, with this cruel King."

The two children felt the same way and all three were rather solemn during the remainder of the meal.

When they had eaten, the servants escorted them to their rooms. Cap'n Bill's room was way to one end of the castle, very high up, and Trot's room was at the opposite end, rather low down. As for Button-Bright, they placed him in the middle, so that all were as far apart as they could possibly be. They didn't like this arrangement very well, but all the rooms were handsomely furnished and being guests of the King they dared not complain.

After the strangers had left the courtyard the King and Googly-Goo had a long talk together, and the King said:

"I cannot force Gloria to marry you just now, because those strangers may interfere. I suspect that the wooden-legged man possesses great magical powers, or he would never have been able to carry himself and those children across the deadly desert."

"I don't like him; he looks dangerous," answered Googly-Goo. "But perhaps you are mistaken about his being a Wizard. Why don't you test his powers?"

"How?" asked the King.

"Send for the Wicked Witch. She will tell you in a moment whether that wooden-legged person is a common man or a magician."

"Ha! that's a good idea," cried the King. "Why didn't I think of the Wicked Witch before? But the woman demands rich rewards for her services."

"Never mind; I will pay her," promised the wealthy Googly-Goo.

So a servant was dispatched to summon the Wicked Witch, who lived but a few leagues from King Krewl's castle. While they awaited her, the withered old courtier proposed that they pay a visit to Princess Gloria and see if she was not now in a more complaisant mood. So the two started away together and searched the castle over without finding Gloria.

At last Googly-Goo suggested she might be in the rear garden, which was a large park filled with bushes and trees and surrounded by a high wall. And what was their anger, when they turned a corner of the path, to find in a quiet nook the beautiful Princess, and kneeling before her, Pon, the gardener's boy! With a roar of rage the King dashed forward; but Pon had scaled the wall by means of a ladder, which still stood in its place, and when he saw the King coming he ran up the ladder and made good his escape. But this left Gloria confronted by her angry guardian, the King, and by old Googly-Goo, who was trembling with a fury he could not express in words.

Seizing the Princess by her arm the King dragged her back to the castle. Pushing her into a room on the lower floor he locked the door upon the unhappy girl. And at that moment the arrival of the Wicked Witch was announced.

Hearing this, the King smiled, as a tiger smiles, showing his teeth. And Googly-Goo smiled, as a serpent smiles, for he had no teeth except a couple of fangs. And having frightened each other with these smiles the two dreadful men went away to the Royal Council Chamber to meet the Wicked Witch.

····◄ Chapter 12 ►··──··

The WOODEN-LEGGED GRASSHOPPER

Now it so happened that Trot, from the window of her room, had witnessed the meeting of the lovers in the garden and had seen the King come and drag Gloria away. The little girl's heart went out in sympathy for the poor Princess, who seemed to her to be one of the sweetest and loveliest young ladies she had ever seen, so she crept along the passages and from a hidden niche saw Gloria locked in her room.

The key was still in the lock, so when the King had gone away, followed by Googly-Goo, Trot stole up to the door, turned the key and entered. The Princess lay prone upon a couch, sobbing bitterly. Trot went up to her and smoothed her hair and tried to comfort her.

"Don't cry," she said. "I've unlocked the door, so you can go away any time you want to."

"It isn't that," sobbed the Princess. "I am unhappy because they will not let me love Pon, the gardener's boy!"

"Well, never mind; Pon isn't any great shakes, anyhow, seems to me," said Trot soothingly. "There are lots of other people you can love."

Gloria rolled over on the couch and looked at the little girl reproachfully.

"Pon has won my heart, and I can't help loving him," she explained. Then with sudden indignation she added: "But I'll never love Googly-Goo—never, as long as I live!"

"I should say not!" replied Trot. "Pon may not be much good, but old Googly is very, very bad. Hunt around, and I'm sure you'll find someone worth your love. You're very pretty, you know, and almost anyone ought to love you."

"You don't understand, my dear," said Gloria, as she wiped the tears from her eyes with a dainty lace handkerchief bordered with pearls. "When you are older you will realize that a young lady cannot decide whom she will love, or choose the most worthy. Her heart alone decides for her, and whomsoever her heart selects, she must love, whether he amounts to much or not."

Trot was a little puzzled by this speech, which seemed

to her unreasonable; but she made no reply and presently Gloria's grief softened and she began to question the little girl about herself and her adventures. Trot told her how they had happened to come to Jinxland, and all about Cap'n Bill and the Ork and Pessim and the Bumpy Man.

While they were thus conversing together, getting more and more friendly as they became better acquainted, in the Council Chamber the King and Googly-Goo were talking with the Wicked Witch.

This evil creature was old and ugly. She had lost one eye and wore a black patch over it, so the people of Jinxland had named her "Blinkie." Of course Witches are forbidden to exist in the Land of Oz, but Jinxland was so far removed from the center of Ozma's dominions, and so absolutely cut off from it by the steep mountains and the bottomless gulf, that the Laws of Oz were not obeyed very well in that country. So there were several Witches in Jinxland who were the terror of the people, but King Krewl favored them and permitted them to exercise their evil sorcery.

Blinkie was the leader of all the other Witches and therefore the most hated and feared. The King used her witchcraft at times to assist him in carrying out his cruelties and revenge, but he was always obliged to pay Blinkie large sums of money or heaps of precious jewels before she would undertake an enchantment. This made him hate the old woman almost as much as his subjects did, but to-day Lord Googly-Goo had agreed to pay the Witch's price, so the King greeted her with gracious favor.

"Can you destroy the love of Princess Gloria for the gardener's boy?" inquired his Majesty.

The Wicked Witch thought about it before she replied:

"That's a hard question to answer. I can do lots of clever magic, but love is a stubborn thing to conquer. When you think you've killed it, it's liable to bob up again as strong as ever. I believe love and cats have nine lives. In other words, killing love is a hard job, even for a skillful Witch, but I believe I can do something that will answer your purpose just as well."

"What is that?" asked the King.

"I can freeze the girl's heart. I've got a special incantation for that, and when Gloria's heart is thoroughly frozen she can no longer love Pon."

"Just the thing!" exclaimed Googly-Goo, and the King was likewise much pleased.

They bargained a long time as to the price, but finally the old courtier agreed to pay the Wicked Witch's demands. It was arranged that they should take Gloria to Blinkie's house the next day, to have her heart frozen.

Then King Krewl mentioned to the old hag the strangers who had that day arrived in Jinxland, and said to her:

"I think the two children—the boy and the girl—are unable to harm me, but I have a suspicion that the wooden-legged man is a powerful Wizard."

The Witch's face wore a troubled look when she heard this.

"If you are right," she said, "this Wizard might spoil my incantation and interfere with me in other ways. So it will be best for me to meet this stranger at once and match my magic against his, to decide which is the stronger."

"All right," said the King. "Come with me and I will lead you to the man's room."

Googly-Goo did not accompany them, as he was obliged to go home to get the money and jewels he had promised to pay old Blinkie, so the other two climbed several flights of stairs and went through many passages until they came to the room occupied by Cap'n Bill.

The sailor-man, finding his bed soft and inviting, and being tired with the adventures he had experienced, had decided to take a nap. When the Wicked Witch and the King softly opened his door and entered, Cap'n Bill was snoring with such vigor that he did not hear them at all.

Blinkie approached the bed and with her one eye anxiously stared at the sleeping stranger.

"Ah," she said in a soft whisper, "I believe you are right, King Krewl. The man looks to me like a very powerful Wizard. But by good luck I have caught him asleep, so I shall transform him before he wakes up, giving him such a form that he will be unable to oppose me."

"Careful!" cautioned the King, also speaking low. "If he discovers what you are doing he may destroy you, and that would annoy me because I need you to attend to Gloria."

But the Wicked Witch realized as well as he did that she must be careful. She carried over her arm a black bag, from which she now drew several packets carefully wrapped in paper. Three of these she selected, replacing the others in the bag. Two of the packets she mixed together, and then she cautiously opened the third.

"Better stand back, your Majesty," she advised, "for if this powder falls on you you might be transformed yourself."

The King hastily retreated to the end of the room. As Blinkie mixed the third powder with the others she waved her hands over it, mumbled a few words, and then backed away as quickly as she could.

Cap'n Bill was slumbering peacefully, all unconscious of what was going on. Puff! A great cloud of smoke rolled over the bed and completely hid him from view. When the smoke rolled away, both Blinkie and the King saw that the body of the stranger had quite disappeared, while in his place, crouching in the middle of the bed, was a little grey grasshopper.

One curious thing about this grasshopper was that the last joint of its left leg was made of wood. Another curious thing— considering it was a grasshopper—was that it began talking, crying out in a tiny but sharp voice:

"Here—you people! What do you mean by treating me so? Put me back where I belong, at once, or you'll be sorry!"

The cruel King turned pale at hearing the grasshopper's

threats, but the Wicked Witch merely laughed in derision. Then she raised her stick and aimed a vicious blow at the grasshopper, but before the stick struck the bed the tiny hopper made a marvelous jump—marvelous, indeed, when we consider that it had a wooden leg. It rose in the air and sailed across the room and passed right through the open window, where it disappeared from their view.

"Good!" shouted the King. "We are well rid of this desperate Wizard." And then they both laughed heartily at the success of the incantation, and went away to complete their horrid plans.

After Trot had visited a time with Princess Gloria, the little girl went to Button-Bright's room but did not find him there. Then she went to Cap'n Bill's room, but he was not there because the Witch and the King had been there before her. So she made her way downstairs and questioned the servants. They said they had seen the little boy go out into the garden, some time ago, but the old man with the wooden leg they had not seen at all.

Therefore Trot, not knowing what else to do, rambled through the great gardens, seeking for Button-Bright or Cap'n Bill and not finding either of them. This part of the garden, which lay before the castle, was not walled in, but extended to the roadway, and the paths were open to the edge of the forest; so, after two hours of vain search for her friends, the little girl returned to the castle.

But at the doorway a soldier stopped her.

"I live here," said Trot, "so it's all right to let me in. The King has given me a room."

"Well, he has taken it back again," was the Soldier's reply. "His Majesty's orders are to turn you away if you attempt to enter. I am also ordered to forbid the boy, your companion, to again enter the King's castle."

"How 'bout Cap'n Bill?" she inquired.

"Why, it seems he has mysteriously disappeared," replied the Soldier, shaking his head ominously. "Where he has gone to, I can't make out, but I can assure you he is no longer in this castle. I'm sorry, little girl, to disappoint you. Don't blame me; I must obey my master's orders."

Now, all her life Trot had been accustomed to depend on Cap'n Bill, so when this good friend was suddenly taken from her she felt very miserable and forlorn indeed. She was brave enough not to cry before the Soldier, or even to let him see her grief and anxiety, but after she was turned away from the castle she sought a quiet bench in the garden and for a time sobbed as if her heart would break.

It was Button-Bright who found her, at last, just as the sun had set and the shades of evening were falling. He also had been turned away from the King's castle, when he tried to enter it, and in the park he came across Trot.

"Never mind," said the boy. "We can find a place to sleep."

"I want Cap'n Bill," wailed the girl.

"Well, so do I," was the reply. "But we haven't got him. Where do you s'pose he is, Trot?

"I don't s'pose anything. He's gone, an' that's all I know 'bout it."

Button-Bright sat on the bench beside her and thrust his hands in the pockets of his knickerbockers. Then he reflected somewhat gravely for him.

"Cap'n Bill isn't around here," he said, letting his eyes wander over the dim garden, "so we must go somewhere else if we want to find him. Besides, it's fast getting dark, and if we want to find a place to sleep we must get busy while we can see where to go."

He rose from the bench as he said this and Trot also jumped up, drying her eyes on her apron. Then she walked beside him out of the grounds of the King's castle. They did not go by the main path, but passed through an opening in a hedge and found themselves in a small but well-worn roadway. Following this for some distance, along a winding way, they came upon no house or building that would afford them refuge for the night. It became so dark that they could scarcely see their way, and finally Trot stopped and suggested that they camp under a tree.

"All right," said Button-Bright, "I've often found that leaves make a good warm blanket. But—look there, Trot!— isn't that a light flashing over yonder?"

"It certainly is, Button-Bright. Let's go over and see if it's a house. Whoever lives there couldn't treat us worse than the King did."

To reach the light they had to leave the road, so they stumbled over hillocks and brushwood, hand in hand, keeping the tiny speck of light always in sight.

They were rather forlorn little waifs, outcasts in a strange country and forsaken by their only friend and guardian, Cap'n Bill. So they were very glad when finally they reached a small cottage and, looking in through its one window, saw Pon, the gardener's boy, sitting by a fire of twigs.

As Trot opened the door and walked boldly in, Pon sprang up to greet them. They told him of Cap'n Bill's disappearance and how they had been turned out of the King's castle. As they finished the story Pon shook his head sadly.

"King Krewl is plotting mischief, I fear," said he, "for to-day he sent for old Blinkie, the Wicked Witch, and with my own eyes I saw her come from the castle and hobble away toward her hut. She had been with the King and Googly-Goo, and I was afraid they were going to work some enchantment on Gloria so she would no longer love me. But perhaps the Witch was only called to the castle to enchant your friend, Cap'n Bill."

"Could she do that?" asked Trot, horrified by the suggestion.

"I suppose so, for old Blinkie can do a lot of wicked magical things."

"What sort of an enchantment could she put on Cap'n Bill?"

"I don't know. But he has disappeared, so I'm pretty certain she has done something dreadful to him. But don't worry. If it has happened, it can't be helped, and if it hasn't happened we may be able to find him in the morning."

With this Pon went to the cupboard and brought food for them. Trot was far too worried to eat, but Button-Bright made a good supper from the simple food and then lay down before the fire and went to sleep. The little girl and the gardener's boy, however, sat for a long time staring into the fire, busy with their thoughts. But at last Trot, too, became sleepy and Pon gently covered her with the one blanket he possessed. Then he threw more wood on the fire and laid himself down before it, next to Button-Bright. Soon all three were fast asleep. They were in a good deal of trouble; but they were young, and sleep was good to them because for a time it made them forget.

Chapter 13

GLINDA the GOOD and the SCARECROW of OZ

That country south of the Emerald City, in the Land of Oz, is known as the Quadling Country, and in the very southernmost part of it stands a splendid palace in which lives Glinda the Good.

Glinda is the Royal Sorceress of Oz. She has wonderful magical powers and uses them only to benefit the subjects of Ozma's kingdom. Even the famous Wizard of Oz pays tribute to her, for Glinda taught him all the real magic he knows, and she is his superior in all sorts of sorcery.

Everyone loves Glinda, from the dainty and exquisite Ruler, Ozma, down to the humblest inhabitant of Oz, for she is always kindly and helpful and willing to listen to their troubles, however busy she may be. No one knows her age, but all can see how beautiful and stately she is. Her hair is like red gold and finer than the finest silken strands. Her eyes are blue as the sky and always frank and smiling. Her cheeks are the envy of peach-blows and her mouth is enticing as a rosebud. Glinda is tall and wears splendid gowns that trail behind her as she walks. She wears no jewels, for her beauty would shame them.

For attendants Glinda has half a hundred of the loveliest girls in Oz. They are gathered from all over Oz, from among the Winkies, the Munchkins, the Gillikins and the Quadlings, as well as from Ozma's magnificent Emerald City, and it is considered a great favor to be allowed to serve the Royal Sorceress.

Among the many wonderful things in Glinda's palace is the Great Book of Records. In this book is inscribed everything that takes place in all the world, just the instant it happens; so that by referring to its pages Glinda knows what is taking place far and near, in every country that exists. In this way she learns when and where she can help any in distress or danger, and although her duties are confined to assisting those who inhabit the Land of Oz, she is always interested in what takes place in the unprotected outside world.

So it was that on a certain evening Glinda sat in her library, surrounded by a bevy of her maids, who were engaged in spinning, weaving and embroidery, when an attendant announced the arrival at the palace of the Scarecrow.

This personage was one of the most famous and popular in all the Land of Oz. His body was merely a suit of Munchkin clothes stuffed with straw, but his head was a round sack filled with bran, with which the Wizard of Oz had mixed some magic brains of a very superior sort. The eyes, nose and mouth of the Scarecrow were painted upon the front of the sack, as were his ears, and since this quaint being had been endowed with life, the expression of his face was very interesting, if somewhat comical.

The Scarecrow was good all through, even to his brains, and while he was naturally awkward in his movements and lacked the neat symmetry of other people, his disposition was so kind and considerate and he was so obliging and honest, that all who knew him loved him, and there were few people in Oz who had not met our Scarecrow and made his acquaintance. He lived part of the time in Ozma's palace at the Emerald City, part of the time in his own corncob castle in the Winkie Country, and part of the time he traveled over all Oz, visiting with the people and playing with the children, whom he dearly loved.

It was on one of his wandering journeys that the Scarecrow had arrived at Glinda's palace, and the Sorceress at once made him welcome. As he sat beside her, talking of his adventures, he asked:

"What's new in the way of news?"

Glinda opened her Great Book of Records and read some of the last pages.

"Here is an item quite curious and interesting," she announced, an accent of surprise in her voice. "Three people from the big Outside World have arrived in Jinxland."

"Where is Jinxland?" inquired the Scarecrow.

"Very near here, a little to the east of us," she said. "In fact, Jinxland is a little slice taken off the Quadling Country, but separated from it by a range of high mountains, at the foot of which lies a wide, deep gulf that is supposed to be impassable."

"Then Jinxland is really a part of the Land of Oz," said he.

"Yes," returned Glinda, "but Oz people know nothing of it, except what is recorded here in my book."

"What does the Book say about it?" asked the Scarecrow.

"It is ruled by a wicked man called King Krewl, although he has no right to the title. Most of the people are good, but they are very timid and live in constant fear of their fierce Ruler. There are also several Wicked Witches who keep the inhabitants of Jinxland in a state of terror."

"Do those Witches have any magical powers?" inquired the Scarecrow.

"Yes, they seem to understand witchcraft in its most evil form, for one of them has just transformed a respectable and honest old sailor—one of the strangers who arrived there—into a grasshopper. This same Witch, Blinkie by name, is also planning to freeze the heart of a beautiful Jinxland girl named Princess Gloria."

"Why, that's a dreadful thing to do!" exclaimed the Scare-crow.

Glinda's face was very grave. She read in her book how Trot and Button-Bright were turned out of the King's castle, and how they found refuge in the hut of Pon, the gardener's boy.

"I'm afraid those helpless earth people will endure much suffering in Jinxland, even if the wicked King and the Witches permit them to live," said the good Sorceress, thoughtfully. "I wish I might help them."

"Can I do anything?" asked the Scarecrow, anxiously. "If so, tell me what to do, and I'll do it."

For a few moments Glinda did not reply, but sat musing over the records. Then she said: "I am going to send you to Jinxland, to protect Trot and Button-Bright and Cap'n Bill."

"All right," answered the Scarecrow in a cheerful voice. "I know Button-Bright already, for he has been in the Land of Oz before. You remember he went away from the Land of Oz in one of our Wizard's big bubbles."

"Yes," said Glinda, "I remember that." Then she carefully instructed the Scarecrow what to do and gave him certain magical things which he placed in the pockets of his ragged Munchkin coat.

"As you have no need to sleep," said she, "you may as well start at once."

"The night is the same as day to me," he replied, "except that I cannot see my way so well in the dark."

"I will furnish a light to guide you," promised the Sorceress.

So the Scarecrow bade her good-bye and at once started on his journey. By morning he had reached the mountains that separated the Quadling Country from Jinxland. The sides of these mountains were too steep to climb, but the Scarecrow took a small rope from his pocket and tossed one end upward, into the air. The rope unwound itself for hundreds of feet, until it caught upon a peak of rock at the very top of a mountain, for it was a magic rope furnished him by Glinda. The Scarecrow climbed the rope and, after pulling it up, let it down on the other side of the mountain range. When he descended the rope on this side he found himself in Jinxland, but at his feet yawned the Great Gulf, which must be crossed before he could proceed any farther.

The Scarecrow knelt down and examined the ground carefully, and in a moment he discovered a fuzzy brown spider that had rolled itself into a ball. So he took two tiny pills from his pocket and laid them beside the spider, which unrolled itself and quickly ate up the pills. Then the Scarecrow said in a voice of command:

"Spin!" and the spider obeyed instantly.

In a few moments the little creature had spun two slender but strong strands that reached way across the gulf, one being five or six feet above the other. When these were completed the Scarecrow started across the tiny bridge, walking upon one strand as a person walks upon a rope, and holding to the upper strand with his hands to prevent him from losing his balance and toppling over into the gulf. The tiny threads held him safely, thanks to the strength given them by the magic pills.

Presently he was safe across and standing on the plains of Jinxland. Far away he could see the towers of the King's castle and toward this he at once began to walk.

Chapter 14

The FROZEN HEART

In the hut of Pon, the gardener's boy, Button-Bright was the first to waken in the morning. Leaving his companions still asleep, he went out into the fresh morning air and saw some blackberries growing on bushes in a field not far away. Going to the bushes he found the berries ripe and sweet, so he began eating them. More bushes were scattered over the fields, so the boy wandered on, from bush to bush, without paying any heed to where he was wandering. Then a butterfly fluttered by. He gave chase to it and followed it a long way. When finally he paused to look around him, Button-Bright could see no sign of Pon's house, nor had he the slightest idea in which direction it lay.

"Well, I'm lost again," he remarked to himself. "But never mind; I've been lost lots of times. Someone is sure to find me."

Trot was a little worried about Button-Bright when she awoke and found him gone. Knowing how careless he was, she believed that he had strayed away, but felt that he would come back in time, because he had a habit of not staying lost. Pon got the little girl some food for her breakfast and then together they went out of the hut and stood in the sunshine.

Pon's house was some distance off the road, but they could see it from where they stood and both gave a start of surprise when they discovered two soldiers walking along the roadway and escorting Princess Gloria between them. The poor girl had her hands bound together, to prevent her from struggling, and the soldiers rudely dragged her forward when her steps seemed to lag.

Behind this group came King Krewl, wearing his jeweled crown and swinging in his hand a slender golden staff with a ball of clustered gems at one end.

"Where are they going?" asked Trot.

"To the house of the Wicked Witch, I fear," Pon replied. "Come, let us follow them, for I am sure they intend to harm my dear Gloria."

"Won't they see us?" she asked timidly.

"We won't let them. I know a short cut through the trees to Blinkie's house," said he.

So they hurried away through the trees and reached the house of the Witch ahead of the King and his soldiers. Hiding themselves in the shrubbery, they watched the approach of poor Gloria and her escort, all of whom passed so near to them that Pon could have put out a hand and touched his sweetheart, had he dared to.

Blinkie's house had eight sides, with a door and a window in each side. Smoke was coming out of the chimney and as the guards brought Gloria to one of the doors it was opened by the old Witch in person. She chuckled with evil glee and rubbed her skinny hands together to show the delight with which she greeted her victim, for Blinkie was pleased to be able to perform her wicked rites on one so fair and sweet as the Princess.

Gloria struggled to resist when they bade her enter the house, so the soldiers forced her through the doorway and even the King gave her a shove as he followed close behind. Pon was so incensed at the cruelty shown Gloria that he forgot all caution and rushed forward to enter the house also; but one of the soldiers prevented him, pushing the gardener's boy away with violence and slamming the door in his face.

"Never mind," said Trot soothingly, as Pon rose from where he had fallen. "You couldn't do much to help the poor Princess if you were inside. How unfortunate it is that you are in love with her!"

"True," he answered sadly, "it is indeed my misfortune. If

I did not love her, it would be none of my business what the King did to his niece Gloria; but the unlucky circumstance of my loving her makes it my duty to defend her."

"I don't see how you can, duty or no duty," observed Trot.

"No; I am powerless, for they are stronger than I. But we might peek in through the window and see what they are doing."

Trot was somewhat curious, too, so they crept up to one of the windows and looked in, and it so happened that those inside the Witch's house were so busy they did not notice that Pon and Trot were watching them.

Gloria had been tied to a stout post in the center of the room and the King was giving the Wicked Witch a quantity of money and jewels, which Googly-Goo had provided in payment. When this had been done the King said to her:

"Are you perfectly sure you can freeze this maiden's heart, so that she will no longer love that low gardener's boy?"

"Sure as witchcraft, your Majesty," the creature replied.

"Then get to work," said the King. "There may be some unpleasant features about the ceremony that would annoy me, so I'll bid you good day and leave you to carry out your contract. One word, however: If you fail, I shall burn you at the stake!" Then he beckoned to his soldiers to follow him, and throwing wide the door of the house walked out.

This action was so sudden that King Krewl almost caught Trot and Pon eavesdropping, but they managed to run around the house before he saw them. Away he marched, up the road, followed by his men, heartlessly leaving Gloria to the mercies of old Blinkie.

When they again crept up to the window, Trot and Pon saw Blinkie gloating over her victim. Although nearly fainting from fear, the proud Princess gazed with haughty defiance into the face of the wicked creature; but she was bound so tightly to the post that she could do no more to express her loathing.

Pretty soon Blinkie went to a kettle that was swinging by a chain over the fire and tossed into it several magical compounds. The kettle gave three flashes, and at every flash another Witch appeared in the room.

These hags were very ugly but when one-eyed Blinkie whispered her orders to them they grinned with joy as they began dancing around Gloria. First one and then another cast something into the kettle, when to the astonishment of the watchers at the window all three of the old women were instantly transformed into maidens of exquisite beauty, dressed in the daintiest costumes imaginable. Only their eyes could not be disguised, and an evil glare still shone in their depths. But if the eyes were cast down or hidden, one could not help but admire these beautiful creatures, even with the knowledge that they were mere illusions of witchcraft.

Trot certainly admired them, for she had never seen anything so dainty and bewitching, but her attention was quickly drawn to their deeds instead of their persons, and then horror replaced admiration.

Into the kettle old Blinkie poured another mess from a big brass bottle she took from a chest, and this made the kettle begin to bubble and smoke violently. One by one the beautiful Witches approached to stir the contents of the kettle and to mutter a magic charm. Their movements were graceful and rhythmic and the Wicked Witch who had called them to her aid watched them with an evil grin upon her wrinkled face.

Finally the incantation was complete. The kettle ceased bubbling and together the Witches lifted it from the fire. Then Blinkie brought a wooden ladle and filled it from the contents of the kettle. Going with the spoon to Princess Gloria she cried:

> *"Love no more! Magic art*
> *Now will freeze your mortal heart!"*

With this she dashed the contents of the ladle full upon Gloria's breast.

Trot saw the body of the Princess become transparent, so that her beating heart showed plainly. But now the heart turned from a vivid red to grey, and then to white. A layer of frost formed about it and tiny icicles clung to its surface. Then slowly the body of the girl became visible again and the heart was hidden from view. Gloria seemed to have fainted, but now she recovered and, opening her beautiful eyes, stared coldly and without emotion at the group of Witches confronting her.

Blinkie and the others knew by that one cold look that their charm had been successful. They burst into a chorus of wild laughter and the three beautiful ones began dancing again, while Blinkie unbound the Princess and set her free.

Trot rubbed her eyes to prove that she was wide awake and seeing clearly, for her astonishment was great when the three lovely maidens turned into ugly, crooked hags again, leaning on broomsticks and canes. They jeered at Gloria, but the Princess regarded them with cold disdain. Being now free, she walked to a door, opened it and passed out. And the Witches let her go.

Trot and Pon had been so intent upon this scene that in their eagerness they had pressed quite hard against the window. Just as Gloria went out of the house the window-sash broke loose from its fastenings and fell with a crash into the room. The Witches uttered a chorus of screams and then, seeing that their magical incantation had been observed, they rushed for the open window with uplifted broomsticks and canes. But Pon was off like the wind, and Trot followed at his heels. Fear lent them strength to run, to leap across ditches, to speed up the hills and to vault the low fences as a deer would.

The band of Witches had dashed through the window in pursuit; but Blinkie was so old, and the others so crooked and awkward, that they soon realized they would be unable to overtake the fugitives. So the three who had been summoned by the Wicked Witch put their canes or broomsticks between their legs and flew away through the air, quickly disappearing against the blue sky. Blinkie, however, was so enraged at Pon and Trot that she hobbled on in the direction they had taken, fully determined to catch them, in time, and to punish them terribly for spying upon her witchcraft.

When Pon and Trot had run so far that they were confident they had made good their escape, they sat down near the edge of a forest to get their breath again, for both were panting hard from their exertions. Trot was the first to recover speech, and she said to her companion:

"My! wasn't it terr'ble?"

"The most terrible thing I ever saw," Pon agreed.

"And they froze Gloria's heart; so now she can't love you any more."

"Well, they froze her heart, to be sure," admitted Pon, "but I'm in hopes I can melt it with my love."

"Where do you s'pose Gloria is?" asked the girl, after a pause.

"She left the Witch's house just before we did. Perhaps she has gone back to the King's castle," he said.

"I'm pretty sure she started off in a diff'rent direction," declared Trot. "I looked over my shoulder, as I ran, to see how close the Witches were, and I'm sure I saw Gloria walking slowly away toward the north."

"Then let us circle around that way," proposed Pon, "and perhaps we shall meet her."

Trot agreed to this and they left the grove and began to circle around toward the north, thus drawing nearer and nearer to old Blinkie's house again. The Wicked Witch did not suspect this change of direction, so when she came to the grove she passed through it and continued on.

Pon and Trot had reached a place less than half a mile from the Witch's house when they saw Gloria walking toward them. The Princess moved with great dignity and with no show of haste whatever, holding her head high and looking neither to right nor left.

Pon rushed forward, holding out his arms as if to embrace her and calling her sweet names. But Gloria gazed upon him coldly and repelled him with a haughty gesture. At this the poor gardener's boy sank upon his knees and hid his face in his arms, weeping bitter tears; but the Princess was not at all moved by his distress. Passing him by, she drew her skirts aside, as if unwilling they should touch him, and then she walked up the path a way and hesitated, as if uncertain where to go next.

Trot was grieved by Pon's sobs and indignant because Gloria treated him so badly. But she remembered why.

"I guess your heart is frozen, all right," she said to the Princess. Gloria nodded gravely, in reply, and then turned her back upon the little girl. "Can't you like even me?" asked Trot, half pleadingly.

"No," said Gloria.

"Your voice sounds like a refrig'rator," sighed the little girl. "I'm awful sorry for you, 'cause you were sweet an' nice to me before this happened. You can't help it, of course; but it's a dreadful thing, jus' the same."

"My heart is frozen to all mortal loves," announced Gloria, calmly. "I do not love even myself."

"That's too bad," said Trot, "for, if you can't love anybody, you can't expect anybody to love you."

"I do!" cried Pon. "I shall always love her."

"Well, you're just a gardener's boy," replied Trot, "and I didn't think you 'mounted to much, from the first. I can love the old Princess Gloria, with a warm heart an' nice manners, but this one gives me the shivers."

"It's her icy heart, that's all," said Pon.

"That's enough," insisted Trot. "Seeing her heart isn't big enough to skate on, I can't see that she's of any use to anyone. For my part, I'm goin' to try to find Button-Bright an' Cap'n Bill."

"I will go with you," decided Pon. "It is evident that Gloria no longer loves me and that her heart is frozen too stiff for me to melt it with my own love; therefore I may as well help you to find your friends."

As Trot started off, Pon cast one more imploring look at the Princess, who returned it with a chilly stare. So he followed after the little girl.

As for the Princess, she hesitated a moment and then turned in the same direction the others had taken, but going far more slowly. Soon she heard footsteps pattering behind her, and up came Googly-Goo, a little out of breath with running.

"Stop, Gloria!" he cried. "I have come to take you back to my mansion, where we are to be married."

She looked at him wonderingly a moment, then tossed her head disdainfully and walked on. But Googly-Goo kept beside her.

"What does this mean?" he demanded. "Haven't you discovered that you no longer love that gardener's boy, who stood in my way?"

"Yes; I have discovered it," she replied. "My heart is frozen to all mortal loves. I cannot love you, or Pon, or the cruel King my uncle, or even myself. Go your way, Googly-Goo, for I will wed no one at all."

He stopped in dismay when he heard this, but in another minute he exclaimed angrily:

"You *must* wed me, Princess Gloria, whether you want to or not! I paid to have your heart frozen; I also paid the King to permit our marriage. If you now refuse me it will mean that I have been robbed—robbed—robbed of my precious money and jewels!"

He almost wept with despair, but she laughed a cold, bitter laugh and passed on. Googly-Goo caught at her arm, as if to restrain her, but she whirled and dealt him a blow that sent him reeling into a ditch beside the path. Here he lay for a long time, half covered by muddy water, dazed with surprise.

Finally the old courtier arose, dripping, and climbed from the ditch. The Princess had gone; so, muttering threats of vengeance upon her, upon the King and upon Blinkie, old Googly-Goo hobbled back to his mansion to have the mud removed from his costly velvet clothes.

TROT MEETS the SCARECROW

Trot and Pon covered many leagues of ground, searching through forests, in fields and in many of the little villages of Jinxland, but could find no trace of either Cap'n Bill or Button-Bright. Finally they paused beside a cornfield and sat upon a stile to rest. Pon took some apples from his pocket and gave one to Trot. Then he began eating another himself, for this was their time for luncheon. When his apple was finished Pon tossed the core into the field.

"Tchuk-tchuk!" said a strange voice. "What do you mean by hitting me in the eye with an apple-core?"

Then rose up the form of the Scarecrow, who had hidden

himself in the cornfield while he examined Pon and Trot and decided whether they were worthy to be helped.

"Excuse me," said Pon. "I didn't know you were there."

"How did you happen to be there, anyhow?" asked Trot.

The Scarecrow came forward with awkward steps and stood beside them.

"Ah, you are the gardener's boy," he said to Pon. Then he turned to Trot. "And you are the little girl who came to Jinxland riding on a big bird, and who has had the misfortune to lose her friend, Cap'n Bill, and her chum, Button-Bright."

"Why, how did you know all that?" she inquired.

"I know a lot of things," replied the Scarecrow, winking at her comically. "My brains are the Carefully-Assorted, Double-Distilled, High-Efficiency sort that the Wizard of Oz makes. He admits, himself, that my brains are the best he ever manufactured."

"I think I've heard of you," said Trot slowly, as she looked the Scarecrow over with much interest; "but you used to live in the Land of Oz."

"Oh, I do now," he replied cheerfully. "I've just come over the mountains from the Quadling Country to see if I can be of any help to you."

"Who, me?" asked Pon.

"No, the strangers from the big world. It seems they need looking after."

"I'm doing that myself," said Pon, a little ungraciously. "If you will pardon me for saying so, I don't see how a Scarecrow with painted eyes can look after anyone."

"If you don't see that, you are more blind than the Scarecrow," asserted Trot. "He's a fairy man, Pon, and comes from the fairyland of Oz, so he can do 'most anything. I hope," she added, turning to the Scarecrow, "you can find Cap'n Bill for me."

"I will try, anyhow," he promised. "But who is that old woman who is running toward us and shaking her stick at us?"

Trot and Pon turned around and both uttered an exclamation of fear. The next instant they took to their heels and ran fast up the path. For it was old Blinkie, the Wicked Witch, who had at last traced them to this place. Her anger was so great that she was determined not to abandon the chase of Pon and Trot until she had caught and punished them. The Scarecrow understood at once that the old woman meant harm to his new friends, so as she drew near he stepped before her. His appearance was so sudden and unexpected that Blinkie ran into him and toppled him over, but she tripped on his straw body and went rolling in the path beside him.

The Scarecrow sat up and said: "I beg your pardon!" but she whacked him with her stick and knocked him flat again. Then, furious with rage, the old Witch sprang upon her victim and began pulling the straw out of his body. The poor Scarecrow was helpless to resist and in a few moments all that was left of him was an empty suit of clothes and a heap of straw beside it. Fortunately, Blinkie did not harm his head, for it rolled into a little hollow and escaped her notice. Fearing that Pon and Trot would escape her, she quickly resumed the chase and disappeared over the brow of a hill, following the direction in which she had seen them go.

Only a short time elapsed before a grey grasshopper with a wooden leg came hopping along and lit directly on the upturned face of the Scarecrow's head.

"Pardon me, but you are resting yourself upon my nose," remarked the Scarecrow.

"Oh! are you alive?" asked the grasshopper.

"That is a question I have never been able to decide," said the Scarecrow's head. "When my body is properly stuffed I have animation and can move around as well as any live person. The brains in the head you are now occupying as a throne, are of very superior quality and do a lot of very clever thinking. But whether that is being alive, or not, I cannot prove to you; for one who lives is liable to death, while I am only liable to destruction."

"Seems to me," said the grasshopper, rubbing his nose with his front legs, "that in your case it doesn't matter—unless you're destroyed already."

"I am not; all I need is re-stuffing," declared the Scarecrow; "and if Pon and Trot escape the Witch, and come back here, I am sure they will do me that favor."

"Tell me! Are Trot and Pon around here?" inquired the grasshopper, its small voice trembling with excitement.

The Scarecrow did not answer at once, for both his eyes were staring straight upward at a beautiful face that was slightly bent over his head. It was, indeed, Princess Gloria, who had wandered to this spot, very much surprised when she heard the Scarecrow's head talk and the tiny grey grasshopper answer it.

"This," said the Scarecrow, still staring at her, "must be the Princess who loves Pon, the gardener's boy."

"Oh, indeed!" exclaimed the grasshopper—who of course was Cap'n Bill—as he examined the young lady curiously.

"No," said Gloria frigidly, "I do not love Pon, or anyone else, for the Wicked Witch has frozen my heart."

"What a shame!" cried the Scarecrow. "One so lovely should be able to love. But would you mind, my dear, stuffing that straw into my body again?"

The dainty Princess glanced at the straw and at the well-worn blue Munchkin clothes and shrank back in disdain. But she was spared from refusing the Scarecrow's request by the appearance of Trot and Pon, who had hidden in some bushes just over the brow of the hill and waited until old Blinkie had passed them by. Their hiding place was on the same side as the Witch's blind eye, and she rushed on in the chase of the girl and the youth without being aware that they had tricked her.

Trot was shocked at the Scarecrow's sad condition and at once began putting the straw back into his body. Pon, at sight of Gloria, again appealed to her to take pity on him, but the frozen-hearted Princess turned coldly away and with a sigh the gardener's boy began to assist Trot.

Neither of them at first noticed the small grasshopper, which at their appearance had skipped off the Scarecrow's nose and was now clinging to a wisp of grass beside the path, where he was not likely to be stepped upon. Not until the Scarecrow had been neatly restuffed and set upon his feet again—when he bowed to his restorers and expressed his thanks—did the grasshopper move from his perch. Then he leaped lightly into the path and called out:

"Trot—Trot! Look at me. I'm Cap'n Bill! See what the Wicked Witch has done to me."

The voice was small, to be sure, but it reached Trot's ears and startled her greatly. She looked intently at the grasshopper, her eyes wide with fear at first; then she knelt down and, noticing the wooden leg, she began to weep sorrowfully.

"Oh, Cap'n Bill—dear Cap'n Bill! What a cruel thing to do!" she sobbed.

"Don't cry, Trot," begged the grasshopper. "It didn't hurt any, and it doesn't hurt now. But it's mighty inconvenient an' humiliatin', to say the least."

"I wish," said the girl indignantly, while trying hard to restrain her tears, "that I was big 'nough an' strong 'nough to give that horrid Witch a good beating. She ought to be turned into a toad for doing this to you, Cap'n Bill!"

"Never mind," urged the Scarecrow, in a comforting voice,

"such a transformation doesn't last always, and as a general thing there's some way to break the enchantment. I'm sure Glinda could do it, in a jiffy."

"Who is Glinda?" inquired Cap'n Bill.

Then the Scarecrow told them all about Glinda, not forgetting to mention her beauty and goodness and her wonderful powers of magic. He also explained how the Royal Sorceress had sent him to Jinxland especially to help the strangers, whom she knew to be in danger because of the wiles of the cruel King and the Wicked Witch.

····◄ Chapter 16 ►····

PON SUMMONS the KING
to SURRENDER

Gloria had drawn near to the group to listen to their talk, and it seemed to interest her in spite of her frigid manner. They knew, of course, that the poor Princess could not help being cold and reserved, so they tried not to blame her.

"I ought to have come here a little sooner," said the Scarecrow, regretfully; "but Glinda sent me as soon as she discovered you were here and were likely to get into trouble. And now that we are all together—except Button-Bright, over whom it is useless to worry—I propose we hold a council of war, to decide what is best to be done."

That seemed a wise thing to do, so they all sat down upon

the grass, including Gloria, and the grasshopper perched upon Trot's shoulder and allowed her to stroke him gently with her hand.

"In the first place," began the Scarecrow, "this King Krewl is a usurper and has no right to rule this Kingdom of Jinxland."

"That is true," said Pon, eagerly. "My father was King before him, and I—"

"You are a gardener's boy," interrupted the Scarecrow. "Your father had no right to rule, either, for the rightful King of this land was the father of Princess Gloria, and only she is entitled to sit upon the throne of Jinxland."

"Good!" exclaimed Trot. "But what'll we do with King Krewl? I s'pose he won't give up the throne unless he has to."

"No, of course not," said the Scarecrow. "Therefore it will be our duty to *make* him give up the throne."

"How?" asked Trot.

"Give me time to think," was the reply. "That's what my brains are for. I don't know whether you people ever think, or not, but my brains are the best that the Wizard of Oz ever turned out, and if I give them plenty of time to work, the result usually surprises me."

"Take your time, then," suggested Trot. "There's no hurry."

"Thank you," said the straw man, and sat perfectly still for half an hour. During this interval the grasshopper whispered in Trot's ear, to which he was very close, and Trot whispered back to the grasshopper sitting upon her shoulder. Pon cast loving glances at Gloria, who paid not the slightest heed to them.

Finally the Scarecrow laughed aloud.

"Brains working?" inquired Trot.

"Yes. They seem in fine order to-day. We will conquer King Krewl and put Gloria upon his throne as Queen of Jinx-land."

"Fine!" cried the little girl, clapping her hands together gleefully. "But how?"

"Leave the *how* to me," said the Scarecrow proudly. "As a conqueror I'm a wonder. We will, first of all, write a message to send to King Krewl, asking him to surrender. If he refuses, then we will make him surrender."

"Why ask him, when we know he'll refuse?" inquired Pon.

"Why, we must be polite, whatever we do," explained the Scarecrow. "It would be very rude to conquer a King without proper notice."

They found it difficult to write a message without paper, pen and ink, none of which was at hand; so it was decided to send Pon as a messenger, with instructions to ask the King, politely but firmly, to surrender.

Pon was not anxious to be the messenger. Indeed, he hinted that it might prove a dangerous mission. But the Scarecrow was now the acknowledged head of the Army of

Conquest, and he would listen to no refusal. So off Pon started for the King's castle, and the others accompanied him as far as his hut, where they had decided to await the gardener's boy's return.

I think it was because Pon had known the Scarecrow such a short time that he lacked confidence in the straw man's wisdom. It was easy to say: "We will conquer King Krewl," but when Pon drew near to the great castle he began to doubt the ability of a straw-stuffed man, a girl, a grasshopper and a frozen-hearted Princess to do it. As for himself, he had never thought of defying the King before.

That was why the gardener's boy was not very bold when he entered the castle and passed through to the enclosed court where the King was just then seated, with his favorite courtiers around him. None prevented Pon's entrance, because he was known to be the gardener's boy, but when the King saw him he began to frown fiercely. He considered Pon to be to blame for all his trouble with Princess Gloria, who since her heart had been frozen had escaped to some unknown place, instead of returning to the castle to wed Googly-Goo, as she had been expected to do. So the King bared his teeth angrily as he demanded:

"What have you done with Princess Gloria?"

"Nothing, your Majesty! I have done nothing at all," answered Pon in a faltering voice. "She does not love me any more and even refuses to speak to me."

"Then why are you here, you rascal?" roared the King.

Pon looked first one way and then another, but saw no means of escape; so he plucked up courage.

"I am here to summon your Majesty to surrender."

"What!" shouted the King. "Surrender? Surrender to whom?"

Pon's heart sank to his boots.

"To the Scarecrow," he replied.

Some of the courtiers began to titter, but King Krewl was greatly annoyed. He sprang up and began to beat poor Pon with the golden staff he carried. Pon howled lustily and would have run away had not two of the soldiers held him until his Majesty was exhausted with punishing the boy. Then they let him go and he left the castle and returned along the road, sobbing at every step because his body was so sore and aching.

"Well," said the Scarecrow, "did the King surrender?"

"No; but he gave me a good drubbing!" sobbed poor Pon.

Trot was very sorry for Pon, but Gloria did not seem affected in any way by her lover's anguish. The grasshopper leaped to the Scarecrow's shoulder and asked him what he was going to do next.

"Conquer," was the reply. "But I will go alone, this time, for beatings cannot hurt me at all; nor can lance thrusts—or sword cuts—or arrow pricks."

"Why is that?" inquired Trot.

"Because I have no nerves, such as you meat people possess.

Even grasshoppers have nerves, but straw doesn't; so whatever they do—except just one thing—they cannot injure me. Therefore I expect to conquer King Krewl with ease."

"What is that one thing you excepted?" asked Trot.

"They will never think of it, so never mind. And now, if you will kindly excuse me for a time, I'll go over to the castle and do my conquering."

"You have no weapons," Pon reminded him.

"True," said the Scarecrow. "But if I carried weapons I might injure someone—perhaps seriously—and that would make me unhappy. I will just borrow that riding-whip, which I see in the corner of your hut, if you don't mind. It isn't exactly proper to walk with a riding-whip, but I trust you will excuse the inconsistency."

Pon handed him the whip and the Scarecrow bowed to all the party and left the hut, proceeding leisurely along the way to the King's castle.

Chapter 17

The ORK RESCUES
BUTTON-BRIGHT

I must now tell you what had become of Button-Bright since he wandered away in the morning and got lost. This small boy, as perhaps you have discovered, was almost as destitute of nerves as the Scarecrow. Nothing ever astonished him much; nothing ever worried him or made him unhappy. Good fortune or bad fortune he accepted with a quiet smile, never complaining, whatever happened. This was one reason why Button-Bright was a favorite with all who knew him—and perhaps it was the reason why he so often got into difficulties, or found himself lost.

To-day, as he wandered here and there, over hill and down

dale, he missed Trot and Cap'n Bill, of whom he was fond, but nevertheless he was not unhappy. The birds sang merrily and the wildflowers were beautiful and the breeze had a fragrance of new-mown hay.

"The only bad thing about this country is its King," he reflected; "but the country isn't to blame for that."

A prairie-dog stuck its round head out of a mound of earth and looked at the boy with bright eyes.

"Walk around my house, please," it said, "and then you won't harm it or disturb the babies."

"All right," answered Button-Bright, and took care not to step on the mound. He went on, whistling merrily, until a petulant voice cried:

"Oh, stop it! Please stop that noise. It gets on my nerves."

Button-Bright saw an old grey owl sitting in the crotch of a tree, and he replied with a laugh: "All right, old Fussy," and stopped whistling until he had passed out of the owl's hearing. At noon he came to a farm-house where an aged couple lived. They gave him a good dinner and treated him kindly, but the man was deaf and the woman was dumb, so they could answer no questions to guide him on the way to Pon's house. When he left them he was just as much lost as he had been before.

Every grove of trees he saw from a distance he visited, for he remembered that the King's castle was near a grove of trees and Pon's hut was near the King's castle; but always he met with disappointment. Finally, passing through one of these groves, he came out into the open and found himself face to face with the Ork.

"Hello!" said Button-Bright. "Where did *you* come from?"

"From Orkland," was the reply. "I've found my own country, at last, and it is not far from here, either. I would have come back to you sooner, to see how you are getting along, had not my family and friends welcomed my return so royally that a great celebration was held in my honor. So I couldn't very well leave Orkland again until the excitement was over."

"Can you find your way back home again?" asked the boy.

"Yes, easily; for now I know exactly where it is. But where are Trot and Cap'n Bill?"

Button-Bright related to the Ork their adventures since it had left them in Jinxland, telling of Trot's fear that the King had done something wicked to Cap'n Bill, and of Pon's love for Gloria, and how Trot and Button-Bright had been turned out of the King's castle. That was all the news that the boy had, but it made the Ork anxious for the safety of his friends.

"We must go to them at once, for they may need us," he said.

"I don't know where to go," confessed Button-Bright. "I'm lost."

"Well, I can take you back to the hut of the gardener's

boy," promised the Ork, "for when I fly high in the air I can look down and easily spy the King's castle. That was how I happened to spy you, just entering the grove; so I flew down and waited until you came out."

"How can you carry me?" asked the boy.

"You'll have to sit straddle my shoulders and put your arms around my neck. Do you think you can keep from falling off?"

"I'll try," said Button-Bright. So the Ork squatted down and the boy took his seat and held on tight. Then the skinny creature's tail began whirling and up they went, far above all the tree-tops.

After the Ork had circled around once or twice, its sharp eyes located the towers of the castle and away it flew, straight toward the place. As it hovered in the air, near by the castle, Button-Bright pointed out Pon's hut, so they landed just before it and Trot came running out to greet them.

Gloria was introduced to the Ork, who was surprised to find Cap'n Bill transformed into a grasshopper.

"How do you like it?" asked the creature.

"Why, it worries me good deal," answered Cap'n Bill, perched upon Trot's shoulder. "I'm always afraid o' bein' stepped on, and I don't like the flavor of grass an' can't seem to get used to it. It's my nature to eat grass, you know, but I begin to suspect it's an acquired taste."

"Can you give molasses?" asked the Ork.

"I guess I'm not that kind of a grasshopper," replied Cap'n Bill. "But I can't say what I might do if I was squeezed—which I hope I won't be."

"Well," said the Ork, "it's a great pity, and I'd like to meet that cruel King and his Wicked Witch and punish them both severely. You're awfully small, Cap'n Bill, but I think I would recognize you anywhere by your wooden leg."

Then the Ork and Button-Bright were told all about Gloria's frozen heart and how the Scarecrow had come from the Land of Oz to help them. The Ork seemed rather disturbed when it learned that the Scarecrow had gone alone to conquer King Krewl.

"I'm afraid he'll make a fizzle of it," said the skinny creature, "and there's no telling what that terrible King might do to the poor Scarecrow, who seems like a very interesting person. So I believe I'll take a hand in this conquest myself."

"How?" asked Trot.

"Wait and see," was the reply. "But, first of all, I must fly home again—back to my own country—so if you'll forgive my leaving you so soon, I'll be off at once. Stand away from my tail, please, so that the wind from it, when it revolves, won't knock you over."

They gave the creature plenty of room and away it went like a flash and soon disappeared in the sky.

"I wonder," said Button-Bright, looking solemnly after the Ork, "whether he'll ever come back again."

"Of course he will!" returned Trot. "The Ork's a pretty good fellow, and we can depend on him. An' mark my words, Button-Bright, whenever our Ork does come back, there's one cruel King in Jinxland that'll wish he hadn't."

Chapter 18

The SCARECROW MEETS
an ENEMY

The Scarecrow was not a bit afraid of King Krewl. Indeed, he rather enjoyed the prospect of conquering the evil King and putting Gloria on the throne of Jinxland in his place. So he advanced boldly to the royal castle and demanded admittance.

Seeing that he was a stranger, the soldiers allowed him to enter. He made his way straight to the throne room, where at that time his Majesty was settling the disputes among his subjects.

"Who are you?" demanded the King.

"I'm the Scarecrow of Oz, and I command you to surrender yourself my prisoner."

"Why should I do that?" inquired the King, much astonished at the straw man's audacity.

"Because I've decided you are too cruel a King to rule so beautiful a country. You must remember that Jinxland is a part of Oz, and therefore you owe allegiance to Ozma of Oz, whose friend and servant I am."

Now, when he heard this, King Krewl was much disturbed in mind, for he knew the Scarecrow spoke the truth. But no one had ever before come to Jinxland from the Land of Oz and the King did not intend to be put out of his throne if he could help it. Therefore he gave a harsh, wicked laugh of derision and said:

"I'm busy, now. Stand out of my way, Scarecrow, and I'll talk with you by and by."

But the Scarecrow turned to the assembled courtiers and people and called in a loud voice:

"I hereby declare, in the name of Ozma of Oz, that this man is no longer Ruler of Jinxland. From this moment Princess Gloria is your rightful Queen, and I ask all of you to be loyal to her and to obey her commands."

The people looked fearfully at the King, whom they all hated in their hearts, but likewise feared. Krewl was now in a terrible rage and he raised his golden sceptre and struck the Scarecrow so heavy a blow that he fell to the floor.

But he was up again, in an instant, and with Pon's riding-whip he switched the King so hard that the wicked monarch roared with pain as much as with rage, calling on his soldiers to capture the Scarecrow.

They tried to do that, and thrust their lances and swords into the straw body, but without doing any damage except to make holes in the Scarecrow's clothes. However, they were many against one and finally old Googly-Goo brought a rope which he wound around the Scarecrow, binding his legs together and his arms to his sides, and after that the fight was over.

The King stormed and danced around in a dreadful fury, for he had never been so switched since he was a boy—and perhaps not then. He ordered the Scarecrow thrust into the castle prison, which was no task at all because one man could carry him easily, bound as he was.

Even after the prisoner was removed the King could not control his anger. He tried to figure out some way to be revenged upon the straw man, but could think of nothing that could hurt him.

At last, when the terrified people and the frightened courtiers had all slunk away, old Googly-Goo approached the King with a malicious grin upon his face.

"I'll tell you what to do," said he. "Build a big bonfire and burn the Scarecrow up, and that will be the end of him."

The King was so delighted with this suggestion that he hugged old Googly-Goo in his joy.

"Of course!" he cried. "The very thing. Why did I not think of it myself?"

So he summoned his soldiers and retainers and bade them prepare a great bonfire in an open space in the castle park. Also he sent word to all his people to assemble and witness the destruction of the Scarecrow who had dared to defy his power. Before long a vast throng gathered in the park and the servants had heaped up enough fuel to make a fire that might be seen for miles away—even in the daytime.

When all was prepared, the King had his throne brought out for him to sit upon and enjoy the spectacle, and then he sent his soldiers to fetch the Scarecrow.

Now the one thing in all the world that the straw man really feared was fire. He knew he would burn very easily and that his ashes wouldn't amount to much afterward. It wouldn't hurt him to be destroyed in such a manner, but he realized that many people in the Land of Oz, and especially Dorothy and the Royal Ozma, would feel sad if they learned that their old friend the Scarecrow was no longer in existence.

In spite of this, the straw man was brave and faced his fiery fate like a hero. When they marched him out before the concourse of people he turned to the King with great calmness and said:

"This wicked deed will cost you your throne, as well as much suffering, for my friends will avenge my destruction."

"Your friends are not here, nor will they know what I have done to you, when you are gone and cannot tell them," answered the King in a scornful voice.

Then he ordered the Scarecrow bound to a stout stake that he had had driven into the ground, and the materials for the fire were heaped all around him. When this had been done, the King's brass band struck up a lively tune and old Googly-Goo came forward with a lighted match and set fire to the pile.

At once the flames shot up and crept closer and closer toward the Scarecrow. The King and all his people were so intent upon this terrible spectacle that none of them noticed how the sky grew suddenly dark. Perhaps they thought that the loud buzzing sound—like the noise of a dozen moving railway trains—came from the blazing kindling; that the rush of wind was merely a breeze. But suddenly down swept a flock of Orks, half a hundred of them at the least, and the powerful currents of air caused by their revolving tails sent the bonfire scattering in every direction, so that not one burning brand ever touched the Scarecrow.

But that was not the only effect of this sudden tornado. King Krewl was blown out of his throne and went tumbling heels over head until he landed with a bump against the stone wall of his own castle, and before he could rise a big Ork sat upon him and held him pressed flat to the ground. Old Googly-Goo shot up into the air like a rocket and landed on a tree, where he hung by the middle on a high limb, kicking the air with his feet and clawing the air with his hands, and howling for mercy like the coward he was.

The people pressed back until they were jammed close together, while all the soldiers were knocked over and sent sprawling to the earth. The excitement was great for a few minutes, and every frightened inhabitant of Jinxland looked with awe and amazement at the great Orks whose descent had served to rescue the Scarecrow and conquer King Krewl at one and the same time.

The Ork, who was the leader of the band, soon had the Scarecrow free of his bonds. Then he said: "Well, we were just in time to save you, which is better than being a minute too late. You are now the master here, and we are determined to see your orders obeyed."

With this the Ork picked up Krewl's golden crown, which had fallen off his head, and placed it upon the head of the Scarecrow, who in his awkward way then shuffled over to the throne and sat down in it.

Seeing this, a rousing cheer broke from the crowd of people, who tossed their hats and waved their handkerchiefs and hailed the Scarecrow as their King. The soldiers joined the people in the cheering, for now they fully realized that their hated master was conquered and it would be wise to show their good will to the conqueror. Some of them bound Krewl with ropes and dragged him forward, dumping his body on the ground before the Scarecrow's throne. Googly-Goo struggled until he finally slid off the limb of the tree and came tumbling to the ground. He then tried to sneak away and escape, but the soldiers seized and bound him beside Krewl.

"The tables are turned," said the Scarecrow, swelling out his chest until the straw within it crackled pleasantly, for he was highly pleased; "but it was you and your people who did it, friend Ork, and from this time you may count me your humble servant."

··—··‹ Chapter 19 ›··—··

The CONQUEST of the WITCH

Now as soon as the conquest of King Krewl had taken place, one of the Orks had been dispatched to Pon's house with the joyful news. At once Gloria and Pon and Trot and Button-Bright hastened toward the castle. They were somewhat surprised by the sight that met their eyes, for there was the Scarecrow, crowned King, and all the people kneeling humbly before him. So they likewise bowed low to the new Ruler and then stood beside the throne. Cap'n Bill, as the grey grasshopper, was still perched upon Trot's shoulder, but now he hopped to the shoulder of the Scarecrow and whispered into the painted ear:

"I thought Gloria was to be Queen of Jinxland."

The Scarecrow shook his head.

"Not yet," he answered. "No Queen with a frozen heart is fit to rule any country." Then he turned to his new friend, the Ork, who was strutting about, very proud of what he had done, and said: "Do you suppose you, or your followers, could find old Blinkie the Witch?"

"Where is she?" asked the Ork.

"Somewhere in Jinxland, I'm sure."

"Then," said the Ork, "we shall certainly be able to find her."

"It will give me great pleasure," declared the Scarecrow. "When you have found her, bring her here to me, and I will then decide what to do with her."

The Ork called his followers together and spoke a few words to them in a low tone. A moment after they rose into the air—so suddenly that the Scarecrow, who was very light in weight, was blown quite out of his throne and into the arms of Pon, who replaced him carefully upon his seat. There was an eddy of dust and ashes, too, and the grasshopper only saved himself from being whirled into the crowd of people by jumping into a tree, from where a series of hops soon brought him back to Trot's shoulder again. The Orks were quite out of sight by this time, so the Scarecrow made a speech to the people and presented Gloria to them, whom they knew well already and were fond of. But not all of them knew of her frozen heart, and when the Scarecrow related the story of the Wicked Witch's misdeeds, which had been encouraged and paid for by Krewl and Googly-Goo, the people were very indignant.

Meantime the fifty Orks had scattered all over Jinxland, which is not a very big country, and their sharp eyes were peering into every valley and grove and gully. Finally one of them spied a pair of heels sticking out from underneath some bushes, and with a shrill whistle to warn his comrades that the Witch was found the Ork flew down and dragged old Blinkie from her hiding-place. Then two or three of the Orks seized the clothing of the wicked woman in their strong claws and, lifting her high in the air, where she struggled and screamed to no avail, they flew with her straight to the royal castle and set her down before the throne of the Scarecrow.

"Good!" exclaimed the straw man, nodding his stuffed head with satisfaction. "Now we can proceed to business. Mistress Witch, I am obliged to request, gently but firmly, that you undo all the wrongs you have done by means of your witchcraft."

"Pah!" cried old Blinkie in a scornful voice. "I defy you all! By my magic powers I can turn you all into pigs, rooting in the mud, and I'll do it if you are not careful."

"I think you are mistaken about that," said the Scarecrow, and rising from his throne he walked with wobbling steps to the side of the Wicked Witch. "Before I left the Land of Oz, Glinda the Royal Sorceress gave me a box, which I was not to open except in an emergency. But I feel pretty sure that this occasion is an emergency; don't you, Trot?" he asked, turning toward the little girl.

"Why, we've got to do *something*," replied Trot seriously. "Things seem in an awful muddle here, jus' now, and they'll be worse if we don't stop this Witch from doing more harm to people."

"That is my idea, exactly," said the Scarecrow, and taking a small box from his pocket he opened the cover and tossed the contents toward Blinkie.

The old woman shrank back, pale and trembling, as a fine white dust settled all about her. Under its influence she seemed to the eyes of all observers to shrivel and grow smaller.

"Oh, dear—oh, dear!" she wailed, wringing her hands in fear. "Haven't you the antidote, Scarecrow? Didn't the great Sorceress give you another box?"

"She did," answered the Scarecrow.

"Then give it me—quick!" pleaded the Witch. "Give it me—and I'll do anything you ask me to!"

"You will do what I ask first," declared the Scarecrow, firmly.

The Witch was shriveling and growing smaller every moment.

"Be quick, then!" she cried. "Tell me what I must do and let me do it, or it will be too late."

"You made Trot's friend, Cap'n Bill, a grasshopper. I

command you to give him back his proper form again," said the Scarecrow.

"Where is he? Where's the grasshopper? Quick—quick!" she screamed.

Cap'n Bill, who had been deeply interested in this conversation, gave a great leap from Trot's shoulder and landed on that of the Scarecrow. Blinkie saw him alight and at once began to make magic passes and to mumble magic incantations. She was in a desperate hurry, knowing that she had no time to waste, and the grasshopper was so suddenly transformed into the old sailor-man, Cap'n Bill, that he had no opportunity to jump off the Scarecrow's shoulder; so his great weight bore the stuffed Scarecrow to the ground. No harm was done, however, and the straw man got up and brushed the dust from his clothes while Trot delightedly embraced Cap'n Bill.

"The other box! Quick! Give me the other box," begged Blinkie, who had now shrunk to half her former size.

"Not yet," said the Scarecrow. "You must first melt Princess Gloria's frozen heart."

"I can't; it's an awful job to do that! I can't," asserted the Witch, in an agony of fear—for still she was growing smaller.

"You must!" declared the Scarecrow, firmly.

The Witch cast a shrewd look at him and saw that he meant it; so she began dancing around Gloria in a frantic manner. The Princess looked coldly on, as if not at all interested in the proceedings, while Blinkie tore a handful of hair from her own head and ripped a strip of cloth from the bottom of her gown. Then the Witch sank upon her knees, took a purple powder from her black bag and sprinkled it over the hair and cloth.

"I hate to do it—I hate to do it!" she wailed, "for there is no more of this magic compound in all the world. But I must sacrifice it to save my own life. A match! Give me a match, quick!" and panting from lack of breath she gazed imploringly from one to another.

Cap'n Bill was the only one who had a match, but he lost no time in handing it to Blinkie, who quickly set fire to the hair and the cloth and the purple powder. At once a purple cloud enveloped Gloria, and this gradually turned to a rosy pink color—brilliant and quite transparent. Through the rosy cloud they could all see the beautiful Princess, standing proud and erect. Then her heart became visible, at first frosted with ice but slowly growing brighter and warmer until all the frost had disappeared and it was beating as softly and regularly as any other heart. And now the cloud dispersed and disclosed Gloria, her face suffused with joy, smiling tenderly upon the friends who were grouped about her.

Poor Pon stepped forward—timidly, fearing a repulse, but with pleading eyes and arms fondly outstretched toward his former sweetheart—and the Princess saw him and her sweet face lighted with a radiant smile. Without an instant's hesitation she threw herself into Pon's arms and this reunion of two loving hearts was so affecting that the people turned away and lowered their eyes so as not to mar the sacred joy of the faithful lovers.

But Blinkie's small voice was shouting to the Scarecrow for help.

"The antidote!" she screamed. "Give me the other box—quick!"

The Scarecrow looked at the Witch with his quaint, painted eyes and saw that she was now no taller than his knee. So he took from his pocket the second box and scattered its contents on Blinkie. She ceased to grow any smaller, but she could never regain her former size, and this the wicked old woman well knew.

She did not know, however, that the second powder had destroyed all her power to work magic, and seeking to be revenged upon the Scarecrow and his friends she at once began to mumble a charm so terrible in its effect that it would have destroyed half the population of Jinxland—had it worked. But it did not work at all, to the amazement of old Blinkie. And by this time the Scarecrow noticed what the little Witch was trying to do, and said to her:

"Go home, Blinkie, and behave yourself. You are no longer a Witch, but an ordinary old woman, and since you are powerless to do more evil I advise you to try to do some good in the world. Believe me, it is more fun to accomplish a good act than an evil one, as you will discover when once you have tried it."

But Blinkie was at that moment filled with grief and cha-grin at losing her magic powers. She started away toward her home, sobbing and bewailing her fate, and not one who saw her go was at all sorry for her.

·····◄ Chapter 20 ►·····

Queen Gloria

Next morning the Scarecrow called upon all the courtiers and the people to assemble in the throne room of the castle, where there was room enough for all that were able to attend. They found the straw man seated upon the velvet cushions of the throne, with the King's glittering crown still upon his stuffed head. On one side of the throne, in a lower chair, sat Gloria, looking radiantly beautiful and fresh as a new-blown rose. On the other side sat Pon, the gardener's boy, still dressed in his old smock frock and looking sad and solemn; for Pon could not make himself believe that so splendid a Princess would condescend to love him when she had come to her own and was seated upon a throne. Trot and Cap'n Bill sat at the feet of the Scarecrow and were much interested in the proceedings. Button-Bright had lost himself before breakfast, but came into the throne room before the ceremonies were over. Back of the throne stood a row of the great Orks, with their leader in the center, and the entrance to the palace was guarded by more Orks, who were regarded with wonder and awe.

When all were assembled, the Scarecrow stood up and made a speech. He told how Gloria's father, the good King Kynd, who had once ruled them and been loved by everyone, had been destroyed by King Phearce, the father of Pon, and how King Phearce had been destroyed by King Krewl. This last King had been a bad Ruler, as they knew very well, and the Scarecrow declared that the only one in all Jinxland who had the right to sit upon the throne was Princess Gloria, the daughter of King Kynd.

"But," he added, "it is not for me, a stranger, to say who shall rule you. You must decide for yourselves, or you will not be content. So choose now who shall be your future Ruler."

And they all shouted: "The Scarecrow! The Scarecrow shall rule us!"

Which proved that the stuffed man had made himself very popular by his conquest of King Krewl, and the people thought they would like him for their King. But the Scarecrow shook his head so vigorously that it became loose, and Trot had to pin it firmly to his body again.

"No," said he, "I belong in the Land of Oz, where I am the humble servant of the lovely girl who rules us all—the royal Ozma. You must choose one of your own inhabitants to rule over Jinxland. Who shall it be?"

They hesitated for a moment, and some few cried: "Pon!" but many more shouted: "Gloria!"

So the Scarecrow took Gloria's hand and led her to the throne, where he first seated her and then took the glittering crown off his own head and placed it upon that of the young lady, where it nestled prettily amongst her soft curls. The people cheered and shouted then, kneeling before their new Queen; but Gloria leaned down and took Pon's hand in both her own and raised him to the seat beside her.

"You shall have both a King and a Queen to care for you and to protect you, my dear subjects," she said in a sweet voice, while her face glowed with happiness; "for Pon was a King's son before he became a gardener's boy, and because I love him he is to be my Royal Consort."

That pleased them all, especially Pon, who realized that this was the most important moment of his life. Trot and Button-Bright and Cap'n Bill all congratulated him on winning the beautiful Gloria; but the Ork sneezed twice and said that in his opinion the young lady might have done better.

Then the Scarecrow ordered the guards to bring in the wicked Krewl, King no longer, and when he appeared, loaded with chains and dressed in fustian, the people hissed him and drew back as he passed so their garments would not touch him.

Krewl was not haughty or overbearing any more; on the contrary he seemed very meek and in great fear of the fate his conquerors had in store for him. But Gloria and Pon were too happy to be revengeful and so they offered to appoint Krewl to the position of gardener's boy at the castle, Pon having resigned to become King. But they said he must promise to reform his wicked ways and to do his duty faithfully, and he must change his name from Krewl to Grewl. All this the man eagerly promised to do, and so when Pon retired to a room in the castle to put on princely raiment, the old brown smock he had formerly worn was given to Grewl, who then went out into the garden to water the roses.

The remainder of that famous day, which was long remembered in Jinxland, was given over to feasting and merrymaking. In the evening there was a grand dance in the courtyard, where the brass band played a new piece of music called the "Ork Trot" which was dedicated to "Our Glorious Gloria, the Queen."

While the Queen and Pon were leading this dance, and all the Jinxland people were having a good time, the strangers were gathered in a group in the park outside the castle. Cap'n Bill, Trot, Button-Bright and the Scarecrow were there, and so was their old friend the Ork; but of all the great flock of Orks which had assisted in the conquest but three remained in Jinxland, besides their leader, the others having returned to their own country as soon as Gloria was crowned Queen. To the young Ork who had accompanied them in their adventures Cap'n Bill said:

"You've surely been a friend in need, and we're mighty grateful to you for helping us. I might have been a grasshopper yet if it hadn't been for you, an' I might remark that bein' a grasshopper isn't much fun."

"If it hadn't been for you, friend Ork," said the Scarecrow, "I fear I could not have conquered King Krewl."

"No," agreed Trot, "you'd have been just a heap of ashes by this time."

"And I might have been lost yet," added Button-Bright. "Much obliged, Mr. Ork."

"Oh, that's all right," replied the Ork. "Friends must stand together, you know, or they wouldn't be friends. But now I must leave you and be off to my own country, where there's going to be a surprise party for my uncle, and I've promised to attend it."

"Dear me," said the Scarecrow, regretfully. "That is very unfortunate."

"Why so?" asked the Ork.

"I hoped you would consent to carry us over those mountains, into the Land of Oz. My mission here is now finished and I want to get back to the Emerald City."

"How did you cross the mountains before?" inquired the Ork.

"I scaled the cliffs by means of a rope, and crossed the Great Gulf on a strand of spider web. Of course I can return in the same manner, but it would be a hard journey—and perhaps an impossible one—for Trot and Button-Bright and Cap'n Bill. So I thought that if you had the time you and your people would carry us over the mountains and land us all safely on the other side, in the Land of Oz."

The Ork thoughtfully considered the matter for a while. Then he said:

"I mustn't break my promise to be present at the surprise party; but, tell me, could you go to Oz to-night?"

"What, now?" exclaimed Trot.

"It is a fine moonlight night," said the Ork, "and I've found in my experience that there's no time so good as right away. The fact is," he explained, "it's a long journey to Orkland and I and my cousins here are all rather tired by our day's work. But if you will start now, and be content to allow us to carry you over the mountains and dump you on the other side, just say the word and—off we go!"

Cap'n Bill and Trot looked at one another questioningly. The little girl was eager to visit the famous fairyland of Oz and the old sailor had endured such hardships in Jinxland that he would be glad to be out of it.

"It's rather impolite of us not to say good-bye to the new King and Queen," remarked the Scarecrow, "but I'm sure they're too happy to miss us, and I assure you it will be much easier to fly on the backs of the Orks over those steep mountains than to climb them as I did."

"All right; let's go!" Trot decided. "But where's Button-Bright?"

Just at this important moment Button-Bright was lost again, and they all scattered in search of him. He had been standing beside them just a few minutes before, but his friends had an exciting hunt for him before they finally discovered the boy seated among the members of the band, beating the end of the bass drum with the bone of a turkey-leg that he had taken from the table in the banquet room.

"Hello, Trot," he said, looking up at the little girl when she found him. "This is the first chance I ever had to pound a drum with a reg'lar drum stick. And I ate all the meat off the bone myself."

"Come quick. We're going to the Land of Oz."

"Oh, what's the hurry?" said Button-Bright; but she seized his arm and dragged him away to the park, where the others were waiting.

Trot climbed upon the back of her old friend, the Ork leader, and the others took their seats on the backs of his three cousins. As soon as all were placed and clinging to the skinny necks of the creatures, the revolving tails began to whirl and up rose the four monster Orks and sailed away toward the mountains. They were so high in the air that when they passed the crest of the highest peak it seemed far below them. No sooner were they well across the barrier than the Orks swooped downward and landed their passengers upon the ground.

"Here we are, safe in the Land of Oz!" cried the Scarecrow joyfully.

"Oh, are we?" asked Trot, looking around her curiously.

She could see the shadows of stately trees and the outlines of rolling hills; beneath her feet was soft turf, but otherwise the subdued light of the moon disclosed nothing clearly.

"Seems jus' like any other country," was Cap'n Bill's comment.

"But it isn't," the Scarecrow assured him. "You are now within the borders of the most glorious fairyland in all the world. This part of it is just a corner of the Quadling Country, and the least interesting portion of it. It's not very thickly settled, around here, I'll admit, but—"

He was interrupted by a sudden whir and a rush of air as the four Orks mounted into the sky.

"Good night!" called the shrill voices of the strange creatures, and although Trot shouted "Good night!" as loudly as she could, the little girl was almost ready to cry because the Orks had not waited to be properly thanked for all their kindness to her and to Cap'n Bill.

But the Orks were gone, and thanks for good deeds do not amount to much except to prove one's politeness.

"Well, friends," said the Scarecrow, "we mustn't stay here in the meadows all night, so let us find a pleasant place to sleep. Not that it matters to me, in the least, for I never sleep; but I know that meat people like to shut their eyes and lie still during the dark hours."

"I'm pretty tired," admitted Trot, yawning as she followed the straw man along a tiny path, "so, if you don't find a house handy, Cap'n Bill and I will sleep under the trees, or even on this soft grass."

But a house was not very far off, although when the Scarecrow stumbled upon it there was no light in it whatever. Cap'n Bill knocked on the door several times, and there being no response the Scarecrow boldly lifted the latch and walked in, followed by the others. And no sooner had they entered than a soft light filled the room. Trot couldn't tell where it came from, for no lamp of any sort was visible, but she did not waste much time on this problem, because directly in the center of the room stood a table set for three, with lots of good food on it and several of the dishes smoking hot.

The little girl and Button-Bright both uttered exclamations of pleasure, but they looked in vain for any cook stove or fireplace, or for any person who might have prepared for them this delicious feast.

"It's fairyland," muttered the boy, tossing his cap in a corner and seating himself at the table. "This supper smells 'most as good as that turkey-leg I had in Jinxland. Please pass the muffins, Cap'n Bill."

Trot thought it was strange that no people but themselves

were in the house, but on the wall opposite the door was a gold frame bearing in big letters the word:

WELCOME.

So she had no further hesitation in eating of the food so mysteriously prepared for them.

"But there are only places for three!" she exclaimed.

"Three are quite enough," said the Scarecrow. "I never eat, because I am stuffed full already, and I like my nice clean straw better than I do food."

Trot and the sailor-man were hungry and made a hearty meal, for not since they had left home had they tasted such good food. It was surprising that Button-Bright could eat so soon after his feast in Jinxland, but the boy always ate whenever there was an opportunity. "If I don't eat now," he said, "the next time I'm hungry I'll wish I had."

"Really, Cap'n," remarked Trot, when she found a dish of ice-cream appear beside her plate, "I b'lieve this is fairyland, sure enough."

"There's no doubt of it, Trot," he answered gravely

"I've been here before," said Button-Bright, "so I know."

After supper they discovered three tiny bedrooms adjoining the big living room of the house, and in each room was a comfortable white bed with downy pillows. You may be sure that the tired mortals were not long in bidding the Scarecrow good night and creeping into their beds, where they slept soundly until morning.

For the first time since they set eyes on the terrible whirl-pool, Trot and Cap'n Bill were free from anxiety and care. Button-Bright never worried about anything. The Scarecrow, not being able to sleep, looked out of the window and tried to count the stars.

..—..◄ Chapter 21 ►..—..

DOROTHY, BETSY and OZMA

I suppose many of my readers have read descriptions of the beautiful and magnificent Emerald City of Oz, so I need not describe it here, except to state that never has any city in any fairyland ever equalled this one in stately splendor. It lies almost exactly in the center of the Land of Oz, and in the center of the Emerald City rises the wall of glistening emeralds that surrounds the palace of Ozma. The palace is almost a city in itself and is inhabited by many of the Ruler's especial friends and those who have won her confidence and favor.

As for Ozma herself, there are no words in any dictionary

I can find that are fitted to describe this young girl's beauty of mind and person. Merely to see her is to love her for her charming face and manners; to know her is to love her for her tender sympathy, her generous nature, her truth and honor. Born of a long line of Fairy Queens, Ozma is as nearly perfect as any fairy may be, and she is noted for her wisdom as well as for her other qualities. Her happy subjects adore their girl Ruler and each one considers her a comrade and protector.

At the time of which I write, Ozma's best friend and most constant companion was a little Kansas girl named Dorothy, a mortal who had come to the Land of Oz in a very curious manner and had been offered a home in Ozma's palace. Furthermore, Dorothy had been made a Princess of Oz, and was as much at home in the royal palace as was the gentle Ruler. She knew almost every part of the great country and almost all of its numerous inhabitants. Next to Ozma she was loved better than anyone in all Oz, for Dorothy was simple and sweet, seldom became angry and had such a friendly, chummy way that she made friends where-ever she wandered. It was she who first brought the Scarecrow and the Tin Woodman and the Cowardly Lion to the Emerald City. Dorothy had also introduced to Ozma the Shaggy Man and the Hungry Tiger, as well as Billina the Yellow Hen, Eureka the Pink Kitten, and many other delightful characters and creatures. Coming as she did from our world, Dorothy was much like many other girls we know; so there were times when she was not so wise as she might have been, and other times when she was obstinate and got herself into trouble. But life in a fairyland had taught the little girl to accept all sorts of surprising things as matters-of-course, for while Dorothy was no fairy—but just as mortal as we are—she had seen more wonders than most mortals ever do.

Another little girl from our outside world also lived in Ozma's palace. This was Betsy Bobbin, whose strange adventures had brought her to the Emerald City, where Ozma had cordially welcomed her. Betsy was a shy little thing and could never get used to the marvels that surrounded her, but she and Dorothy were firm friends and thought themselves very fortunate in being together in this delightful country.

One day Dorothy and Betsy were visiting Ozma in the girl Ruler's private apartment, and among the things that especially interested them was Ozma's Magic Picture, set in a handsome frame and hung upon the wall of the room. This picture was a magic one because it constantly changed its scenes and showed events and adventures happening in all parts of the world. Thus it was really a "moving picture" of life, and if the one who stood before it wished to know what any absent person was doing, the picture instantly showed that person, with his or her surroundings.

The two girls were not wishing to see anyone in particular, on this occasion, but merely enjoyed watching the shifting scenes, some of which were exceedingly curious and remarkable. Suddenly Dorothy exclaimed: "Why, there's Button-Bright!" and this drew Ozma also to look at the picture, for she and Dorothy knew the boy well.

"Who is Button-Bright?" asked Betsy, who had never met him.

"Why, he's the little boy who is just getting off the back of that strange flying creature," exclaimed Dorothy. Then she turned to Ozma and asked: "What is that thing, Ozma? A bird? I've never seen anything like it before."

"It is an Ork," answered Ozma, for they were watching the scene where the Ork and the three big birds were first landing their passengers in Jinxland after the long flight across the desert. "I wonder," added the girl Ruler, musingly, "why those strangers dare venture into that unfortunate country, which is ruled by a wicked King."

"That girl, and the one-legged man, seem to be mortals from the outside world," said Dorothy.

"The man isn't one-legged," corrected Betsy; "he has one wooden leg."

"It's almost as bad," declared Dorothy, watching Cap'n Bill stump around.

"They are three mortal adventurers," said Ozma, "and they seem worthy and honest. But I fear they will be treated badly in Jinxland, and if they meet with any misfortune there it will reflect upon me, for Jinxland is a part of my dominions."

"Can't we help them in any way?" inquired Dorothy. "That seems like a nice little girl. I'd be sorry if anything happened to her."

"Let us watch the picture for awhile," suggested Ozma, and so they all drew chairs before the Magic Picture and followed the adventures of Trot and Cap'n Bill and Button-Bright. Presently the scene shifted and showed their friend the Scarecrow crossing the mountains into Jinxland, and that somewhat relieved Ozma's anxiety, for she knew at once that Glinda the Good had sent the Scarecrow to protect the strangers.

The adventures in Jinxland proved very interesting to the three girls in Ozma's palace, who during the succeeding days spent much of their time in watching the picture. It was like a story to them.

"That girl's a reg'lar trump!" exclaimed Dorothy, referring to Trot, and Ozma answered:

"She's a dear little thing, and I'm sure nothing very bad will happen to her. The old sailor is a fine character, too, for he has never once grumbled over being a grasshopper, as so many would have done."

When the Scarecrow was so nearly burned up the girls all shivered a little, and they clapped their hands in joy when the flock of Orks came and saved him.

So it was that when all the exciting adventures in Jinxland were over and the four Orks had begun their flight across the mountains to carry the mortals into the Land of Oz, Ozma called the Wizard to her and asked him to prepare a place for the strangers to sleep.

The famous Wizard of Oz was a quaint little man who inhabited the royal palace and attended to all the magical things that Ozma wanted done. He was not as powerful as Glinda, to be sure, but he could do a great many wonderful things. He proved this by placing a house in the uninhabited part of the Quadling Country where the Orks landed Cap'n Bill and Trot and Button-Bright, and fitting it with all the comforts I have described in the last chapter.

Next morning Dorothy said to Ozma:

"Oughtn't we to go meet the strangers, so we can show them the way to the Emerald City? I'm sure that little girl will feel shy in this beautiful land, and I know if 'twas me I'd like somebody to give me a welcome."

Ozma smiled at her little friend and answered:

"You and Betsy may go to meet them, if you wish, but I can not leave my palace just now, as I am to have a conference with Jack Pumpkinhead and Professor Wogglebug on important matters. You may take the Sawhorse and the Red Wagon, and if you start soon you will be able to meet the Scarecrow and the strangers at Glinda's palace."

"Oh, thank you!" cried Dorothy, and went away to tell Betsy and to make preparations for the journey.

·····◀ Chapter 22 ▶·····

The WATERFALL

Glinda's castle was a long way from the mountains, but the Scarecrow began the journey cheerfully, since time was of no great importance in the Land of Oz and he had recently made the trip and knew the way. It never mattered much to Button-Bright where he was or what he was doing; the boy was content in being alive and having good companions to share his wanderings. As for Trot and Cap'n Bill, they now found themselves so comfortable and free from danger, in this fine fairyland, and they were so awed and amazed by the adventures they were encountering, that the journey to Glinda's castle was more like a pleasure trip than a hardship, so many wonderful things were there to see.

Button-Bright had been in Oz before, but never in this part of it, so the Scarecrow was the only one who knew the paths and could lead them. They had eaten a hearty breakfast, which they found already prepared for them and awaiting them on the table when they arose from their refreshing sleep, so they left the magic house in a contented mood and with hearts lighter and more happy than they had known for many a day. As they marched along through the fields, the sun shone brightly and the breeze was laden with delicious fragrance, for it carried with it the breath of millions of wildflowers.

At noon, when they stopped to rest by the bank of a pretty river, Trot said with a long-drawn breath that was much like a sigh:

"I wish we'd brought with us some of the food that was left from our breakfast, for I'm getting hungry again."

Scarcely had she spoken when a table rose up before them, as if from the ground itself, and it was loaded with fruits and nuts and cakes and many other good things to eat. The little girl's eyes opened wide at this display of magic, and Cap'n Bill was not sure that the things were actually there and fit to eat until he had taken them in his hand and tasted them. But the Scarecrow said with a laugh:

"Someone is looking after your welfare, that is certain, and from the looks of this table I suspect my friend the Wizard has taken us in his charge. I've known him to do things like this before, and if we are in the Wizard's care you need not worry about your future."

"Who's worrying?" inquired Button-Bright, already at the table and busily eating.

The Scarecrow looked around the place while the others were feasting, and finding many things unfamiliar to him he shook his head and remarked:

"I must have taken the wrong path, back in that last valley, for on my way to Jinxland I remember that I passed around the foot of this river, where there was a great waterfall."

"Did the river make a bend, after the waterfall?" asked Cap'n Bill.

"No, the river disappeared. Only a pool of whirling water showed what had become of the river; but I suppose it is under ground, somewhere, and will come to the surface again in another part of the country."

"Well," suggested Trot, as she finished her luncheon, "as there is no way to cross this river, I s'pose we'll have to find that waterfall, and go around it."

"Exactly," replied the Scarecrow; so they soon renewed their journey, following the river for a long time until the roar of the waterfall sounded in their ears. By and by they came to the waterfall itself, a sheet of silver dropping far, far down into a tiny lake which seemed to have no outlet. From the top of the fall, where they stood, the banks gradually sloped away, so that the descent by land was quite easy, while the river could do nothing but glide over an edge of rock and tumble straight down to the depths below.

"You see," said the Scarecrow, leaning over the brink, "this is called by our Oz people the Great Waterfall, because it is certainly the highest one in all the land; but I think—Help!"

He had lost his balance and pitched headforemost into the river. They saw a flash of straw and blue clothes, and the painted face looking upward in surprise. The next moment the Scarecrow was swept over the waterfall and plunged into the basin below.

The accident had happened so suddenly that for a moment they were all too horrified to speak or move.

"Quick! We must go to help him or he will be drowned," Trot exclaimed.

Even while speaking she began to descend the bank to the pool below, and Cap'n Bill followed as swiftly as his wooden leg would let him. Button-Bright came more slowly, calling to the girl:

"He can't drown, Trot; he's a Scarecrow."

But she wasn't sure a Scarecrow couldn't drown and never relaxed her speed until she stood on the edge of the pool, with the spray dashing in her face. Cap'n Bill, puffing and panting, had just voice enough to ask, as he reached her side:

"See him, Trot?"

"Not a speck of him. Oh, Cap'n, what do you s'pose has become of him?"

"I s'pose," replied the sailor, "that he's in that water, more or less far down, and I'm 'fraid it'll make his straw pretty soggy. But as fer his bein' drowned, I agree with Button-Bright that it can't be done."

There was small comfort in this assurance and Trot stood for some time searching with her eyes the bubbling water, in the hope that the Scarecrow would finally come to the surface. Presently she heard Button-Bright calling: "Come here, Trot!" and looking around she saw that the boy had crept over the wet rocks to the edge of the waterfall and seemed to be peering behind it. Making her way toward him, she asked:

"What do you see?"

"A cave," he answered. "Let's go in. P'r'aps we'll find the Scarecrow there."

She was a little doubtful of that, but the cave interested her, and so did it Cap'n Bill. There was just space enough at the edge of the sheet of water for them to crowd in behind it, but after that dangerous entrance they found room enough to walk upright and after a time they came to an opening in the wall of rock. Approaching this opening, they gazed within it and found a series of steps, cut so that they might easily descend into the cavern.

Trot turned to look inquiringly at her companions. The

falling water made such din and roaring that her voice could not be heard. Cap'n Bill nodded his head, but before he could enter the cave, Button-Bright was before him, clambering down the steps without a particle of fear. So the others followed the boy.

The first steps were wet with spray, and slippery, but the remainder were quite dry. A rosy light seemed to come from the interior of the cave, and this lighted their way. After the steps there was a short tunnel, high enough for them to walk erect in, and then they reached the cave itself and paused in wonder and admiration.

They stood on the edge of a vast cavern, the walls and domed roof of which were lined with countless rubies, exquisitely cut and flashing sparkling rays from one to another. This caused a radiant light that permitted the entire cavern to be distinctly seen, and the effect was so marvelous that Trot drew in her breath with a sort of a gasp, and stood quite still in wonder.

But the walls and roof of the cavern were merely a setting for a more wonderful scene. In the center was a bubbling caldron of water, for here the river rose again, splashing and dashing till its spray rose high in the air, where it took the ruby color of the jewels and seemed like a seething mass of flame. And while they gazed into the tumbling, tossing water, the body of the Scarecrow suddenly rose in the center, struggling and kicking, and the next instant wholly disappeared from view.

"My, but he's wet!" exclaimed Button-Bright; but none of the others heard him.

Trot and Cap'n Bill discovered that a broad ledge—covered, like the walls, with glittering rubies—ran all around the cavern; so they followed this gorgeous path to the rear and found where the water made its final dive underground, before it disappeared entirely. Where it plunged into this dim abyss the river was black and dreary looking, and they stood gazing in awe until just beside them the body of the Scarecrow again popped up from the water.

The LAND of OZ

T he straw man's appearance on the water was so
sudden that it startled Trot, but Cap'n Bill had
the presence of mind to stick his wooden leg out
over the water and the Scarecrow made a desperate clutch and grabbed the leg with both hands. He managed to hold on until Trot and Button-Bright knelt down and
seized his clothing, but the children would have been powerless to drag the soaked Scarecrow ashore had not Cap'n Bill
now assisted them. When they laid him on the ledge of rubies
he was the most useless looking Scarecrow you can imagine—
his straw sodden and dripping with water, his clothing wet and
crumpled, while even the sack upon which his face was painted

had become so wrinkled that the old jolly expression of their stuffed friend's features was entirely gone. But he could still speak, and when Trot bent down her ear she heard him say:

"Get me out of here as soon as you can."

That seemed a wise thing to do, so Cap'n Bill lifted his head and shoulders, and Trot and Button-Bright each took a leg; among them they partly carried and partly dragged the damp Scarecrow out of the Ruby Cavern, along the tunnel, and up the flight of rock steps. It was somewhat difficult to get him past the edge of the waterfall, but they succeeded, after much effort, and a few minutes later laid their poor comrade on a grassy bank where the sun shone upon him freely and he was beyond the reach of the spray.

Cap'n Bill now knelt down and examined the straw that the Scarecrow was stuffed with.

"I don't believe it'll be of much use to him, any more," said he, "for it's full of polliwogs an' fish eggs, an' the water has took all the crinkle out o' the straw an ruined it. I guess, Trot, that the best thing for us to do is to empty out all his body an' carry his head an' clothes along the road till we come to a field or a house where we can get some fresh straw."

"Yes, Cap'n," she agreed, "there's nothing else to be done. But how shall we ever find the road to Glinda's palace, without the Scarecrow to guide us?"

"That's easy," said the Scarecrow, speaking in a rather feeble but distinct voice. "If Cap'n Bill will carry my head on his shoulders, eyes front, I can tell him which way to go."

So they followed that plan and emptied all the old, wet straw out of the Scarecrow's body. Then the sailor-man wrung out the clothes and laid them in the sun till they were quite dry. Trot took charge of the head and pressed the wrinkles out of the face as it dried, so that after a while the Scarecrow's expression became natural again, and as jolly as before.

This work consumed some time, but when it was completed they again started upon their journey, Button-Bright carrying the boots and hat, Trot the bundle of clothes, and Cap'n Bill the head. The Scarecrow, having regained his composure and being now in a good humor, despite his recent mishaps, beguiled their way with stories of the Land of Oz.

It was not until the next morning, however, that they found straw with which to restuff the Scarecrow. That evening they came to the same little house they had slept in before, only now it was magically transferred to a new place. The same bountiful supper as before was found smoking hot upon the table and the same cosy beds were ready for them to sleep in.

They rose early and after breakfast went out of doors, and there, lying just beside the house, was a heap of clean, crisp straw. Ozma had noticed the Scarecrow's accident in her Magic Picture and had notified the Wizard to provide the straw, for she knew the adventurers were not likely to find straw in the country through which they were now traveling.

They lost no time in stuffing the Scarecrow anew, and he

was greatly delighted at being able to walk around again and to assume the leadership of the little party.

"Really," said Trot, "I think you're better than you were before, for you are fresh and sweet all through and rustle beautifully when you move."

"Thank you, my dear," he replied gratefully. "I always feel like a new man when I'm freshly stuffed. No one likes to get musty, you know, and even good straw may be spoiled by age."

"It was water that spoiled you, the last time," remarked Button-Bright, "which proves that too much bathing is as bad as too little. But, after all, Scarecrow, water is not as dangerous for you as fire."

"All things are good in moderation," declared the Scarecrow. "But now, let us hurry on, or we shall not reach Glinda's palace by nightfall."

....——< Chapter 24 >·...——..

The ROYAL RECEPTION

At about four o'clock of that same day the Red Wagon drew up at the entrance to Glinda's palace and Dorothy and Betsy jumped out. Ozma's Red Wagon was almost a chariot, being inlaid with rubies and pearls, and it was drawn by Ozma's favorite steed, the wooden Sawhorse.

"Shall I unharness you," asked Dorothy, "so you can come in and visit?"

"No," replied the Sawhorse. "I'll just stand here and think. Take your time. Thinking doesn't seem to bore me at all."

"What will you think of?" inquired Betsy.

"Of the acorn that grew the tree from which I was made."

So they left the wooden animal and went in to see Glinda, who welcomed the little girls in her most cordial manner.

"I knew you were on your way," said the good Sorceress when they were seated in her library, "for I learned from my Record Book that you intended to meet Trot and Button-Bright on their arrival here."

"Is the strange little girl named Trot?" asked Dorothy.

"Yes; and her companion, the old sailor, is named Cap'n Bill. I think we shall like them very much, for they are just the kind of people to enjoy and appreciate our fairyland and I do not see any way, at present, for them to return again to the outside world."

"Well, there's room enough here for them, I'm sure," said Dorothy. "Betsy and I are already eager to welcome Trot. It will keep us busy for a year, at least, showing her all the wonderful things in Oz."

Glinda smiled.

"I have lived here many years," said she, "and I have not seen all the wonders of Oz yet."

Meantime the travelers were drawing near to the palace, and when they first caught sight of its towers Trot realized that it was far more grand and imposing than was the King's castle in Jinxland. The nearer they came, the more beautiful the palace appeared, and when finally the Scarecrow led them up the great marble steps, even Button-Bright was filled with awe.

"I don't see any soldiers to guard the place," said the little girl.

"There is no need to guard Glinda's palace," replied the Scarecrow. "We have no wicked people in Oz, that we know of, and even if there were any, Glinda's magic would be powerful enough to protect her."

Button-Bright was now standing on the top steps of the entrance, and he suddenly exclaimed:

"Why, there's the Sawhorse and the Red Wagon! Hip, hooray!" and next moment he was rushing down to throw his arms around the neck of the wooden horse, which good-naturedly permitted this familiarity when it recognized in the boy an old friend.

Button-Bright's shout had been heard inside the palace, so now Dorothy and Betsy came running out to embrace their beloved friend, the Scarecrow, and to welcome Trot and Cap'n Bill to the Land of Oz.

"We've been watching you for a long time, in Ozma's Magic Picture," said Dorothy, "and Ozma has sent us to invite you to her own palace in the Em'rald City. I don't know if you realize how lucky you are to get that invitation, but you'll understand it better after you've seen the royal palace and the Em'rald City."

Glinda now appeared in person to lead all the party into her Azure Reception Room. Trot was a little afraid of the stately Sorceress, but gained courage by holding fast to the hands of Betsy and Dorothy. Cap'n Bill had no one to help him feel at ease, so the old sailor sat stiffly on the edge of his chair and said:

"Yes, ma'am," or "No, ma'am," when he was spoken to, and was greatly embarrassed by so much splendor.

The Scarecrow had lived so much in palaces that he felt quite at home, and he chatted to Glinda and the Oz girls in a merry, light-hearted way. He told all about his adventures in Jinxland, and at the Great Waterfall, and on the journey hither—most of which his hearers knew already—and then he asked Dorothy and Betsy what had happened in the Emerald City since he had left there.

They all passed the evening and the night at Glinda's palace, and the Sorceress was so gracious to Cap'n Bill that the old man by degrees regained his self-possession and began to enjoy himself. Trot had already come to the conclusion that in Dorothy and Betsy she had found two delightful comrades, and Button-Bright was just as much at home here as he had been in the fields of Jinxland or when he was buried in the popcorn snow of the Land of Mo.

The next morning they arose bright and early and after breakfast bade good-bye to the kind Sorceress, whom Trot and Cap'n Bill thanked earnestly for sending the Scarecrow to

Jinxland to rescue them. Then they all climbed into the Red Wagon.

There was room for all on the broad seats, and when all had taken their places—Dorothy, Trot and Betsy on the rear seat and Cap'n Bill, Button-Bright and the Scarecrow in front—they called "Gid-dap!" to the Sawhorse and the wooden steed moved briskly away, pulling the Red Wagon with ease.

It was now that the strangers began to perceive the real beauties of the Land of Oz, for they were passing through a more thickly settled part of the country and the population grew more dense as they drew nearer to the Emerald City. Everyone they met had a cheery word or a smile for the Scarecrow, Dorothy and Betsy Bobbin, and some of them remembered Button-Bright and welcomed him back to their country.

It was a happy party, indeed, that journeyed in the Red Wagon to the Emerald City, and Trot already began to hope that Ozma would permit her and Cap'n Bill to live always in the Land of Oz.

When they reached the great city they were more amazed than ever, both by the concourse of people in their quaint and picturesque costumes, and by the splendor of the city itself. But the magnificence of the Royal Palace quite took their breath away, until Ozma received them in her own pretty apartment and by her charming manners and assuring smiles made them feel they were no longer strangers.

Trot was given a lovely little room next to that of Dorothy, while Cap'n Bill had the cosiest sort of a room next to Trot's and overlooking the gardens. And that evening Ozma gave a grand banquet and reception in honor of the new arrivals. While Trot had read of many of the people she then met, Cap'n Bill was less familiar with them and many of the unusual characters introduced to him that evening caused the old sailor to open his eyes wide in astonishment.

He had thought the live Scarecrow about as curious as anyone could be, but now he met the Tin Woodman, who was all made of tin, even to his heart, and carried a gleaming axe over his shoulder wherever he went. Then there was Jack Pumpkinhead, whose head was a real pumpkin with the face carved upon it; and Professor Wogglebug, who had the shape of an enormous bug but was dressed in neat fitting garments. The Professor was an interesting talker and had very polite manners, but his face was so comical that it made Cap'n Bill smile to look at it. A great friend of Dorothy and Ozma seemed to be a machine man called Tik-Tok, who ran down several times during the evening and had to be wound up again by someone before he could move or speak.

At the reception appeared the Shaggy Man and his brother, both very popular in Oz, as well as Dorothy's Uncle Henry and Aunt Em, two happy old people who lived in a pretty cottage near the palace.

But what perhaps seemed most surprising to both Trot

and Cap'n Bill was the number of peculiar animals admitted into Ozma's parlors, where they not only conducted themselves quite properly but were able to talk as well as anyone.

There was the Cowardly Lion, an immense beast with a beautiful mane; and the Hungry Tiger, who smiled continually; and Eureka the Pink Kitten, who lay curled upon a cushion and had rather supercilious manners; and the wooden Sawhorse; and nine tiny piglets that belonged to the Wizard; and a mule named Hank, who belonged to Betsy Bobbin. A fuzzy little terrier dog, named Toto, lay at Dorothy's feet but seldom took part in the conversation, although he listened to every word that was said. But the most wonderful of all to Trot was a square beast with a winning smile, that squatted in a corner of the room and wagged his square head at everyone in quite a jolly way. Betsy told Trot that this unique beast was called the Woozy, and there was no other like him in all the world.

Cap'n Bill and Trot had both looked around expectantly for the Wizard of Oz, but the evening was far advanced before the famous little man entered the room. But he went up to the strangers at once and said:

"I know you, but you don't know me; so let's get acquainted."

And they did get acquainted, in a very short time, and before the evening was over Trot felt that she knew every person and animal present at the reception, and that they were all her good friends.

Suddenly they looked around for Button-Bright, but he was nowhere to be found.

"Dear me!" cried Trot. "He's lost again."

"Never mind, my dear," said Ozma, with her charming smile, "no one can go far astray in the Land of Oz, and if Button-Bright isn't lost occasionally, he isn't happy."

EXPLORE the WORLD of OZ.

SIMON AND SCHUSTER

EXPLORE the WORLD of OZ.

Explore the World of Oz.

SIMON AND SCHUSTER

EXPLORE the WORLD of OZ.